BREAKING IN BABY FACE BY STEVEN SAYLOR
WRITING AS AARON TRAVIS

A professional wrestling mogul takes a young and innocent Adonis under his wing and shows him a lot more than the ropes.

THE SEX VACATION BY ANDREW HOLLERAN

The celebrated writer tells in exquisite detail about making his fantasy vacation come true—in Orlando's infamous Parliament House motel and cruising palace.

ELLIOTT: THE SPORTS ARCADE BY ANNE RICE
WRITING AS ANNE RAMPLING

Excerpted from her renowned novel *Exit to Eden*, this tale of fun and games on an S&M resort island paradise features "boy toys," domination, and contact sports.

PAST MASTER BY D. V. SADERO

Set in San Francisco's leather underground, this violent tale pits two "tops" against each other in a quest for power—and very hot sex.

AND OTHER VITAL WORKS OF GAY EROTICA—INCLUDING MICHAEL BRONSKI'S LANDMARK ESSAY "WHY GAY MEN CAN'T REALLY TALK ABOUT SEX."

JOHN PRESTON, one of the gay community's most eloquent and beloved advocates, published more than forty books before his death in 1994, among them the novels *Mr. Benson* and *Franny, The Queen of Provincetown*, the acclaimed anthologies *Hometowns*, *A Member of the Family*, and *Friends and Lovers*, and the first two volumes of *Flesh and the Word*.

MICHAEL LOWENTHAL is a writer and editor in Boston whose work has appeared in *Flesh and the Word 2*, *Men on Men 5*, and other anthologies.

D1552536

BOOKS BY JOHN PRESTON

FICTION

Franny, the Queen of Provincetown, 1983, 1995
Mr. Benson, 1983, 1992
I Once Had a Master and Other Tales of Erotic Love,
    1984 (short stories)

THE MISSION OF ALEX KANE
Volume I: *Sweet Dreams*, 1984, 1992
Volume II: *Golden Years*, 1984, 1992
Volume III: *Deadly Lies*, 1985, 1992
Volume IV: *Stolen Moments*, 1986, 1993
Volume V: *Secret Dangers*, 1986, 1993
Volume VI: *Lethal Secrets*, 1987, 1993

Entertainment for a Master, 1986
Love of a Master, 1987
The Heir, 1988, 1992
In Search of a Master, 1989
The King, 1992
Tales from the Dark Lord, 1992 (short stories)
The Arena, 1993
Tales from the Dark Lord 2, 1994 (short stories)

Edited

Hot Living: Erotic Stories About Safer Sex, 1985
Flesh and the Word: An Erotic Anthology, 1992
Flesh and the Word 2: An Erotic Anthology, 1993
Flesh and the Word 3: An Anthology of Gay Erotic Writing, 1995

NONFICTION

The Big Gay Book: A Man's Survival Guide for the Nineties, 1991
My Life as a Pornographer & Other Indecent Acts, 1993
Hustling: A Gentleman's Guide to the Fine Art of Male Prostitution, 1994
Winter's Light: Reflections of a Yankee Queer, 1995

with Frederick Brandt

Classified Affairs: The Gay Men's Guide to the Personals, 1984

with Glenn Swann

Safe Sex: The Ultimate Erotic Guide, 1987

Edited

Personal Dispatches: Writers Confront AIDS, 1989
Hometowns: Gay Men Write About Where They Belong, 1991
A Member of the Family: Gay Men Write About Their Families, 1992
*Friends and Lovers: Gay Men Write About
    the Families They Create*, 1995

Edited with Joan Nestle

*Sister and Brother: Lesbians and Gay Men Write About
    Their Lives Together*, 1994

EDITED BY
JOHN PRESTON
WITH
MICHAEL LOWENTHAL

FLESH
AND THE
WORD 3

AN ANTHOLOGY OF
GAY EROTIC WRITING

A PLUME BOOK

PLUME

Published by the Penguin Group
Penguin Books USA Inc., 375 Hudson Street, New York, New York 10014, U.S.A.
Penguin Books Ltd, 27 Wrights Lane, London W8 5TZ, England
Penguin Books Australia Ltd, Ringwood, Victoria, Australia
Penguin Books Canada Ltd, 10 Alcorn Avenue, Toronto, Ontario, Canada M4V 3B2
Penguin Books (N.Z.) Ltd, 182–190 Wairau Road, Auckland 10, New Zealand

Penguin Books Ltd, Registered Offices:
Harmondsworth, Middlesex, England

First published by Plume, an imprint of Dutton Signet,
a division of Penguin Books USA Inc.

First Printing, June, 1995
1 3 5 7 9 10 8 6 4 2

REGISTERED TRADEMARK—MARCA REGISTRADA

LIBRARY OF CONGRESS CATALOGING-IN-PUBLICATION DATA:

Flesh and the word 3 : an anthology of gay erotic writing / edited by John Preston, with Michael Lowenthal.

p. cm.

ISBN 0-452-27252-1

1. Gay men—Literary collections. 2. Erotic literature, American. 3. Gays' writings, American. I. Preston, John. II. Lowenthal, Michael. III. Title: Flesh and the word three.

PS509.H57F566 1995

810.8'03538—dc20

94-42651

CIP

Printed in the United States of America
Set in Garamond No. 3 and Futura

DESIGNED BY STEVEN N. STATHAKIS

CONTENTS

x CONTENTS

MICHAEL
LOWENTHAL

EDITOR'S

NOTE

JOHN PRESTON HAD A TERRIBLY MESSY DESK. HIS COMPUTER, a hulking behemoth that looked big enough to run the Pentagon, took up much of the useful space. Beyond that there were piles upon piles of manuscripts, correspondence, newspapers and porn magazines. He was always working on about a dozen books at once, and the sprawling mass of paper could get extremely confusing. John always fretted about the need to "clear my desk."

Sometime after we had become close friends, John devised a method to speed the clearing of his work space: He would box up various works-in-progress and mail them to me so they would sit on my desk. I was expected to read each manuscript—not too quickly, lest it boomerang back to his pile—and return it with a detailed editorial evaluation that John hoped would make his own job more simple.

The pile of papers that would become *Flesh and the Word 3* was one of the manuscripts John sent me; I dutifully sent back my report about a month later. That month, sadly, was the one in which John's

AIDS caught up with him. He seemed perfectly well when he packaged the manuscript and mailed it, but by the time I returned it, he was barely able to sit in his desk chair and face the computer. John asked me if I would finish *Flesh and the Word 3*, and I agreed immediately.

Porn aficionados know that, despite what some fuzzy-minded egalitarians will try to tell you, size does matter. And John Preston left some *big* shoes to fill.

It isn't just that John was probably the best-known gay pornographer, having won legions of fans with his prodigious publications including *Mr. Benson, The Heir,* the *Master* books, and of course the first two *Flesh and the Word* collections. John *believed* in pornography. Porn was like a religion for him, and although Episcopal in upbringing, he preached this faith with the fervor of a Southern Baptist minister.

John had initially gravitated to porn as one of the only visible aspects of a gay world that, when he was coming of age, remained painfully hidden. But even as gay men and lesbians became more and more open, and as a proud gay culture flourished in more socially sanctioned artistic forms, he continued to value pornography as the "gay vernacular"—an essential, natural language of expression.

John also had a good sense of humor about porn. While it was work for him—an essential component of his livelihood—he never lost sight of the fact that erotic writing is essentially about play. To the end, he was tickled and amazed that he had been able to make money doing something that was so much fun.

In completing the present volume, I have tried to honor John's enthusiasm for the material, and his wonderful ability to take the form seriously but not too seriously. I have attempted to present this sexually charged writing the way he, as the High Priest of the form, would have.

A number of individuals helped make my task an easy one. Matt Sartwell, who edited the first two volumes, lent his expert advice again. John's agent, Peter Ginsberg, has nurtured the series of anthologies from the beginning and his belief never wavered. His support and advice were invaluable as I carried on the project. I want to thank the contributors, who were generous with their patience and input. Thanks also to Susan Ackerman for her insightful comments on drafts of the introductions.

Finally, as always, I thank Chris Hogan for his love.

JOHN PRESTON

INTRODUCTION

IN MY INTRODUCTION TO THE FIRST *FLESH AND THE WORD* anthology, I explained that my hope in publishing the book was to make some of the best gay sexual writing available by making it legitimate. The difference was not one of substance or content, I emphasized, it was simply one of presentation. By virtue of being published in a fancy edition from a division of one of the world's largest publishers, what had previously been "dirty" material found only in darkened shops would now be "erotica" that you could pick up at the local chain bookstore.

It worked. Shortly after the book was released, *The New York Times Book Review* and *USA Today* ran essays about *Flesh and the Word* and the trend of mainstream collections of erotica. Gay writers who had been confined previously to publications like *Drummer* and *Honcho* now found their work being referred to in the icons of the national media.

The response from readers was equally encouraging. *Flesh and the Word* quickly sold out its initial print run. At the time I'm writing this, the book is in its sixth printing.

I worked quickly to compile *Flesh and the Word 2*, which allowed me to introduce a whole new group of gay sexual writers to their waiting audience. And before *Flesh 2* even hit the stands, the publisher offered a contract for this third installment in the series. What began as a gamble had become an institution.

I was gratified by the success of the series, but through all the excitement I remained adamant about my original point: The writing was the same as always, it was only the presentation that was different.

Now, as I complete this third volume, I find that there *is* a difference in the work. Having gay pornography printed in "mainstream" anthologies from a major publisher has not only affected the way reviewers and readers view the genre, it has affected the way gay writers themselves think of porn. This changes what gets written, and who is willing to write it. The very character and the quality of the submissions have changed.

Pornography has always been related to the market for writing. What gets classified as pornography depends on the desire and ability of an audience to obtain such works. Two hundred years ago, when books were limited to a wealthy elite, their content was not questioned by authorities. But with the spread of literacy and the advent of less expensive printing techniques, and as more and more people had access to books, the content of these works had to be kept in check. As Lynn Hunt writes in her introduction to *The Invention of Pornography*,

> pornography as a regulatory category was invented in response to the perceived menace of the democratization of culture. . . . It was only when print culture opened the possibility of the masses gaining access to writing and pictures that pornography began to emerge as a separate genre of representation.

The current shift in perception is essentially the same, but in the opposite direction. Two centuries ago, when large numbers of people suddenly had access to books, previously accepted works became "pornography." Now, works that have long been termed pornography are being accepted by virtue of their widespread availability.

This is a major change in the history of pornography, because it also affects who produces the work. Sexual writing has been marginalized for so long that only marginal writers wrote it. To write in a devalued form was to be devalued as a writer.

My own career is a good example of this phenomenon. I started to write pornography because I felt I wasn't entitled to write the good stuff. I had been told in college that I was too working class, too crude to sip sherry at department receptions with the English majors. But pornography wasn't important. It was as unsophisticated as I had been led to believe I was. It seemed like a good place to start.

The wonderful thing about the *Flesh and the Word* books is that, in a very real way, they have made gay pornography "the good stuff." The anthologies are beautifully designed, distributed internationally, and backed by an impressive publicity department. They are taken seriously. And so "serious" writers want to be published here.

The new prestige these anthologies have bestowed on gay sexual writing has prompted young writers like Will Leber and Michael Lowenthal, people who have studied creative writing at leading colleges and universities, to publish their first fiction in these books. The anthologies create an instant audience of fifteen thousand readers, or more. Compare that with the couple of thousand who comprise the circulations of most literary magazines, and it's easy to see why an aspiring writer would find *Flesh and the Word* an appealing outlet.

It's not just young or unknown writers who are drawn by the prospect of exposure. One writer included in this volume, somebody with a number of mainstream books to his credit, submitted his story with a cover letter that said, "Because the *Flesh and the Word* books are getting so much attention, and have become such a showcase for new and established talent, it would be a great boost to my career (and ego) to be included."

By "legitimizing" gay pornography, the *Flesh* books have also created a justification for established writers to branch out and try their hands at explicitly sexual writing. Accomplished novelist Larry Duplechan wrote one of his first determinedly pornographic stories specifically for *Flesh and the Word 2*. Martin Palmer, who has published stories in *Men on Men 3* and other prestigious venues, wrote an explicit sexual essay specifically for this volume.

It's another measure of the accomplishment of the *Flesh and the Word* books that almost all the writers included here are publishing under their real names. Not too long ago, every gay erotic story that got published was signed with a pen name. Even if the author wasn't too concerned about preserving his reputation, magazine editors simply assumed that no one would want his real name attached to such filth. Now that pornographic writing is recognized in a legitimate volume, writers want to take credit for their work. Numerous authors who have long hidden behind false names have insisted on "coming out" when their stories appear in the anthologies. They direct that their stories be signed with their real name "writing as" their pen name. They want to cash in on the prestige.

All this talk of new writers and new forms is not to overlook the writers who are still the bread and butter of gay pornography, those who write for the commercial skin magazines like *Honcho, Drummer, Advocate MEN*, and *Fresh MEN*. These magazines are the places where gay sexual writing still thrives, and they are vitally important. I have made a point of opening the current volume, as I did in the second book, with a section for "traditional" stories. But I find that in this category, too, writers are pushing themselves to break through the formulaic requirements of commercial publications to create better and better stories.

More than anything, these anthologies have been about creating new spaces for gay sexual writing and writers. They have been about creating physical room: shelf space in bookstores and column space in book review media. They have also been about new literary spaces. Each volume includes established writers like Anne Rice, Andrew Holleran, and Steven Saylor, but I've presented a few writers each time who have never before had their work published in a book.

The anthologies also expand the boundaries of erotica as a category. I have included the "hot" sections from mainstream novels as well as excerpts from little-known 'zines. I have included short stories, nonfiction memoirs, and in *Flesh 2* even a screenplay. The current volume includes one essay with academic footnotes and ends with a piece of astute cultural analysis. When readers find all of this included in a book of gay pornography, their preconceived notions about the form are struck down. What was once a dark backroom in the house of literature is becoming a well-lit parlor.

With this third volume, the ongoing project of expanding the space for gay erotic writing continues. The forces that would end our project are many. Repressive academics like Catherine MacKinnon and Andrea Dworkin assault our right to express our explicit fantasies. Censors in government are a constant threat to the distribution and sale of the works that do get published. AIDS has taken away some of our most daring sexual writers and constantly threatens to stifle the erotic imaginations of those who survive.

But the more space we create, and the more spaces within spaces, the more difficult it will be for the forces of opposition to succeed. In the end, I am confident that we will triumph, because there is no force more vital or more urgent than our sexuality. I invite you to join the writers included in this volume in celebrating that force.

Portland, Maine
1994

PART ONE

THE
TRADITIONALS

LARS EIGHNER

THE EXPERIENCE

THE SECOND WEEK OF MY VACATION I GOT MICHAEL TO drive me to the office to pick up my paycheck. He came in with me, although he was wearing only some skintight cutoffs and a denim vest that didn't cover much of his chest. We hadn't stopped since we left the lake, and I had to piss.

While I was peeing, Thom came into the men's room. I stared at the ceiling. I knew Thom's dick was so long it would take him about two minutes to fish all of it out of his trousers. Thom stood at the urinal right next to the one I was using. He'd never done that before.

"Man," Thom whispered although no one could have overheard him, "your new boyfriend gives me a hard-on."

"Geez, Thom, you're straight." That's why we got along, I guess. In his position as the office stud he didn't feel threatened by me.

"Yeah. But if every guy looked like him—Mike, is it?"

"No. He insists on Michael."

"Well, I don't know how you do it. You've always had great looking guys, guys I'd never guess, you know. But Michael's a god and he's
about to turn me queerer than you are."

"That's the thing, you see, because Michael is almost as straight as
you are."

"You aren't having sex with him?"

"Of course I'm having sex with him. But it's not really his idea.
Actually, it wasn't even my idea."

"Whose idea was it?"

"Our dicks'."

Although I sort of let Thom think I'd been having sex with Michael all
along, I hadn't really before my vacation started. I had scheduled my
vacation to coincide with spring break at the university before I met
Michael. I'd planned to go to the coast, but Michael said we would have
as much fun at the lake.

As he drove us to the lake, that first day of my vacation, Michael
took his shirt off. It was a warm day. He was about as big as a man can
get without steroids. I threw a boner immediately.

Michael had big, round, firm, low pecs. You can work out forever,
but if you aren't born with low pecs you'll never be a bodybuilder. And
Michael had them, low pecs, and peaking biceps. He had convinced me
he was straight.

And he did have a girlfriend who was beautiful and not nearly so
stupid as she should have been. I'd met her. And he was screwing her,
or he was a pretty good liar because there were a couple of tense weeks
when he said she missed her period although he was 99 percent certain
they'd always taken precautions. So it seemed completely pointless for
my dick to be hard and I wished it would go down.

He was blond, incredibly blond, and every time he raised his arm
to brush his hair out of his eyes I had to fight the impulse to bury my
nose in the golden fuzz of his deep armpits—and from there I would
have been within lapping distance of his big brown, sensitive nipples. I
knew they were sensitive. They were each as big as a quarter and the
hard part always stayed hard. I think the truth of it was he believed he
was straight. He knew I was gay. I'd invited him to bed more than
once.

I cannot explain—I do not think he could explain—why he was
attracted to me. But he wanted to be my friend, he was determined to

be my friend no matter what. I felt very guilty about that because if I had been him I would not have given me the time of day.

I wanted my cock to go down. In fact my main interest in Michael was his body. That was another thing I felt guilty about. I wouldn't have had time for him if he had not looked so good. And I told him that. But it didn't seem to matter.

I told him all I wanted was to have sex with him. And he told me it would never happen, but that was no reason we could not be friends and if I'd go along with it we would have everything but sex. And that was the idea of the trip to the lake. He wanted me to have a good time.

He was attracted to me—and if I knew what it was about me that attracted him, I'd bottle it and get rich. The truth was, we were dating. I don't know what to call it except dating. I was living in a rat hole. I did not have transportation. I was absorbed in my work. I had sex, of course. But I never had much fun. So Michael started taking me out. Movies, concerts, all of that. Stuff I had not done in years. I was liking it. I was grateful. I did not want to screw it up.

My cock did go down before we got to the lake. Michael pulled off the road and cut across some low grass. He brought the car to a stop a few feet shy of a cliff where limestone fractured into tiers, like a contoured wedding cake. I had never been to that part of the lake before.

We climbed down to the water. We were utterly invisible to the rest of the world. Michael set the cooler down, laid out his towel, and stripped off his jeans.

This was not the official skinny-dipping part of the lake. But most everybody takes skinny-dipping for granted. I dropped my pants, too, and of course I threw another boner in a matter of seconds. I laid out my towel and folded my clothes, just as if my dick was not stiff. But there was no hiding it.

"Mac, is that an accident or not?"

"What?" I asked. I wasn't being evasive. I did not know what accident he meant.

"Did you want to get a hard-on just to show me?"

"No, Michael, really, I did not mean it." He would believe me, partly because it was the truth and partly because he did trust me.

He hopped in the water right away and swam across the little inlet and back. When he hauled himself out of the water, my hard-on had not gone down a bit, which was not really very surprising because he looked as hot wet as he did dry.

"Does your dick stay hard all the time," he asked, "or is it me?"

I sighed. "Michael, it's you. Man, you can't look like you do and not have had this happen before with other guys."

"Well," he said, "there was this guy at the bus station once. You know I'd just got off the bus and had to piss. And the whole time he watched me and jerked off."

"That's all?"

"Yeah. I'm not trying to tease you, you know."

"I know."

"I don't want to have a homosexual experience."

That was the story. He was in Navy ROTC. He expected to have a career in the Navy. And in fact I think he said he wanted to do intelligence work. So maybe it was not so farfetched that he expected to be hooked up to a lie detector some day. Anyway, he said he wanted to be able to say truthfully he had never had a homosexual experience.

"I don't want to tease you," he said. "If you want to get in the water, or something. I mean I can't help it if you look at me."

He wouldn't put it in so many words, but if it would do me any good he would pose for me while I jacked off—in the water or behind a rock or any way that he could not see precisely that I was jacking off. But he did not want to tantalize me. Would his posing make me happy, or would it only make matters worse? Of course, it had happened a couple of times he hadn't known about.

Once he'd slept on my sofa and I'd watched him have a wet dream. He crushed a cushion against his bare chest. His thighs twitched. His abs tensed and his hips thrust. His dick was trapped against his right thigh—he'd kept his jeans on. He moaned softly and squirmed for a couple of minutes, and of course I pulled down my Hanes and started beating off even though he would see me if he opened his eyes.

Maybe I hoped he would open his eyes. He made a little coughing sound in the back of his throat, tossed the pillow away, grabbed for his nuts, and curled up into a ball. When he relaxed again, he spread his legs and I could see dark blue splotches on the right thigh of his faded jeans. I shot off on the carpet and didn't clean it up because once it was over I didn't want to wake him.

And we had showered together once at the gym. His dick got bloated and red in the steamy spray and my dick got hard as I watched him wash his nuts and spread the cheeks of his ass as he backed up to the shower to wash his butthole. I knew he was going to shampoo his hair because he'd brought shampoo into the shower, and I soaped my cock every which way just short of actually beating off. And sure enough, when he put the shampoo in his hair he clamped his eyes shut.

I beat my meat as hard as I could, as fast as I could. There was a guy in the locker room who could see me, who was watching what I was doing and he started tugging on the pouch of his jock. But I shook my head and motioned him away. No one else came into the shower or saw me, at least I think not. I just couldn't help myself. I managed to shoot off just as Michael finished rinsing his hair.

Now I say that Michael didn't catch me that time, and I don't think he did, but I could be wrong. When he opened his eyes my dick was still pretty heated and I was dripping come. But with the steam and soap and water and all, Michael didn't notice, or at least he could tell himself he hadn't noticed which was just as good. Maybe he smelled it. At any rate, he said, loud enough to echo from the far wall of the shower, "I don't want a homosexual experience."

Over Michael's shoulder I could see the guy in the locker room, who I had forgotten about. He now had a good view of Michael's tiny, tight, golden ass. His jock was pulled down and his dick was stuck in a wadded up towel. I'm pretty sure he came at just that second.

"I don't want a homosexual experience," Michael said again, a little softer. And then very much softer, almost a whisper, "I guess you've been with a lot of guys, so tell me, how do I measure up?" Michael held up his meat with his thumb and forefinger. It was droopy, but still pretty bloated.

"You've got a big dick, Michael," I said. "Don't even worry about that." Although that was the truth and I was very sincere about it, perhaps I was not quite as enthusiastic as Michael thought I should be. He reminded me of a kid in school who used to draw these pictures of dragons and castles and all, and no matter how much you said you liked them, and they were pretty good, it was never enough. He'd keep explaining the picture and showing you little elves he'd hidden in the forest and stuff. And that was Michael with his dick.

Michael stepped back a bit. He placed his hands behind his head, his fingers interlocked. He bent his knees a little. He pumped up every muscle in his body and when he thrust his hips forward his dick sprang up like a diving board after a fat man jumps off. "How about this way. Is it okay when it's hard?"

It was more than okay. It looked like ten inches to me, really thick in the middle of the shaft. The purple-tan head of Michael's cock pointed straight up, and his cock was hard enough to break bricks. Although my balls were still sore from shooting off, my own dick got hard again.

"Yeah, it's great, Michael. I'd suck you off right here if you'd let me. Don't ask me to get any more excited about it, or I'll make a grab for it."

"I'm sorry," Michael said. "I didn't mean to tease you. I just wanted your opinion." His dick stayed hard until we were dried and dressed and he didn't even try to cover it up when he walked through the locker room.

I hopped into the lake and began to stroke my cock. The water was clear, but it was choppy enough, I suppose, that he could convince himself I was scratching my nuts. Or at least that would be what he told himself when he took the hypothetical, imaginary polygraph.

It was early in the season and the water was cold. My nuts shrank, but my dick didn't. Michael flexed one bicep and then the other, and then did a crab.

"Any requests?" he asked.

"Yeah, how about that one you did in the shower that day. You know, when you asked me if it was big enough."

He thought a moment and then he did it. Again when he thrust his hips forward, his dick sprang up. "Like that?"

"Yeah, exactly like that."

"You don't have to be way out there, you can get a little closer."

I picked my way from rock to rock closer to Michael until the water was barely covering my navel. It was perfectly obvious I had been jerking off the whole time and now my fist was splashing the water as I jacked on my dick.

Michael turned his back and spread his lats. Then he pushed against the wall of rock, leaning low against it, with one knee bent and the other leg stretched out. He did a few deep-knee bends. And then he squatted and spread the cheeks of his ass. He was showing me his butthole.

My jaw dropped. Straight guys don't know they have buttholes, right?

"Are you finished?" he asked, over his shoulder.

I'd been so surprised I'd stopped splashing the water with my fist. "No," I said.

"Take your time," he said.

Michael lay on his back on his towel. His cock was still hard. He put one forearm over his eyes. "Consider me asleep," he said.

I couldn't believe he meant what I hoped he meant. Maybe that was only his way of saying I could look at him as long as I wanted. As I moved closer I could see he was rubbing around the base of his cock.

When I got out of the water there was a big splash and Michael spread his thighs. I spread my towel at the foot of his and began to creep up between his legs.

Now I had a great view of his massive hard cock and his yellow-haired balls. The come-tunnel bulge on the underside of his cock was thick as my thumb and his nuts rolled around slowly in his bag. My hand brushed against his inner thigh and Michael sighed.

I licked my lips and went down on his dick, sucking a pearl of precome out of it on the first stroke.

"Aw shit, not that," he said, as if I really had woke him up. With both hands he pried my face out of his groin. "Don't suck my dick like a little fag," he said.

The fingers of my right hand were still wrapped around the base of his cock. Michael grabbed my middle finger in his fist and I thought for a moment he would bend it back until it broke. Instead he raised his knees and guided my finger to his asshole. "Stick it in," he said.

Michael stroked his cock. He opened his palm in front of my face. "Spit on it," he said.

Michael's pecs got bigger and redder. He stroked his cock with his right and twisted his tit with his left. I probed the smooth lining of his bowels, my finger searching for the right spot. Then he let his cock go and his body went limp. "Fuck, your finger's no bigger than mine. It's not big enough."

His cock hand went up behind his head. It must have been under the edge of his towel the whole time. He must have had it there all the time. He handed it to me.

"Put this on, Mac," he said. "You know, I gotta get dicked."

My hips were trapped between Michael's feet as he squatted over me. He flicked the purple tit of the condom with the puckers of his asshole. "You really want it?" Michael pulled on my tits.

I was delirious, like in a fever. All I had wanted was to worship him, but now I just wanted to stick my dick in his butt. "C'mon, c'mon, give it to me." I thrust upwards, but he raised up so my dick was still just touching his asshole. "You gonna give it to me or not?" I asked.

"Yeah, give me a second. Not every day you'll get some straight butt. Some virgin butt. Fuck, I don't know if I really am a virgin. I've put everything up my ass I can think of, except dick."

It looked like he was about to shit on my cock, even more so because of the way he squatted, his ass hanging down from his knees. He bounced against my dick a couple of times, and then he stood up. "It's no use," he said as he stroked his huge white cock.

I was horny sick and my hand went right to my cock. "Stop that," he said and he pushed my hand away from my crotch with his foot. "I can't give it to you. You have to take it." Michael lay down on his towel and drew his knees up to his chest. "Fuck me, Mac."

He pressed his feet against my shoulders and his hands went to his groin, cupping his balls up against his belly as if he had been racked. "Fuck me," Michael said, "I can't stand it anymore."

I pressed my cock against his tiny blond-furred hole. He squirmed and rocked his hips just as I began to wedge the tip of my dick into his muscle.

"Oh shit," he said. "C'mon Mac, make it happen." He struggled for a while, his face twisted up like a medieval gargoyle. Michael took a deep breath and relaxed, just a little, for just a moment, and my cock plunged into him.

"Fuck me, Mac. Fuck me hard." Michael's feet slid off my shoulders and he locked his legs around my waist. He bruised my butt with his heels as he tried to force my dick deeper into his asshole. His tight, muscular hole clung to my cock. Michael's head rolled from side to side and his biceps flexed as he pinched his tits. "Dick me, man, really dick me."

I was going to lose it—I'd been so close a couple times when I was jacking off in the water. I tried to warn him, but I could only pant in his face.

"Gonna come, Mac. Come on, pinch my tits. Come on, shoot off in me."

All my weight was on him as I twisted his tits. I could feel his cock against my belly button. I could only hold out for a couple of thrusts before my dick started to shoot.

"Aw, good dick," he said as I lifted my shoulders off his chest. "D'ya come?"

"Yeah."

"A lot?"

"Yeah, a whole lot."

He squished his fist on the head of his cock, so fast his fingers were a blur. "Just a little more. Fuck me a little more."

My cock was so sensitive it was like sticking it in fire, but I rocked on my knees a little.

"Fuck, you're making me come, you're making me come." Michael's dick started shooting big globby thick wads onto his chest and belly. "Oh fuck," he said. "Oh fuck." Then he shit my cock and went limp.

"Aw, Mac, let me see it." Michael sat up. The condom was still hanging on my droopy cock. He bounced my sheathed cock on his fingers. "This is it. This cock's been up my ass. Man, I've been fucked. I've been dicked."

Michael pulled the purple condom off my dick and poured the contents onto his rippled stomach. He ran his fingers in circles through the pools of our sperm like a kindergartner fingerpainting. I looked at the dead condom for a while and then held it up. "Where did this come from?" I asked. "You must have been planning this, but I thought you didn't want any homosexual experiences."

"Well, I don't want any homosexual experiences. I just couldn't think of how to get you to dick me without having one."

"Do you suck him off?" Thom asked. He'd been standing at the urinal, but I hadn't heard him peeing.

"Yeah, among other things." Well, I'm not sure that was a lie exactly. Michael had come in my mouth a few times, but he never did let me really blow him. He didn't want any homosexual experiences. He just wanted dicking.

"Look at me, Mac."

I'd been staring at the ceiling. After Thom and I had come to understand each other, I'd made it a point to avert my eyes whenever we ended up peeing together. I looked at Thom. His dick was hard. My hand went right to it.

"If I knew his girlfriend, I'd want her," he said. Thom took my dick in his hand. "The idea of putting my cock where his has been just makes me so fucking hot."

Thom had turned me down a couple of times, but I could tell by the way he handled my cock that he was very sorry about that. "I'll do it back," he said. "Don't think 'cause I'm straight that I don't know how to suck dick."

Thom did know how to suck dick. And Thom was good at it. But not right then. Right then Michael came into the men's room and tried to flush Thom's head down a urinal.

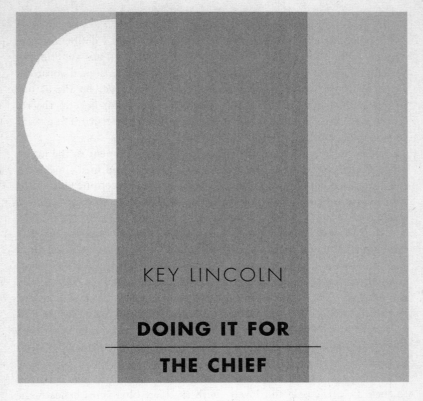

KEY LINCOLN

DOING IT FOR

THE CHIEF

INDEPENDENCE DAY, 1974. OUR MINESWEEPER IS ANCHORED in Monterey Bay—has been since 0800—and by now most of the crew have gone ashore for their first liberty since we left the Canal. They'll straggle in tonight, some of them pleasantly squiffed but few having found the pussy they talked about all the way up here.

The reason I'm still aboard is that Chief Boylan hates my guts. No big deal. It's the natural dislike of a vinegary old career bosun's mate for a brash college kid who's only in for the duration. I made it worse by putting in for officer's training, and he finds that infuriating. He thinks officers are all a bunch of faggots anyway. From my limited experience, he's not far wrong.

Being confined to ship doesn't faze me. At the very least it gives me the chance to jack off without a crowd of sailors popping in and making lewd remarks, cramping my style. Ever since those warm, lazy hayloft afternoons in Pinchwood, Nebraska, I have liked to do my thing leisurely and alone.

Somebody else has pulled skeleton duty, too, and I doubt if I'd lay eyes on anyone prettier at the fireworks in Monterey. This is a crumpet we call Pip, a fresh young quartermaster 3rd class who signed aboard at Pensacola three weeks ago. Of course, laying your eyes on Pip is one thing; laying your hands on him is quite another. For he's on the reserved side, kind of remote and mysterious—and so beautiful you want to smack his face.

Besides, he's already practically on special assignment to the junior officers' mess. They have their pets among the enlisted men, invariably the cute ones. The night we left Tobago, I saw Pip coming out of the wardroom, blushing and tucking his blue chambray shirttail into his dungarees.

Pip is nearly my height (five feet and almost ten inches), but he's willowy and undeveloped, whereas I'm stocky and hard-muscled from working on the ranch and playing high school football. Over his whole slim figure his skin is smooth, soft, hairless except at the crotch, and the color of—oh, I don't know—maplenut ice cream? His face is gentle, a trace feminine, with its plump cheeks and long, curved eyelashes. His eyes are almond-shaped, as if there might be a smidgen of Japanese blood in him. Yet the irises are gray, romantic—and disconcerting. They blow my mind.

His penis makes me wonder for the first time if it would be fun to suck dick. It's pale and lovely, with shadowy blue veins beneath the surface. While the ship was rolling in a heavy sea in the Caribbean, Pip was naked and holding on to a bunk to stay upright, and his cock was swinging with a flip so saucy it just took my breath away. Nobody said anything about his seductive nudity, but I can't believe I'm the only swabby fixating on Pip's pretty prick.

You can see I'm real hot for him. At night, with everybody snoring all around me, I lie awake and fantasize myself in the same bunk with him. My cock head presses against my pillow between my thighs, and I imagine I'm slipping it between Pip's ass cheeks. I'd be mortified if anyone saw me doing this: I move my hips like I'm fucking him, and by the time I shoot my load into a handkerchief or a T-shirt, I half believe, in my delirium, that my tightly squeezing palms are Pip's virgin butt hole.

And so this morning under the warm shower, I'm fantasizing about him as I fist my cock. However, with an effort of will I hold off my orgasm, even to the extent of grabbing my wrist as if I'm two different persons, pulling it away from my pulsating shaft just before I will get the familiar tension in my nuts that means the climax is irreversible. After all, I have the whole afternoon and most of the evening to tease myself, and I want to make the most of it.

I feel my pulse returning to normal. My cock begins to soften, though its nerve ends still crave the touch of my fingers. I have the feeling of being in control of myself.

Well, just one more stroke. I feel my dick hardening again and begging for a second and a third stroke. I am caught up by it. I can't let go of it. I can't stop. I can't stop! I shoot a white arc of semen about two feet in the air and fall back against the bulkhead of the shower-stall.

Oh, well, I think in the afterglow, *it* was *fun.* I'll write a letter to my mother this afternoon. I rinse and, without drying, wrap the terry-cloth towel around my wet waist. I like to feel the water evaporating on my skin. I'll probably get horny again around twilight, before the guys start stumbling aboard.

Just then, Pip saunters into the head, looking rumpled, sleepy, and more human, less a vision from another planet. He nods indifferently and clops on his sandals over to a sink.

He's wearing a pair of boxer shorts with his name stenciled just above his curvaceous butt and a T-shirt that shows the imprint of his beadlike tits. Stretching languorously in front of the mirror like a house cat, he yawns and slips his hands up under his shirt to stroke his smooth midriff. The sight of his slender beige waist between the shirt and boxers starts my cock warming again and my heart pumping.

Should I make a comradely pass that I can back away from if he takes offense? After all, the guys are all the time pretending to put the make on one another as they horse around in the shower. I'd just be bantering. The chance might not present itself again till we hit Pearl Harbor, and maybe not even then. You don't have any privacy in the Navy. *So go for it, Lincoln!*

Heart jerking, I step up behind him, press my cock against the crack of his buns, and slip my arms around his waist. The feeling on my cock flesh of that resilient butt, even through the towel and skivvies, is mind-boggling. I start to panic, then think to myself, *Yeah, I can go this far and still come across as butch.*

But I have trouble controlling my own body. The fingers of my left hand slide, by an instinct of their own, up under his T-shirt to his BB-sized bare left tit, and my right hand, before I can draw it back, is fingering his limp cock through the thin cotton. I haven't touched another guy like this since I joined the Navy. But my heart is thumping in terror as well as sexual excitement, because I don't know how he will react. He could have my ass in the brig.

He's uttered a gasp of surprise, and his whole body jerks, as if I hit a ticklish spot. But he doesn't pull away from me! He begins to move both his chest and crotch in a voluptuous rhythm that makes both tit and prick rub against my fingers. And the sensation of his ass crack rubbing my cock practically turns off my headlights.

His warm, gentle hand touches mine—*to brush it away*? No! He's drawing my hand with tantalizing slowness in between the loose flaps of his fly, and I feel for the first time the full, naked, suede-smooth, lengthening, warming, stiffening shaft. I am so fucking dizzy, I'd fall down if I weren't holding on to him.

He arches his head back against my left shoulder, where his fragrant brown hair tickles my neck. I feel goose pimples run down my left arm, while my cock goes as hard as a hawser in the warmth of his butt cleavage. His dick heats up. It thickens, hardens, and now lengthens dramatically. *God, the kid has a bigger one than I do!* I imagine the ensigns playfully teasing it while he stands bashfully at attention. I feel his pulse beating through the velvety skin. I feel the rigid core, against which the skin is sliding smoothly as I fist it.

He moans, and whispers, "Fuck me, man," in a throaty, urgent way, as if he can't wait a second longer. He pulls down his shorts and then takes my hand again in his warm grasp, and I feel myself cupping his moist, hot, hairless balls.

"Come on, Linc!" he urges, rubbing his butt crack up and down against the underside of my stiff cock. "There's nobody here."

"What are you *doing*?"

"Oh, Jesus!" he groans. "Don't play with me. I know you want it, and I'm so hot to be screwed, I can't see straight!"

"The chief'll catch us!" I whine.

"Shi-i-it!" says Pip contemptuously through those cherubic lips. "That fucker's in the galley drinking torpedo juice."

I feel his hand clutching for my towel, and I let him pull it off me. My bare cock is sliding like a cooked frank between his bare buns, which he's spreading, leaning over the sink. *I'm gettin' the fuck outta here!* I tell myself. But instead, I feel the tip of my cock nuzzle his smooth, hairless, half-open fuck slit. I am feverishly stroking his nipples, partly because I'm not quite sure how to proceed at his ass.

And then I see the chief's outraged face in the mirror, and I just about die!

In his South Boston accent Boylan orders us into his private cabin and bolts the hatch. My hands and knees are shaking. Pip, on the other hand, seems calm, but that may be the effect of shock.

We stand in front of the chief's desk while the leather-skinned little man sits there, leaning back, looking us over with his watery pale blue eyes. Pip has pulled up his shorts, and I've redraped my towel about me, covering even my belly-button in my effort to regain my virginity. But the way the chief stares at my crotch makes me painfully aware that I still have a knob there.

"You know what this means?" He woofs the question like an attack dog. Then he thunders the answer: "Portsmouth!" He nods and smiles grimly, as if carrying out his bound duty in this case is going to be a distinct pleasure. I just can't keep my knees and hands from trembling. I see myself behind bars. I see myself returning home to Pinchwood in disgrace.

He picks up a black ballpoint pen and makes spirals with it to get the ink flowing. When it still fails to work, he puts it down. "Unless . . ." He narrows his eyes.

Pip leaps into the pause. "I'll do anything," he says meekly.

I wait for the chief to blow up at the brazen offer to deal. But he stops looking for another pen. "And you?" He scowls at me as if he'd just as soon pitch me out with the galley slops.

"Oh, yes, *sir*!" I blurt out. "Anything!" I rather have in mind something like a permanent assignment to swab the head or wash the chief's skivvies, and that doesn't seem too painful to agree to. He's got us by the short hairs.

The chief leans way back in his chair. "Strip!" he says through clenched teeth. His eyes are slits, and his mouth has taken a determined dip downward.

We stand uncomprehending.

"Get naked, you smartass college sons of bitches!" snarls the chief, his voice taking that Navy tone that says, *Don't try to get reasonable with me!*

Pip quickly pulls off his T-shirt and peels down his boxers. I nervously shed my towel, my skin crawling with the implications of what the chief is saying. As reckless as I've been with Pip, I've really had little experience. Well, the truth is, I haven't had *any*, if we're talking about sucking cock or taking dick up my ass.

Now the chief seems to have trouble speaking. He opens his mouth several times. Finally, in a surprisingly choked contralto, he says, "Make love—to one another!"

We stand paralyzed. "Go ahead," he says primly, as if we're naughty children. "You were doing it in the head. Do it in front of me."

Is this some kind of trick? If I show I'm homosexually aroused, will it go worse for me? Maybe he'll take pictures and use them as evidence? I look at Pip, and he looks at me. Now he seems just a bare-assed, frightened kid. My cock has retracted into a soft nub.

But Pip's dick, though flaccid, still hangs long. And now it seems to fatten, blush, and arch out from his slender thighs. The pink of his cockhead is peeking out of the foreskin.

Staring at it and at his round balls in their long, hairless pink sac, I feel my crotch warming up again, and I know my cock is betraying me, lengthening and filling. Pretty soon it will hang at full length and then swing up hard till it taps my belly button.

With that old guy looking on? I can't do this, I tell myself. I close my eyes. I feel Pip's smooth hands take hold of my cock and force it down level with his own. I feel the soft tips touch. I feel the slipperiness of his precum flowing over my cock head. I feel his satiny foreskin slide over my knob. His hands slip around my waist and slide up to my shoulders. He exerts only the mildest of pressure downward against my deltoids. I could wrestle this kid to submission with my left hand, but I sink to my knees. His wet cock brushes my chest, then my chin, then slides across my forehead, leaving its snail's trail of precum.

The tang of his sexuality is now raw in my nostrils. I lose every vestige of resistance to my powerful urges. I touch my tongue to his bubbling piss hole, then let the warm, smooth, spongy head slide between my lips and fill my mouth. And it's as if I've been doing it all my life instead of for the first time. It's better than anything else I've ever had in my mouth.

I begin to suck him, at first in a kind of wonderment at this live, hot, pungent flesh sliding down my tongue, then with a wild urgency as every part of me responds to the sensation. Pip grips the sides of my head with both warm hands and lunges into me with his hips. I grab the base of his shaft to keep the tip from causing spasms in my throat, and the velvety hard fuck tube feels so intimate against my fingers that my whole body shakes. I milk it and slurp on its luscious head and feather its ridge with my tongue, the way I've seen it in porn flicks in my college fraternity.

Pip—the kid who has seemed to me as remote and cold as a star —is swaying this way and that, moaning as if he's suffering. Pushing as far into my mouth as my fist around the base of his cock will let him, he grabs my other hand and brings it around to his butt. He takes hold of the ends of my fingers, and I feel the soft, gooey wetness of his asshole. He takes my middle finger by the first joint and presses it into the warm hole.

I feel my middle finger slide through the soft, slippery, tight muscle of his ass opening. And then it's in the grip of what seems at first like the warm, gently squeezing electric milking cylinder I used to let my cock be serviced by on the ranch. Now I want like mad to feel my cock in him. I stare speechlessly up into the mysterious gray eyes, silently begging him.

Looking hypnotically into my eyes, his fresh, youthful face turning rosy, Pip presses my shoulders, forces me onto my back on the deck. He stands astride me at my hips and slowly squats. His smooth fingers steady my upright cock, and I feel the tip tuck into the soft indentation of his ass cheeks. At this moment I don't care whether I go to Portsmouth or not. A rich surge of lust starts at my piss hole and begins to move like a hot tide through my hard cock and my body.

Pip parts his buns and does a deep-knee bend. And then I feel my cock head gripped by his soft, warm sphincter. *O Lord,* I am praying giddily, *don't make me cum right away!* I'm grateful that the good Lord made me shoot my nugget in the shower. That may give me some staying power now.

I set my whole mind to staving off my orgasm as I feel the ridge of my cock plop through the slippery but oh-so-tight muscle at his ass entrance. But the pressure on my cock just under the ridge drives me out of my mind. I give up trying to hold back.

Pip's hips descend relentlessly, and I feel the squeezing go all the way down my shaft till his smooth butt is resting against my thighs and balls. My hands have taken a tight hold of his cock as if they are gripping the horn of a saddle, and I slide the loose skin up and down the hard, slippery shaft. Pip moans as if he is dying and then grabs my hands with his and squeezes and pumps them violently.

He whimpers as his brilliant white cum shoots over my face and lands in my hair.

My hips jerk, my cock recoils, and I feel what's left of my semen discharging up into his tight ass.

Now there's a cry like that of a wounded rhino. It's from neither of us. It's from the chief.

When I finally scramble to my feet, I see the old guy leaning over the desk, eyes staring. He giggles weakly. He's looking, not at us anymore, but at a tiny puddle of rusty cum in the middle of the document that would have sent us to Portsmouth, if Navy pens worked.

JOHN M. ISON

WRITING AS
MIKE
MONTGOMERY

MY ROOMMATE

I SHOULD'VE GUESSED HIS TRUE OCCUPATION WHEN HE PAID
me first and last month's rent in crumpled twenties.

Anthony—not Tony—studied Economics at UCLA, and carried
the bookbag to prove it. When I asked him how he supported himself
through school, he grinned. He had glorious teeth. I noticed his smile
and failed to notice how he evaded my question. "Work-study program,
you know, flexible hours." He shrugged with the shoulders of an ancient
Egyptian water-carrier. If he'd said "Athletic scholarship," I wouldn't
have doubted him. Through his pale-blue Polo shirt I could see a gymnast's chiseled torso, the result of paring the male body down to the
essentials and sharpening the remains into a sculptor's dream. He wore
baggy chinos in a gesture of modesty that fortunately showed off a
generous basket and a butt that would fit nicely in two cupped palms.
On the feet: Nikes, bleached white. "I won't stiff you on the rent. Shake
on it," he demonstrated before I could object.

Funny. I was thirty-four and nobody's idea of a catch, moneywise or sexually. I've learned to avoid the hustlers, the takers, the liars that thrive in this big city. I've had to, for they play me too well. I've prided myself on choosing friends and coworkers with scrupulous care. With my hours at the store cut in half, I needed to share my apartment for the first time. I promised myself that I'd screen all applicants to within an inch of their lives. That was until Anthony, my first and last applicant, took my hand in a firm but smooth-skinned grip. His direct, blue-eyed stare broke my resolve, and my gaze dropped down to his elegantly-veined forearm that flexed with his final grip on my hand. I withdrew the hand before it broke into a sweat.

I hear moans coming from Anthony's room. His door is ajar. "Want me to close it?" I ask. I hear no response, so I approach the doorway and lean in. My roommate wears no clothes and he kneels by his bed. He grips his thick, uncut cock and beats off. He waves for me to enter. I don't observe this until I'm a couple of feet from him, but Anthony's got a dog collar around his neck. A metal chain stretches from the collar to the right side of the headboard. He looks up at me from a head bowed low, and whispers, "Dad's teaching me a lesson. He wants me to make it up to you by doing anything you want." "Anything?" I ask, in a cool, cruel voice I don't recognize. He nods, but still looks at the floor. "Then suck my cock, and don't fuck up," I reply. As he unzips my pants and swallows my hardening penis, I run my fingers through his blond hair. "If you do, I'll throw your naked ass on the street," I add, tightening my grip on his hair. His open face shrivels up from the pain; I pull harder until his eyes redden and spill with tears . . .

Anthony put me to shame. Not only did he pay his bills on time and never leave one dish in the sink, but he found time to vacuum, scrub the floors and bake a wonderful chocolate cake. "Thought you might like something sweet after a hard day's work," his note read. "Yeah, where are you?" I thought.

He hadn't a clue that I pined after him, I hoped. On late Saturday mornings while I sat on the couch reading the paper, he liked to aerobic dance to the disco radio. He dressed in black spandex shorts while he grooved in the living room. I wanted to collect in my open mouth the sweat that glided down his writhing back and soaked his waistband, or splashed on the floor. I wished that I could brush paint on the soles of his feet and make him dance on canvas. I'd hang the prints on my bedroom ceiling.

Our schedules conflicted. When I came home, Anthony was at work, or at a night lecture. I didn't go out much, usually plopped on the couch and watched TV, or read magazines. I zoned out to the point where I couldn't hear anything else. That is, I used to. One evening, I listened to Anthony's voice reciting the message on his answering machine. After the beep, I heard a deep, masculine voice explaining what he'd like to do to Anthony in exchange for a certain, possibly negotiable fee.

The john's name is Howard, but tonight he's Buck. Works on a construction crew. Boss chews him out, old lady's on the rag and the Packers break his heart. Has a choice: Drown his sorrows at the local pub or take it out on that blond sissy who stares at Buck while he powerdrills shirtless on campus. First thing he wants, when he meets Anthony, is a tonguebath. He's so steamed he never bothered to shower so he needs a hot faggot mouth to wash off the funk. Anthony sticks out a long, red snake tongue and stabs it square in the fur-thatched navel. He's forced to clean out the lint and swallow, then work his way through the hair that covers the stomach and chest and suck up the grime and sweat and dust and heat of his horny master. Take your time, he hears, on my tits. Chew on 'em, you can do better than that, cut those baby teeth on 'em or I'll bust your jaw. Nurse 'em, slut, nurse your daddy's tits and I'll give you the kinda milk you really need. Buck raises his arms and welcomes the dripping mouth of his puss-boy who gags and hardens from the unwashed stink of his worked-out armpits. Sniff 'em, boy, lemme hear you take my smell up your cute little button nose, lemme spoil you with my rank bod. That's it, lick up, gorge on the salty stubble on my neck and chin, that's what daddy tastes like, what manhood's all about . . .

"What, exactly, do you do?" I asked Anthony one morning in the hall-way. I rushed for work and he ambled off to his morning piss. Maybe it was bad timing on my part. He leaned against the wall and rubbed his sleep-coated eyes.

"Uh, gee . . . lots of things," he replied. He started to laugh the way people laugh after a particularly rotten day. "I'm on call." He wiped his mouth of his laughter and coughed, dropping the mask to expose the nervousness beneath. "Why do you ask, Fred?"

"Just curious," I said. "I was wondering who I should call in case you're at work during an emergency."

"There won't be one, don't fret," Anthony grinned. He telegraphed

his opinion in his strange stare: older folks and their worrisome obsessions. "Besides, I'm well taken care of."

Could I believe that? I thought. Despite the constant ringing of
his telephone behind a closed door, despite the voluminous recorded
messages, I'd always seen Anthony alone. For some reason, I couldn't
imagine him otherwise.

*I search for Anthony one night after work. I drive down the stretch of Santa
Monica Boulevard between Fairfax and Vine, watching the pavement break up
into hunks of weed and concrete, studying the steady decay of the boys' bodies
that strut and pose at bus benches or in front of convenience stores. Some have
his taut nipples, his rounded shoulders or his corn-husk-colored hair, but they
also sport tattoos, acne scars or pimples, broken teeth, grimy fingernails, sneakers
that have exploded in the toes from too many laps around the block. They are
friendly to men who drive. They are so friendly they'd flay you alive and leave
you with less than bus fare. I bet none of them know how to make a chocolate
cake, let alone dance to the rhythm of a disco beat. I drive on for several more
blocks before I finally spot him. On a desolate streetcorner, in bun-hugging denim
shorts and motorcycle boots, bumming a cig from some hillbilly with greasy hair
that hangs to his shoulders like strands of maple syrup, stands my Anthony. I
mean, his Anthony. I mean, himself. What's he doing with someone like that
hayseed? Are they conspiring together? Will they meet some poor sucker behind
the wheel of a Continental, drive to some alley or hillside, pull down their pants,
fling their erections in their driver's fat face, pump between his overfed lips and
demand a raise? Or maybe the porker will pay the two of them to get it on
while he watches. Yes. That's it. Jethro will shuck himself of his jeans and
degrade my roommate in the back seat while this executive or CEO or whatever
jerks his flabby rod awake, alive. He'll turn my roommate over, spread his clean,
white cheeks—Anthony, unlike most street trash, knows the importance of
hygiene—spit in the crack, stare at the loopy saliva running down Anthony's
crevice, into his hole, bunching in a ball with sweaty ass-hair. Transfixed, he
won't bother to lube himself up. Possessed of the need to claim this willing boy
for himself, he'll shove his dry dick straight up Anthony's chute. Hillbilly knows
that if he doesn't strike now, he'll never have the chance to own such perfection
again. He'll heed not a sound of Anthony's tortured screams. The john will dig
it all, think it's part of the trip . . .*

Anthony had an annoying, incriminating habit. He always left his book
bag in the living room. While he slept, and I could only toss in my

unmade bed, I sneaked out of my bedroom and counted the number of books he carried in his bag. I expected an uncovering of a ruse, but to my disappointment I pulled out fat, dull volumes full of theory. Underlined, highlighted, dogeared, noted. Thin, lined books transcribing hours of lecture. The adjoining pouch contained no contradictions. A Walkman. Two packs of gum. Several pens and pencils. Not even a small, tasteful jar of Vaseline to elicit suspicion.

Zipping up the bag and replacing it by the coffee table, I was seized with homicidal loathing. I wanted to break into Anthony's room and peel the skin off of his perfect body. While ruining him for life, for anyone else, I'd cry, "What right do you have to own it all? A body, a brain, a heart? What right do you have to stir my envy?"

Strips of him would hang from his lower back like a prisoner's tattered shirt before his first flogging.

The wind howls through a broken window in the abandoned house. I crawl through the hole where a chimney had collapsed and stay down on the broken wood floor littered with nails. I try to sort out the sounds of creaking and wind blowing, and listen for the possibility of pain being inflicted or felt in the next room. All I hear is the pressure of my hand on the floor, that is, the sigh of the boards beneath my palms and my knees. I crawl closer to the hallway and peek through a bedroom door, ajar. A man stands over Anthony, fastening a rope around his neck. He caresses my roommate's cheek with a bare hand, and with the other tightens the noose. Anthony stares straight ahead, accepting the inevitability of the deed. I refuse. I know that I arrived here for a purpose, and that was to rescue my friend. I leap out and tackle his assailant, knock him cold with a few blows to the jaw. As we both tumble to the ground, I fall through a hole in the floor, and find myself swirling in a mudhole, naked, swimming to avoid the downpour of fresh mud from the sky. My cock hardens from the sensation of liquid and dirt possessing my body, caking on my skin the moment I rest. I fight the urge to surrender, to luxuriate in the mud, afraid it will swallow me up, like quicksand. I search for Anthony, wondering whether he saw me fall. He calls to me from a cloud above my head. "You wouldn't understand," he says. As I try to scrub the mud out from under my fingernails, knowing I'm only embedding it deeper into me, I ask, "Anthony, did you love him?"

My clock read 4:30 A.M. when Anthony knocked on my bedroom door. I lost the first good-night's-sleep I'd had in weeks and bolted awake. "Are you all right? What's the matter?"

He laughed, shyly, "It's nothing, really, I feel so embarrassed, but, well . . ." He hung his head, a gesture incongruous with his normally confident image. "I had a nightmare. I get them. Bad ones."

I relaxed. Neither of us had turned on a light, so Anthony could not see the happiness in my eyes as I spoke to him. "Me too. Nothing to be afraid of. It's windy out there, I know that adds to it."

"Thanks, but I was wondering . . . No. That's too much." He turned away from me apologetically.

"Tell me," I said. My voice was flat. I longed to beg him to fill the void my spread arms had made, but I wouldn't.

"May I sleep with you tonight? I'm sorry."

I pulled back the covers in reply. He slipped between the sheets and kicked the covers a few times to feel his way around the new environment. He repeated his apology and rolled from side to side, searching for a comfortable sleeping position. I regretted doing so, but my arms refolded on my chest when he joined me in bed.

"Fred, do you have enough room? I don't want to impose. I need to feel safe right now, for a while."

I could no longer hate him. I realized that my hatred was a wall I built to protect myself from my love for Anthony. If not love, then desire. Or need. Once I'd dismantled that wall, I could bathe in the outpouring of affection I felt for him. It buoyed me, carried me to a safe harbor where I would never know loneliness. I drifted so wonderfully on these thoughts that I almost failed to notice Anthony's warm, wet palm as he placed it on my leg. "Thank you," he whispered, and buried his head in my spare pillow.

We sleep cuddled in a spoon position in my bed. While watching him, while I move with the rise and fall of his back against my chest, I lick the nape of his neck. I inhale the salty sweat from his neck, the greasy cream scent from the blond arrow-shape his hair makes in the back of his head. My cock swells with desire, from the thrill of testing a taboo. Anthony is off limits, but he arches his back and reaches his arms around my buttocks as if I were welcome. Taking the liberty, I cover his neck, his earlobes, his shoulders and upper back with a trail of wet kisses and bites. My fingers tease, twist, pull on his firm nipples; I savor the idea that I might taste them in the near future. His butt bucks into my groin, bumping my cockhead in either recognition or invitation. I run my hands over his thighs, his hips, his hairless chest; between the span of my arms his body writhes and grinds into the mattress, into me. I cannot wait. I spit into my right hand and grip his neck with my left. I lubricate myself and him and spread his cheeks. Raising an arm and diving with outstretched tongue into an armpit, I enter him. He groans and clamps down on my cockhead, but I won't stop. I slaver over the thatched pit and probe deep inside my roommate, who is now mine. Sweat runs in rivulets down my back and between my nipples, sucking his back into my embrace. He breathes shallowly, as if he's unwilling to surrender to the joy, as if he still expects, awaits, pain to envelop him. I prod further, and soon I'm completely inside. I stay there for a bit, massaging his back muscles, licking the delicate spirals of his ears. I coo into his ears. I purr. I praise him, using every phrase I know but the one I ache to use. I will not tell him he's loved, not yet. When, if, I do, it will remind me that I am thirty-four and have never been loved. In time, he gives way and sighs with pleasure, permitting me to pump through his body. As I begin, I pivot him around so that he faces me, raising his legs and running my tongue down the length from thigh to ankle. His arms clasp my neck, his fingers grip my hair. His mouth he keeps open, for breath, for words. I peck at his nipples, his neck, biting harder and leaving bruises the size of my fingertips. He doesn't mind; he jerks his head from side to side, admitting the marks, accepting the touch of my body against his. As I continue to pump him, holding his legs and wishing for him to buck his ass up to my cock, I wait, with the patience of the old or the ignorant, for him to say, "I love you."

I awoke to the smell of frying sausage and burnt toast. My side throbbed as it thawed out from sleeping in one crooked position for hours, and my head ached from the lack of deep slumber. I remembered that I was so afraid of touching my roommate, even innocently, that I curled myself up on the opposite side of my bed, allowing him to splay his body across the sheets.

"You didn't have to do that," I said when I saw the table setting for breakfast.

"It's the least," Anthony shrugged. He was naked except for a barbeque apron that covered his chest and waist. A lobster, streaked with oil, danced a jig on the front. He handed me a full glass of freshly squeezed orange juice. It was milky with pulp. "I wish I weren't so afraid of night. The dark. That kinda stuff."

"Let me take care of you," I blurted out. Hearing the folly of my words, I continued in a rush. "Quit that racket and let me protect you. You don't have to do that anymore, ever. I promise."

He put his spatula down and stared at me. He shook his head.

"You don't understand, do you?" He bit a cuticle and threw me a lopsided grin. As I stared at him, or, rather, the muscles in his forearm flexing as he chewed on his cuticle, I heard the sizzle of frying meat, and knew it would smoke soon.

"I can afford it," I lied. "Let me . . ." I stopped. What I was telling my roommate, what I could never tell him to his face, was this. "Let me love you. Don't laugh." I wasn't sure if I could ask this of anyone.

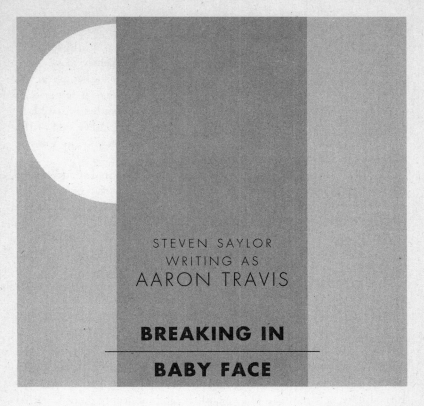

STEVEN SAYLOR
WRITING AS
AARON TRAVIS

BREAKING IN

BABY FACE

"SO THIS IS THE NEW KID?" LARRY MCMASTERS RAISES ONE eyebrow and flicks his gold-plated Bic, igniting the fat cigar wedged in his mouth. He puffs, filling the air with blue smoke, then leans back in his swivel chair.

McMasters is impeccably dressed: gold cufflinks, silk tie, a dark-blue polyester suit specially tailored to fit his enormous shoulders and chest. McMasters is impeccably groomed: His black hair is sheared off in a severe flattop, his manicured fingernails are buffed to a high gloss, oddly out of place with his big strangler's hands. Some people call him handsome. Others are put off by the stony set of his jaw and the predatory glint in his eyes.

His office is plushly carpeted, panelled with fine dark wood. Daylight has faded beyond the skinny blinds. The only illumination comes from the silent bank of video screens set into one wall. Each of the screens plays a continuous loop of videotape; all twelve screens show a wrestling match in progress. Larry McMasters, a millionaire at the age of thirty-eight, is the Bossman, head honcho of the Worldwide Pro Wrestling Confederation. The Bossman can afford expensive toys.

Toys like Mongo Monahan, who stands smiling and smug on the other side of McMasters' desk. Like the Bossman, Mongo is larger than life—six-foot-two, 250 pounds of rock-solid muscle poured into a black tanktop so tight that his shaved nipples peek out on either side of the straps, and a pair of skintight blue jeans that show off a bulge the size of a grapefruit at his crotch.

Despite the dim lighting, Mongo wears his trademark mirror shades, along with the trademark smirk of disgust beloved by wrestling fans around the world. Greasy kidstuff keeps his jet-black hair swept back from his brutally handsome face.

Mongo reaches over and squeezes the shoulder of the tall young blond standing next to him. His voice is deep, gruff and stupid. "Yeah, Boss, this is the one. The kid I told you about." His grip bites into the blond's flesh like metal pincers. The kid tries to smile, but only manages a crooked wince.

"So, kid—Mongo here tells me you're interested in trying out for a spot on the show. Says you got ambitions to be a pro wrestler."

The kid shuffles his feet, clears his throat. "That's right, Sir." His blond hair is cut boyishly long, curling down onto his shoulders, a golden frame for a sweetly angelic face—bright blue eyes, spunky up-turned nose, soft red lips. His smooth cheeks are deeply tanned, with a faint blush shining through. A baby face. Mongo's already told McMasters the kid's age: nineteen. But with a face like that, they'll be carding him at bars until he's thirty.

Below the neck, the kid is hardly a baby. From the rib cage down his white T-shirt hangs loose above his tight, flat stomach, but from the chest up the shirt seems to be two sizes too small. The kid is top-heavy with muscle—big square shoulders, a massive column of a neck, huge biceps that threaten to pop his sleeves. His pecs are enormous. The shirt is stretched thin across his chest, barely able to accommodate the bulging slabs of muscle. Set at the tip of each sweeping curve is a nipple the size of a half dollar, softly swollen and protruding against the thin white cotton.

Inside his faded blue jeans are a pair of big, muscular legs—the denim is frayed thin above the knees from rubbing against his bulging thighs. The kid doesn't show much basket, especially compared to the hamlike bulge that pushes from Mongo Monahan's crotch. But he bulges

very nicely from the rear, where the hard muscles of his ass seem ready
to split the seam of his pants.

McMasters puffs on his cigar and looks the kid up and down. He
likes the innocent, slightly blushing face. He likes the way the boy's
plump nipples show through his white T-shirt. He especially likes the
little bead of sweat that clings to the kid's upturned nose, and the way
he stands there with his arms at his sides, fidgeting, too nervous to look
him in the eye.

"You wrestled before?"

"In high school, Sir. All-state three years in a row. And gymnastics.
Swimming. Track. Football. Weight lifting . . ."

"Yeah," Mongo says, "that's how I met the kid. Working out down
at Sharky's gym. Always hanging around when me and Matt Matthews
were pumping the weights. Turns out the kid's got a thing about pro
wrestlers." Mongo sniggers. "I mean, about pro *wrestling*."

McMasters nods through a wreath of cigar smoke. "So, kid, just
how much do you know about pro wrestling? It's not much like the
wrestling you did in high school—if you know what I mean."

Mongo gives the kid's shoulder a punch and answers for him. "He
knows the score. I been giving him some private training. Teaching him
the ropes. Hell, like the kid said, he's a fucking gymnast. He can fake
a tumble."

"Been training him, huh?" McMasters raises an eyebrow.

Mongo smirks. "Not the way you mean. Not yet." He steps back,
out of the kid's eyeshot, and reaches down to grope himself. He and
McMasters exchange a knowing grin.

"Alright then." McMasters settles back in his chair. "Show me what
you got, boy."

The kid bats his eyelashes, confused.

"Come on, kid," Mongo sneers. "Take off your shirt. The Bossman
wants a look at your bod."

The kid blushes and bites his lip, then reaches up and peels the
T-shirt over his head. Larry McMasters is used to being surrounded and
serviced by some of the finest physiques in the world, but even the
Bossman of the WPWC can't suppress a low grunt of approval. The
symmetry is breathtaking—massive shoulders and chest, flaring lats, a
hard flat belly corrugated with muscle. Skin like satin, burnished with
a deep golden tan.

"You shave your chest, kid?"

The kid seems shocked. "Why, no, Sir."

McMasters nods. Naturally hairless. Smooth as a baby. Probably not a hair on his legs, either. "Okay. Take off your pants."

The kid hesitates, then unbuttons his jeans and slides them down to his sneakers, unties his sneakers and kicks his feet free. Now he's dressed only in cotton socks and a pair of skimpy briefs, white as snow against his honey-colored flesh. Just as McMasters expected—the boy's legs are virtually hairless, long and sleek, superbly muscled. McMasters purses his lips and sucks in his breath.

"What did I tell you?" Mongo says. "The kid's built like a god-damn Greek statue. Yeah, like a fucking statue."

"A *fucking* statue, huh? My favorite kind." McMasters smiles. "You might do, kid. You just might. Turn around."

McMasters squeezes his crotch. Mongo grins and does the same. Both of them run their eyes over the kid's backside, from the long golden hair that brushes against his broad shoulders, down the tapering V of his back to the silky depression at the base of his spine, to the big muscular ass still hidden inside his briefs. On down to the broad thighs, and the kid's unusually developed calves, thick ankles and big flat feet.

"Interesting," McMasters says. "Let's see the rest."

The kid looks over his shoulder. His voice quavers. "The rest, Sir?"

"Yeah, the rest," Mongo smirks. "Don't act stupid, kid."

The Bossman waves his cigar. "You see, kid, I handpick every man who enters the ring. We've got pretty high standards in the WPWC—damned high. I've got some of the finest bodybuilders and pro athletes in the world working under me. My viewers expect the very best. If I'm gonna take you on, I've gotta see exactly what I've got to work with. Exactly what you've got to offer. Pull down your shorts."

The kid darts another quick, blushing glance over his shoulder. Turns his face away. Grabs the waistband of his briefs and peels them down over his thighs. Bends deep to step out of them, thrusting his naked, flexing ass directly under Mongo's smoldering stare. Mongo licks his lips.

The kid stands, straightens his back, squares his shoulders. Naked except for his white cotton socks.

McMasters and Mongo exchange a leering grin. The kid's ass is phenomenal. Two bronzed globes of rock-solid muscle, revealing the skimpiest tan line McMasters has ever seen—just a tiny strip of snow-white flesh like twin arcs across the top of his buns. The remainder of his ass is as honey-gold as the rest of him—shiny brown buttocks, hard and round with muscle, melting down into his sturdy thighs without a crease. Smooth as silk, gently dimpled, perfectly molded to fit a man's hands.

McMasters puffs on his cigar. "Okay, blondie. Turn around."

The kid reaches for his underwear. Mongo is too quick for him. He catches the briefs under the toe of his boot and drags them out of the boy's reach. "The Bossman didn't say nothing about you putting your panties back on."

The kid freezes, bent over with his ass in the air. He twists his neck and looks up at Mongo. The big wrestler stands with his hands on his hips, sneering down at him, the bulge at his crotch straining against the fly of his jeans like a clenched fist. The kid bites his lip, looks away, then slowly stands straight.

"Go ahead, kid." McMasters flicks the ashes from his cigar. "Turn around."

He starts to turn, then stops. Starts again, and makes it halfway. Then finally turns to face McMasters.

The kid hangs his head, blushing furiously. Big veins stand out on either side of his neck. Even his big pecs begin to blush, turning apple-red and shiny in the lurid light. His hands fidget at his sides, as if he'd like to cover himself—but doesn't want to draw attention to the stiff erection springing up from his hips.

McMasters smiles. The kid's cock is a definite disappointment— or would be, if McMasters had any interest in his dick. The important thing is that it's hard—hard as a rock. So hard it looks almost painful, poking up red and swollen from his tidy little bush of golden pubic hair. A short, stubby cock, like a tiny handle sticking up from his groin, ludicrously out of proportion with the big muscles popping out all over the rest of his body.

McMasters makes a point of staring at the boy's puny hard-on and shaking his head in sympathy, as if the kid had just shown him an embarrassing handicap, like a club foot or an ugly birth-mark. "Well," he says, "at least you've got the *body* to make it in the WPWC."

The kid stutters a grateful, "Thank you, Sir."

"Don't mention it." McMasters bolts from his chair, walks up to the kid and slowly circles him, puffing on his cigar, raking his eyes up and down his naked nineteen-year-old body. The kid is blushing all over, lighting up his golden tan with an inner glow. His muscles glisten under a thin sheen of nervous sweat. His cock stays hard as a rock.

"Well, now that we've seen the raw material, let's see what we can do to dress it up."

The kid sighs with relief at the idea of getting into some clothes. "I brought some wrestling togs. Blue and green—"

"No. Uh-uh. I don't think so." McMasters shakes his head. "You don't seem to understand, kid. We don't just put you in some wrestling trunks and send you out into the ring. You gotta have a package, a concept. An idea to build on. We could start with your name."

"My name? It's—"

"Forget it, kid. Not the name your momma gave you. The name *I'm* gonna give you." McMasters steps closer, reaches out and cups the kid's chin. Skin so baby-soft and smooth McMasters wonders if he's ever had to shave it. The kid flinches at the contact.

McMasters tilts his head back, purses his lips. "Baby Face," he announces. "That's it. The whole world is gonna know you as Baby Face. Yeah—Baby Face Billy. Or Bobby. Or maybe . . ."

"Bruce!" Mongo grunts.

"You're a fucking genius, Mongo. That's it—Baby Face Bruce from Billings, Montana!"

The kid chews his lip and stares at the carpet. His shoulders slump. Even his hard-on goes down a little. But he makes no objection. McMasters is the Bossman, after all.

"Now we got the concept. Now we're rolling!" McMasters walks to a big mahogany bureau against one wall and rummages through a drawer, tossing out slinky wrestling thongs and mail-order panties, leather straps and shiny dog collars.

Mongo watches and sniggers, wondering what the Bossman will come up with. Panties are McMasters' favorite fetish, slinky see-through handfuls of nothing purchased from trashy mail-order catalogues— Mongo knows, from personal experience. Once upon a time, under similar circumstances, Mongo himself was pressed into modelling a frilly pink pair for the Bossman's amusement—and ended up bent over the Bossman's desk, the panties pulled down to his knees, squealing and grunting while McMasters plowed his foot-long cock in and out of Mongo's ass. Of course, that was a long time ago—back when Mongo was still a nobody named Joe Smolinsky, just a fresh young kid with muscles and a dream, ready to do anything to break into the pro wrestling circuit. Like Baby Face, standing obediently in the middle of the room, nude and erect and blushing, waiting for the Bossman to dress him up.

McMasters finally finds what he wants. He steps behind the kid. "Raise your arms, Baby Face."

McMasters wraps something around his hips, draws it up between his thighs, pulls it tight. Steps back to take a look.

"What do you think, Mongo?"

"Damn, Boss! It's perfect! What a fucking imagination you got. I don't think it's ever been done before."

The kid looks down, and feels a sinking sensation in the pit of his stomach. McMasters has put him in a diaper!

"Gee, Sir, I don't know if—"

"For chrissakes, kid, stop whining." Mongo rolls his eyes in disgust. "The man is a professional."

"But I feel—ridiculous." The kid blushes deep red from head to toe.

"Don't sweat it, kid." McMasters circles him, staring down at the diaper, adjusting the big metal pins with pink plastic heads. It's a skimpy fit, like a tiny white loincloth—slung low beneath the kid's navel, poking out in front to show the outline of his hard-on. In back it rides up the crack of his ass, showing off his smooth tanned buttocks.

"The long hair may be a problem," Mongo says. "All the babies I ever seen are bald. Maybe we oughta shave it."

The kid turns ghostly pale and makes a funny noise in his throat, like he's about to be sick.

McMasters laughs. "Nah, that can wait. Maybe we'll save it for a grudge match, Mongo, one of these days when we need to pump up the ratings. Let you shave him bald right there in the ring, so all the rednecks can watch."

The kid sighs with relief, but his legs feel wobbly.

McMasters rubs his chin. "There's still something missing. I know what it is!" He reaches into his desk and pulls out a big plastic bottle with a pink label. He pitches it to the kid.

The kid tries to catch it and fumbles—the slippery bottle pops right out of his hands and lands on the carpet with a thud.

"Baby oil," explains McMasters as the kid stoops to pick it up. "Baby oil for Baby Face. Slick yourself up, kid."

Baby Face squirts the stuff into the palm of his hand, smooths it over his big shoulders and down his biceps. McMasters watches, smiling like a shark. "Come on, Brucie boy, pour it on. Like you're basting a chicken. That's it, squirt it all over your tits. And rub it in good."

The kid looks like he's feeling himself up—playing with his big fleshy pecs, cupping the smooth slabs of muscles in his hands, rubbing and squeezing, making his big nipples pop out between his fingers.

"Your legs, too." McMasters steps behind to watch as the kid bends deep, slicking his hands down his thighs, stretching to oil up his calves and ankles.

"Good enough. Hand me the bottle. I'll do your back."

Baby Face stands. McMasters squirts a stream of oil across his broad shoulders and roughly massages the big muscles, probing the resilient flesh under his gliding fingertips, trailing his hands down the kid's spine until his thumbs come to rest in the hard little dimples just above his ass.

"Bend over, Baby Face."

The kid goes stiff.

"Come on, Brucie boy. Grab your ankles. We gotta oil up your bottom."

"But—I could oil it up myself, Sir."

Mongo snorts and rolls his eyes. "Sheeze, kid, you're embarrassing me. Come on. Do what the man tells you."

Baby Face hesitates, straining to get a glimpse of McMasters over his shoulder, then takes a deep breath and bends over, keeping his legs straight, grabbing his ankles. The diaper digs into his crack, baring his buttocks completely. His cheeks blush golden-red as they rear up and make contact with the Bossman's waiting fingertips.

McMasters lets out a sigh of pure lust. The kid's ass feels even better than it looks—taut as a drumhead, smooth as marble. He takes his time oiling it up. Feeling it up. Running his greasy palms all over the hard round globes. Giving Baby Face a nice greasy butt that glistens in the colored light from the TV screens.

He loops his finger under the little flap that runs up the crack of the kid's ass and pulls it aside. The sight of the boy's hole hits him like a fist in the gut. Bent over, with his cheeks stretched wide open, the little hole is completely exposed and slightly protruding, like pouting lips. A trickle of oil runs down the boy's crack and nestles in the wrinkled folds, making the rosebud shimmer.

Virgin ass. Larry McMasters knows it when he sees it. The kid has never been dicked. Virgin boypussy, sweet and tight. Ripe to be split wide open by the Bossman's cock. He imagines his hard dick poised at the opening, nudging up against it. He closes his eyes and can almost feel the tightly clamped ring of flesh nipping at his cockhead as it shoves relentlessly forward and then pops inside—can almost hear the kid squeal and feel him squirm, the way they always do. Virgins squeal loudest of all. . . .

But not yet. McMasters opens his eyes and lets out a sigh of anticipation. He snaps his middle finger against the tiny hole—watches it snap open and shut, hears Baby Face gasp in surprise. Then he steps back, slapping the kid's greasy ass—a friendly swat, just hard enough to leave a glowing red handprint.

"Okay, Baby Dick—I mean, Baby Face. Time for you to strut that ass for me out in the ring. . . ."

Baby Face hits the boards flat on his back and lets out a grunt. Damn! Mongo was never this rough in their practice sessions. For the last thirty minutes he's been tossing the kid around the ring like a rag doll. Slamming him into the turnbuckles, back-flipping him onto the boards, spinning him into the ropes.

And hitting him. Hard. Punches in the gut, chops across the shoulders, even a few stinging slaps across his face. It's almost as if he's really trying to hurt the kid.

Baby Face can't understand it. He knows the rules, the illusion behind the brutal facade of pro wrestling. He and Mongo are supposed to work together, fake the falls, put on a good show. But it seems like Mongo is trying to kill him. And that scares him. Because when it comes right down to it, Mongo outweighs him by at least fifty pounds and packs a lot more experience and muscle. Baby Face is like putty in his hands—it's all he can do just to keep Mongo from breaking him in two.

McMasters watches it all from a folding chair in the corner of the ring. He sits with his arms crossed, legs sticking straight out. The kid occasionally looks to him in confusion, thinking he'll put a stop to Mongo's rampage. But it's obvious from the smirk on his face that this show is just what the Bossman had in mind.

The auditorium is empty except for the three of them, silent except for the kid's gasping and grunting and the echoing crack of flesh against flesh. Dark except for the cone of blinding light illuminating the ring. A spooky place, strangely unreal without a hoard of screaming rednecks to give it life.

The auditorium is just a short distance from McMasters' office,

across a wide expanse of empty parking lot. They could have driven,
but McMasters insisted that they walk—and insisted that Baby Face
take the trip in costume. "You might as well get used to your diaper,
kid. Twenty million raving American rednecks are gonna see you in it
every Saturday night. . . ."

So they strolled to the auditorium, Baby Face blushing and barefoot, glad the parking lot was empty so that no one would see his hard-
on poking against the front of his diaper like a tent-peg.

On the way, McMasters explained a few things. "You may think
that the world of pro wrestling is split between good guys and bad guys.
It ain't so. The split comes between what I call Tops and Bottoms. A
Top may be a good guy or a villain, an angel or an asshole, but whatever,
he's got that certain something that makes the crowd wanna see him
come out on top—like Mongo here. They love to see him mop the floor
with some guy. Same thing with a Bottom. Good guy, bad guy, doesn't
matter. He's got that certain something that makes the crowd go wild
when they see him get the shit knocked out of him.

"Take you, for example. Good-looking kid, clean-cut, all-American.
Definitely a hero type. But my viewers aren't gonna like you one bit.
They're hard-working, beer-belching American rednecks, and to them
you're just another pampered pretty boy who's got it made on his looks.
They're gonna love it when a goon like Mongo throws you down and
stamps on you, drags you up by your hair and backhands you across the
face. I know my audience, Baby Face. They want to see a kid like you
humiliated out in that ring. See you suffer and squirm. They want to
see the look on your pretty face when Mongo pins you down and the
ref counts three, and the pretty boy loses out to the neighborhood bully.
You understand what I'm saying, Baby Face? You were born to be a
Bottom in the world of pro wrestling."

McMasters kept his face hard and stony all through his little
speech—then suddenly smiled as he took a sidelong glance down at the
kid's greasy buttocks, popping out of his diaper and jiggling with each
step that brought him closer to the ring. . . .

Baby Face lands flat on his back again. He just can't take any more.
He aches all over, his muscles are like jelly, he can hardly breathe. If
Mongo would only let up for a second. Just give him one second to
catch his breath. At least his hard-on has disappeared.

He stares up, blinded by the lights. Mongo looms over him, his
sweat-drenched tanktop molded to his muscular torso, his eyes hidden
behind the mirror shades, his jaw clenched in a taunting smirk. The

bulge at his crotch is bigger than ever. He cups his hand and curls his fingers back, gesturing for Baby Face to get up.

"Come on, Baby Dick. On your feet. I haven't even started working you over yet. Come on, you a pussy or something? The man's watching."

Baby Face struggles to his knees, stumbling forward. For just an instant his nose brushes against Mongo's crotch. The odor has a weird effect on him, making his head go light, making him tingle between his legs. He rises to his feet—and immediately Mongo's big meaty fist slugs him square in the belly. The kid doubles over and tries to back away, but Mongo's other hand clutches the back of his neck, holding him in place while he slams the kid's washboard stomach over and over, knocking more breath out of him with each blow until the kid is as limp as a leaky punching bag.

From somewhere far away, the kid hears McMasters laughing. The room spins as Mongo grabs him by the hair and waltzes him toward the ropes, whirling him around, lifting his helpless arms and tangling them in the ropes, putting him into a crucified pose.

"Come on, kid!" McMasters sounds angry. "Put some emotion into it. Ninety-nine percent of this game is acting. Just look at Mongo. A pussycat—but he can sure play one mean son of a bitch, can't he? So let's see some feeling. Show me some *real* suffering!"

Baby Face manages to lift his head. Lips pouting and swollen, eyebrows drawn together, cheeks hollow. Not acting at all.

"Nah, that's not it. Help him out, Mongo."

Mongo grabs him by the hair, wrenches his head back and slaps his face back and forth. The kid is helpless, unable to move, his arms trapped in the ropes. The slaps are real, hard and meaty, making his eyes tear up, making his cheeks sting and burn hotter than the blush spreading across his face—because Baby Face is starting to get a hard-on again.

Mongo notices. So does McMasters. It's time to speed up the audition. Time for Baby Face to learn what it really means to be a Bottom in the world of Larry McMasters.

Mongo slaps him a final time, then yanks the boy's head up, turning his face toward McMasters for the Bossman's approval. The kid's dick pokes as stiff as a broom handle against his diaper. He stares back at McMasters through bleary eyes, then opens his mouth and grunts as Mongo punches him in the belly. "Yeah," McMasters croons, "that's better. Now *that* looks like genuine suffering."

Mongo untangles the boy's arms, grabs him by the hair and walks him toward McMasters. The kid stumbles, held up by the fist in his hair. His hard-on bounces up and down inside his diaper. Mongo spins him around. The kid stands on his own two feet, but just barely, and not for long. Mongo pokes his chest. Baby Face tumbles backward, trips over McMasters' outstretched foot and lands flat on his ass.

McMasters laughs. "Get up, Baby Face."

The kid struggles to his knees, but that's as far as he can manage. He takes a deep, rattling breath and finally finds enough air to eke out a whisper. "Please, Sir. Please, I don't think I can take any more."

McMasters raises an eyebrow. "But you haven't taken anything— yet." He blatantly squeezes the enormous ridge of flesh running down his pants leg. The kid shakes his head to clear it, catches sight of the thing in McMasters' pants and blinks in disbelief.

"You look real good, Baby Face. Damn good." The Bossman's voice is low and crooning. "All smooth and muscular and innocent in your little white diaper. Taking your punishment from big ol' Mongo. Oh yeah, you've got what it takes, Baby Face. The fans are gonna eat you up."

Baby Face just nods, fascinated by the impossible bulge at the crotch of McMasters' pants.

"Just one more thing, kid. One more test. I gotta see you crawl. That's very important, crawling. You'll be doing a lot of it in the ring. Crawling on your hands and knees for big mean studs like Mongo, and Lanny Boy Jones, and Leo Logan and Brick Lewde, while twenty million American rednecks get an eyeful of that big shiny butt of yours. I gotta make sure you got the right look. Gotta make sure you know how to crawl like a genuine Bottom Boy. So do it for me. Crawl for the Bossman, Baby Face."

For a long moment, the kid can't tear his eyes from the swollen ridge running down McMasters' pants leg—the thing reaches almost to his knee! Then he slowly drops onto all-fours and heads toward the opposite corner, keeping his limbs pulled in tight, his chest grazing the floor, raising his ass high in the air, crawling like a baby. Behind him he hears McMasters suck in his breath, and then another sound, a zipper being unzipped.

The kid blushes furiously. His cock throbs between his legs. He crawls all the way to the opposite corner. Then he turns—and stares, unable to believe his eyes.

McMasters' legs are spread wide open, his hands on his knees, his pants undone. His huge cock juts up nude and erect from his open fly —impossibly big, incredibly thick. This is it—the King of Cocks. The heart and soul of the WPWC. The throbbing engine at the core of the pro wrestling world. The key to Larry McMasters' spectacular success, the big stick he uses to keep all his boys in line.

Baby Face stares at it, mesmerized, and then begins to crawl toward it.

Suddenly Mongo blocks his way. The big man plants the tips of his boots on the boy's outstretched fingers, pinning them against the boards. Baby Face gasps and rolls his eyes up, but he can't see Mongo's face—his view is blocked by the eight solid inches of meat sticking out of Mongo's fly.

Mongo has a big, club-like cock, hefty and thick—but just a piker compared to the monster between McMasters' legs. He tears open a foil packet and smears a handful of glistening jelly over his hard-on. Baby Face groans. His asshole begins to twitch.

Mongo pulls his greasy cock to one side and smirks down at him. "Your first time, Baby Dick?"

Baby Face stares up at the hard, lubed cock. He feels a strange warmth in his gut. His asshole itches and tingles. He nods his head.

A mean, nasty grin spreads across Mongo's face. He steps off the kid's crushed fingers and circles around behind him.

Now Baby Face can see McMasters again. His mouth waters. His dick throbs between his legs. Everything goes dark, except for the shiny bars of light reflecting off the huge, spit-slicked truncheon of meat waiting for him across the ring.

He completely forgets about Mongo—until he feels the diaper being unpinned from his hips and ripped away. Mongo kicks his feet apart, forcing him to spread his thighs wide open. Baby Face is naked on his hands and knees, about to be fucked for the very first time.

The air feels cool and moist against the sweaty crack of his ass. Then he feels a sudden sharp twinge at the lips of his asshole. Something blunt and hard presses relentlessly inward against his hole. He instinctively tries to resist, but Mongo's cock is hard as steel, driven forward by the full strength of the man's powerful hips. The clenched hole suddenly snaps and gives way.

Baby Face drops his jaw in a silent howl. His body bucks in a spastic convulsion, then goes rigid as Mongo spears his cock all the way to the hilt. Baby Face is no longer a virgin. Baby Face is impaled on

Mongo's cock. The shock is electric. Mongo's cock is like a lightning rod inserted up the boy's ass, sucking up all his energy from the inside, sapping his will.

"That's it, Mongo." From somewhere far away he hears McMasters laughing. "Ride him over here."

The big cock spears his guts—pulls back with a slurp and spears him again. Baby Face jerks forward. Mongo coils a lock of blond hair around his fist and pumps his cock, riding him like a pony until they reach the Bossman, then reining him in with a sharp tug at his hair. The kid's head snaps up, right in front of McMasters' rampant dick.

The Bossman waves his cock, watching the kid's eyes bob back and forth. "Hungry for your bottle, Baby Dick? Or maybe you're feeling a little too stuffed already."

The kid blushes furiously, staring cross-eyed at McMasters' huge cock.

McMasters chuckles. "You like playing pony, Baby Dick? Yeah, Mongo'll get your insides good and loosened up, all soft and squishy and ready for the Bossman's big toy. Hey—you look like you're about to start crying, Baby Face. Whassa matter, kiddo—you need a pacifier, huh? Something big and warm to suck on?"

The kid grunts, licks his lips—then lets out a little squeal as Mongo delivers a deep jab to his prostate. He squints and stares slack-jawed at the Bossman's meat. The thick shaft stands straight up from the man's lap, spitting and drooling a steady stream of creamy white slag. McMasters tilts the shaft downward and traces the tip of his tool over the boy's wide-open mouth, glossing his smooth pink lips with a coating of shiny semen. He holds his cock poised an inch from the gaping mouth, feeling the boy's warm, moist breath on his cock. "Is Baby Face hungry?"

Baby Face whimpers. McMasters teases him with it, drawing it out of range and batting his cheeks, laughing at the boy's slack-jawed, cross-eyed confusion. Baby Face suddenly goes crazy, opening his mouth wide and sticking out his tongue, lapping frantically at empty air.

McMasters rudely shoves his head away, rises to his feet and kicks the chair aside. The big man peels off his jacket and slings it over the ropes. He undoes his tie and takes off his starched cotton shirt. His undershirt shows off the massive concentration of muscles in his upper body. Larry McMasters is a rugged giant of a man, his body every bit a match for the overgrown truncheon of flesh that pokes like a hairless forearm from his open fly.

Baby Face crouches on the floor—nude, erect, impaled on Mongo's big dick, staring up dazed and hungry. McMasters swaggers toward him, gently slapping the underside of his big dick, making it quiver and drool. "You passed the audition, Baby Face. You're hired. Now it's time for your first job—your first *blow*-job."

Mongo settles back on his haunches, holding the boy's naked, trembling body impaled on his lap. Baby Face squeals and clutches Mongo's hips for balance, keeping his mouth wide open. McMasters has never seen a boy hungrier for it.

McMasters steps forward. Tilts his cock slightly down. Takes aim —and then heaves forward with his hips.

His massive cockhead pops into the boy's mouth, straining his lips to the limit. McMasters pauses for only an instant, savoring the look of shock in Baby Face's eyes, and then drives home, drilling his cock all the way down the boy's neck. Baby Face is skewered at both ends, his throat impaled on the Bossman's throbbing mallet, his ass split open by Mongo's thick eight inches. His body goes rigid from the shock, his holes convulse—and suddenly both men are coming inside him, both monster dicks pulsing and spitting, setting up a shuddering vibration that turns him to jelly. . . .

Eventually . . . after the stamping and sighing . . . the throes of ecstasy . . . the shudders . . . McMasters slowly extracts his glistening cock from the kid's bruised and battered throat. At the same time, Mongo pulls out of his ass. Baby Face crumples exhausted and empty to the floor, belching and farting and seeping juice from both ends.

"Good job," the Bossman mutters, staring down at the boy's gleaming, oil-slicked ass. He gently strokes himself—hard as steel, despite the orgasm that emptied his balls only moments before. "Now it's time to play pony again. Only this time it's gonna be me in the saddle, Baby Face. The Bossman is gonna teach you how to canter and prance and gallop like a good little pony. You get good enough at it, I might even take you outside to show you off—take turns with Mongo, ride you across the parking lot all the way back to my office. Up on your hands and knees, boy—and get ready to whinny. . . ."

Two weeks later, Larry McMasters introduces a new star in the world of pro wrestling. The auditorium is packed with screaming rednecks. Mongo enters first, to a chorus of hisses and boos. Then the challenger: Baby Face Bruce from Billings, Montana. Necks crane, flashbulbs pop —everybody wants a look at the new kid.

The crowd isn't quite sure what to make of him—scattered applause, along with more than a little laughter. Baby Face blushes a bit, but he's gotten used to his diaper. It's all that McMasters has allowed him to wear for the last two weeks. Of course, the crowd can't see the extra-thick butt plug the Bossman makes him wear up his ass, or the electrical tape strapping his cock against his leg—Baby Face never could stop throwing a hard-on during practice.

Life as a pro wrestler is harder than he ever expected. But the rewards are substantial, and the guys, once you get to know them, are all very friendly. Tonight, Baby Face is going to do his best, because after the match, if he's done a good job, McMasters has promised to throw a little welcome party for him. All the guys will be there. McMasters says they'll each have a present for him, a big surprise package, and they'll all gather around to watch as he unwraps them one by one. And the Bossman says he won't have to wear his diaper. In fact, he won't have to wear anything at all. . . .

PART TWO

(SUBVERTING)
FORMULAIC
WRITING

At its worst, gay pornography has all the pitfalls of any genre writing. It is predictable, riddled with tired clichés, written according to lowest-common-denominator formulas. At its best, gay pornography—like gay sexuality in general—subverts the expected and defies common stereotypes.

Sometimes genre writing, rather than constraining authors, provides the greatest possibilities for creativity. Because there are so many expected conceits, it is all the more powerful when these conceits are undermined. Gay sexual writers have a long history of playing with old forms, putting kinks in previously straight stories, adding sex where it's not supposed to be.

In "Monster Cock," Ron Oliver and Michael Rowe combine forces for a queer retelling of the Frankenstein story. By consciously following the overused journal-entry form, and by liberally employing purple period prose, the authors make the story's sexual content jump to the foreground as a brilliant and funny twist. The best historical fiction provides us with a new lens for viewing our own time. Oliver and Rowe's tale does this wonderfully, as their account of the mad doctor, obsessed with creating the perfect specimen, can be read as a cutting commentary on the gay male cult of beauty.

Perhaps the most common charge leveled at pornography is that it is poorly written. Sadly, this is often a justified complaint. Writers emphasize penis size over prose, orgasm over originality. Playwright Robert Patrick consistently defies the stereotype, combining his linguistic genius and his erotic imagination to achieve stunning results. He utilizes rhyme, punning, and other techniques of wordplay promiscuously, flaunting his linguistic talents as if to say, "Yes, I'm a dirty writer, but I'm a *writer* and don't you forget it." "After Hours at the Buono," a chapter that was cut from the published version of his autobiographical novel *Temple Slave*, is a quintessential Patrick tour de force. For its full effect, read the selection out loud.

Another pitfall of much gay sexual writing is that the characters are one-dimensional, cardboard cutouts that bear no resemblance to real people. The most common of these characters is the "regular working guy" who likes to suck cock and maybe even get his "ashes hauled," but insists nonetheless that he is straight. In "Forever Blue," James Medley carries these clichés to their logical extremes. The ostensibly straight character's conflicted desires become actual, clinical multiple personalities: The hunky, blue-collar heterosexual is named simply and archetypically Blue; it's his alter-ego, Red, who is gay. The sexy humor of the situation pokes fun at pornographic conventions at the same time as it fulfills the most basic tenet of sexual writing—it turns us on.

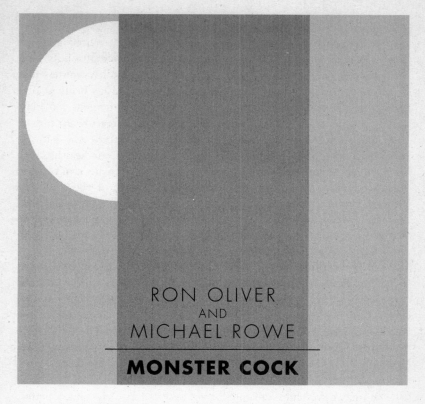

RON OLIVER
AND
MICHAEL ROWE

MONSTER COCK

FROM THE DIARY OF BARNARD WHYCROFT-JONES
MARCH 15, 1889—WHITECHAPEL, LONDON

IT WAS WITH SOME MISGIVINGS THAT I ENTERED THE BULL'S
Head Tavern this evening. Firstly, of course, had any of the assorted riff-
raff and social flotsam looked up from mourning their lost lives over
flagons of cheap ale, they might have recognized my face (one of the
unavoidable inconveniences of my family's social position). But more
importantly, my mission this night was not what one might call morally
unflawed. And while any Christian leanings I might have had in the
past have long since been corrected, it took considerable presence to
remind myself that the task at hand was of paramount importance.

The smoky pub stank of vomit and sour drink. Offering what
doubtless passed in his dull mind as a smile, the sweating innkeeper
slid a warm glass of bitter toward me. I tossed him a farthing, and his
smile dropped like maggots from a shaken corpse. My expensive dress

and gentlemanly demeanour had prepared him for a generous gratuity, but I ignored his naked plea, my focus instead on a young, solidly built man leaning on the far end of the bar. The lad's woollen trousers may have gripped his taut buttocks a little too snugly, and his brilliant blue eyes might have flashed from beneath dark curls a moment too long, but it was his arms, his beautiful arms, which drew me toward him.

Our eyes met in the reflection of the mirror above the bar. He flexed a sinewy bicep to finish the dregs of his ale in one healthy, long swallow. As he replaced the empty glass on the counter, his arm brushed against mine. I could feel the slight electric charge of the skin, and beneath that, the muscles rumbling with a promise of strength. He held it there, just a second too long, and then pulled away and swaggered to the door.

I left my bitter behind and followed him out of the pub.

In the darkness of the docks, hidden by fog and shadows, we silently set about to the business of lust. His rough beard scraped against my face as he pushed his lips to mine, but I pulled back, concentrating instead on licking my way from his calloused palm to his wrist, and further, to taste a chunky bicep awash in sweat. His belt clattered gently as his trousers slid down to the wooden slats beneath our feet, and my hand found its way to his member, engorged in spite of the cold, damp air.

I knelt before him and rolled the foreskin away, exposing a perfect lavender mushroom for my consumption, letting my tongue discover its salty, slightly gamey flavour. He let out a gasp as I took his spear deep in my throat, burying my nose in the dark bush at its root. Drawing back until only the tip rested on my tongue, I lapped at the drippings from his piss slit, each flick causing his cock to leap as if charged with electricity. He reached down to my shirt, his clammy hand trembling at the fasteners, but I pushed him back against the wall. The pleasure was to be only his. That was the way.

My fingers traced a line of sweat up his thigh, to the musty darkness of his hole, and pushed against the puckered flesh within. He exhaled sharply and lowered himself until my index finger slid inside, finding warm purchase at his gland. A few more plunges of his shaft within my mouth and his knees began to buckle. A gasp escaped his lips as his veiny rod tightened, sending creamy gobs spurting from the bulging purple knob to splash my chin, my mouth, and burn my eyes.

I moaned in what he took to be pleasure, but what my faithful boy

Willard knew to be a signal. The dim gaslight caught the flash of Willard's knife.

Let it now be stated, for the record, that my intentions have always been honourable. Even now, as I record these thoughts, my cock hardens within my trousers. I cared for that young man, for that moment we were together there on the dock, for that instant his seed fell on me like the spring rains which would soon be upon us. And as I glance across the room, I am reminded of my feelings towards him, his strong young body and his arms . . .

Those beautiful arms now floating peacefully alone in the still green liquid of my preservation tank.

MARCH 20, 1889

I was plagued in the night by terrifying dreams of spectral voices calling for blood, and awoke this morning shivering in the cold and damp. Willard had not attended the fire upon returning from his vile nocturnal bacchanal of liquor and whoring, and the coals were dead in the grate.

With an oath, I shook the stupid boy, trying to rouse him and he muttered thickly in his sleep. Cursing him for a drunken lout, I kicked aside the sheets and climbed atop the boy, prying apart the twin slabs of his pale, perfect ass.

The fool would warm me with his body if he could not tend the damned fireplace.

I spat on my cock and shoved it into the warm pudding of his asshole. He muttered something that might have been a protest, but I ignored him, and commenced to ream and plough. To my surprise, Willard barely stirred beneath me. I increased the speed of my fucking and slapped his ivory cheeks, first gently and then with increasing sharpness. Still, he stirred not at all. As I screamed my release, the imbecile awoke and cried out drunkenly to watch for timbers falling from the ceiling.

To my intense disgust, I realized the reason for the slippery ease with which I entered Willard. He was slick inside with the spend of another!

(Willard has always enjoyed a tawdry familiarity with sailors and other waterfront scum, and I have long since ceased to marvel at the pleasure with which he attaches himself to such unsavoury society.)

Revolted, I kicked the boy sharply and he fell out of bed, sprawling into a heap upon the cold floor.

I washed and dressed while Willard prepared our breakfast. He tells me that the dockside pubs are full to splitting with packs of merchant marines and roughnecks, members of idle crews whose captains have delayed the departure of their vessels due to an advancing storm of great ferocity. *The Sailor's Almanac* has predicted a barbarous March gale, fit neither for man nor beast, and the winds have already begun to blow from the north. I confess that my pulse quickened when I heard this news.

I have attached the two flawless arms I obtained last week from my dockside specimen, and they fit perfectly. By some pleasing twist of fate, the flesh and musculature of those exquisitely virile arms is uniform, in tone and texture, with the other parts of the Body I have collected.

I imagine the limbs, the torso, the handsome face, all slumbering lifelessly in their cool emerald womb. Waiting.

The spring storms now gather outside this squalid flat, this strangest of all possible Bethlehems. I pray their fury will grow commensurate with my needs.

All I require now is the perfect cock.

MARCH 23, 1889

Heavy clouds in from the ocean today, and still no damned cock. There was the sailor from Naples with a most perfect asshole, ripe and sweet with sweat, and as my cock slid into him I found there was room for my fingers as well. But sadly, he was endowed with one of those slender Italian meats which, while tasty, surely wouldn't fit my needs.

And the Dutch artist, an ill-mannered fellow who needed money to buy his paints and was only too happy to accept mine in return for an hour of his naked body sprawled on top of his not-quite-finished canvas. His plump, uncut organ seemed promising but as it reached its full size, it curved off into uncharted regions as though possessed of a mind of its own.

And the Spanish towel boy from the local baths, whose smooth and gleaming body made one believe, if only for a moment, in the existence of God, but whose massive phallus could not achieve even a passable excuse for an erection.

And the German soldier who seemed ideal until his trousers fell away to reveal bunched rags concealing a most unfortunate war wound.

I could go on, but the misery of the situation overwhelms me. I feel I shall take some of this out on young Willard tonight. He was particularly insolent today, actually hinting to me that his own genitals might suffice. The simpleton's devotion to my work is touching, but I require an able-bodied assistant, not a castrato.

MARCH 25, 1889

I thought all was lost this afternoon.

Toiling among the vials and beakers in my makeshift laboratory in the upstairs room, with Willard away at the fishmonger's and unable to make my excuses, I heard a sharp rap at the door. My rent had been paid in advance for several months, so it could not have been Mrs. Teasdale.

"Who is it?" I called out, alarmed.

I am unaccustomed to visitors in Whitechapel, as no one except Willard and my landlady knows of my residence here. My family, residing at our ancestral seat in Wiltshire, believes me to be on a tour of Africa, seeking tribal cures.

"Police!" came the voice from the other side of the door. "Please open the door, Sir. I'd like a word with you if I may."

"One moment," I called out, arranging my clothing and smoothing down my hair. A cold bolt of fear shot through me as I reached for the doorlatch, but my terror tempered to shock and desire when I opened the door.

The bobby was perhaps twenty-five. His skin was fair, his eyes pale blue, and the hair beneath his absurd helmet was spun gold, like the truncated ruff of a young lion. Discreetly, I took in the powerful body beneath his uniform, my vision arrested by the significant press of manhood beneath the cloth of his trousers.

"May I help you?" I finally blurted out, coming to my senses. "Wherever are my manners? Please, do come in."

"Thank you, Sir," he said, passing me with the clean scent of fresh tar soap. His accent was working class, rough but not displeasing to the ear. I longed to hear more of it, but my terror returned with his next words.

"We are investigating the disappearance of a sailor called Seamus Quinn. A certain Mrs. Eliza Moggs, wife of the owner of the Bull's Head Tavern near the docks, says that a man matching your description was seen leaving the tavern with Mr. Quinn. Do you know him, Sir?"

"Mr. Quinn," I said thoughtfully, tugging at my ear. Fear is its own anaesthetic, and the more I felt, the calmer I appeared. "No, Constable, I don't believe I know the gentleman."

"Do you live here alone, Sir?" he asked, looking about the room with some interest. He smiled knowingly and said, "Your landlady told us that you have a . . . gentleman friend."

It would come to this then, I thought sourly. After my profusion of terrible crimes against God and man in the name of science, I would be arrested for mere sodomy, and all because of that imbecile Willard and his inability to keep those damnable cheeks of his shut.

"Ah, you must mean my manservant Willard," I replied smoothly. "He's out. Would you like a cup of tea? Are you hungry? A biscuit, perhaps?"

The bobby seemed taken aback by my sudden hospitality, but I continued unabated.

"A cool drink? Something refreshing? Please," I said, shoving him down into a chair, "sit down."

The room suddenly seemed very still. He smiled slyly, in dawning recognition, and opened his knees slightly. His pale blue eyes held my gaze, and the diabolically cunning idea which had only recently crept into my brain suddenly seemed completely plausible.

"Quinn probably went back to Ireland," the policeman said, removing his helmet. "Always causing trouble, that lot."

"Oh indeed," I whispered knowingly, marvelling at my own sangfroid. "It's frightening, taking up . . . arms against the Crown."

He shoved one gleaming black boot against my stiffening crotch. "Your manservant?"

"Willard is at the market," I said, kneeling in front of him, my fingers moving like spiders towards the top button of his uniform pants. The swelling I had noticed there earlier had easily tripled in size. He suddenly pressed a calloused hand across mine, holding it down.

"Is the door locked?" he whispered hoarsely, licking his lips.

"Don't worry," I murmured. "Does anyone know you're here?"

He shook his head. "Independent investigation."

I nodded and returned to his crotch, feeling his stiff manhood beneath my fingers, my own cock hardening in response. As I pulled the fabric away, I gasped.

His shaft was as thick as it was long, and yet it was wondrously sculpted. Freed from the confining undergarments, it speared away from his body like a column of flawless marble nestled against a thatch of soft golden hair.

I moved my mouth reverently downward, taking first the pale pink head and then the whole shaft of it into my mouth. The policeman gasped in shock as I pushed the foreskin back roughly with my tongue. I opened my lips slightly, and slipped the hood of his sex back in place. Time enough later for exploration.

For now, I had found the perfect cock.

MARCH 29, 1889

It has all happened so quickly I scarcely dare take time to record this. Suffice to say that the events of tonight have left my hand trembling, and not for the reason one might immediately surmise.

When the storm finally came, it came of a sudden. I had only a matter of minutes to ready the apparatus. I moved the Body from Its hiding place and laid It on an oaken slab in the middle of the room, directly below an open skylight. Its dark form lay still, arms at Its sides, legs slightly apart.

The young policeman's perfect pale cock lying majestically across one sinewy thigh, the fresh stitches barely visible through the blond curls at its root.

Willard, naked beneath his oilskins, clumsily carried a long metal pole up the ladder and through the skylight. As he struggled to secure the rod in its place on the apex of the peaked roof, the clouds opened with a crash of thunder and released their hellish discharge down upon us.

"Willard!" I shrieked over the storm. "Willard!"

The lightning rod in place, the boy stumbled down the ladder, soaked to the skin, and as his coat flapped in the high winds whistling through the skylight I could see his erection gleaming wetly. I motioned him toward me and gently stroked his face, feeling compassion for the idiot for the first time in many years. It must have been the rain.

With one swipe, I tore his garment away, forcing him to his knees before me. I ripped off my own clothing, leaving myself naked against the elements. I grabbed a handful of Willard's wet hair, shoving his face into my groin. My cock, already hardening from the force of the storm, lengthened further still, spurred on by the boy's ministrations. Lightning flashed, illuminating his eyes as they stared up into mine with a strange mixture of fear and exhilaration.

"It is time!" I cried, pulling my throbbing member from his mouth. "The electrodes! The wires!"

Willard staggered away as I climbed upon the slab, hoisting the Body's legs until Its sleeping asshole was exposed to the roaring heavens. My cock slick with rain, I plunged in, screaming with desire.

"Damn you, boy," I shouted. "Faster! Faster!"

Grabbing the edges of the slab, I plundered the anus of the cold wet Thing beneath me, as Willard gathered the necessary wires and hurried across the room. An ominous rumble came from above. The moment was upon us!

The stupid boy slipped on the wet tiles, stumbling face down, crushing his erect cock beneath him. I ignored his cry of pain; he would suffer soon enough. He stumbled blindly to his feet and dragged the cables toward me.

Two long copper wires, insulated with simple gauze, trailed from the lightning rod on the roof, running down through the skylight and coming together in the long velvet sleeve Willard held in one trembling hand.

He reverently slipped the cover off, and held aloft a ten-inch solid copper dildo.

The storm raged. I thrust harder, faster, until I could feel the pressure building within my taut jewels. I looked up into the clouds as the rumble above exploded into thunder, and I knew the moment was at hand.

"Now!" I screamed.

Willard plunged the dildo into my ass, its solid length searing into the depths of my bowels. My head snapped back as I screamed in pain. My shout was drowned by a single bolt of lightning slicing down from the dark skies, slamming into the rod above. The current raced down the pole, along the cables, through the wires, blazing a trail of blue fire deep inside me.

I shrieked again, my body arching, muscles straining, whipped by the pulsing power of the storm.

"One, two, three . . ." counted Willard, eyes glued to the dildo embedded in my ass.

My gland combusted with electricity, and my cock fired like a cannon, crackling jism roaring up the Thing's cold channel.

"Four, five, six . . ." Willard continued, as I shot again and again, my howls of pain and ecstasy pealing up into the storm.

"Six . . . uh . . ." Willard faltered. "Uh . . . um . . ."

"Ten!" I screamed. "Ten, you fool! TEN!!"

Willard suddenly wrenched the dildo from my ass. It sizzled in his wet palm. He screeched in pain, throwing it into a dark corner of the room where it sparked and hissed for a few moments before dying. My cock spasmed one final time before I collapsed upon the Thing, my heart pounding. The rain slowed to a gentle drizzle on my back as Willard waited in silence, rubbing himself.

"Get out," I croaked.

He began to mumble some protest which I silenced with the back of my hand across his face. His shrivelled penis led him to the door and away.

I alone deserved this moment. I alone would greet my Creation at Its first instant of life.

I pulled my still-tumescent organ from the Thing's oozing asshole, and straddled Its firm thighs, watching, waiting. I leaned to Its chest, but heard nothing beating. I touched Its wrist but felt no pulse. My heart sank. Had it all been for naught? Had my parents been right all along, my imaginings merely the phantasms of a diseased mind?

And then, I felt it. A stirring in my loins. But how? I was spent as never before, yet my member was pulsing with a life of its own.

It was not until I exposed my body to the cold light from above that I saw the truth. It was not *my* penis which was even now growing longer, harder, thicker.

It was the cock of my Creation. It was alive.

APRIL 4, 1889

The Creature slept for three days, waking only for short periods during which time I was able to feed It broth from a spoon as one might feed a newborn infant. It sucked water in small quantities from a glass bottle with a soft kidskin nipple. On the fourth day, It began to stir and I fitted It with leather manacles solidly attached to chains of the strongest steel. These in turn I fastened to the metal frame of a bed in the laboratory.

It wears a collar of black leather. It has the face of an angel and the body of a slave.

This morning I ran my hand across the shaft of Its penis for the first time since Its birth. The Creation grimaced and tried to draw away in fear when I first touched It, but the heavy cock hardened immediately and the brute began to grind Its hips in rhythm with my hand. It groaned when I stopped. I caressed Its face gently, tracing my index finger along the sinewy contours of Its thick neck, down Its broad chest, between the powerful pectoral muscles, and across Its abdomen.

I fingered Its heavy scrotum, and, without warning, I inserted my fingers into Its anus.

The Creation reared up and opened Its eyes wide. Panting like a dog, It resumed the rocking motion of Its hips almost as though It sought to impale itself on my hand.

I withdrew my fingers again, and the Creature moaned, clearly in frustration, thrashing about on the bed making a fearful racket. I am relieved that there is no one residing in the flat below.

Quickly stripping off my clothing, I stood before It, myself fully erect. It looked at me with something approaching worship—although this might merely be the expected response of a creature with no memory towards the man who controls all of Its sensations—Its cock hard and red, and clearly aching for release.

It did not protest when I turned It over on Its stomach. I marvelled at Its perfect, broad back (a Brixton labourer), Its narrow hips and flanks (an Eton batsman), Its creamy white ass (a young Balkan dancer whose tour ended abruptly in a seedy Soho rooming-house). Its body glistened with sweat, and I stroked It the way one might comfort a frightened stallion.

I straddled the Creation's ass, pressing my knees into Its hips, my hard cock between Its cheeks. It moaned, and reared up to receive my stiff prick. In one brutal thrust, I rammed my cock deep into Its asshole.

It bucked violently, grinding Its own cock against the sheets. The muscles of Its anus clamped around my cock and squeezed so artlessly that I howled and exploded, shooting my seed deep into Its bowels. An answering howl sounded from the Herculean figure chained beneath me, and for a moment I was afraid that I had somehow damaged It.

I pulled out, and climbed off the bed.

The Creation was dusted with a rosy flush I had not noticed before. I approached It cautiously, and gently turned the Creation over on Its back. Its hair was soaking in sweat, Its eyes closed.

I glanced down at Its prick, and my breath caught in my throat. Its penis had dwindled to a still-impressive flaccid state. Its chest and groin area, and indeed the sheets beneath it, were drenched in pools of glistening cum.

I touched Its cock, testing the post-coital sensitivity. The Creation flinched and cried out. I smiled, and touched It again, eliciting another howl of discomfort. I touched It again, and again. Each time, the same tortured groans. I felt my own cock harden in response.

Note: I must pace myself, and I must not lose my scientific objectivity, however difficult that might be, given the delicious range of uses to which I might put this creature.

Leaving It there on the bed, panting and groaning, I turned and suddenly heard Willard's rapid footsteps in the next room. A door slammed and the fool clattered down the stairs to the street.

Odd. Very odd. But I can work better without the distraction of Willard who, since the Creation's birth, has been snappish and watchful.

I do not have time to coddle him, and I *will* punish him if he persists with his wilfulness.

APRIL 16, 1889

Dawn rises through the tattered curtains of this frigid flat, but it may as well be midnight. In the days (or is it weeks?) past, I have neither ventured out of doors, nor wondered what current affairs inflame the dull imaginations of the human sheep on the streets below.

Willard has been sulking for days. He refuses to speak to me, merely starting the fire and setting my meals at the table. Two days ago, he deliberately threw a glass upon the floor, shattering it to pieces, then glared at me as if demanding punishment.

In a way I gave it to him: I ignored the stupid boy.

I continue to explore the nether regions of lust and perversion with my Creation. It is a willing sexual slave and, although It inhabits the solid, rippling body of an adult, It possesses the curiosity of a child and the same willingness to learn.

And I have so much to teach.

APRIL 17, 1889

Awoke to the sound of the Thing grunting, and the low, idiotic laughter of Willard in the laboratory. Not bothering to dress, I crept through the flat and eased the door open to find the young imbecile naked, teasing the Beast by waving his ruddy meat inches from Its mouth.

The Brute strained against Its bonds, grunting as Its tongue tried desperately to taste the boy's jutting cock, and Willard laughed dully, enjoying the sport. I watched for a moment, feeling my own loins stir, but my anger rose before my cock, and it propelled me into the room.

"Willard!" I roared, pulling his leather belt from the pile of clothes on the floor. "How many times have I told you not to touch my work?"

I swung the belt in a wide arc, striking the smooth flesh of his shoulders with a satisfying crack. The young fool stumbled away from the beast, whining unintelligibly as I continued to lash him, raining blow after blow on his naked body, raising welts upon his stringy biceps, his thighs, and across his hard cock. He fell to the floor, crawling away, and I gave him a final kick out of the room, my foot all but vanishing into his well-worn asshole.

Suddenly, a shadow climbed the wall, and I froze.

Turning in fear, I saw that the Creation had, in Its desperation, managed to rip one of the chains free from the bed. It reached towards me, the brawny hand quivering with unrestrained fury.

I tried to speak. Surely It would heed Its master's voice! But I could not find my tongue. The hand reached closer and closer, and the Beast locked Its dark eyes with mine. But where I should have seen hatred, I saw something else. Something strange.

Its cold hand grabbed at my cock. I half-expected it to be torn from its root, but to my surprise, the fingers wrapped around my flaccid shaft with an almost familiar ease, pleading it into erection. The Creation looked curiously at the pulsing member in Its hand, a child with a toy, and leaned closer. It sniffed the smooth knob and extended a tentative tongue to touch, then lap at the crystalline droplet at the tip.

Before I dared move, It had engulfed my cock with Its mouth and slid the shaft deep into Its throat. Death had robbed Its throat of a gag reflex, and I might have been swallowed whole had the Thing's nose not slammed into my pubis, startling It like a young dog at a looking-glass. It took a moment to consider this finitism, and resumed sucking,

Its strong throat muscles massaging my engorged phallus with languid strokes.

I watched Its face, a mask of contentment, as It nursed at my groin. Although I was still frozen with fear, I felt my nerves tingling, the shivering prelude to the passionate abyss into which this unnatural copulation drew me . . .

When at last I arched my back, groaned and thrust one hard and final time, the Thing would not release me, instead holding my spurting cock within Its mouth, drinking deeply until my seed was spent.

I shook uncontrollably and dropped to my knees. Never before had I felt such an explosion, such sheer, unadulterated release. Light seemed to dance on the edge of my vision, my legs and arms numb, my skin afire . . .

The Beast leaned back on Its haunches, watching my face keenly. Some of my thick white cum glistened on Its chin. It used Its free finger to wipe it up and let the strand dangle over Its open mouth.

It lowered the seed onto Its tongue, and swallowed the last of me. A smile crossed Its face.

APRIL 21, 1889

So tired.

In these days since I gave the Creature some limited freedom, It has ignored all of my attempts to educate It. It showed no interest in the books I presented; instead, It sniffed at them, licked them and then rubbed them against Its groin. Unsatisfied, the Brute then tore the valuable first editions to shreds and let loose an acrid stream of piss across the remains.

In Its past life, It may have been a critic.

My only rest comes when the Thing ejaculates. As It sinks onto the floor, hot wet jism still oozing from Its massive organ, I replace the manacles and gag. Only then can I try to sleep, to eat, to write my reports. But within minutes it seems the Satyr is awake again, Its obscene cock engorged, pounding at the air, demanding my attentions. I cover my ears with my shaking hands but Its agonizing howls slice through me and in spite of my efforts, I feel my own shaft stiffen with desire.

Dear God, what have I done?

[NO DATE GIVEN]

No sleep. No food. The Fiend is insat i a

MAY 11, 1889

I am lost. By the feverish light of this one stinking candle, I see that the walls are smeared with fresh blood, and the furniture is smashed to kindling. What monstrosity have I wrought here? What in the name of God have I allowed to happen? I hold the torn, twisted body of Willard in my arms. He weeps and raves, deliriously repeating the Catholic act of contrition over and over.

The boy has clearly been driven mad with pain. His lips have been cruelly bitten, and his rectum hangs in tatters. But it is Willard's eyes which truly strike fear in me. They appear bottomless, as though he opened the door to hell and found himself unable to close it.

I can barely hold this pen in my hand, so violent is my trembling, but if I am to die tonight as well, I must tender at least an explanation; surely this foulness I have unleashed is beyond an apology.

This is what happened:

I went to the Globe Theatre with three friends, gentlemen of like-minded persuasion whom I knew from my days at Oxford. Lest word reach my family in Wiltshire, I explained to my companions that my African tour had been interrupted by the sudden illness of a friend (oh, horrible irony!).

Throughout the performance, I was troubled by some presage of doom, a nagging misgiving that something was not well at the flat.

I had induced the Creation to swallow some laudanum this afternoon, and It was sound asleep when I left. Willard had been sulking since the night of his flogging, but he appeared to understand all of my instructions.

I attributed my premonition to exhaustion and no small measure of guilt, and proceeded to enjoy the mediocre performance, and an excellent supper afterwards. My friends commented on my pallor. I laughed, berating the "rainy season" in Kenya at this time of year.

After the supper, I took a hansom to a safe distance from the flat. I walked the remaining distance through the gelatinous fog. Swathed in my cloak, my head down, I mercifully encountered no one en route save two catcalling bawds on opposite street corners. I am satisfied that they would be hard-pressed to identify me.

As I approached the flat, my feelings of distress intensified to an almost physical degree. I mounted the stairs outside, slipping for a moment on what I first took to be a dark patch of oil. To my horror, upon closer examination, it appeared to be blood.

I raced up the three flights of stairs. The door to my flat was hanging on its hinges, the wood in splinters. The force which had ripped the heavy oak to pieces had obviously erupted *from the inside*.

The bloated yellow moon flooded the flat with ghastly clarity. The rooms had been torn apart. All of my laboratory equipment was smashed, and an ocean of glass crunched beneath my boots.

The crude wooden furniture had been rent as though it were paper. I heard Willard moaning in a corner. I found a candle among the debris and, lighting it, looked closer at my poor boy.

Upon seeing me framed in the glow of candlelight, he began shrieking, peal after peal, as though to wake the dead. I clasped him in my arms and he calmed immediately.

He prays and weeps in the corner as I write this.

By some miracle, the Monster (for there is no doubt in my mind now as to the identity of the Thing that did this) has left my diaries and the dozen or so leather-bound volumes of my medical notes untouched.

I must close this entry here, and attend to Willard.

MAY 26, 1889—CAMPBELVILLE GATE, MILTON-BY-SEA, CORNWALL

These notes are now from memory, and if they seem scattered I must be forgiven. At times in the past few days, I felt my mind would surely snap. Perhaps it has, and perhaps my recollections, fantastic as they sound, are simply fictions. But surely nothing this horrifying could be anything but the truth.

It seemed ironic to me that while I had conspired to conceal my family name to commence this experiment, it was now that same name which prompted Sisters of Perpetual Pain Hospital to take Willard immediately. He looked tiny and frail as the sisters fluttered above him like doves, stripping off the remains of his simple clothes, strapping him down with leather restraints and wheeling a metal table laden with cruel medical instruments up to his bed. I found myself taking his cold hand in mine and he moved his lips as if to speak, but the words seemed to catch in his throat. He could only smile before his eyes closed. I replaced his limp hand across his chest and bade the good women to care for him well.

Riding in the coach, my mind raced. What had once been my private madness now rampaged unbound. The lights of London glittered, a buffet for the horrible appetites of this Monster of my creation. I felt sure the guilt would drive me insane.

Turning a corner, I saw a crowd had gathered in front of St. Pancras train station and a police wagon waited nearby, horses stomping and rearing with fear. Something about the scene chilled me and I ordered the driver to stop. Pushing past the curious fools with some lie about my medical credentials, I made my way to the bobbies kneeling within the crowd.

The victim was a burly, bearded trainsman, not yet thirty, with a firm and naturally muscled body, much of which was covered in blood. I pulled away the cloak laid over him by the police and the crowd reared back as one, a collective gasp of horror taking their breath away.

It was as I feared. The blood, the horrible mutilation, the heavy ivory cream lacing the wounds. And rising from his body, the familiar gunpowder smell of the Creature's sex.

The trainsman opened his eyes then and, for a second of perfect clarity, seemed to look toward me, beyond me, and whispered, "Monster . . . cock . . ."

And died.

I backed away as the police covered the now still form. The crowd hushed and behind me I heard the steady shuffling of a train leaving the station. Beyond me. The trainsman's gaze . . .

The midnight train was leaving St. Pancras station, whistle blowing and steam rising. In the rear window, a face grimaced back at me, horribly contorted.

The face of my Demon.

I leapt up and ran through the crowd, feet pounding toward the train. But my cries went unheard by the conductor, drowned by the steam engine's blasted whistle. The Creature's face glared with what was surely mockery and then disappeared into the darkness of the car. Anger supplanted my fear and with a mighty leap I thrust myself toward the departing train. I just barely grabbed the edge of the platform. The train picked up speed and it took all of my strength not to tumble off and be left crushed on the tracks behind.

With what I thought was the last of my energy, I pulled myself up onto the platform. I caught my breath and watched the lights of the station disappear in the distance. A sudden scream from within the train galvanized me and I charged through the door. I hurried into the rear car, and through the train, following the horrified expressions of the passengers as they gaped at what had passed seconds before.

A locked door stopped me at the coal car. I pounded against the steel panel, kicking at the latch with my heavy boots, but made not a scratch. Wrenching a fire axe from the wall, I raised it in a wide arc, ready to smash this last barricade between myself and the murderous fiend when I felt something wet on my forehead. I reached up and touched it. Sticky. Warm. A red stain on my fingertips.

And above me, a trap door smeared with blood.

I slammed the door open with the axe and lurched up, finding myself atop the speeding train. The wind tore at my clothes, whipped hair into my eyes. The Beast was nowhere in sight. Suddenly, I felt a mighty blow at my back, knocking me sprawling onto the roof. My weapon clattered off the edge and into the darkness. I rolled onto my back and saw, silhouetted there against the velvet sky, the naked beauty of the Devil I had unleashed.

It revolted me, Its face and body stained with the trainsman's life and my poor Willard's blood. Even in the darkness, the Beast must have sensed my disgust. It seethed above me, and from deep within Its chest came a rumbling of air as It tried to form words, Its voice the grating of concrete as a mausoleum door closes.

"Me. In. You."

I heard but did not understand at first. It was only as the horrifying possibilities of those three words penetrated the haze of terror around me that I found myself shaking with fury.

"No!"

I threw myself at the Monster and we tumbled together off the top of the train. Our bodies hurtled through the dark sky, locked in combat. The train sped off into the night as we smashed against the hard ground along the tracks, hurtling down a deep embankment into blackness.

Landing hard in a shallow pond, my head slammed against a rock. Dazed, blood trickling into one eye, I could only watch as the Thing rose up from the water just a few feet away. It slowed but a moment, smelling the air, before It saw me. It shambled toward me, Its perverse, huge phallus lilting with undisguised lust.

Somehow it seemed to have grown, as though nourished by each murderous intercourse. Steam rose from the shaft, the fist-sized head sheening, the slit dilating like a lover's mouth with every beat of the Fiend's heart.

It moved closer. I slipped my fingers into my pocket, wrapping them around the firm, hard handle of the scalpel I had taken from Willard's bedside table. But as It loomed over me, moonlight etching Its taut, obscenely perfect form into sharp relief, I faltered.

I knew not whether to kill the Beast or to fuck it.

God help me, I did both!

LATER

Now I sit here at my family's deserted summer home, watching the waves. The air is very damp here. No matter how warmly I dress I continue to tremble almost constantly. Noticed grey in my hair this morning for the first time.

What did the Monster mean when it said "Me. In. You."? At first I thought it was a demand to fulfill Its needs, to thrust Its cock into my ass. But on reflection, a more frightening notion comes to mind. That It somehow thought to reverse the balance of power? Preposterous of course. I was Its *God*. It was, simply, my Creation.

Naturally, I disposed of Its body. I cut it into small pieces, wrapping them in butcher's paper and burying the parts across the city. The legs in Covent Garden, the head in South Kensington, the ass in Piccadilly. But I couldn't bear to be rid of it all. I've kept a souvenir.

It's in a wooden box beneath the bed.

I am entitled. I made it.

LATER, NIGHT

Awakened by a sound. Probably a tree branch hitting the window. Will check in the morning.

EXCERPTED FROM THE PRIVATE JOURNALS OF
DR. JAMES ABERCROMBIE MAY 29, 1889—
ST. ANNA'S HOSPITAL, MILTON-BY-SEA, CORNWALL

". . . pains me to remember that I came to this tiny coastal village fifteen years ago in the sincere hopes that the salt air would act as a restorative to my dear wife's delicate condition. How I miss my darling Amanda. I cannot help but feel that she would be a comfort to me in the perplexing affair in which I find myself embroiled. I have been instructed by my superiors at St. Anna's Hospital that the official report pertaining to the death of The Hon. Barnard Whycroft-Jones, eldest son of Lord and Lady Campbelville, is to be falsified. When I objected on moral and professional grounds, I was informed that it was the express wish of Lord Campbelville and that my many years at St. Anna's were too valuable to be thrown away for a trifling matter such as this one.

So the young man died of a "heart attack," and I have put my name to this lie.

Even now, my gorge rises, and I confess to this diary what I have been ordered to keep forever to myself. I could have lived out the balance of my allotted years without ever having shared in this unspeakable horror. That Whycroft-Jones was murdered is not, to me, in question, but the manner in which he died is the stuff of nightmares. I cannot but remember his terrified countenance. Were it not for that gruesome member thrust so deeply into his throat, I would have believed that the man had died of fright.

I shudder to imagine what the fellow saw or heard in his last moments.

I do not understand the Campbelville family's refusal to pursue justice for their murdered son. But, as I have been continually reminded by that jackass Harcourt, it is no longer my affair. Perhaps it is time to tender my resignation at St. Anna's and return to private practice in London. This village is a landscape of painful memory for me, and I am lost without my precious wife . . ."

FROM THE NOTES OF WILLARD GREER
JUNE 4, 1889

Mistur Wikrofft Joons gots berried tooday I watcht itt. I wuz sadd. Everbuddy wor blak, evn the rich wuns.

Wen it got dark, I goed bak to the grayvyard an took my shuvl. An I got Mistur Wikkrofft Jonns out the grouned and tuk hym bak to are olde playce.

I wanto tuch him but I haveta wate. I foun the big medal cock with all the wirs attashed. Beder hurrie to gett the wirs upp on the ruf.

Thers a big storm toonite.

ROBERT PATRICK

AFTER HOURS

AT THE

BUONO

WE PLAYWRIGHTS WERE ANGERED BY AN UNDERGROUND paper's suggestion that we made actors ball us for roles. God knows actors were available, liking, as a class, to be told what to do, but balling them had no more to do with casting than with breeding.

For instance:

One night after hours, my bosses Joe and Johnny slipped away to their house behind the Espresso Buono cafe-theatre, marooning me at one of the little mushroom tables with a moronic yackety-yacking so-called actor, a jock, musclebound and bowlegged, agog in a monologue about his "career action."

I sat trapped at the table by his dumbness and my numbness, when preppy-dressed ex-sailor Augie wobbled in, faggy and foggy, high and looking to get down.

"Hi," he said. "Where's the auction? I mean 'action'?" he cracked as Jock yacked. Augie had been so beautiful for so long he'd interrupt anyone.

"You're after hours," I admonished.

"I'm after anyone's," he astonished, brushing his flanneled panel against my face. He wagged his head at the mumbling dumbo and asked, "How's for instance, about his?"

I found the actor so boring I hadn't considered goring him. Seeing him through hoggy Augie's eyes, I perceived it might be intriguing to bury my stiff in his symmetry. I nodded approval to Augie.

I hove my chair nearer the nerd. Augie hooved another to his other side and sat. We sent fondling feelers out to his bowling-ball shoulders, his hardwood thighs.

He slipped from our paws, acting (badly) as if nothing had happened, and stepped onto the low stage (currently decorated with a fake campfire and a real bedroll), and continued his monologue about managerial manipulations.

Augie and I shrugged our own shoulders at each other. Reaching over the chair still warm from the actor factor, I clutched Aug's crotch. In hot jockies, his basket rose like a biscuit. I had some trouble digging out his dinger and duffel-bag, and he made it harder on me, so to speak, fingering my denims 'til what was in 'em finally funnily flipped up and flapped out.

He watched it twang and spring. "So that's why they call you 'Bob,' " he surmised.

Then while our so distant, *soi-disant* star kept up his self–pep talk with his blue eyes closed to our carousing but focused under his pink-petal lids on a rosy future, Aug and I alternately bent and savored each other's sabers, absorbed each other's orbs.

The after hours dull lull had been agony 'til Aug and I peeled each other's shirts up and shorts down and I tongued the sweet sweat and salt silt along his rung and then fell back to see the blond dive for my wand and felt my file fill his grin as he ground my groin. We turned each other on like jukeboxes.

Titillated by Aug's "Ugh-ugh's" and elated by Jock's tits as his rising nipples tented his T-shirt (he was obviously hearing our whoring), I lifted Aug's vaginal lips from my lap and nodded at the stage, where Jock in his ego-ecstasy all but butt-danced. If his career had rolled like his rear, he might have made it.

Augie smiled like a lizard and nodded. Both our dickheads were already nodding in agreement. Simultaneously rising, our thighs trouser-trussed, Aug and I shuffled and rustled, our divine rods tugging us stageward, until Aug stood before and I behind Jock's blind behind, which was waving in anticipation of memorable openings.

Augie unbuckled him and I disrobed his globes, then knelt and licked through his slick slit into his slot. He may have acted like an ass, but there was musk beneath his mask. Reaching around, I found his moist mast pilastered against his flat front above a shaved scrotum —prickly pair!

I felt Augie's lips slipping down the stiff's staff. Through Jock's jean-hobbled splayed legs, kneeling Aug displayed in my direction an erection lively as a diving-board.

Sticking a digit up the idjit, I ducked through his wishbone legs and sucked Aug's fishbone.

That triggered and envigored us. Shucking bunched pants with socked feet, we kicked them behind us like pawing stallions and then pulled the goon-with-the-wind, his tongue still sales-talking, down to lie mostly prone but partly perpendicular on the prop bedroll.

I straddled his prattle and squatted, plunging first my root into, and then my rut across, his face's fosse, to test, as he tossed, the lingering tingle of his lingual tangle on my shoot and then my chute.

He might as well have been unconscious under my haunches. Whether slicking my anus or sipping my heinous dick, he kept eyes clutched tight and jaw wagging while I was dragging my sac back and forth over his nose to get my gut or my gat onto the mucilagenous massage of his mouth.

As I sambaed on my slippery, slobbery saddle, Aug stood astride the lug's legs, stroking his own stoker with a fast fist and laddy-like licking a finger on the other hand which he put behind and up himself to open his soul's hole. The locus of his focus was Jock's tapered taper, shiny as a shin, thrust from his fork where his eggs hung between his bowed legs. With a pyramidal head peering amid folds of foreskin, it was the kind of pylon on which it is easiest to pile. Clearly Aug was agog to get on the fool's tool and get off.

Lifting his shirttails he shifted his socked feet to put his pawed pod over the lean loin. I continued to hole and pole the mug's mug and gazed glazed as Aug spread his bread and descended open-ended to intercept the sap's spiny scepter into his pink sphincter (I peeked and all but peaked at the sight of his winy blind undereye).

Aug hit the hot height and crouched on it, crutched on it, then by expert exertion he weighed in and slid down and grunted as Jock's dome hit home and his own yoni yawned in feigned boredom to admit it and then snapped at its neck like a snake. Aug's eyes oozed as his fundament filled with wonderment.

I was intensely sensitive that inches behind Aug's dancing dick a snug duct had been dicked. The thought of the electric ants that Jock must feel crawling on his awl, the certainty of the buffed stuffed sensation that must be rushing all Aug's awareness to the burning blush of his punctured juncture, flushed blood to bloat my whole bod.

We were no longer Aug, Bob, and Jock, but hot-air balloons of those goons, held down only by long tugging dicks. Jock was a joke, but the scent he sent to mingle with ours as we mangled had something virile and virulent in it. He was a fit armature for this twelve-limbed topless bottomless monster that had come into being, this multiple incestuous insect of sex that not only ate its mate after coupling, but coupled by cannibalism.

It didn't matter that Aug was an old friend and Jock a stranger. They had become mere animated objects to couple, triple, ripple with to exacerbate and eradicate the red web of overheated nerves that had replaced me. What little humanity I retained was pleased to notice they were as kill-crazy as I, and whatever animal madness I imagined I couldn't imagine either of them denying me access to any axis.

I plunged my threat down Jock's throat and closed my buns on his nose. Fucking his face with my front and my back with his beak, I redoubled my bolero.

Ganched to the liver on the lever of our lover, froggy Augie bounced, his dick filling up as his crack hit Jock's sac, draining as he elevated his velvet nates, his banana throbbing, his apples bobbing as he cooed and rode the rude rod.

While tangle-tongue tickled my pucker and pickle by turn and twist, I bowed down and mouthed Aug's log. I bit his sweet meat as his sweet meat beat. His column's volume swole each time his hole swallowed pole; the head of him kicked like a chicken-heart, a heartbeat, a hard-beat, a thick meat thermometer with its own pulse. Aug threw off his upper clothes as he jacked Jock off with his ass. My head of necessity nodding in automated affirmation, I sucked Aug like a giant soda straw. In fact, he fucked my face, though his purpose was the porpoise he bucked upon, fucked upon, as he lobbed his throb into Bob, bopping me up and down as he went to town, shining his rim with the ream he rodeoed on.

I, my mouth stuffed, my south buffed wide by Jock's snorting nose, tingling tongue, and chucking chin, my tight end scoured and not scared to get skewered, I lifted my head from Aug's suck-soaked hod, bounded around, and must have shown indifferent Aug a great shot of rosy hole as

I clawed my cleft apart and backed my act onto Augie's honed, toned bone, gauging it in, gouging it up me bouncing ounce by ounce, feeling Aug's bully budging into my belly, taking his ticking tusk into my pulsing pit. The strength with which his lethal length seethed soothed the sheath I eased on it and he smoothly shoved more bore up my tunnel with each of his own gut-wrenching trips to the top tip of his sole polar ecstasy that was now empowering auxiliary ecstasies for Jock and me. With all the ache I could take, I shoved and felt the fluff of Aug's bush push against my tush as he fell and felt our bull's bush on his balls.

Aug's and my gorges were now as engorged, his and Jock's plugs as engulfed, as was physically plausible. My own wood stood. I sighed inside. My worm was firm, my fold filled, my crack felt Aug's sac. I was content as a hen on hot eggs. But my bloated toad was croaking, aboil with bile. I fell forward on our bellicose's belly, as flat as his flute (now up Aug) had stood against it back when we were all sane. I was a cock, I was all cock, all cocks, Jock's cock up Aug, Aug's cock hunting my heart, my own cock, man-sandwiched between my and Jock's taut torsos. I wriggled to rub the underside, wonderside of my slimy salami on talky Jock's shaven haven, bristle grinding my gristle, my thick dick and big bag bunched betwixt my and Jock's bulks, while fool-filled Aug's whole pole still swole my hole.

This meant Aug's bat got bent flat at a painful angle in my hold. I twisted; he misted. As he moaned on Jock's mound, I frictated as need dictated. Only our swiny sweat kept me from setting Jock aflame as I struck my match on his sandpaper snatch, the grip of my anal lips hurting Aug's quirt again and again.

This stimulus made Aug tremulous and, incensed, he winced, tensing, jamming Jock up his rudder so utterly that he jumped frontward, cuntward, shoving his egg up my cup. Growing bolder, he clutched my shoulder and continued his sinewy reflex, impaled and impelled by suffering and sex, wooing pleasure, pursued by pain. Whipped by a carrot behind, his own carrot ahead, he fellow-fucked me and himself on a roll composed of his and Jock's hoses, oozing, using us as accessories to his pierced and piercing pleasure, bartering his prepuce and perineum, battering my prostate where I lay like a prostrate apostate so that I buckled, chuckled and, with Augie's Hun's hands clutching my clavicle to assist in his pistoning, I attended to my own mounting urges, squeezed the boob's boobs and sucked fuel from his still-mobile mouth-hole while Augie hit and hit and hit my spot, and my smothered pud rubbed bloodily in stubble and, using Jock's navel for an anvil and his nipples for grips, awash in an awful stew of stinging smells, distantly as Aug's lance glanced my gland I began to feel a big brass band up in that avenue where the long arm of Augie's law beat me with its fist, and my penis between us ballooning bigger than Babylon. With a thrashing, trashed ass and an enormous clash of symbols, I now raped and reaped, screwed, mooed and spewed lewdly and loudly; my reservoir sprung at the bung by Aug's ring-battering ram, I was damned near de-livered of a kingdom of un-dammed come.

With each shot on the hummock of Jock's stomach, my rubbery clutch clinched at each active inch of Aug's pumping lump, choking its poking so that with a screech in my breech, pain and pressure came together and his rose-nosed hose wheezed and sneezed, cramming cream into my tugging gut, causing his own stinging ring to ripple and shift on Jock's shaft and wring simultaneous chimes of slime from our victim, who to occupied and preoccupied Aug's orgasming surprise suddenly at last came to lust, hugged Aug's hams with clamped hands, and dicked Aug wickedly, no longer massive and passive, but randy and demanding, roughly stuffing, royally and oilily rutting Aug's butt-gut which put Aug to butting my glutted rut.

And "Ach!" cried Jock, "Ugh," cried Aug, and "Oy!" cried I.

So our trio with concerted *brio* came together and then came apart, and with me shriveling, Aug dribbling, and Jock still driveling, we rolled like rocks away from the openings of sacred tombs and shrank in sighs like *soufflés*.

And I swear that through the whole schleppy epic episode, hung, young, shocked, blocked Jock never once stopped yapping his inane, insane aspirations.

In the morning, nacre-naked, Johnny strolled in out of Joe's little place in the rear. He saw us wedded, wadded together and tip-toed back out to fetch back Joe.

Joe arrived bare-hairy. They stood, Apollo-Johnny and Jovial Joe, laughing like gods at the cluster of crusted clowns curled up like pale anchovies beside the cold campfire.

Their delight at our plight seemed oversized until I realized it was laughter of recognition because they, too, were clothed only in socks and flaking, gluey goo.

"Ain't it grand," said Joe, "how theatre folk stick together?"

As we peeled free, he dodged Johnny's swat at his twat, made up fierce cups of jo and, singing, steamed us all eggs in clean white cups.

But despite our gorgeous orgiette, I never cast Jock!

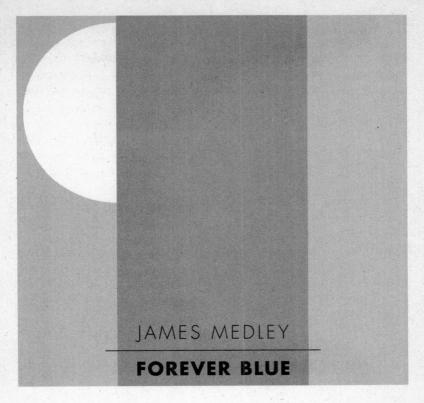

JAMES MEDLEY

FOREVER BLUE

I THOUGHT MY LIFE WAS PRETTY WELL SET WITH A STRAIGHT shot toward retirement when I achieved my tenure at Saint Angus. I was thirty-five and this was the life I had always envisioned and aspired to; a gentle, tweedy professor of languages at a small, prestigious New England college, brick and ivy, tree shaded, surrounded by my books and writing, occupying myself exclusively with the world of letters.

Which was the case until I met a young man named Blue. I don't know if it was the Lady Chatterley thing or Pygmalion, a medieval fairy tale of classes attracting the opposite, whatever, but I became hopelessly addicted to this man.

Blue wasn't a student (I had assiduously avoided having any affairs with my collegiate charges) but a groundskeeper. The first time I saw Blue he was raking leaves on the campus circle, a broad lawn surrounding the statue of the school's founder. It was chilly, a typical Eastern fall day.

Two of my more advanced female students were sitting with me on a park bench, sharing lunch. I had always encouraged my students to express themselves as freely as they chose around me. This was the sort of relationship I cultivated at the weekly gatherings in my modest cottage just off the campus. Blue was working about twenty feet away. He had been hired recently and I had never seen him before.

"Doesn't he have a nice butt?" one of the girls observed.

"Real cute," said the other. "Did you know that, Mr. Haley?"

"Know what?" I asked, idly looking at the object under discussion.

"That's what a girl always notices first about a guy, his butt," she said.

I allowed as to how I remembered having read it somewhere. Of course I knew it quite well, but only if he was facing away from me and I couldn't see his crotch. Though I've been called stodgy, I wasn't exactly celibate. I contented myself with monthly trips to Boston where I got my ashes hauled by anonymous men at the baths. Up to this time, that had been enough.

"And a cute face too," the first girl said. "Wonder if he has anything between those big ears?"

"Wonder if he has anything between those big legs," her companion remarked. As I said, they *were* advanced.

While they chattered on between themselves about their plans for the Christmas break, I studiously appraised the young man they had referred to. He was strikingly handsome, curly black hair and blue eyes, what I've heard referred to as "Black Irish." He wore matching blue pants and shirt, tight, so that his torso was definitely on display. He reminded me of the young Marlon Brando in *Streetcar*, without the sneer. His lips were full and fleshy, sensuous. He exuded an animal sexuality from every pore in his body, that sort of magnetism not necessarily accompanied by striking good looks, a lusty rawness quite close to the surface and unconsciously expressed. The way his hips moved with his arms in an agile, graceful way, illustrated his masculine maturity. And he did have a beautiful ass.

Not a slender little college boy ass but a real man-ass, muscular and firm, tight and heavy, a working man's ass. The seam of his pants rode up his crack and cleaved deeply into his trench. I thought he might not be wearing any underwear.

It had been three weeks since my last trip to Boston and just the sight of his bulging groin gave me an intense erection. More evidence of his lack of underwear was hanging down his right leg, his impressive equipment perfectly visible beneath the starched cotton. I wadded up my lunch bag and stood, collected the lesson plans I'd intended working on and adjusted my jacket over my swollen pouch and said good-bye to the girls. I would have to pass right in front of Blue on the way to my next class and I was going to try to keep my eyes off him.

It truly was an accident that I dropped the books and my folio of papers fell open. The wind whipped the scattered sheets across the lawn and, in a clear stream of litter, right to where Blue was working. I began to collect them hastily from my end and I saw that Blue had dropped his rake and was picking up the flying pages from the other.

We met in the middle. "Thank you," I said, painfully conscious of his bright eyes on me. They had the gleam of a single-edge razor in them, sharp and piercing. He was so close I could feel his body heat and smell him a little. Even in the chill, his armpits were wet and the dark stain stuck to his ribs, looking like a raft of logs stitched together. His palm was calloused and warm when I took the pages from him.

"S'okay," he said. Then he just stood there. He stood there as though he were expecting something further, his eyes chaining me as if we had an invisible rope between us. I was pinioned by his gaze. Those cool blue eyes held me as surely as the butterflies in the science collection. He knew.

I mumbled some inane apology about being late for class and hurried off. I wished my room wasn't on the second floor right above where Blue was working. I uncharacteristically tried to deliver a lecture from the window where I could see him. I bungled a lesson that I had given a hundred times when he glanced up and saw me. Our eyes locked again and I gave up, told my students to read twenty pages and dismissed the class. I watched him for twenty minutes until he left with a backward glance. He smiled at me.

I was in the shower that night when the doorbell rang and it was Blue. I answered the persistent gongs with a towel wrapped around my middle.

"I wanna fuck you," he said as soon as I opened the door. Just like that. "I wanna fuck you." No prelude, hesitation, or uncertainty.

I gulped about twenty times and held the door wide, my whole body blushing in as many shades of crimson. Blue walked in as assuredly as if he lived there. He was in the same clothes he wore while working, only now they were rumpled and disheveled. His hair was tangled and it looked like he'd been in a fight. He stumbled against the wall a bit, steadied himself. I could tell he'd been drinking heavily. He didn't seem himself at all.

"Where's your bathroom?" he demanded. "I gotta piss first." The smell of liquor on his breath practically floored me.

I was speechless and pointed down the hall. "Show me," he said in an authoritative fashion, harshly.

I led the way to my bathroom which was still steamed up from the shower. My legs became Jell-O and it felt as if all my innards had come unglued and were racing around in my body. There was a pit of mud in my stomach threatening to slide farther down.

Blue walked to the front of the toilet and put his hands on his hips like a marine drill sergeant. "Take my cock out and hold it for me," he ordered in the manner of that same simile, although a little slurred.

My hands shook as I fumbled with his zipper. When I succeeded in dragging Blue's dick out, I thought my heart would burst out of my chest. He had an uncut fire hose for a cock and as much foreskin as I've ever seen on any man. It formed a huge nozzle over the flaring knob and lube-drool oozed out in copious amounts. His dick was veiny and the shaft was like a roadmap of blue worms.

"Skin me back," Blue mumbled. His liquored-up breath was hot in my face. His rod was feverish in my hand. I clutched the shaft and pulled back his dick-skin, and it felt like thick rubber and was slippery on the bone. I felt his slimy flesh skimming over the veins as I drew back his foreskin and unhooded his bright red knob. He was lubing as much as some guys come, drooling strands of clear viscosity actually dripping from his cock-head.

I directed the greasy knob and squeezed his erection. He started gushing out a real horse-cock piss that splattered loudly in the narrow space. I eased the fleshy foreskin back up over his swollen crown and his cock-nozzle flared out like tent flaps under the force of his flushing yellow stream. I flung the last leaking drops onto the floor by flicking his half-hard dick from his belly to his thighs.

Then he reached over and stroked my boner through the towel which had tented out at the sight. He held his own fat fucker in his fist and growled, "I'm gonna get this in you."

He pulled off my towel and dug his calloused palms up my crack. He pulled my hard cock into his groin and forcefully spread my cheeks apart. His liquor breath assaulted my senses.

"Suck me till I'm good and wet," he ordered. "Don't wanna dry-fuck you." He pushed my shoulders down until my face was in his crotch. Then he started to slap my cheeks with the heavy fucker till they were red and burning. He batted a home run on my lips. He held my chin while he jabbed his cock in the general direction of my mouth. Then he put three fingers of each hand in my mouth and pulled my cheeks apart. He held my mouth open while he pushed his dick into my face. Piss was still seeping out and he muscle-jerked his cock and a late stream hosed off down my throat. I swallowed every drop.

I got a lip-lock on his hardness and he pulled his fingers out of my mouth and placed his palms on each side of my head. He fed me dick by grabbing my hair and pulling me onto his log. His fleshy cock-skin rode a wave before my lips as he shoved in farther.

My cock is a barometer of my sexual excitement, jerking in the air like a demented puppet when I'm most aroused. Right then, it was banging on my belly like a drum.

Suddenly, Blue pulled me off his cock. "That's enough, man, I come quick the first time," he growled. "Where do you want to take it?"

I hadn't said a word this whole time. My body had taken over somewhere back there about the time he'd said he wanted to fuck me and my mind still hadn't caught up. Even at the baths, in the hottest steam room orgy, I'd never felt as depraved as I felt right then.

Just the thrill of undressing this man was practically enough to bring me off. I unbuttoned his uniform shirt, felt the wiry tendrils of his matted chest hair. I can only use the word breasts for those slabs of muscle which planed off his chest. They were firm and hard, barely yielding as I kneaded them. His nipples rose like rubber eraser caps and grew thick and even harder as I twisted them.

His belly was concave to his ribcage and wavelike ripples undulated as I stroked him. The pants came down. No underwear. His dick was hard. His balls were like pink grapefruits, swinging in their bag like a sack of groceries. His ass. Good God, his ass.

His ass felt firm as marble, but warm and big. His round spheres were lightly dusted with downy soft hair, like giant peaches and just as ripe.

I swagged a bottle of lotion off the sink and greased him up. I slapped a handful of the yellow cream between my cheeks and oiled myself up for him. "Here. Now," I said. I bent over the toilet and splayed my legs wide apart. I held onto the lid and felt his knob pressing against my tightly clenched pucker.

He savagely drove his cock into me. With no tenderness or mercy, he set up a quick rhythm inside my rectum and I saw the proverbial stars. Thunder, lightning, volcanic explosions, all the standard hyperbole are inadequate to express what it was: a fuck of epic proportions. Blue drilled my ass in a demented fury, a really fast-plugging, deep-dicking madness.

Come blew out of my dick almost straightaway. Without even touching myself, I shot off all over the toilet and the floor. When he came, I thought I would be blasted into the next county. The force of his gushing ejaculation nearly drove me off his cock.

"Now let's go to bed," he said, hauling his hose out of my tortured hole.

And in bed, Blue and I became lovers, the opposite of our near doglike coupling of earlier. There was an urgent need in his passion to be held, touched, kissed. I wanted to crawl inside his body. It was like he wanted to devour my skin right off me, the way he bit and chewed at every patch of my flesh. I had never been confronted by such desperate hunger to be loved, transcending the raw physicality. It was as if he hadn't had sex in months and now craved to be satiated. Something inside him was like a little boy, abandoned in a cave or falling down a well, then discovered. I drowned in his maleness.

When I fucked him, he fell apart in my hands. There was some delicate construction of himself inside this man-boy, his body's need outside and apart from that macho image of his appearance. A maw of wanton lust opened at his core and he was not content until I had fed inside his body for half the night.

The funk of his hole was intoxicating. Thirsty for the heady brew, I slurped at the juices of his ass. I tasted my own come, so recently expended, warm from the tender insides of him. His asshole clenched my tongue like a prick and I distended it to the fullest and stabbed him with it.

Under the covers and during the night, Blue held me fast to him. My butt was snuggled tightly to his groin, held in his hard embrace, and I felt as protected as a child. Even in sleep, his mouth nibbled lightly at my shoulder, half-conscious little bites and tender murmurings escaping his fleshy lips.

When I awakened, he was gone.

I dressed hurriedly, already late for my first class. Blue was again raking leaves, this time on the opposite side of the small campus. I approached him warily.

"Will I see you tonight?" I asked.

"Can't," was all he said. He returned to his chore. I hurried off to the classroom. During the week I saw him every day but he didn't speak to me. He would only give me that monosyllabic response of "can't" each time I asked if we could be together again.

I masturbated incessantly to his memory. Seeing him around the campus and remembering how he'd come onto me that night was rapidly driving me insane. I went about my duties in a perfunctory fashion, attending to the bare minimum of my responsibilities. I was preoccupied with Blue, could think of little else. A million explanations for his strange behavior crept through my brain, threatening my mental stability.

Perhaps he was going through some ridiculous period of self-denial, some half-formed self-hatred for the way he was. Maybe I had turned him off somehow. But that didn't seem possible, given that he had practically eaten me alive. Maybe he was fearful of commitment, but I'd made no mention of anything beyond another frantic coupling. My mind fretted and worried at the nagging notion that possibly Blue was just prick-teasing me. He was doing a fucking great job of it if that was the case.

My obsession with Blue grew even more powerful the second week, still with the "can'ts."

"Why, Blue, why?" I demanded of him. We were standing alone behind the gymnasium and he was trying to repair the antique furnace which piped heat into the building. The machine was about ten foot square and we were hidden between it and the wall of the gym. I couldn't help myself; I grabbed him and pulled him onto me, hard. I stuck my tongue down his throat and he pulled back as if he'd been bitten by a snake.

"I'm straight, Mr. Haley, don't do that," he said, offended.

"I suppose I was dreaming week before last, huh? You didn't fuck me and I didn't fuck you, right? Nothing happened?" Exasperated.

"That was Red, I'm sorry about that. I should have told you."

"What the hell do you mean, Blue? The man I went to bed with was none other than your own sweet self. I know every vein in your cock. I can tell you what your asshole tastes like. I oughta know, I spent half the night in there."

"Red's another part of me, he gets out sometimes. The doctor's working on it."

"Multiple personalities?" I gasped.

"Yeah," he replied, somewhat bashfully. "Red's gay and that's happened a couple of times before. Sometimes he sees something he likes and just takes over. Especially when I've had a few too many."

I stood there as speechless as the night that Blue/Red had said he wanted to fuck me. I could think of nothing to say, so I asked him, "Do you know what Red's doing when he's, ah—in charge like that?"

"Nope," he said in an embarrassed way. "And let me tell you, I waked up in some pretty funny places, with some pretty weird stuff going on."

"Like what?"

"Like I was tied up on a bed and this dude wouldn't let me go, said I asked him not to. I tried to explain but it didn't do no good. He fucked me."

"And you didn't like it?" Incredulous. Because with me he'd acted like he'd died and gone to heaven when I got my cock up his ass.

"I hated it, Mr. Haley. I felt raped."

"Jesus, Blue, I don't know what to say. Somehow sorry doesn't seem to fit."

"S'okay. I'm getting better about handling him every day."

I walked off with my mind fractured. I'd read the classic literature regarding such things but had never encountered a person with that condition. And he'd been so positive about being straight. That's why I got a double whammy shock when Blue, in the person of Red, showed up at my house that very night.

He wasn't drunk this time, and nowhere near as brazen. I opened the door, looking askance at him. "Blue?" I said tentatively.

"Red," he said. "Nice to see you again." He shook my hand. "I don't have much time, can we make it again?"

I practically ripped the clothes off him, leaving a trail of tossed garments all the way to the bedroom.

Lying on top of his meaty torso, with his cock drilling into my belly and lubing all over me, I kissed all over his face and our tongues dueled. When Red stuck his tongue in my ear, it was as if he were in my brain.

I pulled him on top of me, my cock pressed up into his silken cleavage. He was his own impetuous self again, as randy and goat-rutting as Pan. I held his lithe flanks tightly between my hands and pressed his high-hung ass down onto my cock. His hole was tight and clenched my rod with rippling muscles, milking me off. I pressed deeply into his yielding flesh and jabbed repeatedly into him. He moaned and crooned over and over, "I love you, man. I love you, man."

I skimmed my feverish hands all over his hard body, twisting and squeezing his nipples till they were thick and hard. Red jacked furiously on his meat, squatting and fucking himself on my tool like a bucking colt.

It felt as if I was getting ready to come. Red knew because he pulled his butt off my cock and got on his knees straddling my legs. I arched my back and punched out my hips and Red started sucking on my meat. I was going to come any minute.

I wanted to shoot off. It felt so good. It felt so exquisitely tormenting, after so long without, after nearly creaming his ass, to have him blow me. He was giving me quick little dick-licks to the head of my sensitive cock, all upward tongue strokes like he was licking on an ice-cream cone. Then his soft lips sucked my cock up and down, slowly, slowly, ever so slowly, nearly making me come, almost ready to shoot.

But not until he'd lifted my legs to his shoulders and worked his cock into my hole. His veiny shaft spread me apart and I felt him tunneling to my spark plug. Red clenched his teeth and set his lips in a firm straight line, worked them in and out and closed his eyes. The muscles in his body tossed like ocean waves in a storm as he deep-dicked me in a tight rhythm.

I reached for Red's broad sweating chest and squeezed his hardened nipples and he groaned. I couldn't hold out much longer as he mauled my guts with his pounding prick. He masturbated me while he fucked me. Paroxysms of pleasure washed over me like a surging tide, and I gave myself over to the beginning of an exploding, shattering ejaculation. Deep within me I felt his plunging cock grow even more rigid than before, swelling and filling me from side to side.

"Here it comes, man! I'm shooting!" he gasped. "Take my load, baby! Take that come!"

I felt his gushing jizz flooding my guts in spurting bursts, creaming my asshole with his spunky seed. He started jacking my cock faster. My hole rode a river of raw nerves, surging forward and back, slammed and banged and fucked as I felt his glory start to shoot. He pressed his spewing fucker hard against my trigger, jabbing at my button and making me come.

I started ejaculating then, great long ropes of thick come arching out of his pumping fist and shooting across my chest, to my shoulders, and in my face and hair. Red milked more dick-honey out of me than I'd have thought possible.

He filled my hole with so much gooey come that I felt it sliming out and running over my balls. The longer he pumped his juice into me, the more I thrashed and trembled with paroxysms of an exquisite, near torturous orgasm battering my senses.

We shuddered to a mutually convulsive and anguished climax and he collapsed his spent body atop me, cemented there with my shot-off spunk. The final globules of Red's powerful ejaculation drained into my well-fucked body, and we lay still, clasped in a sweaty bearhug.

Then Red licked the come off me and kissed it into my mouth. I sucked hungrily on his sweet, fleshy lips.

"I won't be seeing you again, Mr. Haley," Red said while he was dressing. I asked him why. "Blue's getting married, the doctor said that should cure his little problem with me. He told him I should get weaker and disappear."

"And you believe that?" I asked, furious.

"Nah, there's another reason."

I asked the question with my silence.

"—love the guy."

"You mean you're in love with Blue? With yourself?"

"Wouldn't you be, hunk like that?"

"But—but. But that's you, Red, you're Blue."

"Not really, just his wild side. I want him to settle down, have some kids, a family. Besides, think how good looking those kids are going to be."

He left and I resigned myself to never having him again. I said at the beginning that my life came apart. For weeks I was disconsolate. Blue had come to be more than a one-night stand, a trick. Like an addict deprived, I was even more obsessed with his absence around the campus than the torment his unattainable presence wrought upon my mind. He had simply disappeared and, though I discreetly asked several administrators, not one knew of his whereabouts.

Then one morning I was having coffee in the cafeteria, idly reading the paper. I thought my heart would stop when I saw the notice of a marriage, the picture of an attractive girl, her fiancé smiling. Blue. The words beneath.

"To Mr. Blue Samuels."

I tore out the announcement, noting the date and time, within the week. The ceremony would take place in a small Baptist church with which I was familiar. I vacillated a hundred times about attending. In the end I welcomed the occasion as cathartic, telling myself that by going, I could view it as a finality.

The wedding was not lavish, simple and dignified, though the bride was resplendent in her gown. Blue looked more stunning than I'd ever seen him. His white suit was dazzling under the brilliant lights, like the sun, hard and dangerous to look at.

I reached him in the receiving line and he shook my hand. He didn't seem too surprised to see me there. For just the briefest moment, something danced in back of his eyes. A tiny mischievous grin played about his lips for only a second before dying.

"Best wishes, Blue," I choked out.

"I'm coming back to work," he said. "I'll see you soon, Mr. Haley."

PART THREE

INITIATION

Gay men have no automatic lineage. Unlike straight men, who can be initiated into the rituals of heterosexual manhood by their fathers and brothers, we must create our own models and our own rites of passage. We self-consciously assume the roles of teacher and student, mentor and protégé . . . and, in some instances, master and slave.

In "Raven," Jeff DeCharney uses a classic situation to depict how a mentoring relationship benefits both parties. A battle-weary and jaded teacher encounters a young man eager to discover the "edge" of experience. In the course of the story, the young man matures by testing his limits, and the older man is rejuvenated with a sense of his own purpose. This contemporary story is told with conscious reference to the medieval tales of the Knights Templar. As in the older tradition, it is important that the young man is given multiple chances to prove his commitment to his teacher and to the initiation process itself. Thus is the ritual formalized, the compact sealed.

The settings and physical accoutrements of initiation ceremonies are crucial: Native Americans hold ceremonies in sweat lodges and dark kivas; Roman Catholics use holy water and incense; African and other cultures make use of physical markings on the skin. Caro Soles, writing as Kyle Stone, draws on these kinds of traditions in "The Brass Ring." In a liminal space (a hot, dark attic away from the intrusions of "the world"), and with the help of a shamanlike stranger bearing ritual objects, the narrator travels to physical and emotional places he has never been before. Imagination and reality, the physical and the spiritual blend until they are indistinguishable parts of a transformative experience.

V. K. McCarty is a longtime editor at *Penthouse Variations* who adopts a male literary persona to write gay erotica as Victor King. As someone who enjoyed a theater career in New York, and who also became a regular at sex clubs like the Mineshaft—which was self-consciously a theater of sexual initiation—McCarty writes with a heightened understanding of the importance of role-playing in gay sex. In "Basic Training," she shows how the sexual roles of mentor and initiate often go much deeper than playacting.

The three writers represented in this section are all women. This is not by conscious design, but it may indicate some larger truths. Is it because these women observe the defined teacher/student roles in gay male culture and wish they had such clearly established initiatory relationships in their own lives? Or perhaps because they are necessarily outsiders to the gay male tribe, the women represented here fantasize most readily about the idea of being initiated into the kinship.

JEFF DECHARNEY

RAVEN

I'D HAVE KNOWN THIS ROOM WITH MY EYES CLOSED. SMELLS of slightly damp wood warmed by the sun, dust, an undertone of mildew. All it lacked was the pungent tang of boy-sex to take me back to the fifties, to sweaty summer nights with Paul. The anxiety, the excitement, and at the bottom of it all a bond that outlasted lovers, war, booze, the works. And now Paul owned the old house near the lake and had told me to come and make myself at home.

Home. I needed some kind of anchor, all right. Not home, exactly, but a quiet place to think about which way the future pointed.

The window curtain had snagged on a picture frame, an old snapshot, grainy with enlargement. Paul and me at fifteen, horsing around in the old dinghy. As I unhooked the fabric I glanced out the window. The old trees were taller, the leaves beginning to go red and gold, the lake still half obscured.

A movement on the dock caught my eye. A slender body, naked in the sunset, diving cleanly, surfacing with a dog-shake of blond hair.

His face was turned the other way, but the quick glimpse of his neatly muscled ass, white against his tan, was breathtaking.

Smiling, I went back to my unpacking. If nothing else, the addition to the scenery was great. Maybe the kid lived nearby, maybe he sneaked over to Paul's dock for a swim after work. Maybe . . .

There was no maybe about how my cock was reacting to that flash of ass. The hardening flesh moving against my jeans was tantalizing. There'd be time for that later, though. For now I had to get settled in. The flight had been too long, the layover a real pain—literally. The mangled muscles of my left leg ached fiercely and I was limping more than usual.

No, it wasn't 'Nam that did it. It was my own battle with my own demons. A battle that nearly ended with me crushed inside the wreck of my car beside a county road in upstate New York. I was lucky, they said. I could have bled to death. They might have had to take off the leg. There were months and months I wished they had.

I stripped off the jeans and sweatshirt, kicked off my shoes. Gently I rubbed the arroyo patterns of scar tissue that graphically illustrated what havoc metal wreaks on flesh that gets in its way. The place the bones had torn through the skin was still darker, pitted. I'd seen kids medevacked with worse, but this was me—a constant reminder of my mortality and yet a kind of perversely hopeful symbol, too. My life had been changed radically, and mostly for the better. But the damn thing ached, and philosophy wasn't going to soothe it.

The old wood felt good under my feet, and the big old bathtub was just as I remembered it—plenty big enough to soak my six-foot-four-inch frame. Gratefully I sank into the hot water, muscles loosening gradually. Almost dozing I reached for my cock. What was the story about the professor explaining a problem in optics by comparing it to the way you reach for your dick in the tub and it isn't quite where you expect it?

Not bad, I thought, one piece of me that still looks good. What the porn writers call a columnar shaft, with a head like a ripe plum. Not grotesque, but good sized, thick and well proportioned. My fingers grazed my ballsac, loose in the hot water, balls big and heavy.

The blond boy in the water was coming back to me as I stroked, hardening me fast. How I'd like to leave my mark on that creamy flesh, to see those muscles sharply defined by restraint. I wondered what his face was like, how he'd look with eyes half-closed, lips circling my cock as I fucked his throat. My hand clenched like his imagined gag-reflex and come burst out of me like years of dammed-up longing.

Back in my room I eased into a clean pair of jeans, looser now than six months ago, patting my now quiescent rod as I packed it away.

Noises indicated another presence in the house. Paul had mentioned a sometime caretaker who lived over the garage, but hadn't said anything about him. I pictured some elderly local, useful mostly for locking up and checking that the pipes didn't freeze in winter.

I laced up my boots. Barefoot was nice, but it was hard to walk far without support, and I wanted to hike around the lake later on.

Downstairs I saw him through the kitchen door, lowering a case of soda water from his shoulder. It was the boy from the lake. Slim, but the muscles moved well. Early twenties, streaky blond hair, white teeth, gray-green eyes. The smile was slightly self-conscious, either because he knew who I was or because of my obvious meat-market appraisal. His nipples were small and brown, hardening even as I watched him. A golden down fuzzed his chest and arms. I waited for him to speak first. Why give away the advantage?

"Er, Mister Raven, my name is Mike, Mike Larsen. Paul said I should stock up the fridge for you and lay in some cases of club soda. . . . And I really am glad to meet you. I've read all your books; I think they're great."

Read all my books? Somehow I doubted it. The academic ones were too obscure. What he meant was my series of historical thriller/romances aimed at the gay male S&M audience.

"Paul said to tell you I'm at your service. Anything you want or need while you're here, just let me know. And, Mr. Raven, Sir," he swallowed hard and looked directly at me, "this is from me, not him. When I say anything, I mean anything." His eyes were a little unfocused, as if he needed not to look down but couldn't look me straight in the eye. The tips of his ears grew pink.

Did he really mean that? Somehow I doubted he knew what he was asking to get into, whatever Paul had said to him. But then they never do, not exactly. Just the heat in the guts when they remember prisoner games or being wrestled to the ground by a bigger kid. This one was old enough to know himself as a gay man, but he didn't look like anybody'd ever worked him seriously.

I looked at him for a long minute, unsmiling. The green eyes fell and the blush on his ears deepened.

"For starters," I said, "a long cold soda water, slice of lemon. On the porch. No ice." As he dove into the fridge I walked away.

The sunset I had seen beginning from the window was dulling into twilight. Lightning bugs were blinking on and off, insects were humming in the grass. I sat on the porch rail, inhaling the sweet autumn smell, missing the leaf smoke from now-illegal bonfires. It was autumn all the same, a season I love. And the first for years I hadn't been teaching. That part of my life was over. The books were selling well, and I was starting to work on something more mainstream.

I leaned back against the rugged post and wondered about this boy. I was certainly interested. I could almost taste the sweet, unused savor of his skin, and how it would sharpen with the anxious tang of fear. . . . I caressed that memory, the reality denied me in my students all these years. It had been a long time since I'd handled any but the disappointing poseurs and well-used bottoms of the city scene.

I felt him next to me before I really heard him.

"Sir," he said, clearing his throat, "your drink."

"Sit," I told him, pointing to the porch deck at my feet. He folded himself down gracefully, leggy as a deer, but not quite six feet. Nice size, nice movements.

"How old are you?" I asked him finally.

"Twenty-six, Sir. I worked for a couple of years to earn money for college. My grades weren't good enough for a full scholarship, and I couldn't see taking out a loan. I went to a small school in New Jersey —easy to get to New York on the weekends, you know."

"Do I?" I said, teasing him.

"Well, mostly I'd fooled around with other kids, but it didn't have something . . . It wasn't till I read one of your books and caught that edge between the older guy and the younger one that it got much clearer. I hung out in a couple of the leather bars my last year there, but you can go a whole night without seeing somebody that looks like he's got that edge, you know? I know things have changed a lot since what I've read about the Mineshaft and stuff, but it was so . . . so fake. And besides, I wanted it to be right—to be somebody who knew what he was doing and could tell what I needed, and how do you know that? So mostly I just jerked off a lot."

He'd surprised me there. Perceptive enough to know how hollow so much of the scene was, but sort of romantic enough to wait for the real thing. And what had Paul told him? I asked.

"Well, Sir, he said you'd known each other since grade school. That you went into the marines together, and then he got wounded and you lost track of each other for a few years. That part he didn't say much about except to say you don't drink or smoke anymore or mess with drugs. You like rare steaks and drink gallons of club soda. That you were a hot kid and that you can make a guy do more with a look than most guys can by yelling like a drill instructor. I could kind of get a feel for that from the pictures on your book jackets, but they don't do you justice. I never thought you were so tall, and the beard's new, isn't it?"

He caught his breath and then he did the damnedest thing. He got up on his knees and folded his hands as if he was praying. Looking up at me he said, slowly, the words coming from a deeply treasured pocket of memory, "My lord, the King has killed the body of the Order, but its spirit lives in you and in every knight his schemes have not imprisoned. Teach me, my lord, and that great company shall live in me and others after me, though Philip and his minions know it not."

Not praying, not exactly. The posture of a vassal swearing fealty to his lord. And the words were from the book I'd poured more of myself into than any other, building the character of the fugitive Templar knight out of my own deepest pain. Not my best book, it was too raw for that, but my best loved.

He looked so damned vulnerable kneeling there. I resisted the urge to reach down and run my fingers through his silky, rough-cut hair. The gesture would have dishonored his intensity. Lust and tenderness and violence combined to make a growing bulge in my crotch, inches from his face.

I made the only gesture that was fitting. My hands, bigger, darker, folded around his, accepting his homage. When I let them go he sat back on his heels and I lifted his chin so I could see his eyes. They widened, but to his credit he didn't look away.

"If I say yes, you'll be into something serious. I'm not into kid's games or playing dress-up. I don't sit down and plan scenes so the bottom calls the shots. I only want to deal with people who are strong enough for real submission, no reservations. If you can give me your whole self I can take you places you've never dreamed of. If not, I'd rather not even bother. I'm too old to fuck around with a spoiled kid. But if you're man enough, we'll see. Understand?"

"Yes, Sir, I think so, Sir."

I tapped him sharply on the cheek. He started, but he recognized it—the symbolic gesture that reminds the would-be knight what he may have to endure to reach his goal. Pride shone in his face for a moment, then changed to serious purpose.

"Stand up. Straighter. Hands by your sides, fingers loosely curled. Head up, chin tucked, feet at a forty-five degree angle. Not great, not great. If you were standing against a wall not even air should be between you and it, even at the small of your back. Got it?"

Eager. He was definitely eager.

"Now, hands behind your back, feet shoulder-width apart. That's parade rest. You will assume this position while waiting for orders."

I took another long pull at the soda water. Slowly, slowly I got up and walked around him. He stood very still, but every nerve ending was alert. I settled back on the rail.

"Strip."

He blinked. He must have expected it, but the moment itself was electric.

"Now. Do it."

He shoved off his sneakers. Hands shaking a little, he unbuckled his belt and unzipped the baggy workpants. They fell to the porch deck and he balked for just a second, but the rising mound of his jockey shorts betrayed him. No way he was going to be able to act cool—not in that condition.

I let him stew a little as he disentangled his erection and yanked off his shorts. He stumbled as he got his feet free and looked at me uncertainly.

"Pick 'em up and fold 'em. Neatly."

Now that was a truly beautiful boy. Not as hard muscled as an older man might be, but athletic and trim. The golden down made a tangled nest for his cock. It might be as long as mine, uncut, but not as thick. White like his ass, blue veined, deeply indented head, slit already weeping. His balls were compact, not as big as they might be, but they made a nice fist between his legs. Altogether a nice package. What else might there be for me to unwrap?

"Now bend over the rail and grab the bottom bar. Legs spread. Ass up."

So very young, but a man for all that. There was heat under the coolness of his skin, like a fever beginning. I stroked his neck, rubbing up into his hair. It was every bit as soft as I had imagined and its clean, sunny smell lingered as I brought my hand up to my face.

I ran my hands down his back, stroking him, gentling him like an unbroken colt, but mostly soaking up the feel of him, sleek and strong, and smelling the metallic sweat of apprehension start to break.

He was certainly afraid, but still he seemed to mold his back to my hands, arching slightly like a cat into each stroke. Not relaxed, but going with my hands.

His ass shivered at my touch, that marvelous galvanic response like a nervous animal's. But all I did for the moment was to stroke its curves and savor its texture: the silkiness of skin, the crisp hairs around the asshole. The puckered opening itself, eager and fearful at the same time.

Slowly and quietly I removed my belt. There are times to heighten expectation with the sound of leather on cloth and there are times for surprise. I wanted this to come out of the blue.

I never double up a belt. It makes a louder noise maybe, but it makes for a clumsy instrument. And a canvas like this deserved finesse.

At the first stroke his head reared back, but there was hardly any sound from him, only startled exhalation. The stripe rose deep red against the white. It would welt beautifully. Another blow, then half a dozen fast cracks. The galvanic quivering increased as the stripes began to weave their pattern. My hand caressed the heated flesh, making him flinch almost more than the impact of the belt. Then with measured deliberation I laid down the last dozen, dropped the belt and hoisted his hips higher, licking the emerging welts, tasting the unique sweetness of bruised flesh.

As I let him go, the head of his cock scraped the rough wood and his control gave way. Come spurted out into the dusk.

I grabbed the back of his neck and shoved him roughly to his knees.

"That, Mister, is the last time you come unless I tell you. Got it?"

"Yes, Sir," he mumbled, face and ears flaming.

"Louder, Mister, I want to hear you answer."

"Yes, Sir. Not unless you say to, Sir."

"Now. Stay there. On your knees, legs apart, eyes down, hands on the top of your head, fingers laced together. That's the position I want to find you in when I come back and any time I point to the floor and say 'Boy.' Unless, of course, you decide to quit, in which case I don't want to see you around except to do the basic chores. Got it?"

"Yes, Sir, no, Sir. I'll be here, Sir."

Moving slowly to minimize the limp, I descended the steps and strolled around the house. The same old trail wound down the slope to the dock. The dock where Paul and I first wrestled, not knowing any other way at first to touch the way we wanted to. The dock where I had first seen this young faun, this Mike, who had erupted into what I thought would be a quiet, meditative visit to my old haunts.

Would he be there when I got back? I thought so. Would he come back again to weave this into an ongoing pattern? I didn't know, and just for now I didn't plan beyond tonight. Not exactly proper AA philosophy, but living in the present all the same.

I moved on, feet remembering the contours of the path, but thoughts oblivious to my surroundings.

He was still there. The night air had begun to chill him, goose-flesh competing with the darkening welts across his ass. My cock responded, lengthening and hardening as I unbuttoned my fly.

Almost fully hard, I leaned against the post, inches from his face. I pulled his head closer and slapped my cock across his mouth, once, twice. He stared, mesmerized, almost crosseyed from proximity, concentrating as if memorizing every vein, as if he would be quizzed on the exact quality of my circumcision.

"Want it, Boy?" I whispered.

"Yes, Sir." He was whispering, too.

"Yes, Sir," he repeated, louder, leaning toward me.

I handed him the condom, its wrapper still warm from my pocket. He was a little clumsy, as you might be tying someone else's tie, but his face was reverent as he smoothed the sheath along my rod.

"Over the rail."

His eyes widened again, but he obeyed, legs spread. Pulling apart his asscheeks with my hands I spat once on the wrinkles of his asshole, causing that shiver again.

I was hard as the porch rail, hard as iron. I rammed forward, harsh and nearly dry, up to the root. A whimper escaped him, and I reached down, spreading his hands on the rail, my reach longer than his, my arms heavier. The warmth had come back to his neck; its flush was like a ripening peach. Deliberately I took its softness in my teeth, biting down enough to leave a mark.

As roughly as I'd entered him I pulled out, tossed aside the condom, and jerked myself off across his back, rubbing the thick come into his hair. His ass quivered, bereft, but he didn't move. Not until I yanked his head back and pushed him to his knees. The tears and snot didn't spoil his face at all.

"Take the weekend. Think. Feel. Out of my sight. If you're back here Monday, when I wake up, we'll see."

I let the screen door slam, and made my way back into the kitchen. I rinsed myself off in the sink and rustled up a steak and salad. Thank you, Paul. You always did seem to know what I needed better than I did myself.

CARO SOLES
WRITING AS
KYLE STONE

THE BRASS

RING

IT SEEMS EVERY TIME I TURN AROUND THERE IS SOMEBODY there—my Mom, my Dad, even Uncle Allan and his new girlfriend with the fake eyelashes. After living away from home in residence for a year, it's tough. So when I found the attic in my parents' new house, it was almost too good to be true. Now I can pull the steps up after me and masturbate in peace.

It's warm up there, the air still, like it's just the way it's always been. I like to think it's the same air the other guy breathed, the one who sold my folks this place, the one who watched me all the time while he talked to them with those eyes that saw right down inside. Neil Jenkins, that's his name. He's got a deep tan, like he spends a lot of time outdoors. It's that look, you know? Fit. In charge. His shirt was open and he wore a gold key on a chain around his neck. I got hot just being in the same room. My parents didn't seem to notice. All they saw was a well-dressed guy in his forties with a house to sell. I saw a great body radiating sex, an iron will and years of experience making guys do exactly what he wanted. I saw the ass muscles hard against the pull of his trousers. I saw the swell of his big cock, filling in the rest with my overheated imagination. And when I went up to the attic that first time, it was like he was still there. I filled my lungs with the stale air and imagined a little bit of him inside me. I came in my jeans.

We've been in this house a couple of weeks now. It's August, and the heat and humidity build every day like the whole place has suddenly become part of South America. They leave me alone, pretty much.

Today, finally, there's no one home. Mom and Dad are visiting friends in our old town, about sixty miles east of here. I've got the whole afternoon and evening to myself. I wait till I'm sure they won't come back for something they forgot, like they usually do. I give them twenty minutes. Then I go to the upstairs hall, climb up on the chair from my room and fold down the attic steps.

This is the first time I've had the chance to really kick back and dream a little, without keeping one ear open for sudden intrusions from below. I just stand there, taking it all in. There is a round window at each end of the room and the late afternoon sun pours in through the dancing leaves of the trees outside. Rough wooden planks are nailed down across the joists to form a solid floor beneath my bare feet. Exposed rafters meet over my head and the smell of wood and dust tickles my throat. Carefully, I take a deep breath and feel an odd shudder pass through my body.

It's hot. Stifling. I take off my T-shirt and cutoffs and sit down on the unfinished floorboards. The rough wood bites into my ass as I move. One hand is already on my cock as I stretch out full length on my back. My body is beaded with sweat and the weight of all that heat pushes down on me like a lover.

I close my eyes. My hair is long and when I turn my head, splinters tangle in it and hold me. I know if I move sharply, I can break free, but I like the sensation. Like fingers, pulling me down. I spread my legs farther apart, bend my knees. The floor pushes back against the soles of my feet. I can feel it against my balls. My shoulders prickle as I squirm, my hand pumping, my heart beating in my ears. Dust motes vibrate in the air. I can almost feel them, tiny pricks on my hard tits, whispers like breath on the hairs on my groin. I turn my face into my armpit, smell my own ripe scent. My tongue lolls out to taste the tang of my hot flesh.

My eyelids pulse red as my nuts grow tight and I push my shoul-

ders hard against the floor, trying to steady myself for the wild rush
building inside. My left hand reaches out to catch hold of a metal post
that goes from the floor to the ceiling. My eyes snap open. I am panting,
my chest rising and falling in gasps. My cock begins to jerk and as I
cry out into the heat, I spurt my hot juices up and out and over my
hand, the floor, part of my thigh. I start to laugh and pull my knees
up to my chest, feeling the air whisper and sigh against my asshole. I
stop the crazy laughing and just lie there, coming down, watching the
dancing shadows in the room settle around me, till I see only a dusty
attic, filled with heat and my own desire.

Slowly I sit up, not bothering to wipe myself off. The smell of sex
drenches the air. I like that. It suits this place, this neglected eyrie that
is the only part of the house that is all mine. I walk to the window
overlooking the neighbors' front yard and take pleasure in pressing my
naked body against the glass. What would they think if they looked up
and saw me? My cock, still half erect, smears come, mingled with dust
and cobwebs, across the window pane.

"Morons!" I shout, and my voice in this hot space, surprises me. I
turn away from the window.

As my eyes readjust, the attic seems to swim for a moment in the
green-gold light. I see a trunk, standing on end against the wall by the
opposite window. I've never seen one like it before, except in movies.
It's like the kind they had on the *Titanic*, a steamer trunk to hold all
the different clothes you need to dress for the afternoon, for dinner, for
dances—silk cravats and pearl studs and cufflinks, spats and boiled shirts
and fancy vests and velvet smoking jackets. It stands open, displaying
on one side the rows of small drawers, covered in faded lavender roses,
and on the other, a curtain of the same material. As I walk over to
examine it, I wonder why I didn't notice it the first time I was here.

The musty odor of mildew and dust tickles my nose and I open
the first drawer. Inside is what looks like old T-shirts and underwear.
Faintly disappointed, I take out the garments and put them to my nose.
The smell that suddenly shocks my senses is strong and new and now
—sweat and the faint odor of piss where a damp cock would have pushed
against the material. I feel aroused by the thought and the association.
I rub the underwear over my own sweaty body as I open the next drawer.

The smell of leather pushes against me and I drop the shorts to
pick up the gleaming black straps and belts and braided throngs. The
leather slides and twists under my fingers, creaking and crying out with

the voices of all the men who have felt the sting of it against their bare flesh. Instinctively I know what each is used for, feel the slap of the broad paddle on my ass, hear the crack of the belt against my shoulders. The sensation is so strong I tense, as if expecting pain.

I open another drawer, and find gleaming metal cock rings, spring clamps and small weights and a series of padlocks. In the next drawer are handcuffs, metal ones like policemen carry. Black ones of molded plastic. Clips and clamps and a studded leather collar. There's a dildo, too, that looks so much like a real cock I feel my mouth water. My asshole tingles with need.

I choose a long supple strap with smooth metal rivets along each side. I walk around for a few moments slapping the leather against my hands. The feel and smell and sound all combine to give me goose bumps of pleasure in the heat.

Then I notice a glint of metal on one of the upright beams on the other side of the room. On closer inspection, I find it is one of a series of large brass rings attached to the beam and to the bare rafters above my head in the center of the room. I am so absorbed in my discovery that I don't hear the slight groan of the wooden steps behind me. It is the change in the air that I finally become aware of. The abrupt tension hardens my cock. I stop. Carefully, I turn my head.

"I see you've found the brass ring." It's Neil Jenkins, the man who used to own this house. He looks different somehow. He smiles, seeing my questions. "I didn't move far," he says.

"I didn't hear you come in." I am suddenly embarrassed in my nakedness. I start to reach for my shorts, but he stops me with a gesture.

"It's hot," he says. "For what we'll be doing, you don't need clothes. Am I right?"

"Yes, Sir." My response startles me. I'm not in the habit of calling people "Sir."

He smiles, his dark eyes lighting for a moment as he takes in my body. I'm not very tall, about 5'8", and he towers over me, but I run every day and work out three times a week. I'm proud of how I look. As he sizes me up, I can almost feel the lick of heat from his eyes. My cock stirs. I am beginning to find his scrutiny uncomfortable and shift my weight to my right leg.

"Stand still." His voice has changed. It's deeper, rough with command.

I am not used to this. At once I feel a rush of anger that he is giving me orders. "What is this? You don't own this house any more, you know. You can't come up here—"

"Shut up!"

"What?"

"You heard me." His large hands are at his waist, undoing his belt. A large stainless steel clip hangs from the buckle. I feel the first flicker of fear.

I take a step towards my shorts and T-shirt, instinctively wanting the protection of clothes. As I bend over to grab my cutoffs, his belt whistles through the still air and cuts across my ass. I jump, shocked by the pain. The heat from the blow tingles as I gape at him, my mind tumbling with confusion. "What the hell . . ."

"Shut up and listen." He draws the black leather belt through his hands as he talks, staring at me all the time, his jaw tense, his eyes glinting with menace. He means every word. "Stand up straight and pay attention. I'm not used to having to repeat myself."

Instantly I straighten up. I can feel my long hair damp on my shoulder blades. Sweat drips down my sides. My ass burns, my cock twitches.

"First time I laid eyes on you I knew you needed to feel a man's hand," he goes on. "I knew you needed some guy to twist your balls and wipe that self-satisfied smirk off your face. I also knew you'd find your way up here, and when you least expected it, I'd be here."

"How did you know—"

"No questions, boy." He comes over and puts a hand on my chest, his broad thumb roughly pushing my left tit. I shiver in the heat, ripples of pleasure making the nipple hard. I almost cry out as his other hand reaches for my cock and squeezes. "Legs apart." His fingers continue to probe and feel. Wherever he touches me, the gold-brown hairs on my body stand up and quiver. He runs his hands down my sides, over my thighs, between my legs. He takes my long hair in one fist and pulls it back sharply, making my eyes water and my chin lift. With his other hand he strokes my throat. His fingers force my jaw open. His thumb hooks over my lower teeth and pulls down, opening my mouth.

I don't know how to react to this, standing there naked in front of him, my legs apart, staring at his strong weathered face. My impulse is to talk during sexual encounters, but this isn't like anything I've ever experienced before. I am an animal being examined at the county fair. He grunts and pushes me away. He unbuttons his shirt.

"Those rings you were so curious about," he says, and his deeply tanned chest ripples as he rolls his broad shoulders out of the shirt. "Grab one."

I look up and see the brass rings, one just above my head, another at the same height on the exposed rafter about three feet to the right. They're big, not like the padded ones gymnasts use, but just wide enough for a man's hand. I reach up and take hold of one. It's worn smooth, as if from frequent use. I feel the tug of muscle as I stretch.

"The other hand."

By now I'm almost on tiptoe. I shake back my hair and watch him pull up the steps and fasten them in place with a series of bolts I hadn't noticed before. No one can get up here, now. No one.

I smell my own sweat on the air as I watch him take off his shoes and socks. He peels off his white linen trousers and folds them neatly. He is wearing a jock strap, the white cotton stark against his tanned hard belly. Black pubic hair curls defiantly around the scanty pouch. He trails the belt through the dust as he comes towards me. I see the glint of the gold key on a chain around his neck. He doesn't say anything for a few moments, just keeps looking at me. Hard. I feel the flush all over me. My cock stands at attention, waiting. I cough.

"Shut up." He walks behind me and I feel his breath on my neck as he lifts my long hair and pushes my head forward. His arms embrace me from behind. His hands follow the contours of my chest as his fingers flick my nipples.

I twitch.

His hands slide up into my armpits. He licks the damp hair there, his saliva pasting it to my skin. He runs his hands down my sides and I can smell my sweat lingering on his skin. His fingers fasten around my hips. I catch my breath as he draws my ass close to his hard cock. My feet are barely on the ground now and my arms are beginning to ache with the strain of my own weight.

"Pretty boy," he murmurs in my ear. "You've been aching for it, haven't you?" When I don't answer, one hand grabs my balls and squeezes. I yell. "Answer me when I ask a question!"

"Yes, Sir." The attic blurs through my tears, but the excitement in my stomach keeps building. For some reason, it doesn't occur to me to let go of the rings. In fact, I clutch them even more tightly, feeling the metal slippery with my sweat.

The leather belt goes around my hips and I hear a snap, click, and am lifted backward, my ass in the air, my feet off the ground. I look over my shoulder and see the strap attached to another ring on the rafters, clipped onto the belt that's holding me. The weight on my arms is greater, now. My muscles cry out in protest. All my effort is concentrated on hanging on.

And now I feel the nudge of a finger against my hole. I try to relax, but it's hard when my whole body cries out against the pain. He slides inside, one finger, two, three. My muscles contract around his hard flesh, trying to expel this invasion, but he pushes further, deeper.

"Relax, boy. Just let it happen." His deep voice thrums in the air, entering me like sex, pouring through me like hot melting wax.

I almost lose my grip on the rings as he pushes further, forcing my asshole to open wide, wider. Slowly, slowly I let him possess me, like no other man ever has. Not like this, not like this!

"Oh God! Oh shit! Ahhhhhhhh!" I stop, my breath coming in gasps. But Neil controls me, now. Utterly. Completely. I feel melded to him. Part of him. His whole hand is in my bowels. I feel the pulsing of his blood, the beating of his heart deep inside me. My face is bathed in tears but I'm aware only of our union, this absolute intimacy I have never experienced before. I have opened myself to this stranger, given him my soul to play with. I will never be exactly the same.

I have no idea how long we remain like this. Time fades as the sunlight shifts outside the dusty windows. I hang in the still air clinging to the brass rings, attached to the leather straps, attached to the man whose hand moves now and then inside me, whose wrist is sealed in by my quivering sphincter muscle. His other hand moves on my back, stroking, soothing, calming. His fingers gently play with my damp hair, move around to explore my hard tits. I know if I let go, he will catch me. But I hang on, because he wants me to. I know this, too.

Then, with the same exquisite slowness, he begins to withdraw. Inch by inch. Rearranging my universe every few minutes, until finally, he is gone. We are separate. A great cry of loss escapes me. The belt around my hips is pulled up. I hear the click of the metal as the clip is unfastened and I am lowered to the ground. I am trembling. He walks around in front of me. I let go of the rings and collapse sobbing into his arms.

"That's just the beginning," he says. "You're a good boy. A good pupil."

"Thank you." I'm still sobbing, but feel calmer, now. I notice my own come on my thighs. When did that happen? How many times?

He holds my head between his hands and kisses me, his tongue exploring, tasting, claiming. Then, with a final kiss, he lays me gently on the ground, gets dressed and leaves.

I lie on the floor, naked, drifting, coming down. I realize how dark the room is. Did I fall asleep? I look up and can't see the brass rings any more. Disappointment washes over me. It was just a dream. Turning my head, I see the steamer trunk in the shadows. I remember the dull sheen of leather, the glint of silver studs I saw in that wonderful fantasy. I sit up and wince. Twisting around, I look back at my ass and see bruises. What kind of a dream leaves marks?

I stand up and look more closely at the beams above my head. They are rough, unfinished, naked. There is no gleam of brass now, nothing to show what I went through. Nothing, except the marks on my ass, the marks on my soul.

I look through the gathering dusk at the steamer trunk. It's too dark to see details any more. Still naked, I walk over to check it out. It's closed. When I try to push the two sides open, the way they were before, nothing happens. Surprised, I run my hand along the front and find a round metal fastening with a small keyhole in the middle. The trunk is locked. I remember the gold key around Neil Jenkins' neck and I smile.

V. K. MCCARTY
WRITING AS
VICTOR KING

BASIC

TRAINING

"YOU'RE EXQUISITE LIKE THAT, MY BOY," I WHISPERED INTO HIS ear, exaggerating the articulation so he could understand me through the blindfold. So beautiful teasing him with the sibilant S-sound. As I watched his poised devotion before me on the carpet, I thought back through the odyssey of his surrender and of his careful grooming for my explicit pleasure. He shifted the weight on his knees, weary from waiting, and licked his lips, carefully holding his head up at the desired angle. He was, quite simply, irresistible.

I tell you, it all begins with the touch. That exquisite response hidden in the touch. Indescribable and inescapable. A boy exposes that, surrenders it to me, and he is mine.

Paul was waiting for me with his voluptuous flesh answering back and his liquid eyes in an Off-Broadway experiment called, "The Erotic Connection." Those were daring nights in the theatre; it might be hard to comprehend today how dangerous and thrilling every exposure was in those days. I'd seen a flyer for this thing at one of my downtown

magazine store hangouts, Physique Memorabilia, and hoped there might
be some plump, tan pecs on display or perhaps a flash of spongy German
underpants, something like that.

The actors came on stage after the performance to rap with the
audience and there was Paul—butch, bashful, and ripe for training. He
sold his soul to me with a smoldering stare across the footlights to my
first-row seat. He'd been the one who stripped down in the last scene
and delivered his sweet nostalgic monologue with all of us staring at
his young meat, but now he was clad again in painter's pants and a tank
top. Maybe he did it to everyone, but I really felt that my eyeing him
was making his nipples stand up under the ribbed jersey. He seemed to
flinch if I arched my eyebrow and again as I licked one side of my
moustache, and I watched his mouth trail open as I rubbed my cock,
quietly palming it a little further down my crotch. Our courtship was
as simple as that. I left my card for him at the box office and he'd left
a message for me before I got home.

We met the next night in Central Park. I'd packed a good deal of
innuendo onto a business card, curious to figure out if he could really
live up to the leather pants he'd worn in the show. I hoped he'd be
complimented by the idea of a command performance but I was none
too forthcoming in my instructions about how to find our corner of the
Rambles, the L-shaped opening in the woods which was our theatre of
operations back then.

Of course you could get to where we cruised more directly from
two other entrances a little further up on Central Park West, but I
usually preferred to make a slower approach with a jay, around the lake
from the Seventy-second Street entrance, particularly fond as I was of
that bushy patch near the grape arbor with the Puerto Rican boys pranc-
ing and posturing in their lipstick and perfumed chinos. Mind you, this
was many years before Yoko Ono put in the Strawberry Fields gardens
she could see from her Dakota window to remember John Lennon. The
Frederick Olmsted forest primaeval was a little denser in those days.

It said a lot about him that he even knew which lampposts I meant.
After several cigarettes of wondering whether he'd show up, he came
sauntering across the grass through patches of lamplight. He seemed so
youthfully confident, and unaware of the danger around us in the night,
yet disarmingly shy as he glanced about to keep his bearings.

Others had spotted him, too, and I watched him handle that for a
while, enjoying the good end of my Camel before coming out of the
shadows. He was a little taller than I remembered and possessed of a

charming combination of hesitancy and petulance, trying not to move as he presented himself to me right there where I'd settled, leaning on the end of a park bench.

After taking him in a spell, I rested a hand on his neck and he responded with the most endearing melting under my fingers, as if he were adjusting me on his throat. His eyes never moved from mine as I jerked up a little flannel out of his jeans, unsnapped his shirt, and let my hand wander down to find his barely discernible nipple. Clamping it neatly between my thumbnail and finger, I watched his eyes go through changes under the growing pressure. I was waiting for a pooled tear to drop, or a lip to tremble, but instead he eventually shifted and groaned; and I took his upper arm to support him.

Fine specimen, that boy.

And such a sweet surprise it was to find behind his fly buttons the cock ring propping up his plump flesh for my plunder. We locked eyes again, sex-rushing in the knowledge that we were indeed playing the same game. As I pressed his meat against the ridge of the ring, our stare crackled with intensity and I felt his tactile response rippling through him into my hands.

Kneading the whole package of him suddenly up into my arms, I bundled him over the back of the bench and yanked his opened jeans down in back. Frantic cock appeared amazingly quickly in a crude circle around us. I fisted his dick soundly under him and bent him way over the plank, managing to get mine out, spit on it, and roger him without too much fumbling if I do say so myself.

With each thrust I rammed at him, he convulsed, wrenching his torso back and forth, stretching his delicious ass on my cock. He jerked from side to side as I squeezed and milked his hard-on, flashing his hair up at me. The real beauty of it was that he was giving me the pain. In the systematic climb through the threshold of an intense orgasm, in the flooding of that precious moment, he was crying under me, opening his ass for me.

Broadway, as we walked it afterwards, seemed most mundane.

We stopped at my smoke shop and he stood submissively beside me while I bought more rolling papers. I jammed my hand into his ass, two fingers probing for the delicate flesh between his balls and now-tender asshole. Maybe I'll guiche him, I thought, so I could grab him there.

He closed his eyes tightly, ignoring the Arabs eyeing him behind the counter. Then relaxing his eyelids, he slowly raised his head high, letting out a low sigh. Lovely gesture, I thought.

Papers purchased, we continued down Broadway. I felt like a sleek panther striding down the boulevard dragging home the captured gazelle. What a glorious stretch of flesh he was.

Enough of this gentle wooing, I laughed to myself, and marched him straight over to my favorite leather place to purchase a collar for him.

Tom smiled as we entered. He was quite familiar with my boys and my preferences.

"We've come for a collar."

"But of course—" Trays of assorted leather and studs appeared on the counter. I chose one and let Paul finger it.

He reached up to put it on. Tom spoke even before I could.

"Hey, don't do that. He won't like you doing that."

"I'll take it."

I sent Paul to my studio to wait at the door contemplating the package in his hands while, besotted romantic that I am, I stopped at the florist for one red rose and the liquor store for champagne.

"Are you ready for this?" I drilled him.

"Yes, I am," he stammered, kneeling with his rose. He reached up in slow ritual to accept the collar. I slapped his hand. He jumped back, one knee thumping his confusion on the floor.

"Yes, what, Paul?"

"Anything you want—"

I slapped his face.

"Yes, Sir?"

There it was, I liked that. But I slapped him again, still holding the collar in my other hand.

"Close your eyes."

The dropped lids squeezed tears onto his flushed cheeks—and I was snared in that moment. I grabbed a fist of his hair, arched back his head, and sucked a little snack out of his blond neck and cheeks, licking away the salty offering. Then threw back his head.

"Hands over your head, boy. Yes. Higher." I flicked the collar across his stomach and savored his flinch.

"Taut torso, Paul. Straight back!" Instant response.

"Legs open." His knees stumbled apart.

"Now: right in left. Grab your right wrist in left fist." Oh, yes.

"Right hand open." The palm flashed.

"Higher, higher. Arms higher." I prodded the armpits. He stretched himself taut.

"Good boy . . . head up. Good boy." What a picture. To complete it, I stretched the collar across the throat. And buckled it snug, right across where I'd marked him.

His face relaxed, eyes closed, so very peaceful.

"You're lucky, Paul. As it happens, I find this position you're in most endearing, but most people have to learn it from a bartender who knows what I like. So just remember this: You can present yourself to me like this, exactly like this, and I will always acknowledge you . . . eventually. Do you understand?"

"Yes, Sir."

The first few weeks with Paul were a positive sensate marathon. I couldn't stay in a bad mood. Every time aggravation or anger would convolute inside me, the feeling would blossom into arousal for Paul, and the desire to abuse him would burn in my stomach. I would suddenly lust to press him into brick walls, crushing his balls in my gloved hand. Lust to watch his mouth tremble as I fogged his cheek with my threats.

Midsummer nights found Paul taking his training sessions blindfolded. It made for a good frame of mind about heeling, that bonding skill so dear to my heart. It was like the little boy who learns to instantly connect rudeness to Daddy with a hot bottom.

And good behavior has its rewards. One night under an almost full moon, I'd treated him to a particularly grueling time of it in my favorite secluded part of the dog park out east in the fifties. I was so pleased with him, I strapped his hands together over his head and bound him to the fencing separating us from the FDR below and the river beyond. And sucked him off.

Patches of moonlight flashed gently in his sighing face. I let his cock swell slowly in a limp, hot mouth, sliding almost imperceptibly back and forth at random, feeling each heartbeat fill the mucous opening. Then, wetting space for my hand with each stroke, I penetrated my mouth with him, kneading the swelling flesh with rolling fingers.

Finally, with his glossy skin stretched taut over the iron shaft, veins arching out, I grabbed his hips and jammed my throat onto the flaming rod. His cock roughly skimmed the roof of my mouth, trembled a moment at the impasse, and suddenly broke down into the inner depth.

Paul groaned and shuddered impulsively and I ground his ass against the wrought-iron web. My throat gripped the cockhead impaled inside and lust was ours.

The bond between us stormed, flesh stretched on flesh, mine this time. His load was melodramatic and young-tasting, there with the East River noises around us and the car lights flashing below. I let him down and he hung in my arms in the midnight grass in sweet surrender.

Now, as I look back on it, I think it was the last months we were together that were the best. Having him at home so deliciously accessible, keeping him in welts and saddlesore, took the edge off my constant drive to sniff out cute ass, and I remember for the first time in my life musing on the notion of growing old with someone.

But our little honeymoon of storms and challenges had to burn itself out first.

Paul was able to submit, open to me, and assimilate behavior quite a while without my being able to introduce any really satisfying corporal discipline. But I began to itch more and more to punish him more severely than the little spanking scenes he begged for so often. He was so obedient and attentive there was really no excuse to abuse him. But he deserved punishment every moment he brought his aggravatingly arousing pussy-mouth into my presence.

My first experience of really welting his ass, instead of just teasing him with my riding crop, concerned the bathing suit lines I wanted on him. He thought he was pleasing me, in each of the ripe sunny days, by tanning himself in Central Park, wearing only the T-strap I'd made him out of my old car-polishing chamois. It cupped his cock like my hand and ran tight up his ass. He used some musky unguent oil for this ritual and presented himself to me each night fragrant and bronzed. Fine meat, that boy. Such sweet fine meat. Made me jealous and hard to think of other men savoring it in Sheep's Meadow.

However, I fancied the sight of his ass bleached white, naked, and inviting defilement. Inside the frame of his jock, I wanted flashing white boy-buns to target on in the night. So I made him promise to cultivate bathing-suit lines—to my personal specifications, of course.

He stood in the mirror for me, looking over his shoulder, and with my trusty Swiss knife, I scraped the desired shape on his bum, licking up the tasty welts I'd raised.

Later, so he could choose appropriate attire for the sun, he watched again in the mirror, blushing this time, as I renewed the fading marks in slick wet dry-mark slashes. He repeated to me how he would please me and I enjoyed the entire incident. Then the rain began and it seemed like endless days were passing before I could view the prescribed humiliation.

Nevertheless, one September day the moment was ripe. Ripe for unjust abuse. I called his hotel. He wasn't in. I left a message: *"How dare you not be in when I call . . ."*

I called back at midnight. The switchboard said he was in. I said not to ring up, snapped the crop under my arm, and sauntered off to his hotel room, looking for a little trouble.

I knew full well there'd been no opportunity to tan but I wanted to toy with his limits anyway. As it turned out, I needn't have looked so far for an excuse to punish him because my knock precipitated flourishes of bedsprings and whisperings. I could barely contain my smile before he opened the door to find me stone-faced, the riding crop pressed in two fists on my thighs.

I missed whatever gestures and babbling were flooding out of him for the pure pleasure of his totally bewildered face and the sweet affirmation of my collar firmly in place, its studs glistening in the candlelight. Beyond the candle stood a very nervous twinkie-type almost covering himself with a shirt. Not bad looking, actually, he might have been a model. They both squirmed as I calmly watched. Slowly and precisely I finally spoke in measured tones of condescension to the guest.

"It is time, young man, for you to take a shower. Go into the bathroom, close the door, and take a nice, long shower." The two of them shot glances at each other. "Don't worry, Paul will be in—momentarily. Now, my boy. Go now." He paused, looking down at himself rather idiotically and fluttered off to the bathroom.

Paul and I stared a moment. He breathed to speak, but I stepped calmly past him and stood at the window, snapping the crop on my thigh in patient rhythm, staring intently at nothing. Another synapse of silence.

Finally I heard three soft steps, the thud of two knees, and a much different silence. Turning, I found the lovely sculpture of humiliation in jockey shorts and candlelight before me on the dirty floor. I could feel my heartbeat in my thighs and fists. Paul was kneeling, hands overhead—stoic, open, beautiful—and such an erection.

I circled him twice, slowly, letting him absorb my presence with his ears. I could think of three or four shapes this momentary scene could take and I loved the embarrassing tension he displayed.

With the crop butt, I slowly edged down the back of his briefs, nudging into the exposed cleavage, reconnoitering my investment.

"Well, Paul. I will certainly enjoy hearing your explanation of what's been going on here. But why don't you start by showing me your pretty white ass—" The crop punctuated for me. "Hm—?"

The delicious curve sliding from his back into the tan cheeks trembled. Even without a bleached target, he made my mouth water.

"Well, what do we have here? Bend over." I caught the back of his neck and completed the descent of his head in one clean gesture, spitting out the archaic phrase, "Alright, boy. Arch and present."

His buttocks flashed high and inviting, his left hand still gripping his right. His face was arched in awkward distortion under my boot and I could feel my balls hitching up under me. His two-syllable reply was unintelligible.

I stroked his tanned, naughty ass. He winced and whimpered.

"Look at this," I taunted, kneading his bad-boy flesh, and brought the candle near.

"Lovely tan, Paul," and with a drool of hot wax I underscored, "simply lovely . . ." His loins arched and sudden voluptuous shivers coursed his back.

"White!" I hissed, pressing down my foot. "I want it white!" The crop hissed as it flourished up.

"White!" and I struck. Paul jumped under my boot, cried out and a livid stroke cried up from his ass. A little shard of nausea bit into me, mingling with the electric desire driving in my arm. I was transfixed by his trembling, remembering the first night in the park and each of his succeeding surrenders. Each encounter he had allowed me further and further into the privacy of his body and heart.

And now his buttocks signing back in a bright red slash the exact shape of each whip stroke. And each writhing convulsion—exquisite. *Danse de la croupe par excellence!* I loved him so much in that moment. Even with the whip poised in my itchy fist, I cared for him so tenderly, so possessively—and lashed down again.

Another scarlet welt answered. This time I placed the crop across his bare flesh before lifting to strike, measuring the stroke, as the Victorians say. His sighing gasp jumped to a hiss as the whip dropped, bouncing off the crease under his cheeks.

I was amazed by the wealth of thought each stroke flashed through my mind and even as I battered his protruding ass, counting off the sixes that ring in my head, I was plotting how to have my cock inside him and feel his irresistible writhing on my erection.

How fondly I look back on it now, all those nights of jagged pleasures, but I guess it had gotten a little Baroque between us when the first really chilly night found us again in the Central Park Rambles. Me with drained balls, on far too much caffeine, and him with arms spread helpless and bound to the accommodating arrangement of tree trunks many of us had used before. And as I rode his nipples and rode my cock, back and forth in frustration, the riding crop flashed again and again, striping his flighty thoroughbred thighs.

Paul's jerking and gasping would nearly drive me over the edge to unload, and then I wouldn't make it again, but the storm of my impending ejaculation was the penultimate experience that windy night.

His arms tensed. He howled suddenly and was just beginning to spout come rather magnificently when one arm, breaking free, flapped up, crashing me across the head.

Puffy pain and aching eyes woke me to the smell of burning leaves. I was buzzing—and raw in my hand. And alone.

It had been two weeks. I missed him terribly.

I was smoking and straightening up and walking around in circles when I literally tripped over his collar. I had condescendingly nailed the hook for it two feet off the floor into the wall, and I now stood with a skinned calf two feet above my toes, glaring at it.

I picked it up, something quite unfamiliar in my hands. It was dusty already. I smelled it. It was cool but still leather-musky. Was I really walking into the bathroom to try it on in the mirror? I remembered him watching me in the mirror, his torso filling the glass with his collar on.

The picture disappeared suddenly as the doorbell rang. I decided not to answer. Paul's image rang in again. The collar was pressing into his throat. But the doorbell destroyed it again.

I stormed off to the door, thrashed back the tiny lever and, growing as fast as my head could reach the hole, Paul's torso and bare throat appeared through the door.

I unlocked it and opened to find him poised in boy-position.

I swallowed down my heart, gathered my voice in my throat . . . and snapped, "You're late."

PART FOUR

TOP
AND
BOTTOM

Top and bottom. Many gay men treat these labels like immutable characteristics, as if we are born with a set of keys dangling from one hip or the other. Other gay men, particularly younger ones, deny these distinctions altogether and say they are only outmoded paeans to straight culture. As in most debates, the truth must be somewhere in between.

At heart, the dynamic of top and bottom is about power. But many people make the mistake of assuming that the top is always in the position of power. A more sophisticated approach leaves the question open: Which is the truer control—the power of topping somebody, or of letting oneself be topped?

D. V. Sadero's "Past Master" plays with these seemingly fixed roles, and with the idea that they can be shifted if the circumstances are right. Sadero pits two leather tops against each other in a battle for revenge and status. Like much of gay pornography, the story is fueled by the notion that a man's true nature will always be revealed through sexual conquest. A man may talk tough about being a top, but when he is properly dominated, the bottom in him will out. Sadero sets his story in San Francisco's leather underground, but the form is very much the classic Western showdown between good and evil. Sadero's moral message is that like the white-hatted Western hero, the *true* sexual master is always noble.

My own story "Tops' Night Out" takes a somewhat more light-hearted look at a similar situation. What happens when four horny friends, all confirmed tops, find themselves in a leather bar with no bottoms in sight? The obvious solution is that two of them have to play bottoms for the night. But how is the reversal to be determined?

A much less familiar porn story—although perhaps all-too-common a situation in real life—is two bottoms together with no top. Writing under the name of Jay Shaffer, his erotic alter-ego, John Dibelka comes up with his own ingenious solution to the problem. Some might wonder how a fuck story can succeed without a character who wants to fuck, but Dibelka has concocted a story that is both funny and hot.

As a woman with a strong feel for gay male erotic sensibility, Anne Rice has always enjoyed playing with roles in her writing. Her extremely popular novel *Exit to Eden*, written under the name Anne Rampling, depicts a private S&M club on a tropical island where members pay to act out their wildest fantasies. The male protagonist, Elliott, has signed up for a term as a sex slave, willingly submitting to the domination of others. But in the chapter included here, Elliott's commanded task as a slave is to dominate another slave himself. In the ultimate playing out of roles, bottom becomes top becomes bottom.

D. V. SADERO

PAST MASTER

THIS ALL HAPPENED YEARS AGO, IN THE SEVENTIES, WHEN THE leather scene in San Francisco was a lot more real than it is now. It was Friday at dusk, the start of the three-day Memorial Day weekend. I was hosting a big party with my bike club, for local guys and out-of-towners, in my flat. A few guys had already arrived. I saw it was time to stock up on the beer. Larry from across the hall volunteered to go with me. We went around the corner to Folsom Street, pushed some leather curtains aside and stepped into our favorite bar. Which was already deep in leathermen.

Eyes went all over us. Especially over Larry. He was in his middle twenties, real good looking, blond and with a great build and a long dong showing under his jeans.

The bar owner was a friend and he'd said he'd sell the club all the cases of beer we wanted for our party, at cost. We ordered four for a start, as much as we could carry, and the bartender went into the back to get them.

Suddenly Larry stood up straight from where we were leaning against the bar. I watched him cross the room and tap a dude on the shoulder. The guy was tall and thin, wearing a black leather jacket, jeans and close-fitting chaps, which showed off a small, hard, high-riding butt, one of the prettiest I'd seen in a long time. The man turned around. He was good looking in kind of a gaunt way, with a real tanned, bony face and a head of straight black hair.

Larry brought him to me at the bar, where the four cartons of longnecks were waiting in two stacks.

"Hey, Beer Can," he said, "this is my ol' buddy from Los Angeles, name's Rex."

We went through the usual, and I reckoned him to be about thirty-five and even better looking close by than far off. He had a smoldering animal sexiness about him, striking me as the kind of guy who would be really worth turning on. I could smell a mix of leather, sweat, grease and dust, which is only the best perfume there is, for my money. So I asked him, "You biked up from L.A.?"

"Yeah. Thought I'd come see the city again."

As we talked we openly checked each other out. He had a set of keys hanging down the left side of his jeans, and so did I. I kind of hooked my left hand in my belt and cupped my hand around my keys and played with 'em like they were a man's balls.

He stopped talking and smiled, slow and crooked and hot. "Guess we're both serious about which way we go."

"Guess so," I said. "Too bad."

"Yeah, it is." And he looked me up and down again, more like a compliment than trying to get me going. And I loved it. I was thirty and not ugly, just that I'd taken some sudden flying exits off my Harley, hit a few sand patches and grease puddles. So I was a little mashed and scarred here and there. But it's a look that goes with leather, I've always thought. And it fit my build, which was from my job as a longshoreman, not from a gym. Always been the massive type, not fat, but solid beef with a hairy chest.

I guess Larry was feeling left out, 'cause he suddenly said, "Yeah, ol' Rex and I were real close back in L.A. Great to see you again, Rex, after what—gee, three years now."

Larry sounded a little nervous, actually, and I wondered just what kind of "real close" they'd been. Because I was sure Rex was a pure top. All the vibes said that. And Larry always came on as a top. Real insistent about it, got salty if anybody even gave him a little pat on the butt. Forever bragging about scores who'd never put out for nobody until they met him.

Maybe, I figured, Rex and Larry had just been buddies. Except that, well, there had to be more, judging by the way they were carrying on right now: Rex never took his eyes off Larry, who was coming on two or three times more macho than I'd ever seen him act before.

And making a jerk of himself, I thought. But then I never much liked Larry. We lived in the same building, hit the same bars, went on the same runs, a lot of the same parties. But Larry, besides talking about what a tough stud he was all the time, liked to steal tricks and make loud jokes about it afterward. See, our apartment building was a big old barn of a place, so it was easy to hit on somebody coming to see somebody else. Too easy: no class to it, so nobody did it. Except Larry. So I tolerated him, nothing else.

Larry asked Rex, "You got a place to stay?"

Rex said, "Nope. First thing I needed when I got off the road was this." He held up his beer bottle.

"Hey, come stay at my place," Larry said. "The whole building's gonna be a party tonight. That's what these cases of beer are for."

"Sounds good to me," Rex said.

Larry and I each carried two boxes of beer down the sidewalk. Rex revved up his black Harley. We walked around the corner and Rex came alongside. We told him to turn right at the next street.

It was just a dead-end alley. He gunned his motor and next we saw of Rex, he was waiting for us in front of the building, among a bunch of parked motorcycles.

It was a big old two-story house, or had been a long time ago. When the area filled up with factories and warehouses, the house was made into a mess of flats and apartments. With cheap rent. On all sides were concrete factory walls, two and three stories high. Not any too attractive to most people, but for men wanting to live their lives noisy but private, it was great. All the tenants were leathermen and bikers.

We went inside, down the hall and into my place. Lots more guys had shown up, and they grabbed beers right out of the boxes.

Larry left, taking Rex across the hall to his apartment. I grabbed a beer myself, lit a big cigar, and wandered from room to room saying hello and all. I recognized a lot of the guys from Folsom Street, but I was glad to see a big crowd of out-of-towners piling in: lots of tight

chaps and bulging crotches and black boots. All kinds of men, all looking great. And everyone was nursing a mood, letting his lust build
higher and higher. Wasn't a sweatless ball in the place, and mighty few
hanging loose.

I stuck my hand in my pocket to get some matches to relight my
cigar. And I discovered a wad of money there, money that wasn't mine.
I figured I must have picked up Larry's change from when he'd paid for
the beer at the bar. Which he'd done only to impress Rex, I was sure.
Well, Larry was someone I didn't enjoy owing money to. I crossed the
hall and was about to knock on his door when I heard Larry's voice
saying my name. I have to admit I stood there and listened.

Another voice, Rex's, said, "Seems like a great guy."

"If you like a slab of beef with legs," I heard Larry say. "And a
beat-up face. Ugly freako prick on him, too. That's why he's called Beer
Can. His cock is about the same dimensions as a tall can of beer. And
red bull balls; really gross, man. And very hairy, all over."

"Sounds hot to me," Rex said.

"Ugh."

Feeling real glad that I'd never liked Larry, I made sounds with
my boots like I was walking up the hall, then knocked on the door.

It surprised me that Larry, not his slave, answered the door. I saw
why: Rex was sitting on the couch with his long legs spread wide. Billy,
Larry's slave and naked as usual, was kneeling between them. Young
and with about the same height and build as Larry, Billy was nice
looking but pale from never getting any sun, and had bruises all over
him. Which was another thing about Larry that rubbed me the wrong
way: He just used Billy for sex and housework, and knocked him around
when he was feeling mean. No development, no meaningful discipline.
Billy was his third slave in the last year. The other two had run away,
one of them with some secret help from another tenant in the building.

Rex waved from across the room, and I waved back. I gave Larry
his money.

Suddenly Rex pressed Billy's head down into the gaping fly of his
501s. Rex flexed his body up again and again, grunting with each thrust,
until he let out a groan of relief and relaxed back onto the couch.

In a short while, Rex pushed Billy's face away from his cock, then
patted Billy on the head. As Rex stood up, I saw a helluva boner sticking
out of his jeans. Even though it had begun to soften, it stood tall and
pale, with a blazing red, long and pointed cockhead on it.

"Real nice," Rex said to Larry. "Thanks. . . . I kind of need a shower; the road dust is making me itch."

"Billy," Larry said, "show Rex the bathroom, get him towels and stuff."

They left the living room, and I said to Larry, "Isn't Rex shooting his wad a little early?"

"Rex can pop his rocks half a dozen times a night," Larry said. "He had a bad case of roadburn after all those hours on the iron coming up here. So I had Billy service his dick."

"Heavy top," I said, "right?"

"Yeah, he is . . . most of the time."

" 'Most of the time'?" I asked, real doubtful, but also, frankly, with some hope: Topping Rex would be a real hot treat.

"Maybe I have plans for him," Larry said.

"Yeah?"

"Listen, Beer Can, I'll tell ya what it's all about. See, four years ago, down in L.A., I met Rex. He's a very smooth mover, especially when he's got a naive kid all crazed about him. I was just twenty and didn't know shit. Rex took me over, man, punched every button I had."

I began to wonder if Rex was as neat a guy as I'd been thinking he was. "Anyway," Larry went on, "tonight I'm laying a little trip on Rex, going to dish out some of what I had to take. That's why all this 'ol' buddy' bullshit. And when I get down to it with Rex, I want you to be there, second top with me."

I'd second topped with Larry only once before. In action, to my way of seeing it, he'd had no feel for the interplay in a scene. That session had gone nowhere. But now, tonight, if he was going to put a game on Rex, well, I figured I'd enjoy myself a lot. I've always felt that stud ass is the best kind.

"Sure," I said. "Just tell me when."

"Okay. Rex and I'll party a while, get him softened up."

Back across the hall I found my apartment rooms real crowded. I went to my bedroom, which I was keeping locked, for my own personal use later. There I took off my jeans and put on a leather codpiece. Wearing just that, with my chaps and boots, I went back to the party.

It was shaping up fine. Leathermen and bikers in every room, bare chested men talking with arms slung over each other, dancing together, guys off in corners laughing and trading big slurpy tongue-thick kisses.

Lots of hard bare-ass sticking out of black skintight chaps, and some guys already stripped down to just their leather jocks.

The noise level was a lot higher than it had been before, what with the rock music, lots of deep male voices shouting over it to be heard, the roar of motorcycles coming and going, and every bit of sound echoing off the tall blank cement walls all around.

"Mr. Beer Can, Mr. Beer Can?"

I turned to find the slave, Billy. "Yeah?"

"My master is in the blackroom now, with Mr. Rex. He wants you to join him."

"Okay," I said. I lit another cigar and headed down the stairs to the basement. Billy followed.

It was big, the same size as the building. About half of it was filled with the usual junk that ends up in basements. The other half had been made into a blackroom by and for the guys in the building and improved over the years. The door was open. I went in, pulled the door closed behind me and slammed the bolt into place.

The floor was all paved with those thin mats like you see in school gyms for students to wrestle on. Some chains and hooks dangled out of the darkness above the one glaring light hanging high above us. The walls were painted black, except one, which was solid gymnasium lockers. Above our heads the party was making a soft, steady sound, like heavy surf when you hear it from far away.

Billy sat cross-legged in the dimness of a far corner, facing the wall. Larry was at my left, out on the mats, blond hair gleaming under the harsh light, and Rex was to my right. They were wearing chaps and boots and nothing else. They had about the same height, weight and muscularity, but Rex, deeply tanned, was a lot darker than Larry. Larry's cock was beginning to fill out and straighten. Rex's meat hung longer than Larry's but wasn't as thick. With that pointed tip, Rex had a real penetrator, a cock that could open up the tightest hole and slide in deep.

Larry said to me, "Beer Can, Rex and I have an old score to settle. We want you here as a witness." Larry gave me an almost invisible wink.

So, Rex thought I was a neutral, had no clue I was Larry's second top. I looked at that fine small ass on Rex, felt a jolt of blood surging into my cock, and decided that even if Larry was, as usual, playing it low and dirty, I'd go along with it this one time. What the hell, from what I'd heard tonight about Rex, he wasn't all that classy a guy himself. And anyway, Rex was just exactly what I wanted: black hair, great looking face, tanned body, and his quiet, cool, confident manner. All that and his ass, too. My slowly stroking hand told me my huge fat cock was super-hard, and I could feel my big balls all tightened up, clutched high and snug in my hairy crotch. My whole big body was thirsting for stud hole.

Larry said to Rex, "Let's make this winner take all."

Rex asked, "What do you mean by 'winner take all'?"

"The winner has the loser as a slave for the rest of the night," Larry said.

Rex shrugged. "Winner take all," he said.

"Think about it, Rex," Larry said. "You could end up fucked by me, by Beer Can, by everyone at the party. Fucked and maybe all kinds of other stuff, too. I might even order my slave to piss all over you, for a start."

"Winner take all," Rex said again, as indifferent as before.

Which sorta threw Larry for a moment. Then he said to Rex, "Whatever happens here tonight, let's start with a handshake."

Rex stepped toward Larry with his right hand outstretched. Larry put his hand out, and something happened that I didn't see clearly. There was a little struggle, with Larry trying to spin Rex around, and when Rex jerked away, a handcuff was hanging from his right wrist. The other cuff was wide open, like the jaws of some great big insect.

"So that's what your handshake is worth," Rex said, voice low with contempt. "You were trying to get my hands cuffed behind my back, huh? Okay. Fine with me. Beer Can, put the other cuff on me." Rex turned his back toward me and put his wrists almost together, just above that fine, firm little butt of his. I locked the other handcuff around his left wrist and stepped back.

I was surprised Rex would voluntarily accept such a handicap. I thought it was a great fuck-you gesture, but definitely not a good idea. I mean, he had to be aware of what a lowdown schemer Larry was.

Larry began talking to Rex in a real nasty kind of way: "You put me through hell, man. All that humiliation you made me endure, the whippings and the punishments. Until I ran away and became the master I always really was. And am."

"Yes," Rex said, "you are. I was training you that way, but you were too vain and stuck on yourself to see what I was doing, all the trouble I was going to. By now, if you hadn't chickened out and run off, you'd be a master. And you'd be a man."

"That's what you say," Larry sneered.

"I never lied to you," Rex said. "I saved your runaway punk ass from street hustling. You begged to be my slave, to take you over, train you. I brought you into my home and my life, and I tried to make a man out of you. And if you got a lot of punishment, it's because you needed it. You were incredibly full of shit, man, and you needed it beat out of you, because you didn't understand anything else. Because I tried teaching you first, tried hard, before I kicked your ass. And you left too soon. You're still phoney, still full of shit, still not a man."

I began to see that Larry's description of his relationship with Rex hadn't been exactly accurate. I told myself I'd forgotten the big rule: There's always two sides to any story. Still, this was all between them, and I was here just to get my cock a deep taste of Rex's fine stud butt.

"I'm a born master," Larry growled, now as angry as Rex. "And because I was young and didn't know about life, you took advantage of me. So I got talked into letting you fuck my face and my ass and beating me and chaining me up and all that."

"Take advantage of *you?*" Rex asked, amazement and fury in his voice. "When you left you stole money and credit cards out of my wallet, and took some of my leathers, the ones you're wearing now, in fact, and also my Harley, which you ditched in an alley up here in San Francisco."

Yeah, I thought, that's what Larry would do, all right. . . .

"I deserved all that," Larry said, "after what you put me through. That and more. And tonight I'm going to take it all. . . . Beer Can, let's get him!" With that, Larry charged at the handcuffed Rex, right arm moving into position for a blow to the face.

"Man," I shouted, "I'm neutral!"

Now that I'd heard Rex's side of the story, and from what I knew about Larry, and having seen him do that shitty number with the handcuffs, I wasn't about to take his side. There was plenty of good stud ass in the world. Much as I wanted Rex's, I didn't want it like that. Of course, if Larry beat him fair and square. . . .

Larry swung his right arm with a killer punch. Rex, showing great reflexes, pulled his upper body back, and the blow missed. But the force of it carried Larry around in a half-circle and put him off balance. He regained control fast, but by then Rex had stepped through the ring formed by the handcuffs and his arms. Now his hands hung down in the front of his tanned, sweat-glowing body, and the handcuff chain made a silvery loop in front of his big balls.

Rex took two steps toward Larry, who backed off.

"Beer Can, you bastard, help me!" Larry yelled. When I didn't move he called out, "Billy, get over here!"

Billy had stopped facing the wall some time before, disobeying Larry's orders but unable to resist looking. He got to his feet, as tall as Larry and Rex, but he was no fighter and looked terrified. I pointed a finger at him. "You!" I roared. "Siddown! This is between them." Billy returned to his corner, face covered with a look of relief.

Larry didn't curse me out or order Billy back again. That's because Rex was moving toward Larry, who, now almost cornered against two black walls, began cursing and shooting out feints with his fists clutched so tight they were dead white. Rex took some hard blows but he kept coming. They clenched, and then they were wrestling more than fighting. Suddenly they froze, Rex behind Larry. Rex's hands were closed into hard fists, one on either side of Larry's neck, and the handcuff chain was sinking deep into the flesh over Larry's throat.

As Larry sank to his knees, he frantically grabbed at Rex's arms, at the chain. Rex pulled it tighter. "Unlock 'em," Rex shouted at Larry, "unlock 'em fast!"

Larry dug into a hidden pocket in the top front of his chaps and brought out a little flat key. His face was turning dark. After desperately searching, he found the lock, and the cuffs fell away from one hand. Rex grabbed the key, shoved a gasping Larry to the floor and freed his other hand.

Breathing kind of hard himself, dripping sweat and combing his black hair back in place with his fingers, Rex stood over Larry, who was writhing around and breathing real noisy.

"You crummy piece of shit," Rex said. "I don't know why I wasted one fucking second of my life on you. Imagine, loving a punkass jerk like you. I must have been crazy." He turned away, went over to the wall lockers and found a towel. He wiped the sweat off his face and chest.

Billy looked almost like he was in shock. I went to him and said, "Relax, it's all over. Go upstairs to my humidor on the refrigerator, and bring me back a couple of cigars, the big ones." Billy ran out. I had no idea if Rex smoked, but he deserved some kind of reward, far as I was concerned.

Rex, now wiping down his leathers, had his back to Larry, who was pulling himself to his feet using the lockers and, at the same time, as I later figured out, he was getting something out of one of them that had its door unlocked and half-open. I didn't see what it was until the horsewhip sang through the air and slashed around Rex's arms and torso. The tip snapped a dab of flesh off Rex's left chest.

Rex turned around in a flash, trying to jerk the horsewhip from Larry's hands. He didn't succeed.

Larry backed up, giving a weird kind of laughing sneer, a deep "Haaaaa!" that made the shivers travel through all the muscles on my back. He snapped the whip a few times more in Rex's direction. And once at me, firing it upward from the floor. "*Neutral*, hah? You lying son of a bitch!"

I sidestepped just in time, and instead of the whip cracking me square in the balls, it just whizzed up hot along my thigh.

"Put it down, Larry," I said. "It's two against one."

"I can beat the living shit out of both of you with this," Larry growled. "You don't stand a chance."

The three of us stood all tensed. A line of red was making its way down Rex's fine chest.

Larry held us off with flourishes of his horsewhip while he edged toward the door. Of course, being Larry he wasn't going to make good on any threat. He was going to cut and run, shitass as ever.

I charged Larry. As I expected, the horsewhip whirled around me, binding my arms to my sides, setting my back blazing with pain so intense I was paralyzed by it. But only for a moment. Half stumbling, half running, I moved hard and fast at Larry.

He made the mistake of holding tight to the horsewhip, which, being wound around me, he couldn't use. I wrenched my right arm free, and I gave him a good strong tap in the solar plexus. Larry let go the whip, which snaked off me to the mats. Half paralyzed because he couldn't get his breath, Larry fell flat on his face in front of Rex.

Rex stripped down again. Obviously he wasn't thinking about leaving now. Both of us were naked except for chaps and boots. Larry groaned, and he struggled to get to his feet, but with one boot I kept pulling an arm or a leg out from under him, which caused him to keep collapsing back to the floor. Rex put the handcuffs on Larry, behind his back. "It's going to be a long night," Rex said.

Now Rex took up the whip. He stood back, aimed and laid a stroke across Larry's butt. Larry choked back a yell. The second time he roared aloud. The third lash made him scream. Now his buns were scarred with three red welts, one below the other, almost exactly parallel. I could see that Rex had a lot of practice at using a whip.

Rex threw the whip aside. He forced a space for himself between Larry's legs and knelt down, spreading Larry's thighs apart. He roughly spread Larry's buns wide, and spat a big goober onto his asshole.

"No!" Larry yelled. "No! No!"

Rex levered himself forward and pushed his long, shiny-hard cock into Larry's ass.

"No! No! Aaagh!"

At that moment I saw a movement out of the corner of my eye. It was Billy, standing just outside the door and gaping at the sight of his master being fucked. I told him to come inside and pull the door shut after him. He gave me the two cigars.

I put one aside and lit the other. I stood watching and smoking, also stroking my very hard, thick cock. I felt extra excitement because Larry was fighting and groaning with every deep, hard stroke Rex gave him. His pale body writhed and twisted under Rex's dark form. From the look on Rex's face, I could tell he was enjoying every moment of it, fucking Larry in ways that would give him the most pain, just so he could get off on Larry's yells and struggles.

I saw Rex's hands slide around under Larry's ribs on both sides, and by Larry's suddenly louder screams and sharp movements of his body, I knew Rex had a hold of his nipples. Larry arched and jerked and roared while Rex worked him over, real harsh, with his prick and his fingers both. Rex looked to me like he was riding one of those white dolphins in an aquarium show.

Rex stopped all of a sudden. I thought he was going to shoot. But all he did was pull out, get to his feet and wipe his stiff cock thoroughly with a towel. Then he turned to Billy. "Who is your master?" he asked, startling the slave.

Like he was hypnotized, Billy said, "You are, Sir."

"Prove it. Do what I say. Take off his leather and his boots."

Billy bent down slow and real careful, clearly scared of Larry but wanting to please Rex. He worked fast, being used to dressing and undressing this man, and Larry, messed up, made only half-hearted gestures and whispered threats.

Once Billy was done, Rex waved him away. He went over to Larry and shoved at him until he was up on his knees and facing Rex's still stiff meat. "Suck cock," Rex said.

Larry said no. He fought to escape Rex's grip on his shoulders. I knelt down kind of half on the side and half behind Larry, and I took his big balls in a really strong grip, one he couldn't jerk his way out of. "Suck the man's dick," I said, increasing the pressure on Larry's hot, sweaty 'nads. It was the least I could do for a nice guy like Rex.

Larry's mouth jumped at Rex's cock. Keeping a hold on his testicles, I hunched up behind him and then pressed the big stubby head of my "beer can" against his butthole.

I thought Rex might have ruined Larry's hole, but there was a lot left. Enough so that when my ol' cockhead slid inside his rectum, Larry screamed and his body stiffened. " 'Ugly freako prick,' huh?" I growled down at the head of blond hair. " 'Ugly red bull balls,' huh? 'A slab of beef with legs,' huh?" With each phrase that I grunted, I jammed my cock in further. Larry let out a yell every time, which got me hotter and hotter.

"Keep sucking!" Rex said, and he made Larry do that while I went on forcing my prick into him. It was juicy inside, from Rex's fucking him, and in a little while I was moving it back and forth. Larry hardly screamed at all, just groaned sharply every time I plunged all the way in, and shuddered when I pulled back almost all the way out.

When I was going good, Rex backed off, letting Larry flop flat to the floor. Now I fucked him hard as I could, which made him scream again. Trick-stealer, liar, stuck on himself, son of a bitch—each thrust was not just for the sex of it but also for punishment and revenge.

I didn't come either, didn't want to waste my fuckjuice on Larry. Anyway, his body reeked with fear-sweat which even my cigar smoke —I'd never stopped smoking during the sex—couldn't cover up.

So I stood up. Rex pushed Billy toward me. He had a towel in his hands and cleaned me off.

Rex shoved at Larry's body with his boot until he turned over onto his back. He turned to Billy. "Is he still your master?"

"No, Sir. You are."

"Piss on him."

Billy looked up at Rex in surprise. Rex stared back at him.

Billy stepped up to where Larry lay, groaning and half conscious. He skinned back his foreskin to show a pale cockhead cut real deep by one huge piss slit.

"Billy," Larry said, trying to rise. "Don't! Don't do it!"

With his black boot, Rex gave Larry something between a kick and a shove, and Larry collapsed back on the mat, all the time ordering Billy not to do it.

Billy had to close his eyes, but he managed to get a stream going.

"Not just on his belly," Rex ordered. "Up and down, wet his balls. . . . Yeah, like that. . . . Now piss on his face. . . . Yeah . . . yeah . . . yeahhhhh." Every time Larry tried to get out of the way, we kicked him back into place.

A little bit later, after we'd forced Larry to suck his ex-slave's cock, we all went back upstairs. By Rex's order, Billy was wearing Larry's leathers and boots and jeans, which all fit pretty well. Rex was all dressed, T-shirt and jacket and everything. I'd put my codpiece back on, so I was like before, with just my leathers and boots besides, nothing above the waist.

I admit I was self-conscious about the red whip mark across my back. Rex had examined it and said I was lucky it was superficial, more from the whip leather moving across my flesh than sinking into it. Still, I didn't want my friends and everybody getting the wrong idea about me. You know how fast gossip travels.

But I think everybody understood there'd been some kind of struggle and who'd won it, because Larry, naked and pale and with handcuffs holding his wrists close to each other behind his back, was walking in front of me and behind Rex, who, like me, was smoking a cigar. The three welts across Larry's ass gleamed in what little light there was.

We marched Larry through the rooms of my place, and though it was fairly late and a lot of guys were getting it on in various combinations on various pieces of furniture and on the rugs, a lot of them checked out the little parade we made. We led Larry into the spare room, took off the handcuffs and shoved him onto the bed. I left the door wide open. The first guys to go in there, I noticed, were other tenants in the house. No doubt to get even for the times Larry had done them dirty.

The party ran most of the night. Every time I saw Rex he was getting sucked or fucking, with Billy standing nearby, towel in hand, eager to be called to help. When it was real late, Rex gave a whipping demonstration on a really muscular volunteer, which got us all hot and bothered again.

I was so busy having my own good time—with my cock being kind of locally famous, and a fair number of guys, if I say so myself, wanting to service it—that I pretty much forgot about Larry. Though I'd noticed there was always a line of men outside the bedroom door. And I'd heard he'd tried to escape a couple of times.

Around dawn, when everyone had left or was snoring on couches and rugs and wherever, I went into the spare room. Larry was lying face-down on the bed, naked and with his legs spread wide. "Party's over," I said. "Time to go home."

He made a groaning sound.

I got him up and out and into the hallway. "Hope your door is unlocked, 'cause I have no idea where your keys are." It was.

I didn't see Larry all Saturday or Sunday. Rex and Billy stayed at my place. Rex and I went to bars and parties and stuff all weekend.

On Monday afternoon, Memorial Day, I guess Larry heard the noise of a certain Harley starting up. Because he popped out of his door, still naked and his blond hair all over the place. He looked real beat. "Rex," he gasped out, sounding kinda intense. "Where's Rex?"

"He's about to leave. I just said good-bye to him."

Larry ran down the hall and out the front door, yelling "Rex! Rex! Wait! Take me with you! Master! Take me with you. Please! Master! Master!"

For an answer, as I heard when I followed him down the hall to the front door, Larry got a big increase in the roar of the Harley. It was almost too much for my ears, the way it echoed off the concrete walls. Larry, bare-ass naked at the front door, with me holding him back, kept yelling that he wanted to go with him, that Rex was his master. I'm not sure if he saw that Rex already had Billy, in full leather, as a pas-senger on his Harley.

In the quiet of the afternoon, the sound of the motorcycle took a while to die away into just traffic noise. Larry began weeping. I led him back inside and shoved him into his apartment.

I never saw Larry again. When I came home from work on Tuesday, he was gone. I don't know if, wherever he ended up, he went on playing superstud and being a shitass or whether maybe he learned something.

I'm still friends with Rex. He moved up to San Francisco, bringing his slave Billy back here with him. Rex and I have been hanging out together for years. We're no kids any more, and the leather world isn't what it was . . . but we still get our kicks and have some laughs.

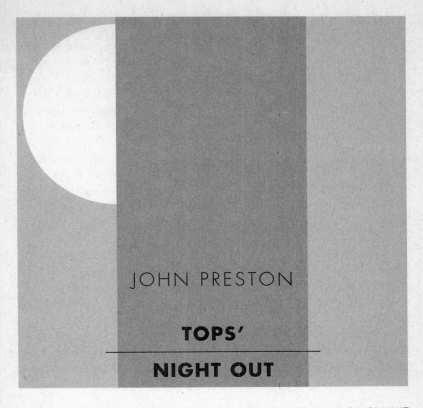

JOHN PRESTON

TOPS'

NIGHT OUT

"THIS IS A WASTE OF MY TIME." ROOSEVELT LET HIS COMPLAINT roll out with that lazy-sounding exaggerated homeboy accent of his.

I made the mistake of turning and meeting his stare. Rosie and I both wear reflector sunglasses when we go to bars. If I look straight at him I create an infinity effect. My image bounces off his glasses, back into mine, back to his . . . I get dizzy if I look at Roosevelt straight on.

I turned away. But the view wasn't very pretty. The Ramrod was almost empty.

"Never is decent ass on a Monday night," Roosevelt grumbled. "When am I going to learn my lesson and stay home?"

"What'd you do there? Watch television?" I knew that Rosie hated television.

"Hell, no," he answered. "I'd read some Audre Lourde." I didn't touch that one. Roosevelt prided himself on being the meanest top in town. As much as I wanted that title for myself, I had to admit he had a good claim to it. I just couldn't picture the big man curled up with a book of poetry.

"Life is hard," Rosie sighed.

The problem was that not much of it was hard at all. And it didn't look as though much was going to be. There were only two other customers in the Ramrod, and they weren't going to do Rosie and me any good.

Thor and Zen sauntered over to us and we all four exchanged sharp nods. That's what top men do when they greet one another. We don't shake hands or say hello, we bow our necks in one sharp action. It made us look like a bunch of Asian diplomats, as we gave a curt shake of the head to one another.

It almost seemed appropriate for us to do that, since Zen was one of our group. He's Japanese, a graduate student at the university. He spoke flawless English, though it tended to be a bit too formal. His great role model had been Yukio Mishima. It was that writer's example that lead him into his life as a leather top as soon as he got to this country.

"Saw you dance the other night," I said to him. He stripped at a vanilla club to earn spending money. He was pretty good at it, sometimes even wearing some pieces of traditional Japanese samurai clothing to give his performance a bit of international flavor.

Zen smiled. He liked the attention his dancing got him and it pleased him whenever one of us commented on it. But the smile wasn't really all that sincere. Zen was more comfortable when he was scowling, giving his own imitation of the way a warrior would look back in the old country. Of course, his version of that was pretty firmly updated. Mishima may have been all for traditional Japanese values, but he had also been awfully interested in American and German motorcycles.

Zen had on leather pants, over-the-calf riding boots, leather shirt, motorcycle cap. The only thing that was even a little out of place was his leather backpack. But if you knew Zen, you knew he carried that around because of his ropes. Zen is heavily into being a bondage master. Bottoms in the bar always whisper about how lavish and extreme his technique is. He needs lots of rope to carry it off and doesn't trust that his tricks will have the right kind, so he stores it in the pack and just brings it along.

Of course, there weren't any bottoms in the bar that night. We all looked around the empty space and then had to look back at one another.

It was just us. I avoided Rosie's reflector glasses and scanned Thor instead.

Zen may have been motivated by Mishima, but Thor's inspiration was a lot more basic. I swear the man must have seen too many Tom of Finland drawings when he was a baby queer. He decided that he'd become the living embodiment of the artist, and he pretty much succeeded. Thor was over six feet tall. He had close-cropped blond hair and a carefully trimmed moustache. He had shoulders that you could barely put your arms around, but a waist that was almost impossibly small. His butt filled his pants nicely. The whole thing was an hourglasslike effect—big at top, narrow in the middle, big again in the hips. Though there weren't many hourglasses that showed off a rod like his. The thing snaked down his tight khaki uniform pants—left side, of course—and sometimes you could swear that it was going to reach his kneecap. Thor wore his own version of regulation costume: khaki pants, like I've said, and a khaki uniform shirt to match. He had a Sam Browne belt that crossed his chest and underscored his massive pectoral development. He didn't think it was right to display military or police insignia if it wasn't authentic—all four of us claimed we were big into authenticity—so his shirt was plain. His boots were highly polished, not the rough bikers' stuff that the rest of us wore. He was a picture of Aryan arrogance that helped him scoop up slave tricks with ease, when they were there.

Roosevelt was still grumbling about the fact that they weren't. Rosie is a striking looking man. He claims he wears nothing but leather when he goes out—not even cotton underwear or socks. I've never seen him with any other kind of clothing, so why would I doubt him? His pants were a statement. His cock and balls were caught in a codpiece that was studded with snaps around the edges. On some nights, when Rosie stood in decent light, you could get a look at his black curly pubic hair that escaped through the spaces between them.

As he always did, Roosevelt had a leather tunic on underneath his jacket, the pullover kind of thing that had a lace up front to it. And he wore his signature—a leather baseball cap, worn backwards in the fine tradition of the 'hood.

I completed the group's picture of perfect tophood. My name is Gino. Like my mama told everyone when I was growing up, I was a perfect Italian boy—black curly hair, thick bones that supported decent muscles, bright-blue eyes, and a smooth olive complexion. I have my own signature now that I'm all grown up: a heavily hairy chest that I always show off. It's what gets the guys interested in me, along with my dense beard and thick moustache. As usual, I had on a denim shirt that was unbuttoned down to the waist. Everyone liked the way that my sporty pink tits stuck out from the forest of my hair, inviting anyone who was interested to take a lick. I had on my leather jacket over my shirt, my jeans, my chaps, my boots, the usual.

We were the four hottest topmen in town. We knew it. And we knew that no one else was in the bar to appreciate us.

"What the hell we going to do?" Thor finally asked.

"You could give me your white ass for the night," Roosevelt shot back.

"Hell, you know I won't do that," Thor tried to laugh off Roosevelt's crude proposition, but Rosie wasn't smiling.

Zen wasn't smiling, either. "I think that someone in this group must submit to the will of the others. Some one must succumb to the greater good of our collective desires."

I snorted before I answered, "We're tops, Zen. We don't bottom for anyone."

"Somebody's got to do *something*," Roosevelt complained. "Hell, I'm so horny I could die."

"I'm not sure I'm ready to do that," Thor said, "but I admit I'd like to have something happen."

"We could leave it to a little game of cards," I offered.

They all looked at me. I could tell they were all hoping that I was going to offer to bottom for the three of them. Not likely. But I did have a suggestion. "Why not go back to my place. It's quiet. I got some beer. You know I have the best dungeon in town. We'll play a few hands. The winners get to top the losers."

"Like strip poker," Thor said.

"Yeah, like who loses his clothes loses his ass, too," Rosie said, warming up to the idea. He had told me he used to play in some mean poker games when he had been in the Marine Corps a few years ago. He probably figured he could work this to his own advantage.

"We can work out the details when we get there," I said.

"There's no reason to stay here," Zen said tentatively. I watched while all three of them glanced from one to the other, and then to me. There was a change in all our attitudes. We had just been buddies hanging out before, now we were all checking one another out, looking at one another like the potential piece of slave meat each one of us could be.

I know I wasn't the only one who was getting a hard-on. Zen was rubbing his crotch. Thor's big snake was beginning to crawl down his trousers and there was a pronounced expansion in Rosie's codpiece.

I got their juices going. Now I just had to get them.

"We don't want this to get too elaborate," I said as I was shuffling the cards.

We'd moved a card table and chairs into my game room. My place is pretty well done up. I'd put padded leather all over the walls. It meant there was never a problem with noise; that was absorbed by the material. It also meant that the powerful odor of all the leather we four were wearing was merged with the aroma of animal skin from the walls. There was plenty more leather in the room as well—a fine collection of paddles and restraints and crops was on display, all the usual top stuff was hanging from the hooks. There were chains hanging from the ceiling and there was a nice little setup I'd created myself with a carpenter's horse; again I'd padded it with leather. You could put a bottom right over it and go to town after you'd attached his wrists to one set of legs and his ankles to the other.

It'd take too long to catalog the whole arrangement. Let's just say it represented a small fortune in mail-order purchases and a dog's lifetime in my own carpentry and other handiwork.

"Shouldn't be nothing more simple than getting a couple of you to suck my dick," Roosevelt said.

I ignored him. "If we play full hands of poker, it'll get too complicated, and it could take too long. Let's do this: I'll deal single cards, face up, to each of us. Aces high. Whoever loses has to remove a piece of clothing. The first two people who're naked are the bottoms for the night."

"Something this important shouldn't be left to chance," Rosie complained.

"It's a question of leaving your destiny to be my slave to the fates," Zen said quickly. "You should just simply submit to your fortune."

"Hell, I'm not going to do any such thing when it's obvious all three of you were born to kiss my ass," Roosevelt answered. They glared at each other. When the crisis eased, I continued.

"Really, it's the best and easiest way. We'll find out soon enough just whose destiny is at stake here."

Zen nodded his agreement. Thor shrugged his. "Deal the cards," Roosevelt finally said. "And make sure you let me cut that deck before you do, every hand."

I slammed the pack on the table. He halved them. I put the deck back together and began the game.

The first hand went to Rosie. He lost with a six of diamonds. "Take it off," Thor said, a bit too lightly. I don't think he understood what had started here.

Roosevelt stood up and grabbed hold of his codpiece. He ripped it open with a single pull and his cock and balls bobbed out. "Meet your master," he growled.

Well, at least it wasn't *that* big. God knows it wasn't small though. Rosie bragged about the size of his dick all the time. I thought it might be a monster, but it was just a good-sized cock. The colors of his genitals were what fascinated me. There was purple mixed in with the dark black skin on his shaft and the wrinkled pouch of his scrotum. When he reached down and pulled back his foreskin in the kind of defiant gesture I expected from him, I could see that the head of his dick was pink, bright pink.

Thor and Zen were just as interested in Rosie's brash display of his masculinity as I was. I could see a mixture of lust and apprehension in their faces. Was this the tool that was going to be used on them? Or was this the toy they were going to get to play with?

Things settled down after Rosie's dramatic gesture. I kept dealing the cards and everyone seemed to win or lose in a kind of steady and balanced way. But an air of seriousness had entered the room once Rosie's cock was first exposed, and the way it hung down between his legs kept us all focused on that.

There started to be increasingly serious questions about the rules of the game. Was each boot a separate piece of clothing? Each sock? What about belts? We agreed they did each count, but that wallets or anything in our pockets didn't.

We were all barefoot about the same time, with our belts on the floor. Rosie was a little luckier than the rest of us, but it didn't help him in the end since he really didn't wear socks under his boots. We all had a couple things on him because of that. Thor was the first one to go on a run of bad luck. It made sense that he was the one who began to ask the most serious questions. "Just how long is this session going to last?" he wanted to know as he unbuttoned his uniform shirt. His big mounds of pectoral flesh looked good underneath the tight T-shirt.

"Till the rosy fingers of dawn creep over the horizon," Rosie said, totally serious.

"Till morning?" Thor asked for clarification.

"Yep," I said as I shuffled the cards once again. "It's for the whole night."

"Shouldn't we talk about limits?" Thor asked. I looked up at him and saw that he was sweating. Moons of moisture were soaking his T-shirt around his armpits. "I mean, come on, guys, there have to be some limits."

"There are no limits in an authentic sadomasochistic experience," Zen announced.

"No limits," Rosie said gravely.

I put the cards down for him to cut them. When I picked up the deck and began to deal again I said, "No limits."

Thor was getting very uncomfortable. When the deuce of hearts showed up in front of his seat, I had to agree he had every right to be. The T-shirt came off.

I'd never seen Thor without a shirt on. No matter how good he had looked in his tight clothes, he looked even better in the flesh. He was virtually hairless with only a bit of blond fur under his arms and a downy covering on his forearms. His skin was perfect, so smooth it looked like it would feel like velvet. He had been to the beach a lot, evidently, and he had a nice tan. The V of his torso seemed even more distinctive when he sat stripped to the waist. The muscle definition was sharp; his abdominals were clearly etched underneath his skin. His pectorals weren't just nicely built up, they were hard pieces of beef.

The biggest surprise was his nipples. He might have built the rest of his body up to meet the standards of Tom of Finland pornography, but only God and good genes would have given him tits like those. They were very big, flat brown circles. I'm used to men who've had their tits worked on pretty well, who have the kind I do, the ones that stand up erect like little cocks when you get horny. But Thor's were just level loops of tender-looking flesh with only the slightest tip in the center of each one. It seemed like an affront for such virgin nipples to be displayed in front of three topmen who would have trained them so well, given half a chance.

I got a whiff of Thor's sweat when he'd lifted his arms up over his head to remove the T-shirt. It was good clean perspiration, mixed with that undeniable scent of fear. It was a common odor in my game room. It made my cock twinge.

A couple more hands went against Zen. He kept getting the low card until he was down to just his boxer shorts. He was much more stoic about his fortune, though, and didn't display any of Thor's anxiety.

"Some good looking skin at this table," Rosie said as he looked at their naked chests.

Zen's body wasn't as built up as Thor's, but it was hard and just as hairless. His nipples were much smaller, but much more perky. They looked nice and delectable. "Can't you just taste those things?" Rosie asked me.

I was thinking that Zen's legs were his more interesting feature. The muscles were incredible and I figured they promised a fine, firm ass.

Rosie and I could be easygoing about it all. It certainly looked like we were the ones who were going to come out on top of this game. Rosie still has his codpieceless pants on and his leather pullover shirt, as well as his hat, which he vowed would be the last thing he'd remove. I had my shirt and pants, having just lost my chaps in a previous hand.

I shuffled the cards loudly and let Rosie cut the deck. "Looks like a good night to me," I said as I dealt the hand.

When I finished, Thor was looking at the three of clubs, the low card on the table, and he began to blush furiously.

"Come on, boy. What's your problem? Lose the pants," Rosie demanded.

"I don't have any underwear on," Thor finally admitted.

There was a sudden silence in the room. The first bottom had been chosen. The three of us winners smiled at one another.

"Remove your clothing, slave," Zen told Thor as he reached for his backpack.

"Come on, guys, the joke's gone far enough." I wasn't surprised when Thor tried to get out of the thing, but there was no way we were going to let him.

"Take off your fucking pants, asshole," Rosie said. There was so much menace in his voice that Thor didn't hesitate any longer. He stood up and pulled down his zipper. The khakis fell to the floor, and I nearly did, too.

I've seen lots of men sport big baskets when they're dressed only to discover that the real thing wasn't quite so impressive when they got naked. In Thor's case, his cock was even bigger than it looked when he was in his clothes. It was a long fucker with a head that flared out to almost twice the girth of the shaft. He also had the lowest hanging balls I'd ever seen, huge eggs that dangled down in a long, long pink sac. The damn things even cast a shadow on his thighs from the overhead lights. There was only a tuft of blond hair crowning the entire package, which was framed by a swath of remarkably white skin that was set apart by his sharply defined tan line. Thor had learned the trick of always wearing the same brand of bathing suit when he went out in the sun, so there was never any blurring between his pale midsection and his chestnut tan.

"Man," Rosie said with that exaggerated drawl of his. "Goddamn."

Zen was all over Thor. The blond man didn't resist when his hands were tied behind his back by the end of a long piece of rope Zen had taken from his pack. But then Zen brought the rope down the crack of Thor's ass and to the front where he looped it around Thor's cock and balls. "That hurts!" Thor complained.

Crack! Zen slapped him hard across the face. "You are a slave to two of us, which two you don't yet know. You do not criticize any of our actions." Zen glared at him until Thor averted his gaze in what really was a nice looking bit of submission.

"No limits," I reminded him.

Zen went back to work. He wrapped the rope around Thor's entire cock and ball package, then just around the base of his cock, then around just the balls, and finally around each one of the big ovals, separating them and making the skin on his scrotum tighten up from the tension.

There was still enough rope that Zen could wrap it around Thor's neck, like a collar. He yanked hard, forcing Thor to lower his head to relieve the tension, then tied the final knot. Thor looked perfect in that position, his head bent down, his shoulders slumped.

He had quite a view of himself, too. He was forced to stare right at his crotch and when he did, he couldn't help but see that his own huge cock was standing straight up in the air, hard as a bone. Some people might excuse the hard-on by saying it was caused by the tension of the situation. We weren't buying that though. "It's unfortunate that so many men fight their natural inclinations to slavery," Zen said quietly as he ran his fingertips over Thor's chest.

Rosie reached over and grabbed hold of Thor's erection. "Sometimes you just can't hide the truth of what's good for you," he said.

Zen decided to give us all a rear view. He roughly turned Thor around. No one had to say anything this time. We were looking at a work of art and we knew it. Thor's butt was beautiful. It was perfect.

"Let's play some cards," Rosie said. "I gotta get that stuff."

Zen sat down. I shuffled. Rosie cut. I dealt the cards.

It looked like it was all over when Zen got a three of spades and both Rosie and I turned up with face cards. Rosie certainly thought so. He leaned back in his chair and waited for the unveiling.

Zen didn't show any emotion. He stood up, put his hands on the waist of his boxers and pulled them down. To display a pair of briefs. He laughed when he saw the dismayed expression on Rosie's face.

"I danced at the club, remember? When I strip, I wear layers of underwear, it incites the gathering. Underneath this I have a thong. Underneath that, a g-string. I have three pieces of clothing to go, Roosevelt, the same as you.

But Rosie didn't keep all three of his for very long. We alternated losing the next hands. I lost my shirt. "The hair on your Caucasian torso is disgusting," Zen sneered when I was stripped to the waist. Rosie lost his shirt. Then he lost his pants. He was sitting there with nothing but his cap on his head.

I could tell he was getting worried. Zen was appreciating Rosie's naked body and his half-hard cock much too overtly. There were beads of sweat on Rosie's upper lip as I put down the deck for him to cut.

Zen got a four of hearts—not good. He crossed his arms over his chest, accepting his fate, I guess. Rosie got a ten of clubs and seemed relieved. I figured I was safe, but I dealt myself a three of diamonds. I lost.

I stood up and unbuttoned the fly on my jeans. I pulled them off and stood there in nothing but my jock strap. No one made any comments this time. Zen lost the next hand and was down to his thong. We were close to the end.

The strain was getting to all of us. I felt my cock swell a bit as I thought of fucking Zen's ass, which was just as good looking now that it was exposed as I had imagined it would be. But I also was sweating so much that my jock was damp.

I dealt Zen the king of hearts. He smiled and relaxed. Rosie and I each only had one piece of clothing left. "One of you is my slave," Zen said.

Rosie got the three of spades. He lifted his head up, trying to be proud and dignified about the whole thing. I was smiling. This was going to be my night. I turned over my own card. The deuce of clubs, the lowest card in the deck.

Rosie didn't even wait for me to undress. He reached over and yanked down my jockstrap. "Get on your knees," he ordered.

Zen wasn't waiting either. He stood up and pushed me off my chair and onto the floor.

They lifted the table out of the way and then the chairs. I was sprawled out on my ass, looking up at Thor's naked, trussed torso.

Zen and Rosie didn't even have to talk about what to do next. They both put their boots and their leather jackets back on. Rosie strapped his belt around his waist.

"The problem with Americans," Zen announced, "is that they have no sense of ritual. They don't understand the importance of establishing a proscenium that needs to be crossed into the theater of the soul."

"We'll show them how," Rosie said.

He grabbed Thor and threw him onto the floor beside me. "Kiss Master Zen's feet."

"Come on, Rosie . . ."

Thump. He kicked me on the hip. "It's Master Roosevelt to you, slave. I told you to kiss Master Zen's feet. Do it!"

Thor was willing. He leaned over and put his lips on Zen's boots. He looked handsome as he did, a perfect object of subservience. I think the evidence of his hard-on had done him in. Not that my own was helping me out.

"Jesus, look. They've both thrown rods," Rosie laughed.

I bent over and kissed Zen's other boot. Okay. So I was slave for the night. I had made the bet, and I lost. I was going to be man enough to follow through, maybe even get into it a little.

"Master Zen, you should see this sight," Rosie said from behind me. "These two got great asses. They're big white moons just staring up at me."

"I don't like their paleness," Zen answered.

"That's easy to take care of." I could hear Rosie move over to where I kept the props. Even though I knew what was coming, I wasn't ready when the first blow hit my ass. *Crack!* I steeled myself for the second blow, but it landed on Thor's butt. The stink of our sweat was getting heavier.

"Now lick Master Zen's boots," Rosie ordered. *Crack!* the crop
landed on me again. Jesus, it hurt. I licked the leather under my face
and hoped I was doing a good enough job to convince my new masters
not to get too rough. Thor got another pop across his butt and this time
he couldn't keep from yelling out in pain.

"The red lines help their appearance," Zen said above me.

I hoped that meant a little relief. *Crack!* I bit into Zen's boot when
the next blow struck. "Not enough for me," Rosie said.

Crack! Crack! Crack! The crop alternated as Thor and I writhed
under the blows. Rosie wasn't fooling around. The fucker was beating
the hell out of our butts.

He finally stopped. Rosie seemed to like the results of his work.
He knelt down and I knew when Thor started to moan that he was
getting the same treatment I was—Rosie had lubricated his hands with
spit and was shoving a finger up each of our asses.

He wasn't willing to simply finger-fuck us, though. He used our
buttholes as handles to move us around. "Come on, sluts, move your
asses for me. Show me how pretty your butts can be."

I was forced to rotate my hips in the most obscene way I could
imagine. "That's it," Rosie said softly. "Get into it. You're gonna be
my sluts tonight. Just a couple of whores with pink butts waiting for
me to fuck 'em."

My hip slammed against Thor's smooth skin as we swiveled to
follow the commands of Rosie's fingers. It was mortifying to have to act
this way, becoming just what Rosie wanted us to be. "Work those asses
for Master Roosevelt," he said in his low voice. "Prove what sluts you
really are."

That was the first time I thought I heard Thor cry.

"It's not just the color," Zen said. "This one is too repulsively
hairy."

"We can handle that," Rosie said. He pulled his fingers out of our
holes without any warning. It hurt, and it also left me with a sensation
of emptiness I hadn't expected. I was stunned when I realized I kept
moving my hips, as though I hoped I could seduce Master Roosevelt
into filling me up again.

He laughed at me when he saw what I was doing. Then he reached
down and grabbed me under my armpits and dragged me up. I wasn't
sure what he was doing at first, but then I felt restraints going around
my wrists. My arms were lifted up and my wrists were attached to a
chain that hung down from my ceiling.

Zen was busy putting another set of restraints on my ankles, and then attached them to a length of steel at whose ends I'd attached D-clamps, just for an occasion like this. In a matter of short minutes, I was in total bondage, my arms over my head, my legs forced apart.

Zen disappeared into my apartment. He came right back into the dungeon and I saw that he was carrying the electric clippers I keep in my bathroom to trim my facial hair, a package of disposable razors, and a can of shaving cream.

"Hey, come on guys . . ."

Thump! My protest was cut off when Rosie punched his fist into my stomach. I couldn't breathe. Bile tried to vomit out of my mouth.

"No limits," Rosie said.

Thump! he punched me again.

"And I told you to call me Master Roosevelt."

It took everything I had not to retch this time. I didn't have any fight left when Zen came over with the clippers. He took hold of the back of my neck and forced my head forward. He turned on the clippers and I felt them buzz straight across the top of my head, down my face, across my moustache, and into my beard. He kept on going, clearing a path through my chest hair, and only stopped when the metal hit the base of my cock.

"The slave is looking more acceptable," Master Zen said.

The clippers continued to buzz away as they sheared the first layer of hair off all my body. Then the two of them went to work with the shaving cream and the razors.

It took them almost a half-hour. When they were finished, I didn't even have eyebrows left. I looked down at my body in disbelief. My cock looked bigger now than it ever had, since there wasn't any pubic hair to cover any part of it. My balls looked like a little boy's. My tits looked unnatural without their pelt around them.

"You ever fucked a shaved asshole, Master Zen?" Master Roosevelt asked his partner. "It's one of the real pleasures of life."

They took me down from my upright position and pushed me over to the horse. I was bent over it, with my ass up in the air. I heard the familiar sound of condom packages being opened and smelled the odor of lubricant.

"Wanna go first?" Master Roosevelt asked behind me.

"I think he should see what he's getting, so he can appreciate it," Master Zen replied.

The two of them walked around and stood in front of me. Both

their big hard cocks were sheathed in latex. I could see the precum
leaking into the plastic package that covered Rosie's and I felt my mouth
go dry. It sure looked a hell of a lot bigger now that he was hard than
it had when I first looked at it tonight.

"Suck it," Rosie snarled.

He didn't wait for me to do anything, but forced his erection into
my mouth. He pumped away for a while, shoving so hard and so deep
that I was on the threshold of vomiting again.

I thought I could get my breathing back to normal when he pulled
out, but Master Zen moved right in and took his place. His cock was a
little more manageable in size, but while Master Roosevelt's had been
a straightforward kind of dick, Master Zen's was the kind that stood
straight up against his belly, making it even more difficult to accommodate with my mouth, pressing even more uncomfortably against my
throat.

I couldn't pay attention to much of anything else while Master
Zen's cock was in my mouth. I wasn't prepared when Master Roosevelt's
dick thrust all the way into my butt with one motion. I opened my
mouth to try to scream. It was a mistake. It just let Master Zen's cock
invade my throat even more deeply.

"Nothing like shaved slut ass for fucking," Master Roosevelt said
behind me. "Nothing at all."

He didn't come. He pulled out. If I thought I had felt empty
before, now I felt like there was a void in my belly.

"We gotta have more of this stuff," Master Roosevelt said.

While Master Zen kept on pumping at the front of me, I felt the
weight of Thor's torso being laid on top of mine. His meaty chest and
hard belly were cool as they pressed against my back.

"Spread, Thor."

I felt my fellow slave adjust to follow the command. Thor hardly
had any hair in his crack, but I finally realized that what was there was
getting shaved off. Then Master Roosevelt must have decided to fuck
Thor. I felt the weight on me increase and Thor's breath warmed my
shoulders as he opened his mouth to gasp. The mass that was pressing
down on me began to move with a rhythm as Master Roosevelt began
his fucking.

Thor was into it, there wasn't any doubt about it. I felt his cock
swell up to its gargantuan size as it rode in the crack of my ass. I could
feel the bloated head of it and the smooth column. I sort of moved a

little myself, not entirely disinterested in the possibility that it might slip into my hole. But it was too big to make an entrance without a lot of grease, a *whole lot*, and I had to be satisfied with the sensation of having it stir between the mounds of my butt.

Master Zen removed his cock from my mouth finally. Thor's body was removed from mine and he slid so he was bent over the horse beside me. Thor's tool slipped off me. It skimmered over the surface of my ass, leaving a trail of precum on the surface. The strapping balls dragged behind it.

It didn't take long for Master Zen to take his place inside my asshole and make me forget all about my fantasies about Thor. The reality of Master Zen's cock was much more demanding than any daydream about anyone else's. He didn't enter me with any of the usual niceties, either. He just shoved that curved cock up my chute, ignoring my protests and taking the pleasure he'd won in the card game. I surrendered to what was going on and pretty soon I was lifting my midsection up to meet Master Zen's thrusts. He was a *good* fucker, I had to admit that. There weren't many men that were really *fine* at plugging ass, but Master Zen was certainly one of them.

I turned to look at Thor while the two of us were being fucked in tandem. He was already staring at me. I saw something then that sent a wave of tension through my body, something more painful than even the riding crop had been. It was the look of one slave to another. We were bottoms in this together, Thor was telling me with his expression. We understood one another.

Still the masters didn't come. They pulled out and I could hear the rubbers being ripped off their cocks.

"Paddles or riding crops?" Master Roosevelt asked. There hadn't been any other conversation. I suddenly realized that the two of them were doing their own bonding as masters. They didn't need to explain too much to one another. They understood.

Master Zen didn't even answer, but both he and Master Roosevelt lifted me up off the horse. I thought they were going to let me free, but instead they hoisted me up and attached me to the chains again. This time they found a set of restraints for Thor as well. He was attached to the same chain.

We were chest to chest, cock to cock, face to face. Thor leaned forward and kissed me. I jerked my head away. But then the cat-o'-nine-tails hit my back. *Slash!*

My shoulders burned with sharp pain. My mouth flew open and this time I didn't fight when Thor covered it with his own. The whipping kept on going—I never did know which of the masters did it until it stopped for a moment and then I saw it was Master Zen who moved around so he could start on Thor.

The first time the leather raked across his back, Thor bit my lips so hard I was frightened I was going to bleed. His powerful muscles rubbed against mine as he tried in vain to escape the lash that continued to move from his shoulders to his butt, across the back of his thighs and calves, back up again. Master Zen moved again, and I knew it was my turn to get the same treatment. My buttocks clenched in preparation. Thor's tongue moved down my throat, as though he wanted to feed me some strength to take what was coming.

Slash! My whole body arced against Thor. The pain was merged with the excitement of feeling my rigid tits rub against his smooth ones. His and my cocks were hard as they moved against one another. My hairless skin was slippery from our sweat and our erections glided back and forth over our bellies.

Slash!

"That should be enough attitudinal adjust for them," Master Zen finally said.

"They sure do have a new attitude, don't they," Master Roosevelt laughed.

I knew what he was laughing at—Thor and I were still kissing one another even as our chests were heaving from the exertion of the whipping we'd just endured.

"Come on, boys, we got some more fun for you."

We were released from the chain and directed to kneel back-to-back. Zen quickly tied our wrists together. I was sorry that I couldn't see Thor any more, or have the sustenance of his kisses, but I loved the feel of his ass as it pressed against mine.

Master Roosevelt was in front of me. He had found a couple pairs of tit clamps. I moaned again, but knew enough not to argue this time. He put the clamps on one of my tits, the rough edges eating into my nipples, then the other. A heavy chain hung between the two clamps.

Even as Master Roosevelt was moving to put another set on Thor, Master Zen was standing in front of me jiggling his hand up and down. I knew he'd found some of my most devious toys. They were small lead weights that fishermen use to weigh down their lines. But they had a use for a slave with tit clamps. He slowly attached one after another on the chain that hung between my nipples.

I couldn't hold back the groans now, not as the strain increased with every one of the weights. Thor was moaning, too. I knew that Master Roosevelt was giving him the same treatment.

The thing about any kind of tit torture is that the pain doesn't go away when the pressure's released, in fact, it sometimes increases since the sensation of removing the source of the hurt can create a soreness that you never expect.

Master Zen slowly removed each one of the lead pieces he had attached to the chain. As each one went, the change in tension on my nipples created a new wave of bite in my flesh.

The clamps themselves were left on.

"The boys look like they're not having fun any more," Master Roosevelt said with a voice that carried a full load of ridicule. He knelt beside us and grabbed hold of our cocks. My own was flaccid after the painful assault; I imagined Thor's was, too.

"We had better show them a good time," Master Zen laughed back. He reached over and undid our ropes, but only enough to let us separate our wrists from one another. Then he retied us, so we were still connected but could move a bit to have some space between us.

I made the mistake of thinking that there was going to be a break in the action.

"The two of them get along so well, it would be a shame not to let them experience some more closeness," Master Roosevelt jeered.

Then I saw what he was up to. He had found the huge double-pronged dildo that I kept hidden for special occasions. He was already greasing up both ends of it. "Move away from each other, boys," Master Roosevelt said with the seductive voice that he hadn't used on us since the card game. "Let's have some togetherness."

The two masters knelt on either side of our kneeling figures. I couldn't see who was doing which one of us, but I knew that Thor was experiencing the same sensation as one of the heads of the dildo was being pushed into my asshole. I screamed from the giant intrusion. But there was no mercy. Someone grabbed my balls and twisted them cruelly and pulled them backwards, forcing me to impale myself deeper.

I knew how long that thing was and I was shocked when the surface of my butt touched Thor's. I couldn't believe that the two of us had taken it all in. Once again, I experienced a weird and unexpected response. I felt proud. I was proud of myself and of Thor. We had done it, we had done what the masters had wanted of us.

"Sluts," Master Roosevelt said, but this time I thought there was some affection in the way he said it.

"The rosy fingers of dawn," Master Roosevelt had called them. I supposed they must finally be coming up the sky when the masters began to let the whole thing wind down.

Every square inch of my skin was burning with pain. My tits were on fire with it. My ass had been stuffed with cock and latex and fingers all night and I wasn't sure it could function without something crammed up it.

They made Thor and me lie on the floor, head to foot, each of us with his hands cuffed behind his back. Then Master Zen rolled a condom over my dick, which was miraculously hard, even after the way he'd kept it bound up in rope for so long and then had whipped it when he'd untied it. Sore isn't a word that can convey just what my cock felt like. But it was still alive, I had to admit that.

Master Roosevelt was unraveling a rubber over Thor's massive dick, right by my face. Thor was hard, too. I was impressed; his oversized tool had taken even more abuse than mine. But the masters had obviously done well by us. We were still hard. No matter how tired and sore we were, we could still throw a bone for them.

I wasn't sure what they were doing at first, but then I felt a nudge, a direction far more gentle than they'd used all night, and I realized they wanted us to sixty-nine.

It seemed so gentle to suck in Thor's cock after all the battering the masters had given me. I felt his low-hanging balls slap against my chin as the latex-sheathed monster of his slipped inside me.

I was prepared for anything now, after I'd learned what they were willing to do to us, the extremes they were willing to go to. It took a while to realize there wasn't going to be another beating.

Master Zen's hands massaged my sore back and butt and roved over my thighs. I could see that Master Roosevelt was doing the same to Thor's body.

Thor and I sucked away, getting up more energy than I had thought we'd have left. Pretty soon I felt my juice building up in my belly. I waited to see if the masters would tell me to hold back, but they didn't. Their massage continued, coaxing me and Thor toward the edge.

I felt him go over first. The waves of hot come hit against the rubber and formed a thick pool of ooze that stayed trapped inside his condom. My own orgasm shook through my body. I had been taken to the verge of orgasm over and over again all night, but never allowed to cross over. Now, all the built-up urgency of sex burst through me and crashed into my condom, warmed and protected by Thor's mouth.

The masters lifted us up onto our knees.

"Just 'cause it's nearly over, doesn't mean you're not still my sluts," Master Roosevelt said. "I want you two to show me one more time just what whores you are."

He carefully took off Thor's condom; Master Zen took off mine. They made sure they didn't spill even a drop. Then they brought the rubbers up to each of our mouths. "Swallow it, sluts, swallow your own cum." The slime was already cooling off while Master Roosevelt emptied the latex into my mouth. I let it slide down my throat. I licked my lips.

Master Roosevelt stood up. "Like I said. They're sluts."

They untied us finally and Thor and I collapsed against one another, not ready to stand up yet, still trying to collect ourselves. "It's over," Rosie said to us. Then he turned to Zen, "So, what do you think, Master Zen? Next Monday good for you?"

"Another card game?" Thor asked, a bit of incredulity in his voice. "Hell, I don't know . . ."

"Bullshit," Master Roosevelt broke in. "We saw the way you loved it. You're a born bottom, Thor. You want these dicks of ours more than anyone at the Ramrod."

"Wait a minute . . ." I started to complain.

Rosie laughed out loud. "*You!* Hell, I've got your number."

I went pale. "What do you mean . . ."

"Gino, you try to play with a deck as badly marked as that one in Vegas and someone's going to cut you, they'll cut you real bad."

"What do you mean?" Thor demanded as he rubbed his wrists where Zen's bondage had left him raw.

"You don't know that Gino was playing with a marked deck? He was calling all the shots, deciding just who was going to lose, who was going to win. Hell, he had the whole thing planned out, probably for a long time. He even knew Zen's routine at the dance club and figured out just how many layers of clothes he had on so he could create a bit of tension in those last few hands."

"You mean we didn't win the game? He fixed it?" Zen seemed angry.

"Hell, yes. Gino wanted this to happen all the time!" Rosie roared from laughing.

"You mean he got me naked? He's the one who made me the first slave?" Thor asked.

"You believe it," Rosie said. "It's true, tell them, admit it," Rosie said to me.

I didn't answer. I didn't have to. I wasn't his slave any more.

"Why did he do it?" Thor asked.

"Probably because he's been wanting to bottom out to us and didn't dare admit it," Rosie answered Thor, but he was leering at me while he spoke. "Maybe he wanted to feel your naked butt and he figured it was the only way. I'm not sure. You'll have to ask him sometime."

"I'm going to do a lot more than that," Thor said, a sudden chill in his voice. "You son of a bitch, you owe me! I ended up going through all this just because you cheated at cards!"

"Don't object too much," Zen said. "After all, Thor, it appears you learned something important about your own psyche tonight. And I think it was right here." Zen groped his own crotch; the lewd gesture was unmistakable. Thor blushed, as though he was being forced to admit just how much he had enjoyed bottoming out to the two other men.

Rosie had an idea, though. "Thor, you got the whole week to get something back from him. You still got some top in you, why don't you take it out on him yourself? He's willing."

I just sat there for a minute. "Rosie, it was just one night," that's all I was going to admit. "It's done with."

"No, no, baby, there's next Monday night, too. You're going to be begging for it."

"Rosie . . ."

"Gino, you ever been shaved before?"

"No. Hell, you'd have known if I had bottomed to anyone at the Ramrod. It was a first for me, really."

"When that hair on your body starts to grow in you're going to be on fire. The itch is going to make you so desperate you'll come crawling on your knees and begging us to shave you again. You be good at it and maybe we'll let the hair on your head grow out. You're going to look strange at work with no eyebrows, as it is. You show us how a slave boy likes to please his masters and maybe we'll let you have them back.

"But don't think you're not going to bottom for us again. I know my slaves, Gino. Once a man like you gets the taste of this, you won't lose the hunger."

"I think I shall bring a straight razor next Monday," Zen said.

"I got some better dildos," Rosie answered.

"And we'll need more rope," Zen announced.

I turned to Thor, who now looked interested. He stared at me. I shrugged. There wouldn't be any bottoms to do on Monday night anyway. Why not?

JOHN DIBELKA
WRITING AS
JAY SHAFFER

BETTER

THAN ONE

I DON'T LIKE SNOW.

I have never liked snow.

Rain I can take, and wind, and hail, and serious storms and temperatures well below freezing; all just as long as it doesn't, ever, snow.

Right now it is snowing outside. I plan to stay inside as long as it does.

"Please," Peter begs of me over the phone. "I need your help. I need you here. I can't get this damned report finished without you. You've got to come over *tonight.*"

"Peter," I tell him, "you don't understand. The only thing I've got to do tonight is stay in bed. Bed, Peter. My nice, warm, cozy bed. Doesn't that sound wonderful? And the best thing about it—I don't have to go outside at any point to get here."

"It's only snow."

"I grew up in Phoenix. I don't believe in 'only snow.' The company did this to me."

"I'll make it worth your while," he coaxes. "You have to get me through this. We work so well together. I just cannot do this alone. You're needed, Mister Peel. I need your mind."

I snort. I know he doesn't want my body.

"What are you offering?" I ask him. "What could you possibly give me to make this project worth my while? I'll freeze. Do you understand? I'll get stuck in the snow and I'll die. I'll fall into a drift and stay missing until some stray dog digs me out halfway through next thaw."

"Get over it. You'll live. But you'll have to come over to find out about your bribe. Don't be such a wuss. Put on an overcoat or something and haul yourself up here and help me."

"I don't do snow."

"You're whining. For God's sake, we're not going sledding. It's only five blocks. We'll make beautiful money together."

"*I'm* whining? Listen to yourself. The idea does not appeal."

"Neither did getting fucked, did it, the first time you tried it? Now you can't get enough. Handle it. Be here. Soon."

A dial tone growls in my ear.

Peter, the arrogant asshole, has hung up his phone.

When I was introduced to Peter, I was told he was the City's Leading Bottom. I wasn't too sure what it took to land that kind of title, but I figured holding onto it required some sort of humility.

I was wrong.

It turned out he'd thought up the label himself and was, quite literally, an arrogant asshole. But it also turned out he is brilliant, unpredictable, and sometimes, a whole lot of fun.

All of which tells me this call has meant one of two things. Either Peter is into something way over his head or he has got something truly twisted up his sleeve.

I hang the phone up and get back out of bed, to get dressed. In spite of my deep fear of freezing and all of the rest of my much better judgment, I will now go rescue Peter.

What is five city blocks on a hot, steamy evening becomes a Siberian dogsled gymkhana on winter nights like this. Maria von Trapp can have every last one of these snowflakes that stick to my nose and eyelashes. I trudge and curse. I do not sing.

At least Peter has the sense and decency to greet me at his open door with a hot Irish coffee when I arrive, the valiant survivor of one more skirmish in humankind's ongoing war with nature. I have almost decided to move home and clean pools for a living when the warmth and the whiskey and the look on Peter's face bring my mind back to the problem at hand.

"You were serious, weren't you? About your problem." For some reason, this fact surprises me.

"Never more," Peter answers, closing and bolting his door, taking my coat and galoshes and looking truly humble for the first time I have ever seen. "I'm completely screwed."

I let it pass. "Lead on, MacDuff," I say instead.

Peter takes me to his study, telling me on the way what he has to do and why. The room is a disaster scene; ground zero for a paper bomb. There are files and free pages on every horizontal surface. Graphs are strewn everywhere in no discernible order. Two computer screens stare at each other, one blinking an angry red notice of some kind of error. I crouch and start to sift through printouts while Peter sums his presentation up.

His answer seems obvious to me. I outline it for him. He stares at me, his eyes doing a great imitation of the flashing red computer screen as he starts to shake his head.

"Shit," says Peter. "Fuck. God damn."

"You were too close to your problem," I tell him. "No big deal. Come on. Let's do it. We'll have you all done in an hour."

"I'd have been fucked without your help." He truly seems to mean these words. I'm flattered.

"You generally aren't fucked *with* my help, as we both recall. But you're welcome anyway. Sometimes you're right. About two heads, I mean. Don't let yours get fat."

Peter's eyes flash another message at me; one I'm too engrossed in planning strategy to read. Together, the two of us organize and start to rewrite, redraw graphs and paste in graphics until there are no other thoughts in our world.

The printer is whispering out laser-perfect sheets by the time I come back out of my daze. I ask if there's any more coffee and Peter goes out to the kitchen, returning with a fresh-brewed batch and an unopened bottle of whiskey just as his computer produces an updated acknowledgment sheet. I am surprised, and impressed. Peter has thanked me in print for my "invaluable assistance."

"Thank you," I tell him. He follows my eyes to the paper.

"It isn't much," he answers, "but your name will be seen where the tall carpet grows. You never know which suits are hunting. And I'll split the bonus with you."

"You're far too kind," I tell him while I mix myself another stiff coffee-and-booze, "but don't worry about it. I'm stepping off the ladder. Just decided. I'm going to go home to the desert. Swimming pool maintenance, Peter. That is the wave of my future."

Peter looks taken aback for a moment, before he produces a short, sharp, cold laugh.

"Don't be hasty," he tells me. "You're tired. You make too much money to quit. You'll change your mind."

"Probably. But money isn't everything. I know that's not original, but I also know it's true. There are other things in life. Want to fuck?"

It's an old joke. Peter may be the City's Leading, but it didn't take long for me to become the City's Most Notorious, and while I've got a case of the hots for Peter that even snow can't cool, I'm far from being stupid. So what if he has soulful brown eyes and a thick pelt of golden-brown hair, a tight, compact body and charm out the ying-yang? Two bottoms? Please. Get real.

But this time Peter hasn't answered. He's just standing in front of me, smiling.

"I'd like to explore the possibilities," he says at last.

"Why, Peter. I'm flattered. Now get over it. And yourself. Who would play top? It's not something you can wrestle for when both boys want to lose."

I finish my speech and take a debonair sip of scalding doctored coffee—which I proceed to spew out across my lap and all the papers on the floor at the sight of what Peter is suddenly holding between us.

A wicked-looking, thick and veiny, heavy-duty doubleheaded dildo has appeared, it seems, from out of nowhere to fill and spill over both of Peter's hands. Just looking at it makes my butthole twitch. Tired as I am, this idea appeals.

"Peter," I say carefully, "don't tease me like this."

He smiles the smile that springs at least a million city dicks.

"I told you, you had to come over to find out about your reward," he says.

"It's late. You're overworked," I mumble. My mouth is going dry. I am mopping up coffee, a little at a time, mostly as an excuse to rub my crotch.

"So are you," he says. "I need—we *both* need to relax."

Peter is unbuttoning his shirt. Walking toward me across a field of now-useless notes, he brandishes that incredible toy like the magic wand it just may be.

"Peter—two bottoms?"

His chest is exposed. A carpet of fur uncurls, springs up, waves slightly, waiting to gather his sweat and my spit and thick ribbons of jism. Peter stands in front of me. He starts to peel the shirt completely off, freeing both his hands by dropping his huge double dong in my lap.

"Here," he announces, "you two get acquainted. I'm going to go get some lube." With that, he turns and leaves the room.

I look at the thing in my lap. "Alone at last," I say to it and bark out a short, sweaty laugh.

What to do?

Give in, of course. I will be a mess at work tomorrow, but I'm not the one with the big sale to pitch. Besides—I'll be back-flushing filters soon, skimming off leaves and adjusting acidity, quitting the company, getting a life.

"Are there more like you in Arizona?" I ask as I set it down carefully onto the arm of the chair so I can stand. One more swig straight from the bottle and I am removing my clothes.

I am nearly naked and completely hard by the time Peter returns. He operates a dimmer switch, mellowing most of the lights in the study. He stands in the doorway and sizes me up, raking one hand through the hair on his very flat belly, stroking the other hand up and down his huge, hard cock.

"What a waste," he sighs at last.

"Funny," I answer, undressing the rest of the way while he watches me, "I was about to say just the same thing about you. Why can't we find men as hot as we are, to fuck us?"

Peter arches an eyebrow to remind me conceit is his prerogative, not mine. This man is one pushy bottom.

He lets go of himself and starts toward me again, stopping at his printer's switch to power it down and leaning across his desk to turn off the green glass–shaded lamp. His ass, this way, is perfect. I have no doubt at all that's why he's moving as he is. Dusted with brown hair that grows thicker toward the crack, round, hard cheeks catch the light as he flexes them just enough to split them open and give me a dead-on shot of what may just be the most famous anus in the Western Hemisphere.

How could even I refuse?

My knees land on paper sheets that slide aside as I steady myself. My hands land on Peter's cheeks, gently massaging them, spreading them wider, palming the hair's texture, soaking up warmth and just a hint of ready sweat. My nose lands on his tailbone with the touch of a butterfly and sucks up his musk like an insect sucks up nectar: ambrosia. My chin lands on the back of his ball sack and, finally, I've made Peter groan.

I groan. I exhale a hot breath that flutters his hairs. Peter melts— all across his desk.

I purse my lips. I press them forward. I kiss the lips of Peter's asshole, slightly damp and very hot, and I feel them open to me, just like the lips in the face of a lover. I drop my jaw and spread his cheeks and fuck my tongue into his ass until he has got all I've got to give. I shove my face up his ass, slurping and tonguing and not being very polite, and Peter squirms up to the balls of his feet while he pushes his butt backward, down on my face.

My legs are starting to cramp. Carefully, slowly, I pull Peter with me as I lean over backward to stretch out on the floor with Peter first crouching, then sitting on my face. He leans forward and grabs for my ankles and spreads my legs and thrusts my knees up in the air. His thick-pelted body spreads out across mine. His smooth face spreads my cheeks.

Peter's tongue invades my hole; a hard, hot, squirming, fucking thing that makes me want to scream, and keys the lock that lets me open outward. I feel myself unfold around his tongue, his lips, the fingers he uses to dig deep up in me.

I start to confuse these sensations. Am I a tongue plunging up into an asshole—or an asshole surrounding a tongue? Whose pleasure do I feel? Mine? Or Peter's?

Who cares?

We somehow establish a rhythm. I lose myself to everything but eating butt and being eaten. This is some kind of an eternal struggle, I think. Strike that. I don't think. I can't think. I feel.

I feel Peter coming up for air. I feel Peter touching me with something more than spit on his fingers. I feel my hard, *hard* cock digging into Peter's chest while his digs into mine. I feel his fingers slide inside me. I feel his butthole quiver on my mouth. I feel Peter feel the pleasure his pleasure is giving me.

I feel Peter slide backward until his thick and dripping dick is kissing my lips with its foreskin-crowned tip, and I feel the wet heat of his tongue and his throat on my dick as I open and swallow him all the way down.

We suck the way possibly only we two know how. Nobody blows like a serious bottom. No one more loves to be blown. When you give yourself up to another man's pleasure you sometimes forget what it's like to be spoiled. Peter and I both know just what we want.

I finger Peter's hole just the way he fingered mine, spreading his smooth, hot, hungry wet insides, soothing the muscle to help it relax. I feel myself starting to peak and I freeze; Peter does likewise. We lie still for a moment that goes on forever, waiting for the need to come to pass.

I am delirious. Someone has stolen my brain.

This is like making love to myself.

Slowly and carefully, Peter pulls up and away, stands up to pick up supplies, crouches between my legs, facing me, this time, and smiles. I feel the need. I know the moves. I grab my knees and pull them up and wide and back. Framed between them, Peter goes to work.

He teases me with fingertips and cool, slick, ample lube. He opens me slowly and presses in the dildo's head. I offer no resistance. I open and take it in, and Peter feeds me slowly, finding all my secret bends and how to pass them and move on. I sigh and grunt and rock my hips. He fills me with this phony dick and it's better than most flesh-and-blood fucks I've had.

Now, together, we sense that enough is enough. He stops. I lock my arms around my knees and lift my head to watch his moves.

He rocks back and plants his ass and lifts his own thighs wide. He rolls back and stares at me as his asshole comes into view, pouting it out and then reaching inside himself, planting lube where it will do the most good. Peter plays with his butt for the pleasure it gives him and gives me to watch him. The dim light caresses the fur on his chest and all over his thighs and his ass. Peter glows.

He reaches for the dildo's shaft and rotates it inside me. My eyes roll briefly back, it feels so good. When I focus again he is scooting toward me.

"You ready?" he asks me.

"Never more," I quote.

Peter presses his end home. It disappears. He rocks and rolls. I rock and roll to meet him. We buck together, closing. Closed. The dildo disappears.

Our nuts nudge each other. Our dicks drip and throb. If I touch myself now I'll go off. My gut is full, and so is Peter's. With the hair on his butt cheeks he crushes my own. We reach down together to find our hands, slide our palms over each other, grab our wrists, and pull.

The pleasure is immeasurable.

Peter rolls one way just slightly. I roll just slightly the other. Our pelvises match up much better this way; they slide and lock into the tightest fit possible. The sensation of pressure is everywhere now. Deep up inside me the dildo's head finds a home. Outside my asshole, my crack's full of Peter. We stare into each other's eyes. We pant and grimace, smile and laugh. I massage his wrists. He massages mine. In unison, we start to move.

We grind our hips. We pull back. Shove. We fuck each other gently, both of us knowing exactly what the other wants, both knowing just how to give it. Our cocks stand tall between our eyes, bobbing and weaving and drooling and primed.

I let Peter's hands go and raise myself on my palms, lifting my back and my butt off the floor. I sit down on the plastic prick, fucking myself as I fuck Peter's hole. Peter flips his balls to one side, shoving mine off to the other, and wraps our dicks together in one hot, squirming, lube-slopped hand.

We slide across each other twice this way. Pull back and slide again. Third time's a charm, they say. God. Oh, God. They're right.

With Peter's grip clamping our shafts to each other, the bomb going off in me can't find release. My second explosion hits, slamming up into the first one, still trapped in my dick, making my nuts feel like they are about to burst. I howl, and Peter grunts. Then Peter howls. I smack his hand, hard. He lets go.

Our pricks writhe like snakes fucking, shooting twin streams up like fire-hose fountains. We try to watch and can't; it's too good. We gasp and shudder, fuck each other, feel white-hot sensation shoot out all over us, scalding our skin. Somehow we hear some shots fall with flat *splats* on the papers. Somehow we smell our come, taste our sweat, touch the sky.

And somehow, at last, we come down.

I'm a shaker. Peter's not. I can see his concern but I cannot stop shuddering.

"I'm okay," I tell him. "Christ." I shake. "Believe it." I shudder again.

My seizures pass. We both relax. We lie together, devastated, sending and receiving signals with our ass lips, clamping, relaxing, like wet mouths around a single, solid tongue. We move apart slowly, feeling ever emptier, letting loose until the dildo thumps out softly, free of both our holes at once. Peter can't move anymore. I can't either. Together, with legs intertwined, we doze off.

I wake up before he does, crawl up beside him, kiss him and roll him up onto his side. I spoon myself up to him. He sighs and shoves his butt back at me. I lick some salt out of the fur on his shoulder. I fall asleep dreaming of fucking on thick corporate carpets and of Peter sweeping swimming pools.

ANNE RICE
WRITING AS
ANNE RAMPLING

ELLIOTT:

THE SPORTS

ARCADE

IT WAS DAMNED UNNERVING TO BE OUT OF THE COCOON of her bedroom and borne again into The Club. And the flickering hurricane lamps and the din of the evening crowd in the garden struck a deep, primal chord of fear.

The number of guests suddenly scattered around us seemed even greater than what I'd seen the first day, and I kept my eyes down, feeling a low-grade buzz all through me at being walked this way, slowly and deliberately, past so many inevitable glances.

I followed the path, Lisa's arm prodding me at the turn, her hand out to point if there was a fork.

We passed the buffet tables and the swimming pools, and made our way along a little path out of the main garden and towards a low, glass-domed building. The lower walls were covered with vines, and the lighted dome glowed like a great bubble. I could hear the muted sounds of shouting and laughter.

"This is the arcade, Elliott," she said. "Do you know what that means?"

"No, Lisa," I said in an amazingly calm voice. *But it sounds awful.*
I was sweating already. The welts and stripes from the strap were
itching.

"You're a sportsman, aren't you?" she asked. She pushed me a little
faster along the path, and a young handler with longish red hair and a
pleasant enough smile reached out to open the doors of the strange
building, letting out the noise in a deafening blast.

"Good evening, Lisa," he said loudly. "Packed in there tonight,
and they'll be glad to see this one."

The light seemed dimmer once we stepped in, but it might have
been only the denseness of the crowd, and the smoke. The smell of
tobacco mingled strongly with the malty smell of beer.

Only a sprinkling of women as far as I could tell, though the place
was immense, a giant covered garden of sorts, with a long bar running
along the curved walls. Trainers pushed past us with naked male slaves,
some bound, others walking as I was, some obviously worn out and
covered with sweat and dust.

A dozen different languages easily were being spoken around us. I
could feel the eyes passing over me, lingeringly, and I heard French and
German distinctly, snatches of Arabic, and Greek. Well-heeled men all,
naturally, expensive sportswear, all the little accoutrements of money
and power.

But the appalling part were the shouts coming from up ahead, the
familiar deep-throated noises of men cheering on some competition, then
guffawing and cursing when it went wrong. I wanted to leave now.

Lisa pushed through the wall of men and I saw a tree-lined avenue
of clean, soft white sand before me that led some hundred yards or more
ahead before the crowd swallowed it up. There were large airy fountains
to the far left and the right, scattered park benches, nude female slaves,
all of them extremely pretty, quietly and busily raking the sand, emptying the standing ashtrays, and gathering up discarded glasses and beer
cans.

The avenue itself was a mall, it seemed, lined on both sides with
scattered, neatly whitewashed buildings, each strung with ropes of tiny
lights. There were fenced areas in between the buildings and groups of
men leaned on the wooden railings, blocking the view of whatever went
on inside. Guests moved in and out of the buildings. And hundreds
strolled on the white sand, shirts open to the waist, drinks in hand, only
glancing now and then in the open doorways.

I took a step backwards without realizing it, half pretending I had to get out of the way of two men in swim trunks filing past me, and felt Lisa's fingers biting into my arm. My mouth opened with some half-thought-out plea, like, "I'm not ready for this," but nothing came out.

The crowd thickened around us. I felt claustrophobic as pant legs and boots and coats brushed me. But Lisa had her hand on my arm, and was pushing me towards the first of the long white booths.

It was shadowy inside, and for a moment I couldn't make out what was there. Mirrored walls and ceiling, glossy hardwood floor, and thin white lines of decorative neon etching the ceiling, the stage. Then I saw it was a typical amusement park game. You paid for several black rubber rings and you tossed them up, trying to hang all of them on one projectile to make a perfect score. Only the projectiles here were the bowed heads of the male slaves kneeling on a conveyor belt that moved them very rapidly across the stage.

To the guests it was a coarse, hilarious pastime, getting a number of rings around the neck of the victim before he vanished into the wings. And for all the simplicity of it, it had a real scariness to it: the submission of the kneeling victims, the way their well-oiled bodies had become mere objects as they passed before the crowd.

I stared at the little stage, the bowed heads, the rings hanging from bent necks. I didn't want to be left here. I couldn't. There had to be some way of making it clear. And without considering it really, I backed up until I was suddenly behind Lisa and I kissed her on the top of the head.

"Outside," she said. "And don't waste your pleas. If I wanted you up there I'd put you up there. I don't."

She pushed me towards the door.

The lights of the avenue flickered against my closed eyelids for a second, then I was moving again, being pushed steadily towards another booth on the right.

This was a much larger booth, with the same glossy high-tech decor, with a bar and brass rail along the wall, about thirty feet deep. It wasn't rings this time, it was brightly colored plastic balls, about the size of tennis balls, pitched towards the moving bull's-eye targets that were painted in thick gleaming colors on the backsides of the male victims, who, with their hands tied over their heads, tried desperately to dodge by constant movement what they couldn't see. The balls stuck to the target when they hit. And the slaves shimmied to shake them loose. So deliciously humiliating and not the slightest real pain involved. I didn't have to see the faces of the slaves to realize they were preening as they twisted and turned. Every lovely muscle was fully alive.

I felt the sweat streaming down my face. I gave a little negative shake of my head. Impossible, simply impossible. Checking out. Out of the corner of my eye I saw Lisa watching, and I made my face blank.

The next two booths were similar games, the slaves being made to run on oval tracks above to escape the balls and the rings, and in the fifth booth, the slaves were hung upside down from carousels and did not have to twist or turn themselves.

I wondered if that was what they did with them when they were tired from the other games: put them on that carousel where they hung helpless? Scrumptious sufferers. And this was regular service in The Club, wasn't it, this place, not punishment like being sent below stairs.

Any memory of a sane world in which these things didn't happen seemed untrustworthy at best. We'd stepped into a Hieronymus Bosch painting, full of lurid silver and red, and my only chance of getting out again was the lady who'd brought me in.

But did I want to get out? Of course not. Or let's just say, not this very minute. I'd never thought of stuff like this in all my sexual fantasizing. I was scared to death and secretly entranced. But it was like the old "Purple Cow" poem by Gellett Burgess: "I'd rather see than be involved."

I moved numbly, through the glare of the lights. My senses were flooded. Even the noise seemed to penetrate me, the sweetish smell of the smoke to drug me slightly, the hands that now and then touched or examined me stoking the mixture of dread and desire that I couldn't hide.

Naked women slaves appeared and disappeared like flickering pink flames in the shifting male crowd, as they offered cocktails, champagne, white wine.

"Aren't we geniuses of exotic sex?" Lisa whispered suddenly. It was startling to hear her speak. But the expression on her face was even more surprising. She was taking in the crowd in the same dazed way that I was taking it in, as if we'd been drifting for hours together at a county fair.

"Yeah, I think so," I said. My voice sounded as strange as hers. I was steaming.

"You like it?" she said. No irony. It was like she'd forgotten who we both were.

"Yeah, I like it," I said. I got a powerful, secret satisfaction from the innocence of her face and voice. And when she looked up at me I winked at her. I could almost swear she blushed as she looked off.

It occurred to me, why not grab her and bend her over my arm, kissing her madly, like Rudy Valentino in *The Sheik*? I mean in the middle of all this exotic sex it would be a scream, at least to me. I didn't have the nerve.

I was going to die if she got pushed out of shape with me. Which meant playing one of these alluring little games if she said to do it, right?

As we started to walk again, I watched her out of the corner of my eye, her jutting breasts under that elegant layer of lace, the vest that made her into a little hourglass. This was heaven and hell.

And as she directed me towards one of the small clearings, I realized she might show me all of the diversions before choosing the one that had affected me the most.

But when I saw the game in the clearing, I couldn't too well cover up what I felt.

There was a race in progress here, men all around the four-sided fenced enclosure with feet on the rail as they might be at a rodeo, cheering on the naked slaves who ran in neat tracks on their hands and knees.

But the slaves weren't simply racing each other for the distance. They were retrieving in their teeth black rubber balls thrown down the tracks by the guests at the railing who would not release a second ball until the first one had been retrieved. And the spectators were whipping them on with leather straps.

It seemed some five balls made up the race, because a winner was pulled up by both arms right after he laid a fifth ball at his master's feet. His face was red, dripping wet, as he was applauded, patted, caressed. He was at once taken out of the clearing, a white towel wrapped around him, but the others, panting and shuddering, were whipped into place for the next race.

I saw the punishment. You raced until you won.

And just as I figured, the slaves were glorying in it, really competing with one another. They knelt poised and desperately ready to begin again, eyeing each other, jaws set.

Again, I backed away, trying to appear casual about it. Weren't we going on to the next clearing, the next booth? I mean, come on, there's lots of stuff to see, right? I think I'll go home and read the *New York Times* now. The noise was like a buzzing in my head.

"It's really tough for you, isn't it?" she said, big brown eyes looking up again. Everything melted in me except what never melts, of course. I thought of a lot of little nasty things to say, but I didn't say them. I felt lusciously subject to her. And defiantly I kissed her cheek.

She backed up and snapped her fingers and made a little gesture for me to get moving. "Don't do *that* again," she said. She was really flustered. Her face was pink.

She led the way down the crowded avenue without glancing back. I told myself I didn't want to look at the clearings on either side, but I couldn't resist. More races. Different lengths of races, variations. But it was more fun watching her beautiful little bottom moving under her skirt, the sweep of her hair that came down almost that far, the little seams of flesh behind her naked knees.

The avenue branched to left and right as we neared a thick crowd before a low, lighted stage. Some eight or ten slaves were on the stage, each naked except for a white towel draped over one shoulder.

Lots of tousled hair and polished muscles and smiles, amazingly provocative smiles, as the slaves apparently taunted the crowd with little gestures and "come on" motions of the head.

I soon saw what was happening. The handlers were selling the slaves for the races or games, and the slaves were lapping it up, vying for the high spenders. Two were sold off while I watched, the result of a little informal auctioning among three bidders, and immediately another pair were led up the steps out of a pen, and started the same preening and good-humored taunting. Hoots, shouts from the guests, and occasional threats like, "I'll work that smile off your face," and "You think you want to run for me?" strengthened the convivial tension.

Lisa put her arm around me and pulled me close to her, the feel of her fingers against me pretty maddening. I stole a couple of glances at her breasts beneath the low-collared blouse. I could almost see her nipples.

"Which one is the most attractive, the most sensuous?" she asked, inclining her head as if we were just a couple at a pedigreed dog show. The feeling of being utterly subjugated by her was getting worse. "Think about your answer, and answer me truthfully," she said. "It will teach me things about you."

"I don't know," I said kind of testily under my breath. The thought that she'd buy one of these brutes and start paying attention to him infuriated me.

"Get your mind on exactly what I'm telling you to do," she said coldly. She reached up and brushed the hair back from my forehead, but her expression was flinty, threatening. "Pick the one you really think is the most handsome, the one you'd like to fuck if I let you do it. And don't lie to me. Don't even consider it."

I was pretty miserable. All I felt was jealousy. But I looked at the men, and things inside me were scrambled. My senses took over and shifting gears this fast felt entirely new. They were all very young, obviously athletic, and they were as proud of their stripes, their welts, the pink blush on their butts as they were of their genitals, the muscles in their legs and arms.

"I think the one on this end, the blond, is terrific," she said.

"No." I shook my head as if this wasn't even discussable. "There's no one on the stage who can equal that guy in the back of the pen, the dark one." He was something special even in a place full of people who were special, a young, black-haired, smooth-chested faun, right out of the forest primeval. He should have had pointed ears. His curly hair was short though full on the sides, and only a little long in back; and his neck and shoulders were particularly well shaped, powerful. His partially erect cock was on the way to being as big around as a beer bottle. He looked part demon, especially when he stared directly at me, his lip curling a little, his sleek dark eyebrows coming together for an instant in a playful frown.

"That would be your choice, you'd like to have him?" she asked, appraising him. He was being moved to the front of the pen, his hands behind his neck, his eyes fixed on us as his cock hardened.

I imagined it, screwing him while she watched, and my mind split in half. That had been hard for me at Martin's, very hard, screwing in front of others. Easier to be whipped, humiliated in a dozen ways than to let them see that. There was a sense in me of something being released. He was making my temperature rise.

Lisa made some little gesture to the handler, like the subtle hand bids made at art auctions. Immediately, he motioned for the slave to come up on the little stage, and then down the steps through the crowd towards us.

On close inspection, he was damn near overwhelming. His olive skin had been darkened by a tan, and every inch of him was hard. He dropped his eyes with perfect courtesy as he approached, his hands still behind his neck as he went down on one knee to kiss Lisa's boot with a grace that was slightly surprising. Even the back of his neck was enticing. He threw me a quick up-and-down look. I looked at her, half wanting him, half hating him, unable to detect what she really thought of him.

She took the towel off his shoulder as he rose, and threw it to the handler. Then she motioned for us to follow her.

We came right away to a very noisy clearing, a large open ring where the loose crowd was roughly three deep right up to a half circle of jammed-packed bleachers.

Lisa pushed her way forward, motioning for us to follow until we were at the railing, the crowd closing around us instantly.

Two obviously fresh and sexually primed slaves on hands and knees were just entering the ring, and the spectators began counting in a low chant, one, two, three, four, five . . . as the pair squared off from one another like fighters. Warily, the slaves peered at each other through tousled hair, their bodies glistening under a thick coating of oil, one a dark-skinned, brown-haired slave, the other a silver blond, with a long mop veiling his face.

But what exactly was the game? Just pin the other guy down for the count or rape?

The brown-haired slave sprang with a hiss at the blond one, trying to mount him. Yeah, it was rape. The thick oil allowed the blond to slide free easily, and as he did so he turned and sprang at the darker one, failing to catch hold in the same way. A real scuffle followed, with oily hands slipping desperately off oily limbs. The chanting count continued now past one hundred, and the struggle intensified, the brown-haired slave getting on top of the other, his arm locked around his throat. But he was shorter than the blond slave and no matter how he jabbed, he couldn't pull it off. The blond rolled over on him trying to force him off, and finally got free just as the count ended with 120.

No winners. Both were booed by the crowd.

Lisa turned to me. "Need I tell you what to do?" she asked. She gestured for the handler. The olive-skinned faun gave me another curling smile as I glared at her.

"Pretty damned old-fashioned stuff, if you ask me," I said. The top of my head was coming off.

"Nobody did ask you," she said. "And you picked a champ, by the way. You better be good."

There was a lot of racket from the crowd as the handler pulled us aside for the oiling. The evil little faun was studying me, sizing me up, his lips curling in that same maddening fashion. He was ready to go. I could hear bets being placed, see men arguing and talking in the crowded bleachers.

And my anger gave way to another more savage emotion. Get him. Fuck him, the bastard. I was ready, too.

Champion, she called him. Probably done it hundreds of times. A goddamned gladiator, that's what he was, and I was right off the bus. Okay. I was getting more and more exhilarated, crazy. It was sublimely brutal and it was galvanizing me, yet another doorway opening on something that had always been locked up.

"Remember," the handler said pushing me towards the ring. "On your hands and knees always, and no hitting. And don't waste any time defending yourself. Get him. Now go to it." And he shoved me down and under the rail.

With a loud clack, the count began.

I saw him moving in front of me, glowering at me from under his dark brows, the oil beaded on his hands and his cheeks. Stockier than I am, just a little muscle-bound, not good for him. The count was up to thirty, thirty-one . . .

Suddenly, he lunged at me as if he'd go over my head, and I spun around sharply to the right just in time to see him land in the dust clumsily. But the secret was to mount him now, without a second's hesitation, and I sprang at him before he could recover, making in effect a complete circle from the time he had rushed for me. I got on top of him, and locked my left arm around his throat, reinforcing it with my right. But it was madness trying to hang on, his body slipping and sliding under me as he bucked in fury, his greased fingers scratching uselessly at my hands. I could hear him snarling.

But he wasn't getting away, not from me. It was the gutter fights I'd never had, the alley rapes I'd never committed, nor ever even truly imagined. And he had it coming, the son of a bitch, he would have done it to me. It was divine. I humped him as if I were already in, clamping down on him like a vise. It was working. He couldn't throw me off and he was weakening. His fingers slipped as they grasped at my arms, and my hands. The crowd was roaring. I rammed him hard. He shook his head savagely and tried to roll over, but I was too heavy for him, too mad and determined for him, and I was in. I had him, and I had both arms around his neck again, and he didn't have a chance now.

The crowd broke its counting—110, 111—to scream and applaud. And his frantic bucking only made it better, the friction gorgeous as he tried to get free. I came, spewing into the heat inside him, shoving his head down in the dirt.

They let me rest for a little while after the shower and scrubbing. I sat on a little patch of soft grass with my arms folded on my knees and my head on my arms. I wasn't really tired or worn out.

I was thinking. Why had she chosen that particular game for me? It had been the very opposite of a humiliation, yet the exposure had been dazzling. And the lessons unique. Rape without guilt. Should every man experience that once in his lifetime, his capacity to use another like that, but in a situation where no real moral or physical damage is done?

I could have gotten addicted to that little game. Except that I was already getting addicted to her. It nagged at me, why had she chosen it? It was too tricky, giving me a chance to master the other one. Was she building me up for a real fall?

When I finally looked up, I saw her leaning against one of the fig trees watching me with her head to one side and her thumbs hooked in the side pockets of her suede skirt. She had the strangest expression on her face, her eyes large, her lower lip very kissable, her face girlish and soft.

I had that odd desire to speak to her, explain something to her, the same urge that had come over me in the bedroom, and again the anguish: What the hell would she care? She didn't want to know me, this woman. She wanted only to use me and that was why I was here.

Yet we were looking at each other over the distance of the little bathing place, oblivious to the racket from the ring where the same drama was being reenacted, and I was scared of her again, just as I'd been scared for hours, scared of what was going to happen next.

When she beckoned to me, there was a stirring in my loins that I could almost hear. I had a real premonition, that it wouldn't be any more macho antics right now.

I rose and walked over to her, the anxiety getting worse.

"You're very good at wrestling," she said calmly. "You can do things that a lot of new slaves can't. But it's just about time to whip you again, don't you think?"

I stared at her boots, the tight fit around her ankles. Back to her room, please, I thought. I could take anything if we were alone there again. Just thinking about it . . . I knew I was supposed to answer her, but I could not make the proper words come out.

"Blond slaves give everything away with their faces," she said, her curled finger stroking my cheek. "Ever been whipped at a real whipping post?" she asked. "For a nice large and appreciative crowd to watch?"

So here it comes.

"Well?"

"No, Madam," I said dryly with a little cold smile. Not ever for any crowd. And God, not for this crowd, not in this place! I had to think of something, something that wasn't an out-and-out entreaty. But again, nothing came out.

A handler appeared behind her, flash of hairy wrist, the *de rigueur* strap.

She said: "Take him to the whipping post. Let him walk with his hands at his sides. I like the way he looks that way, better than the other ways. And fully shackle him for the whipping. The works."

Total absence of discernible pulse. And the cold realization that if I said no and refused to move, the son of a bitch would whistle up his assistants and probably drag me to it all the same.

Well, that wouldn't happen.

"Lisa . . ." I whispered, shaking my head just a little.

Her hand came towards me again with a distinct whiff of perfume—flashes of the bedroom, the sheets, her naked under me—and closed warmly on the back of my neck.

"Shhhh. Come on, Elliott," she said, her fingers massaging my neck muscles. "You can take it, and you will, for me."

"Merciless," I whispered, clenching my teeth and looking away from her.

"Yes, exactly," she said.

PART FIVE

CATHOLIC

LUST

Roman Catholicism and homosexuality have long shared a paradoxical but intimate relationship. The church's official stance, of course, is diametrically opposed to the practice of gayness; yet male-to-male sex always seems to lurk just below the public façade.

The locations, rituals, and myths of Catholicism are fertile ground for the homoerotic imagination: candlelit cloisters, dark wooden booths in which secrets are confessed, stories of self-flaggellation and of the "passion" of men being tortured on crosses. And like the armed services, college fraternities, and other sex-segregated institutions, the Catholic priesthood has always been ripe for sexual innuendo. What do all those men *do* together? (The link would appear to be more than innuendo, as recent "inside" accounts have claimed up to 30 percent of Catholic priests are gay.)

Given these affinities, the Roman church's vigorous stance against gayness has been criticized as the worst kind of hypocrisy. And because the church has been such a singular force in opposition to the lesbian and gay rights movement, the relationship between Catholicism and gayness has recently assumed a heightened charge that often has the character of sexual tension. In clashes like ACT UP's Stop the Church demonstration—penetrating the sacred space of St. Patrick's Cathedral in New York—the gay movement and the church have acted with all the bitterness, resentment, and anger of jilted lovers.

David May draws upon these traditional links and tensions in "Hot Under the Collar" to concoct a story rife with religious imagery and themes. May comes to his subject matter with special credentials; he earned his bachelor's degree in medieval religious theater. "Hot Under the Collar" is a darkly erotic revenge tale that can be read as a political allegory about the relationship between gays and Catholics. Narrated by a jaded ex–altar boy, the story focuses on a priest who shows up at the baths in San Francisco. As if in retaliation for all of the Catholic church's oppression of gays, the narrator and a friend subject the priest to the ultimate humiliation. The story ends on a reflective, almost remorseful note. Perhaps it's never possible to shed all of one's Catholic guilt?

"Revelation," by Tom Caffrey, also concerns a Catholic priest, but this time the story is told from the priest's point of view. Worn down by years of service, Father Maguire is disillusioned and doubting his faith. Then a mysterious stranger shows up in the back of the church, wearing jeans and a leather jacket. The sexually charged stranger would seem to be an earthly manifestation of the Divine, the Word literally made flesh. But as the story progresses, we're never sure if he is an angel, or Jesus himself, or perhaps the devil in disguise. The action culminates in a truly unforgettable communion scene that gives a whole new dimension to the term "an act of faith."

DAVID MAY

HOT UNDER
THE COLLAR

BOBO WASN'T WHAT YOU'D CALL PRETTY, OR EVEN HAND-some. But he was hot in the way that was popular ten years ago, especially if you hung out South of Market. He had short brown hair, the requisite moustache, brown eyes. He was hairy and on the husky side, but he worked out and looked good naked: nice round butt, big floppy dick, the perfect tan line.

He got older, which he hadn't counted on. He turned thirty and most of us thought he was hotter than ever. But he wanted to stay young so he could act like a kid his whole life and get away with it. When he realized he wasn't going to get his wish he started taking it out on the world. Life's tough.

I met Bobo early in his career as a sex object. He was growing a beard at the time, and new beards turn me on. We fucked like crazy in the orgy room at the old Eighth and Howard, taking turns on top, slapping each other's butts and yanking each other's tits off; chewing, biting, spitting. When we'd run out of cum we licked the sweat out of each other's pits and washed ourselves off in each other's piss. The good old days.

We got together a few times after that, but sex was never the same, so we sort of became friends instead. When he shaved off his beard I lost interest in sex with him altogether.

But he was still hot. Sex came out of his pores, and he always had that hungry look in his eyes—like he was wondering where his next fuck/meal was coming from. It was intense. I got off just by being with him. We'd cruise together, or do the Cauldron and shit like that. We were cruise buddies, mainly. Once in a while we'd take turns doing the same stud, but we never just had sex with each other anymore. We never talked about it, but we both understood.

When we went out guys would come up to Bobo and ask when they were going to get together with him again. Bobo never really said anything. He'd just nod in his cool way and say, "Later." You never knew if "Later" meant "Talk to you later," or "We'll do it soon," or just "Fuck off." He was cold, really cold. And that was hot. Being seen with him made me hot by association, even if I wasn't the Capital-B Bastard he was.

The weird part about all this was that the guys who came over to talk to him would never call him Bobo, or even Bob. They called him names like Wayne, or Garth, or Drew. And each name had a different personality. One worked in a bank, another was a writer, another a motorcycle cop. But I knew he made deliveries for a printing company and drove a truck because he'd given me a ride home from the tubs in it that first night. So I asked him about it.

"I like sex better if I can be someone else."

"Your real name's Bob, right? Bobo's a nickname?"

"Sort of."

I stopped spending so much time with him after that. A man who won't tell you his name is a man you can't trust. And a man who doesn't like who he is, is a man who doesn't like anyone else either. I still saw him around, and talked on the phone when he called me, but I stopped calling him. We stopped hanging out together.

San Francisco's a small town in a lot of ways. After a while it gets incestuous. You feel like you'll never really meet anyone new because each guy you meet always knows some friend of yours, or has tricked with someone who tricked with you. It can feel creepy sometimes, like you don't have any privacy. Sometimes, though, if you keep your cool, you can hear good shit about some asshole who pissed you off, or an old boyfriend or lover. So meeting Joey shouldn't have surprised me, not after living here so long. But it did.

I still liked hearing Bobo's fuck stories, about how cold he could be. Like he promised a dude he'd go home and fuck him, but first the dude had to give Bobo head in the alley behind the Brig. Then after shooting his load down the dude's throat, Bobo kicked him in the balls and walked off without bothering to button-up his fly. Real cold. I kept thinking "You son-of-a-bitch, Bobo." But I still got off listening to him and could shoot a wad thinking about the shit he'd do.

Bobo had told me about Joey.

"This Catholic priest, see. And I meet him at Rich Street while I'm laying there with my butt up in the air. He's got a nice dick, so I let him fuck me, and then he fucking wants to get married and be *monogamous*! So I told him sure, like that's what I'm looking for with my butt in the air waiting for Mr. Big Dick, right? Anyway, he fucks me, again. I figure a dick as big as his and it doesn't matter what they do once it's in deep, you know? So after we fuck, he asks me out for coffee. Not a beer, man—*coffee*! So I say sure. But he wants us to leave right that second. I get up like I'm packing to leave and give up a room at Rich Street on a Friday night, and tell him to clear out his locker and I'll meet him out front. He says he'll meet me back there in my room, so I tell him I just wanna get outta there, and if I'm not in my room when he gets back to meet me out front.

"He rushes off to get his fuckin' hope chest out of the deep freeze, and I lock the door and mosey down the hall looking for a pretty piece of ass to pump myself. I meet this kid and fuck him a couple times, then I walk around, forgetting all about Joey. A little later I hear this riot goin' on out front. There he is screaming for them to let him back in 'cause I'm being kept there against my will. I wanted to laugh, but I got kinda scared 'cause he was so crazed. But the towel guys call the cops and they tell him to split 'cause he's makin' a disturbance. That's when I hear someone say, 'That guy's a priest.' And someone else says, 'And he's a major pain in the butt.' That's when I knew he was a priest. I laughed so hard. I thought it was great!"

"What did you do, then?" I asked.

"Went back to the orgy room."
See what I mean? Cold.

For a long time I thought that that was all there was to the story. Then
I met Joey.

Joey was what you call a mistake the next morning. It was a week
night and I was horny, so I went out and saw this humpy bearded Irish
man. He wasn't so much tall as massive, heavily muscled and very burly;
the kind you're surprised to see later because you remember him being
taller. And he had a great beard, the sort that waved over the face in a
series of small waves that framed his mouth. When I see a good beard
around a pair of full lips like that, I want to kiss the mouth all night
while I slam my dick down it at the same time.

Joey was a sight in worn jeans, boots, a leather jacket and a plaid
shirt opened to show his massive hairy chest—good old clone drag. He
was leaning against a cigarette machine, giving attitude I thought, but
he was the only man worth looking at that night, so I went right up
to him and said what was on my mind: "Let's go to my place and fuck
our brains out."

"Sure."

Joey, I later realized, was one of those topmen who's a topman not
because he knows how to make a bottom squirm, or because he enjoys
the power of controlling another man's body and sex with his own, but
because he's too scared to get fucked or taste cum himself.

After a guy like that fucks me I treat him like dirt, like he's
the one been screwed. With Joey it was easy, because he wanted
to feel something had happened—as if good sex weren't enough—and
that kind of womanish need for sex to be love always pisses me off.
I mean, I like being in love, too, but when a man invites me
home to fuck, I don't start picking out china patterns the moment I
cum.

It was pretty good sex. Someone must have taught him what to do
with the big meat he had hanging between his legs. While we were
fucking, he told me how good his dick felt buried deep in my bung
hole, and talking trash like that always gets me off.

"That feels so good, baby. I like the way it feels inside your hot
hole."

"Harder, man! Fuck me harder!"

He rammed it into me, hurting me deep inside my guts. His big, hairy balls slapped against my ass. My body was screaming with that hot, heavy pain that only a really good fuck can give.

Then, in all the frenzy, his dick popped out of my hole. He grabbed it in his fist.

"I'll finish jerking off," he panted.

"Get it back in there!" I screamed. "Finish inside me. Now!"

He obeyed, and in a minute his face twisted in pain as he let go of a load of ball juice, filling me up with it. I felt his dickhead swell, and pulse deep inside me as I let loose a hot, sticky wad of my own. I watched it splash against his hairy torso, and drip down onto my beard and face.

Afterwards, while we were laying on the floor and feeling all nice and sticky with sweat and cum, he got philosophical. He started talking about how casual sex was all right 'cause we "really shared something." I got up, turned the radio on and got myself a beer without offering him one. When he started talking about some guy he tricked with at the baths, I got even more annoyed. Do I need to hear about why he's in love with someone he tricked with at the tubs? Then I realized he was talking about Bobo (who he thought was a construction worker named Rich) and I got interested. I handed him a beer and sat down next to him.

"Men like that need love, and sometimes they look for it in all the wrong places."

Like you? I thought.

"Rich was the kind of man who isn't happy with the gay lifestyle, but doesn't know where to turn to have his needs met, so he goes to places like the baths and lets people use him."

I took a swallow of beer to keep from laughing. Father Joey didn't have a clue about who was using who. He kept talking, using words like "lifestyle" and "closure," which always make me barf.

"I could see right away that he and I could really connect, maybe share a life together. He was so vulnerable—"

I almost did laugh this time. Was this dude really talking about my Bobo, the man so cold he can chill a beer in his fist?

"—and I wanted to share that with him. You know, he's so unhappy, I bet he's into drugs. But that's part of the gay lifestyle, isn't it?"

I kept my mouth shut. I knew Bobo. He never did dope. He used poppers sometimes, had a beer once in a while. Most of us did. I wanted to know how much booze did this priest guy put away every day?

"I wonder what happened to him. He must have been taken advantage of somehow. He's the kind of man men can do that to; the kind
who let themselves be tied-up and raped because they think they're
getting loved. It's terrible how gays use each other."

This crap he was handing out pissed me off: Who got raped in a
bathhouse filled with guys willing to be gang-banged, tied-up, fist-
fucked? Father Joey didn't know shit. Maybe it was because I grew up
Catholic (I'd even been a fucking altar boy) and hated the church and
everything connected with it with the deep hatred that comes from
prolonged intimacy—but I began to hate him. Or maybe I just wanted
to take advantage of a "vulnerable" man.

I got down between his legs and took his cock into my mouth and
sucked it down, letting it slide into my throat. When he was hot and
hard again, I sat on his fat meat and rode it, enjoying the way it filled
up my gut and pushed another load of mine out of my balls and up my
hard cock. Then I shot it all over us.

I knew he was ready to cum when I'd finished. I hopped off of his
dick, got myself another beer and let him suffer.

He was still laying on the floor holding onto his dick when I came
out of the kitchen. His eyes begged for more.

"I gotta go to bed now."

He looked hurt. I almost changed my mind, but he got up and
dressed himself before I could. After he dressed, he stood awkwardly in
the middle of the room waiting for something. He got nothing.

"Yeah?"

"I'll see you around," he said.

"Yeah. Sure."

He left and I called Bobo.

"I met your priest," I said. "That Joey guy."

"Yeah?"

"Nice dick. He even knows what to do with it—sort of."

"Give him a little encouragement and he's okay."

"Until he opens his mouth," I said.

Bobo laughed. He enjoyed being unkind more if someone joined
in.

"Just tell him to keep his mouth shut and his dick hard," I added.

"I'll do that."

"Yeah? You gonna see him again?"

"Sure."

"What for?" I asked. "You already had him. You don't even like him."

"I want to break his balls."

I heard the excitement in Bobo's voice. His breathing was heavy.

"Can I help?" I heard myself ask.

"Sure, babe. But why? Since when is this your scene?"

"I hate priests."

I could feel Bobo salivate at the word "hate."

"Yeah," he said. "I can dig it."

I don't know what Bobo said to Father Joey, but it wasn't hard for an operator like Bobo to pee up a guy's back and tell him it's rain. They made a date for Sunday evening, when Joey's "responsibilities" were over for the week.

On Sunday morning I went to Joey's church and took communion from his own shaking hand. I looked right up into his face as he made the sign of the cross (instead of looking straight ahead like you're supposed to) and gave him the biggest shit-eating grin I could manage as I held the wafer firmly between my teeth instead of swallowing it. He almost lost it, then managed to move on to the next in line.

I left right away and spat the wafer and wine onto the church steps.

Bobo and Joey met someplace on Castro. It had been so long since Bobo had been on what he called a "date-date" (as opposed to a "fuck-date") that he was a little uncomfortable with the basic ritual of dinner, a movie and small talk. Not that it was difficult for Bobo to fake his way through the evening. Joey filled all available space with an ongoing monologue. All Bobo had to do was look like he was listening.

After the movie Bobo decided he couldn't take another minute of Joey's bullshit and managed to disappear into the crowd, grab a cab and go to the tubs where he fucked his brains out.

The phone was ringing off the hook when he got home around three the next morning. He made himself a sandwich and tried to decide what to do. Then the ringing stopped, so Bobo finished his sandwich and washed it down with half a carton of milk before going to bed. First he disconnected the phone, though—just to be safe.

After he'd been up a few hours the next day, he remembered he'd pulled the plug on his phone. It was ringing when he reconnected it, but he was expecting it this time and answered it.

"Hello?" he said with a slight quiver in his voice.

"Rich? Are you okay?"

Perfect, thought Bobo. He's worried instead of pissed-off like anyone else would be.

"Yeah. I guess . . ."

"What happened?" asked Joey. His voice was a little more urgent now, a slight trace of anger maybe. Bobo heard the shift in tone and made his move.

"I got scared, Joey. I felt so close to you and couldn't handle it, so I ran. I don't blame you for being mad."

"I'm not mad, honey. I was just worried."

Later on, when Bobo told me the whole conversation, he had me laughing so hard I couldn't breathe.

"What's next?" I asked when I was finally able to talk again.

"More of the same."

Bobo talked to Joey almost every day, and each time they talked Bobo learned more about Joey and his work, and what he did when. Like when he heard confession. Which is when I went to confession.

I sat in the confessional wearing my raunchiest Levis and a leather jacket. I smelled like grease, poppers, Crisco and recycled beer. He waited for me to start the ritual with "Forgive me, Father, for I have sinned." When I said nothing, he got nervous.

"Yes?"

"I want to suck your cock," I whispered. "I want it up my ass. I want you to piss all over me. Make me happy, Father Joey. Treat me like a pig and make me squeal. . . ."

"Stop it!"

"Or should I fuck you, Father Joey? Want to see what it looks like?" I undid my pants and pulled out a hard-on. "See it, Father Joey? Want it? Should I make a glory hole here for you so you can suck all the cum from my balls. Is that what you want?"

I spat on my palm and stroked my cock.

"What do you want?"

"You!"

He saw my fist sliding up and down my meat.

"Stop it!"

"But I'm getting close, Father! Don't you want it? Don't you want my cum?"

I heard him lick his lips behind the screen as I shot my load and watched it splatter over the walls of the confessional.

He bolted from the booth and out of the church. I put my dick back in my pants and strolled off, leaving my wad to dry on the confessional walls.

"You know what they call him?" asked Bobo over beers at the Arena that night. "They call him *Papa* Joe."

"Shit."

"Like he's a fucking rock star or something!"

"Shit," I said again.

"Use it," said Bobo. "It will strike closer."

The next Saturday evening I was back in church, sitting up front in my raunchy jeans.

He was waiting for me. He sat down next to me before Mass started.

"You don't belong here," he said.

"Sure I do. I went to confession." I gave him my best shit-eating grin.

"What do I have to do to make you leave me alone?"

I grabbed my basket in one hand and his in the other. He jumped but didn't leave.

"Meet me tonight," I said. "At the Ambush."

He nodded.

"Don't worry, Papa Joe," I said, grabbing my dick through the threadbare jeans. "I'll save it for you."

I got up and slowly swaggered down the center aisle and out of the church.

They had a date for late that night, which was unusual since it was Saturday, but Bobo had pleaded and Joey had given in.

Joey may have been an asshole, but he wasn't stupid. It'd only be a matter of time before Bobo got caught in one of his lies, or Joey saw us together, or Bobo gave him the clap (which would happen sooner or later since Bobo kept up his whoring while he "dated" Joey), and the jig would be up.

Besides, I was ready to finish it. I figured Bobo would show him up in the bar and break his heart and it'd be over. Bobo would be back on the street looking for his next victim and I'd feel vindicated. Life would go on.

Bobo and I put on leather for the occasion, and waited at the bar. Joey showed up around eleven o'clock. He'd put on jeans and a dress shirt for his "date" with Bobo later on. First he saw me and did his best to look fierce. Then he saw Bobo and smiled. Then Joey saw Bobo was in leather and had an arm around me. Joey looked confused.

"Yo, Papa Joe," said Bobo raising his beer bottle in greeting.

"Rich?"

Bobo looked at me.

"Hey, babe, is he talking to me? Anyone here named Rich?"

"Maybe you're Richie, Bobo."

Joey looked like a man drowning. "Richie?" he asked again. "Is that you?"

"What's the matter, Papa Joe? Don't you know me? I'm the man you *love*!" Bobo put an arm around Joey's shoulder and kissed him. "You wanna suck my cock?"

Before Joey could answer, Bobo turned to me and gave me a deeper, longer kiss.

"This man can *kiss*," Bobo said to Joey. "This man can suck *cock*. *This* man knows how to *fuck*. Things Papa Joe can't do 'cause he's too busy being fucking holy!"

"Why are you doing this to me? Why, Rich? Why?"

"Because it feels good."

The priest got angry now, but at me.

"You put him up to this! You turned him against me." He grabbed me by the collar of my leather jacket. *"You!"*

"Lay off, Papa!" I said breaking free. "He's been a tramp for years. Where do you get off making him as holy as you?"

Bobo laughed. Loud. He sounded like the devil.

Everyone in the bar stopped what they were doing to see what was so funny. Bobo kept laughing, and finally everyone went back to talking to each other again, which was a relief because being at the center of so much attention made me uncomfortable.

I looked back at Joey and saw for the first time that he was trembling from head to foot. At first I thought he was about to kill us, but the trembling continued. Then, in the dark of the bar, I made out that he was moving his lips, but I couldn't hear anything.

Bobo, still laughing, grabbed my arm and nodded towards the door. I followed.

We went to a few more bars, with Joey following us around like a wounded puppy. We ignored him. A couple guys tried coming on to him, but he didn't respond. He just kept looking at us and muttering quietly. When it got close to two o'clock Bobo said we should check out Ringold.

We found a good spot in the alley to view the action from. It felt like it used to, when Bobo and I spent a lot of time together, only now I wasn't sure I wanted a friend like Bobo. I felt a strange sort of intimacy with him, one that scared me—the sort that accomplices to a murder must feel after the fact. I could see now why murderers killed each other: The closeness was unbearable.

Bobo only nodded, smiling at me. As if he understood and enjoyed my discomfort. I hated him.

Suddenly Joey was with us again, but this time he spoke clearly, looking Bobo squarely in the eye. He'd stopped shaking. The crisis was over and now he understood.

"What do I have to do?" he said. "I'll do it. I'll do anything."

Bobo looked at him a moment with no expression. Then a sneer slowly crossed his face.

"Lick my boots."

Next thing I knew Joey was on all fours with his face buried in Bobo's boots.

"Shit, that gets me hot," said Bobo.

After a few minutes passed a small crowd gathered around us. Bobo pulled a key out of his jacket and dropped it on the ground.

"Remove the dog collar from my boot and hand it to me."

Joey obeyed, looking up at Bobo with that same wounded puppy face.

Bobo fastened the collar around Joey's neck.

"Since you forgot your collar, Papa Joe, you can wear this one. But since it's a dog collar, we'll have to call you Rover from now on. See this? It's the only key."

Bobo tossed the key over a fence into a junkyard. If anyone else had done that I'd think he was just mind fucking and expect him to have another key at home somewhere. With Bobo it was not just the mind fuck. There really was no other key.

Now Bobo undid his fly and pulled out a hard dick.

"Come on, Rover, fetch!"

Joey went down as far as he could, but that wasn't good enough.

Bobo grabbed each of Joey/Rover's ears and shoved his meat all the way down. Joey gagged and Bobo kept pumping, riding the fucker's mouth like it was pussy. In a minute he came.

"It's my buddy's turn, now."

Bobo pushed Joey's face into my crotch. Joey, still coughing cum, undid my jeans and went for it. I felt his teeth barely scrape my cock.

"Hey, Rover, no teeth!" I smacked him on the side of his head, then shoved my meat all the way down. "Yeah, fucker, that's better."

I fucked his face with all the rage left in me, and when I shot my spunk down his throat I held his head firmly against my pubes so he'd choke on the load.

We were surrounded now by a small crowd. Lots of them had already pulled out their meat. Bobo grabbed the guy with the biggest dick and pushed Joey's face onto the huge cock. Joey gagged and choked as Bobo pushed his face further down the man's pole. The guy with the big meat knew the score, though, and grabbed each ear and fucked like crazy. When he finished, he kicked Joey to the ground where he started coughing up cum and bile.

"Bad dog! You made a mess! Now lick it up!"

To my horror, he obeyed.

"Hey man, haven't we done enough?"

"Enough? Shit! If you don't like it, fuck off."

But I did like it. I was more turned on than ever.

Next Bobo had Joey/Rover on all fours with his pants down. Guys lined up to fuck both ends. He grunted and groaned, but made no resistance. I saw his ass bleed from the first dry fuck.

The action got wilder. His ass was whipped with a belt, his face slapped. He drank piss, rimmed ass.

Bobo and I stood by and watched. When Bobo was ready again, he stepped up and shoved his dick in Joey's ass.

"Hey man, wait your turn," someone protested.

"He's my slave, fucker."

Bobo slammed the guy's stomach with his fist without missing a thrust from the furious pace of fucking Joey's ass.

"Hey, buddy," Bobo said to me. "You fuck his face again while I do his butt. How about it?"

I stepped up, took my place and shoved it in. I came in minutes, feeling my rage at Joey and all he stood for, released with a final load down his throat. My load was huge, filling his mouth. He choked and I felt his teeth again. I slapped him hard in the head.

I pulled out and held him steady while Bobo fucked him. He was whipping Joey's ass with a belt now, the heavy buckle tearing up the poor fucker's ass.

Bobo came with a scream and collapsed in a pile on Joey's back. Joey remained steady on all fours, supporting Bobo's weight. I looked at Joey's face and saw it was wet with tears.

I walked across the street to get away from the crowd. I stood awhile and watched them, feeling strangely empty, like I was hollow inside.

"Bad dog!" I heard Bobo say. "You got my dick dirty with your shit. That does it, boy. Lick it off! Now!"

I heard Joey get sick as he tried to obey. Someone said, "Make him lick it up."

It was time to leave.

As I reached Folsom Street I saw cop cars and paddy wagons pull into Ringold Alley, blocking the street. The neighbors had had enough of our noisy little orgy and called the cops. And San Francisco cops are always eager to bust a bunch of faggots.

I knew what would happen without hanging around to watch: megaphones, searchlights, men running for cover and scrambling over fences to escape the cops.

Bobo, of course, would get away.

Papa Joe would be arrested and lose everything.

Bobo disappeared soon after that.

There are always rumors when someone picks up and leaves without a word. Some whispered about the "gay cancer" that had not yet made the headlines. Others thought he'd been murdered, and that seemed more likely to me. You can only fuck people over so long before you mess with the wrong dude.

But I didn't care anymore and never tried to find out.

He called a few days after the Ringold episode to tell me he got away by hiding in the junkyard. Like I was worried, right?

"And Joey?" I asked. "What happened to him?"

"Who? Oh, him. Don't know. Got busted, I guess. Hey, I wonder how he liked being in handcuffs?"

Like I said, a Capital-B Bastard. And now I was one, too.

TOM CAFFREY

REVELATION

FATHER JOHN MAGUIRE WAS NOT HAVING A GOOD DAY.
Morning mass had been sparsely attended, with only a handful of the
homeless looking for somewhere warmer than the subway grates to rest
for a few moments. Oddly, some of them seemed to know the complicated ritual of sitting and standing as well as, if not better than, his
usual parishioners. They had listened attentively to his message about
the Crucifixion, their unwashed faces staring up childlike and wondering, then left to resume their hunt for discarded cans and leftover
sandwiches.

The afternoon had not fared much better, spent in the tight confines of the confessional listening to the weekly laundry list of petty
misdemeanors of a young woman by the name of Rose Mahoney. A thin,
lipless girl who whispered her transgressions from behind the screen as
if she were passing on the secrets of life and death, Rose normally came
for her weekly absolution with little of interest to tell him. This week's
admitted sins included the imbibing of several glasses of cooking sherry,

the occasional taking of the Lord's name in vain and, rather unexpectedly, a fleeting lustful thought and temptation to masturbate, for which Maguire rewarded her with three Hail Marys, impressed by her progress.

Once the girl had gone, Maguire had sat in the airless cell for several hours, ignoring the calls of his assistant and thinking. He had remained there until the bells began to ring for vespers, and only then reluctantly dragged himself wearily from the comforting darkness. Rain was pouring down Amsterdam Avenue, and the candles scattered throughout the sanctuary did little to drive out the shadows of the November dusk. The few people who scuttled in beneath their umbrellas greeted him cursorily and headed to their seats, wrapped in unhappiness and damp coats.

When the final bell pealed, Maguire plodded the length of the sanctuary and climbed once more behind the pulpit. As he looked out at the scattered figures waiting for him to begin, the church suddenly seemed too large, the stone walls rising up and disappearing into the eaves. The stained-glass windows, with their colorful depictions of the saints and apostles, frowned down upon him with disapproving eyes. The altar boys moved about the sides of his vision like moths flapping around a flame. His head began to pound horribly, and he thought for a moment that he might faint.

As he was trying to clear the ache in his temple, one of the big wooden doors at the end of the sanctuary opened with a crash and a man entered, bringing the wind and the rain with him. From behind the pulpit, a crack appeared in the gloom that had enshrouded Maguire, and everything else faded into shadow as he looked up and his eyes were drawn to the stranger standing at the back of the church. While he could not see the man's face, he could see that he was tall and muscular, with the powerful body of someone accustomed to hard work. His short black hair was slick with rain, clinging to his head like wet leaves, and he wore dirty jeans and a battered black leather jacket.

He shut the door behind him with a shove of one black boot, then ran a hand through his hair, scattering rain, and leaving it slightly tousled, a stray shock falling across his forehead. He walked slowly up the aisle and took a seat in the last row. Leaning back, he placed his boots on the back of the pew in front of him and put his hands along the back of his own seat. Besides Maguire, no one seemed to take the least notice of either him or his unorthodox behavior, even though one big boot was perilously close to the head of one of the more elderly members of the congregation and one arm hung loosely about the shoulders of George Pederson, the head deacon and a local banker of no small wealth.

Pulling his gaze from the man's face, Maguire continued with the service. Whoever the man was, his apparent invisibility to everyone else was not something the priest wanted to think about. He concentrated instead on the notes in front of him, which he had hastily scribbled a few minutes before the last person had sat down. The theme of his sermon was faith, something he now had very little of, and he was trying his best to muster up some semblance of sincerity. He had had it once, in abundance. As a student at St. Anselm's Seminary he had believed wholeheartedly that the world was a good place that only needed a little of his help to become a wonderful one.

But ten years of patient serving had worn him down. Things had only gotten worse, and the clear, bright joy that he had once conjured up so easily had faded into a heavy stone in the center of his chest. As he watched the parishioners of St. Mary's grow older and increasingly more unhappy despite his weekly attempts to show them that faith could wake them out of a spiritual stupor, he had become more and more bitter and doubtful. Now the ritual of proclaiming a belief in something he couldn't see was beginning to appear to him as the act of a madman talking to spirits.

He managed to finish his sermon without faltering, feeling the whole time the man's gaze on him like a shadow. The service over, he gave the call for communion, and a line began to form as people shuffled slowly into the aisles and came forward to kneel at the mahogany rail in front of the altar. Maguire dutifully approached the first celebrant, attempting to avoid looking into her face. It was when he saw the faces that he was the most saddened; seeing in the eyes and the nervous set of the jaw as they opened their sticky mouths to receive the wine and the host that they were drawn forward more by guilt than by joy. Often he had to fight back an overwhelming urge to smack them forcefully across the cheeks, instead whispering "The blood of Christ, shed for you," playing his part in their weekly pantomime.

He moved swiftly through the row of partakers, administering first the wine and then the wafers, like a spiritual vending machine doling out candy for the soul. They came in waves, falling onto the worn velvet cushions before the rail and retreating again once they were fed, like seabirds scavenging the beach for picnic scraps. When he came to the end of the last row, he saw the hands clasped on the rail, and knew instantly that they belonged to the man from the last pew. The fingers were long and thick, the pale moons of the nails clipped neatly and evenly. Black hairs sprinkled the knuckles, and he could see that the same hair began again at the solid wrists. There was a thin, pale scar running over the back of the left hand, disappearing into the cleft between the middle and ring fingers.

Maguire studied the hands for a moment, wondering what had made the scar and marvelling that such work-hardened hands could be so clean; he had expected to see a fine coating of oil or paint on them. Then he remembered the cup in his hands, and stirred back to life. Moving his gaze up, he saw that the man wore a dark blue shirt, the first two buttons undone to reveal a patch of dark hair at the throat. Looking further, he saw that the man was looking back at him intensely, and that he had large, dark eyes that glinted faintly with gold, like stones streaked with precious metal. His nose was straight and perfectly rounded at the end, and his wide jaw narrowed into a stubble-dusted chin with a small cleft just below full lips.

The man looked at Maguire expectantly, as if he were waiting for the priest to answer a question he already knew the response to. Fighting a strong urge to run, Maguire brought the cup to the man's mouth, noticing suddenly how heavy the chalice felt against his palm, which was trembling. As he tipped the cup forward, he watched the sensuous lips part, allowing the dark wine to flow over them. A drop slipped and began to run down the man's chin, and Maguire wiped it away quickly with the cloth. He did not, as was his usual custom, wipe the edge of the chalice where the man had drunk from it.

Returning the cup to his acolyte, he took a wafer from the pile on the plate, wondering at the thinness of it as he held it lightly between his fingers. He waited for the man to hold out his hands to take the bread, as most of them did, but he simply raised his head and opened his mouth to be fed. Maguire held out the wafer, placing it on the outstretched tongue and reciting, "The body of Christ, broken for you." As he received the host, the man opened his mouth slightly wider, taking in not only the sacrament but Maguire's finger as well. The priest felt the warmth of his lips as the man closed his mouth, then sucked softly, his tongue enfolding Maguire's finger. The rest of his hand was holding the man's chin and he felt the unshaven beard pressing against his palm.

It was over in a matter of seconds, and then Maguire felt the smoothness of the man's teeth as he pulled his hand away. He saw that the man was still looking into his face, only now a slight smile teased at the corners of his mouth. Maguire turned back to the altar quickly, trying to get the sensation of the man's tongue against his skin out of his head. He wrapped the remaining hosts in their cloth and then raised the cup to drain the last dregs of wine. He could still see the faint impression left by the man's lips, the fine lines of his flesh in sharp relief against the cold silver. He paused, then placed the cup at the foot of the cross that stood on the altar. Later he would drink the remaining wine, as the service demanded.

When he turned back to the pulpit, the man was once again seated in the last pew. The choir swept through the final hymn and settled into the threefold amen. Maguire, barely hearing the last note die away, tore his gaze painfully away from the man in the last row and stood for the benediction.

The sanctuary emptied quickly after that, as people rushed home to dinners and evening plans, their consciences cleansed for another week. Maguire busied himself with the ceremony of extinguishing the candles and folding the white linen cloth. As he went about the work of cleaning up, he avoided touching the chalice or looking at the wine. He did not know why, but he could not bring himself to taste what had passed the lips of the stranger in the last row. He had not watched to see where the man went after the service, or whether anyone else had seen him go. The whole incident had disturbed him, and he preferred not to think about it.

A voice behind him broke the stillness of the air. "You feed your flock well, Father."

Maguire whirled around, and saw the man leaning against the communion railing.

"Can I help you?" the priest stammered, suddenly very much aware that he was alone in the church.

The man opened the small gate that gave access to the altar area and walked slowly towards him, his boots tapping a steady rhythm on the floor. He moved with liquid strides, his weight shifting back and forth from side to side like an animal content with the knowledge that it is in complete control of a situation. He stopped several feet from Maguire. "Faith, Father," he said. "I'd like to talk to you about faith."

Maguire cleared his throat. "What exactly did you want to talk about?"

The man smiled, revealing the whiteness of his teeth. Maguire's hand burned in recognition, and he put it behind him, pressing it tightly into the small of his back.

"It's hard, isn't it, Father? To believe, I mean."

Maguire ran his free hand through his hair. He couldn't look the man in the eyes. "It is," he said slowly. "Very hard sometimes."

The man came closer. He ran his hand along the railing as he moved, trailing his fingers along it lightly as he moved.

"Sometimes, you feel as if it isn't worth doing any more," he said. "As if there really isn't any reason to go on doing anything, any of this. You give and give but don't seem to get anything in return."

He stopped in front of the priest. Maguire stared at his boots, fascinated by their shiny blackness, by the way he could move so quietly in such large shoes. The man reached out and ran his hand up Maguire's chest, pushing his chin up so that he was staring right into the black and gold eyes. Maguire realized that the man was a good six inches taller than he. "Am I right, Father?"

Maguire nodded. The man's smile widened. He moved his hand up along Maguire's cheek to his hair, entwining his fingers in it. Bringing his hand towards his chest, he pulled Maguire forward, forcing the priest's mouth against his own. Maguire felt the soft lips press heavily against him, the roughness of the man's unshaven skin scraping his face. He tried to keep his teeth clenched and not let the man in, but in the end he couldn't. He gave way, parting his lips and letting the stranger kiss him deeply, his tongue filling his mouth with wet heat. He tasted the sweetness of the man's mouth, was drawn into the warmth of him by the force of his breath and the pressure of the rough hand on his neck.

The man released him, and Maguire stumbled back, catching himself on the corner of the altar. He steadied himself and caught his breath. His neck ached from where the strong fingers had grasped it, and his mouth burned. The man had bit his lip, and the earthy taste of blood teased at his tongue.

The man was watching Maguire intently, and the priest felt as if he were looking deeply into the center of a pool of dark water, trying to catch a glimpse of something that lived at the bottom and kept scuttling in and out of view. He stared transfixed as the man removed his jacket and began to unbutton his shirt, watching numbly as the fingers slid the buttons from their closings, the fabric slipping apart to reveal a broad chest thick with dark hair. The man pulled the shirttail from the waist of his jeans and undid the remaining buttons until the front of his shirt hung open.

Hair covered his well-muscled torso in fernlike sprays, running down his abdomen in a wide swatch before disappearing into his jeans. His nipples stood out cinnamon-colored against his skin, and a small gold circle pierced the right one cleanly like a halo. He ran a broad hand over the planes of his belly and up to the ring, twisting it silently between his fingertips.

The man reached forward and took Maguire's hand, placing it on his chest. The hair felt rough beneath his fingers, and the skin radiated a warmth that seared his flesh and sent shivers through him. He moved his hand down tentatively, feeling the curves and valleys formed by the man's bone and muscle, covering the expanse of his wide torso with trembling fingers. He put his other hand on the ringless nipple, feeling it press into his palm like a small tongue.

He ran his hands down, stopping when he reached the border marked by the man's waistband. He didn't know what would happen next, but he knew to wait until he was told.

"Sometimes, Father," the man said softly, "faith needs to be restored."

He put his hand on Maguire's shoulder and pushed him down to his knees. From his position on the floor, Maguire was looking directly into the well-worn crotch of the man's jeans. He saw the whiteness of the creases where they slid around the man's heavy cock and full balls, the cloth worn thin and smooth from constant contact with his body. There was a threadbare spot where the fat cockhead swelled out and threatened to break through, and the priest could see a glimpse of flesh through the straining threads. Suddenly he needed desperately to know what was beneath the faded denim.

But the man had other ideas. He lifted one booted foot and placed it on the priest's shoulder, rubbing it against his cheek. Maguire could smell the wetness of the leather enter his nostrils, felt the heaviness of the boot against the bones of his shoulder.

"Worship is such an individual experience, don't you think, Father?" the man said. "We all need something different from our god."

Maguire nodded as the man ran the boot across his face and over his lips. The leather was old and worn soft and smooth from repeated rubbing and exposure to the wind and water. The priest licked tentatively with his tongue, tasting the faintly musty scent of the cowskin and the man's scent mingled with the more recent addition of rain. The stipples of the hide teased his lips, and his mind was filled with the image of the man walking in the boots over city streets and faraway roads, the miles of wear impressing themselves into the leather like an imprint of his travels, the bones of the man's foot softening the resistant leather with each step.

He ran his mouth over the black skin as if kissing the foot that lay beneath it, trying to reach through the tough leather to caress the toes and the skin made rough by miles of walking. He felt the curve of the boot over the toe and then the valley where it joined the sole. Soon he was eagerly washing, slurping at the leather, grinding his mouth against it. He ran his lips along the thick stitching on the sides, caressing the seam with his tongue. As he did it, snatches of thoughts, half formed, swirled through his mind mixed with the peculiar ecstasy he was experiencing from worshiping the man's feet. Was sex perhaps just another kind of religion, just as visceral and heart-stopping as the celebration of the eucharist? Was he in some way drawing closer to his own soul, becoming more alive? He felt that somehow this was true, but the answer danced just out of reach.

His hands were holding the boot tenderly as the man leaned against the altar staring down at Maguire and pinching his tits, twisting the gold ring slowly. The leather was warming under the priest's searching fingers, and he marvelled at how alive it felt. He was also aware that his prick was straining against the pants he wore under his robes. It pressed along his belly painfully, and he wanted very much to touch it. But attending to the man's boots called him, and he knew that stopping now to free his cock would break the spell that held him tightly in its grip.

He noticed, too, that the man had a hard-on. It stretched down his left leg, the fabric bulging out like a pale blue vein beneath the skin of the jeans. Maguire reached forward hesitantly, expecting the man to push him away. But when he looked up, the man simply nodded and he continued, his fingers fumbling uneasily with the buttons. Finally, he managed to get the first one undone. After that, the others came easily, sliding open like the locks of a hidden door. He saw that the dark hair formed a thick patch, and pulled at the sides of the man's pants to better see what grew in the strange garden.

As they slid over his legs, his cock came into view. As thick as Maguire's wrist, it arced downwards, pushed forward by a set of large hairless balls that swung like ripe fruit beneath it, the ballsac stretching under their weight. The oversized head was round and tapered to a blunt point, halved on its underside by a valley that led to a dark piss slit surrounded by tiny pink lips.

Maguire stared at the big prick in front of him, watching the balls rise and fall with the man's breathing. He reached up and cupped the sack in his hand, feeling it roll over the sides of his palm, sensing the life within it. He ran his fingers along the thick shaft, tracing the hairs that covered the first several inches before giving way to smooth warm flesh.

He leaned forward and kissed the heavy knob at the end, his lips parting and his tongue sliding into the mouth of the pisshole, tracing the smooth curve of the head as it ran down and then back up and over the shaft in an arc. He put his mouth carefully around the tip, letting his lips close over it and tasting the thick scent that filled his head.

The man's hand fell on his neck, urging him forward. The head slipped into Maguire's throat, blocking his breathing and forcing him to take in air through his nose. Still the man didn't stop. He pushed several more inches into the priest's gullet. Then he began to work himself slowly in and out, pulling the head along Maguire's tongue until it reached his lips, then drilling back in, each time forcing another inch in. Maguire soon learned to adjust to the thickness and sucked eagerly at the huge tool working his mouth.

The man leaned forward, shoving his entire prick into Maguire's face. The priest shuddered, gagging on the meat that poured past his lips, the hair that scratched at his lips and tongue. Then his nose was pressed against the man's stomach, his chin nestled in the warm ballsac between his legs. The man's full length snaked into him, the vein under his dick beating fiercely against Maguire's tongue and filling his throat with heat.

Again the man worked his way out, and Maguire was able to suck more easily, slurping hungrily at the head as it exited his mouth. The man didn't move, so Maguire continued to bathe the head, rolling his tongue around and around the big crown while kneading the balls in his fingers. He slid his tongue along the veiny shaft, tracing the hardness to its root in the man's crotch. When he felt the prick melt into the softness of the man's ballsac, he began to lick in wide strokes, washing the pouch eagerly. Holding the beating cock in one hand, he burrowed deeper into the musky jungle between the man's legs, sucking at the hair on his thighs, rubbing the precious contents of his sack against his lips.

Maguire slipped one of the fat round balls into his mouth, sucking gently and letting his tongue feel the weight of it. It felt to him like eating the egg of a strange bird, and he thought of the sweet syrup he knew lay at its center. Letting the nut slip out of his mouth, he slid back up the man's prick, licking every inch until he reached the pinnacle once more. A thick stream of cockjuice was flowing from the man's hole, and Maguire lapped at it eagerly. He slid his lips around the tip, milking it slowly and steadily. With his hand he pumped the shaft, matching the motions so that the man's dick became a part of a machine made of flesh and blood and bone, a piston that worked its way in and out of the channel of Maguire's throat.

The man moaned above him, a deep growl that rang in the priest's ears. He was using Maguire's mouth for his pleasure, thrusting quickly and savagely, his big hand pressing the priest's face against his groin until his balls slapped dully against his lips. This excited Maguire, and he felt something in himself open up as the big cock burrowed in his throat. This was something he could feel, something he could grasp on to and believe in with all of his heart. He sucked eagerly and needfully, taking from the man what he so desperately needed.

Suddenly the man pulled out of Maguire's mouth, leaving him gasping for breath, a string of cockslime dangling from his lips like a broken spiderweb. He stood back, smiling, and picked up the chalice from its place at the foot of the cross. Holding it in one hand, he continued to jack his tool, his big hand wrapped so tightly around his shaft wet with Maguire's spit that the head blazed a deep purple. His balls rose and fell like clockwork with the motion of his fist, and the priest stared at them, awed by their raw beauty.

Watching the man jack off reminded Maguire of the pictures of martyrs he used to look at in the seminary library, their bodies pierced and torn but their faces masks of ecstasy, as if the purity of pain were also the perfect joy. The man was wholly caught up in the rapture of his own prick, his face reflecting every pull and tug of his hand, lines of pain and pleasure crossing his lips as he groaned to the machinations of his prick and balls. He stretched his dick out in front of him, his hand pulling it down and out to its full length, the head pointing into the cup he held below it. Drops of precum slid from his gasping slit and fell fat and wet into the remains of the sacred blood of Christ.

Maguire was dimly aware that he should be outraged at this, but instead he was overcome by the purity of the act.

As the priest stared, the man tensed, his hand grasping his balls tightly around the base. The engorged cockhead grew even larger as blood roared into it and a flash of white spilled from its lips, falling in long ropes into the chalice. The man continued to come, his seed streaming out in spurt after spurt, his fingers pumping his balls for the last drops. When he had finished coming, he put one long finger into the cup and stirred slowly, mixing his spunk with the wine. He lifted his hand, drawing out a thin strand of wine-colored cum, then slowly licked the liquid off, sucking his finger deep into his mouth.

Setting the chalice down, he carefully removed his boots and pants, folding them and setting them aside. Completely naked, he shone with a pale gleam of sweat that looked to Maguire's eyes almost like moonlight. His thick legs were covered in the same hair that spread over the rest of his body, and he somehow seemed more complete without clothes than with them, as if the jeans and jacket had been a disguise to hide what he really was.

He picked up the chalice and stepped toward Maguire, his bare feet making no sound on the stone. Leaning down, he offered the cup to the priest, holding it against his lips as if he were now the one administering communion.

"Faith, Father," he said, "comes only to those who partake."

Maguire shut his eyes and drank. The mixture of cum and wine filled his mouth and he gulped, tasting the mingled flavors of the juice and the man's scent. His hands trembled as he tried to hold the man's hand back, to stop the flow that filled his mouth. But the stream came thick and steady, and he nearly choked getting it down.

When he had drained the cup almost to the bottom, the man pulled it away. Maguire opened his eyes and saw that the man was smiling at him and holding out his hands. The priest took the offered hands and was pulled to his feet. The man came forward and lifted the robe from around his head, leaving him wearing the black pants and shirt that were under it.

The man's cock was hard again, jutting out from his body and up towards his belly. He undid Maguire's shirt, pulling the buttons open roughly. He pulled it off and tossed it on the floor. Then he undid the priest's pants, shoving them down his legs. Maguire stepped out of them, standing naked before the man wearing only the silver cross around his neck. The man reached forward and pulled on Maguire's cross, snapping the chain easily. He held it up in front of him, watching it turn in the air slowly like a bird on a string unable to fly away.

"Symbols, Father," he said, "are so important. They help us believe in what we can't see."

Maguire winced as the man grasped his balls tightly and pulled them down and away from his body. Holding the cold metal of the cross tightly against the tender area below the priest's asshole, the man wrapped the chain around his balls and cock, pulling it taut until the metal bit into Maguire's skin. The tiebeam of the cross pressed painfully between his balls, one falling on either side of it. His prick, engorged with blood, stuck stiffly out, the chain encircling it and binding it to the crucifix.

The man turned Maguire and came up behind him. Dipping his hand into the chalice, he took the remaining wine and stroked it onto his dick. His thick fingers slid between Maguire's asscheeks, coating his crack with wine and cum.

"Do you believe in miracles, Father?" he said, his voice low in Maguire's ear.

The priest shook his head. "I don't know," he said slowly. "I've always thought that miracles belonged only to those who talked to angels."

The man laughed. The head of his cock was tickling Maguire's hole, rubbing teasingly against the tight opening.

"Angels come in many forms, Father," he said, and slid his prick deep into the priest's ass.

Maguire's mouth flew open as a searing pain tore through his body, threatening to shatter his bones. But no sound came out, only a short burst of air. He leaned forward across the altar, his head resting at the foot of the cross, his lips open in an unspoken prayer. The man's cock throbbed deep inside his belly, pulsing with heat, each spasm sending new tremors throughout the priest's burning bowels.

The man pulled back, his cockhead ripping through Maguire's guts like hot lead. Then he roared back in, slamming against the priest's ass and pushing the cross lashed to the priest's cock against his nuts. He grasped Maguire around the waist and began pumping at his aching hole steadily, each thrust slapping painfully against his bound balls.

Maguire lay under the man's body like a sacrifice, the pain clawing at his insides. His hands held tightly to the sides of the altar, his heart beating ferociously in his chest like an animal in a trap. He fought to keep the pain from overcoming him, tried to ignore the grasp of the chain around his balls and the cock in his ass.

Then, almost as quickly as it had come, the pain began to fade. It became a part of him. As the big prick beat against him, he let each thrust travel through him, welcomed the pain as pleasure, the fucking as a holy act. He let himself open to what was happening. The man's thrusts became quicker, his nine inches ramming in and sliding out on the wine and come. His fingers gripped the priest's asscheeks tightly, bruising the soft skin.

Having his ass plowed by this strange angel became for Maguire an awakening from the sleep that had plagued him for so long. He felt his own prick stiff and hungry beneath him, rubbing against the altar as the man's weight bore down on him again and again, the trinity of his cock and balls touching his soul.

"Do you feel it, Father?" the man gasped. "Do you believe now?"

Maguire nodded, feeling the flesh inside him stiffen and swell, and he knew it was almost time. The man, sensing it also, plunged into the hungry chute, pushing his head deep into the priest's welcoming hole. Maguire's balls ached as they strained against their constraint. He felt a storm break loose in him, a wave of pleasure wash up and over his mind as he came in long spurts, coating his belly with sticky jism that fell to the stone floor in heavy drops. At the same time, the man let out a roar that echoed through the sanctuary and shot in his bowels, a thick load that streamed out in a rush and flooded his insides with heat. The giant piece swelled and pulsed, and each time Maguire's aching muscles clamped around it, sucking the last drops.

The man pulled out, leaving Maguire's hole satisfied and renewed, and began to put on his clothes without a word. The priest lay spent on the altar, the man's cum slipping down his leg, his own cock half hard and a dull ache in his balls. He did not turn to look at the man, but as he listened to him leave he knew that the next time he needed it faith would come very quickly to him.

PART SIX

OBSESSION

We all have crushes. Certain people or images get lodged in our minds and will not leave, no matter how hard we try to shake them. Our entire existence seems to hinge on obtaining the object of our desire. This kind of self-absorbed attraction can be deeply sustaining. We never feel so alive as when we are in hot pursuit, when all of our thoughts and senses are united in a single, burning goal. But obsession can also be destructive, and it's a thin line between the two.

Gay men grow up assuming that we cannot, and will never, obtain the objects of our desire, because society tells us that that desire is wrong. We become accustomed to fixating on the unattainable—if all sex with men is forbidden, a crush on Marky Mark is no more far-fetched than a crush on the guy who pumps gas at the corner store. When we come out and discover that we *can* be sexual with men, we are prone to forget that there will still be many men who, for whatever reasons, we cannot or should not get involved with. We can easily get swept up in coun-terproductive, even dangerous obsessions.

Martin Palmer does not fit the standard profile of the gay erotic writer. In his late sixties, a practicing doctor in Anchorage, Alaska, he has the refined sensibilities of the southern gentry into which he was born. Yet Palmer has created, in "Love Pitched His Mansion" a remarkable piece of explicitly sexual writing.

The essay is a detailed confession of Palmer's obsessive multiyear relationship with a man who first came to him as a patient seeking a draft deferment from Vietnam. Palmer describes Wayne as ugly, abusive, cold, and reckless, yet all these qualities add to his attractiveness. Driven by his paradoxical attraction, Palmer crosses all the bounds of his professional code as a doctor, of his bourgeois social standing, and—when the men are reunited in the 1980s—of his medical knowledge about safe sex practices. Describing with brutal honesty his dependence on this abuser of people and drugs, Palmer captures the essence of sexual obsession. The writing is all the more remarkable because Palmer describes his thoroughly irrational passion with a doctor's distanced, objective analysis. The results are chilling.

"Bravo, Romeo," is Kevin Bourke's exploration of a more conventional romantic obsession. In tightly compressed language mimicking the urgency of heightened desire, he conveys the feeling of being immersed in that stage of love when the world seems to extend no farther than the other person's body. The ironic subtitle, "Welcome to Sex in the Nineties," comments on the resurgence of romance among a generation of men for whom casual sex is fraught with risk.

Most of us have certain sexual activities or scenes that consistently turn us on. We know what gets us off, and we tend to stick with it. In "Pink Santa Claus," Leigh Rutledge writes about one character's fetish for a certain fantasy scene. Rutledge is a prolific writer whose erotic work is often tinged with romance and wistfulness. This story, although about what some would consider a bizarre sexual obsession, ends up being an extraordinarily tender portrait of two men. While most of us will not share the character's particular fetish, the story speaks to the fantasies many of us do have of being young again, full of all the innocence and hope of children during the holidays.

A fetish quite common among gay men is for bodies shaved smooth of hair. For some, the act of shaving another man becomes an important sexual ritual; to work a dangerously sharp blade over the most vulnerable zones of another man's body is the ultimate act of power and trust. Owen Keehnen explores the power dynamics of the act in "Shaving

Kevin." Here, shaving is a tool of domination, a means of establishing order in a relationship.

"Gerïon" is another story about an obsessive relationship based on power and domination. Patrick Carr writes with all the grittiness and anger of the streets of lower Manhattan, turning them into a contemporary version of Dante's *Inferno*. The narrator, recently withdrawn from heroin, roams the streets looking for something to satisfy him the way the drug could not. He encounters a man who by conventional standards should not be attractive: a filthy street junky panhandling for money. But the narrator can see himself in the young junkie and seizes the opportunity to take out all the pain and frustration of withdrawal on another body. The darkly violent encounter Carr describes, like Martin Palmer's essay, reveals the dangerous edge of obsession.

MARTIN PALMER

LOVE PITCHED
HIS MANSION

"WHAT'S HAPPENIN', MAN." IT WASN'T A QUESTION. IT WAS the usual opening from a man who for me was sex made flesh and blood. He was an asshole, an abuser of men, women, alcohol, cocaine, and animals. And probably kids, if he could get away with it. But there it was: That ploy I hadn't heard for six or seven years. It hadn't changed, and neither had my reaction when I heard it: instant lust.

The year was 1986 and I was fifty-nine years old when he popped into my life once more after disappearing in the late seventies. I encountered him for the first time in 1970 when he, twenty-two years old, came to me as a patient. The war in Vietnam had by then split all of us into for and against, and opposed as I was to it, I was able to get the draft off the backs of several young men by requesting deferral for medical reasons. A few were gay and were straightforward about the claim. Others swore to me that they would mutilate themselves before the draft got them. They weren't political; they were scared and felt desperate at the idea of being sent over to be slaughtered or maimed.

That's the way it was in those times. I looked for any kind of
hangups which could be "psychologically unacceptable" to the armed
services and magnified these in appropriate letters to the draft board.

Some straights were pushed enough to claim to be homosexual.
They knew that I was gay, so that was easy enough to see through. They
were lousy pretenders and would have given gayness a bad name. It was
in this context that Wayne showed up in my office that day.

When I came into the consulting room he was out of his shirt and
jeans (underwear was wuss), thrusting his body, his erection, and a bag-
gie of weed at me all at once, wearing nothing but a sly leer.

A physician sees people in various states of nakedness all the time;
it goes with the job. And all sorts of bodies from the dazzling to the
decrepit, in all kinds of modes. One registers this and one gets on with
what's to be done, from simple physicals to taking up complex diag-
nostic problems.

Ordinarily these are not sexy situations. The work can be as routine
as any office job. Then someone like Wayne walks in and the room
shudders in an earthquake of sexual tension. He was ugly. It was the
kind of ugliness that is lascivious. His body was awkward, but its parts
were perfect and wholly masculine. He wasn't neat and clean and sweet
smelling.

But in some people that's a turn-on. And above all he was knowing.
He always took chances. He aimed at exactly the effect he produced with
a fuck-it recklessness that took my breath away. What he was after that
day was a medical draft deferment and he had no inhibitions about using
any means at hand to get it.

"Like it?" It wasn't a question. He read my expression. I knew he
had seen it often enough on others. "Here." He lay down on the examining table, spread his legs, then reached for my hand to put it on
his dick, its head half out of a taut foreskin.

"Not here," I finally said. I remember my hand shaking a little as
I pulled it back.

So we became lovers. Or, more accurately, began to get it on. Most
of the time it was at my house: in my big brass bed, on the bean bag
seat in the rec room, on the rug, in the tub, the shower, in the wing
chair, the kitchen counter. Or other times in the car, on a bike, in the
woods, a deserted parking lot, in sleeping bags, and once in a boat. It
was before the cocaine avalanche; his drugs then were speed, pot, and
alcohol, and his performances were vigorous. He discovered poppers only

later. It was before AIDS, too, and we did everything two men could do together having sex.

He worked as a cook at a barbecue joint. I'd show up at the hut where the kitchen was to watch him spear and turn big slabs of greasy ribs as he sweated, bare from the waist up, his hair coated with smoke, a muscular neck rising into his damp curls like a giant phallus. His apron usually was blood-smeared and his army boots were slippery with gunk. I liked to grope him as he worked. Grinning, he'd thrust his hips against me, then sometimes we'd slip outside in the muskeg and swamp spruce and finish. His foreskin, thick and sliding, became a fetish with me. It was another defiance of American convention; it was the mark of an outlaw.

He always lived with women who had a house or an apartment and a car. When they were away, for vacation or business or whatever, we went to their place and had sex there. I pass one of the houses that is now a popular Alaskana bookstore, and I see us then in what was the bedroom.

He knew sex thoroughly, having been initiated into it by anyone male or female in his vicinity, including his father, from the time he was nine years old. Fishing trips to remote lakes with his old man had been a sexual rite of growing up. During visits to his brother in another town he seduced his teenage niece. He claimed she had already been broken in by the bikers she ran with. He was only keeping her from feeling lonely. He didn't kiss, or, at least, he didn't kiss men, and he always kept his thick glasses on even while he made out. Without them he looked vulnerable and a little pathetic. His crowd was the six-pack, gun, and pickup truck set and their willing women. Turning me on powerfully, he liked to brag about sessions when two of them fucked one girl at the same time. He said the sensation of their dicks sliding over each other in the same cunt was like nothing else and always made him come like a gusher. Of course, he would add, it was just a great feeling; liking that didn't make him a fucking faggot or anything.

Wayne sneered at faggots, and that included me. To go to a movie or to a bar, to be seen anywhere together or risk running into anyone he knew—hey, no way! I let him get away with it; I was the rabbit mesmerized by his snake. He liked to browse in my books, and after he heard a record of Satie he wanted more. He questioned me a lot about everything from politics to the arts. I was The Headmaster; he got a big kick out of the double meaning. He could mimic anything, especially rednecks and black slang. By then the hook was in me, clear down the throat to the gonads without a chance of coming loose.

It had been like this since the day this man swaggered into my office. I hated him one minute and couldn't do without him the next. I was humiliated; I was excited. I called him up; I tracked him down. He showed up when it suited him. Without the fix that sex with him gave me I felt as unstrung as any junkie. And what was going on in my own life at the time? I was a practicing physician, I had schedules to meet, responsibilities to undertake, my own professional and social world of colleagues and friends to maintain, university matters to attend to. The compleat bourgeois, the mask of sanity. But when he called all other plans were ditched and I was nailed in place until he showed up. Or didn't, more often. At any time, any place my thoughts segued into vivid daydreams of sex, his body. Obsession.

He used the power I gave him ruthlessly: I was a pest, an old queer; God damn it, don't call him—his old lady might get ideas. What the hell! Then, during our sessions he was as eager as I; he gave as good a blow job as he got, got on his back with his legs in the air as quick as any hustler, yelled when he came. God damn! Fuck! Shit! More, more! He ate up gay porno magazines, too, and slurped over his choices. He was just as greedy for gay porno videos, but the ones he brought from the video store had to be heterosex. He favored John Holmes, big dicks, and blond bimbos.

The women he lived with were attractive and stable in most ways except for their helplessness to disentangle themselves from him and their willingness to be degraded, just like me. And so life went on: half slave, half free. But along the way there always came a point at which he fucked things up. Just after we met and I wrote the draft board for him saying that he was unsuited for service, he was drafted anyway. He was a rotten soldier and copped an undesirable discharge within three months, screw benefits and jobs. His old ladies sooner or later kicked him out or left. So what; they were cunts anyway. He'd find another in a couple of weeks. When he got a job that was more than five bucks an hour, he showed up drunk or quit just for the hell of it. Fuuuuck! Nobody was gonna tell him what to do.

Then one day Wayne met Rita, or Rita met Wayne. She was as strong-willed as he was undisciplined, and after he bedded her a few times she saw what she wanted and determinedly set out to change his

ways. That she had an excellent job she liked, had been raised in comfortable circumstances, was willing to experiment but was not about to
give up her own way of life, impressed him. She made it clear that he
wouldn't get her except on her terms, and that made him want her
more. He saw the light, so to speak, and it included the settled life
which he had never had.

He had to change his orbit and it touched mine less and less as
months passed. I had to get used to it and finally I almost did. He
married Rita. She got him a job in the field with a large utility company,
and he got promotions. He and Rita had a son. They bought a big split-
level house in the valley, about fifty miles away. In the late seventies I
lost contact with him. Withdrawal was hell with fantasies. Cutting loose
in this piecemeal fashion was like trying to kick a three-pack-a-day habit
using only nicotine gum. After the years of Tabasco flavors, sex was once
more vanilla. But it was a relief, too, and I had room to breathe, to take
up other matters and other people. After a while I heard nothing more
about him. Finally, Wayne was out of sight. But not out of mind.

"What's happenin', man." That opening; the sound of his voice
again. Instantly I was back to the starting gate.

"Nothing." The old, tense answer; expectant, aroused again.

About an hour later Wayne showed up. When I opened the door
he walked in with that bandy-legged male swagger and stood, one hand
lifting the stained cap he always wore on and off, the other on his hip.
He had on a leather jacket in the cold spring night. He pulled off the
cap and tossed it on the rug by the couch. Balding, chunkier, with
square hands and heavily muscled forearms, his body had gained an
authority that made it even sexier. His dark moustache was thick now
and he had a couple of days' growth of beard shading his chin, starting
instant memories of how it felt on my skin. He looked around the room
then looked me over without saying anything. His Levi's were worn and
tight, with the round, white circle over his left back pocket where he
always shoved his can of Copenhagen. Sitting down on the couch, he
pulled one boot off then the other. His hands on his knees, he sat a few
minutes. He rolled his shoulders and flexed his back tightly, then he
started unbuttoning his shirt, taking his time. We were in business
again.

Three years before this I had seen my first AIDS patient killed
quickly by pneumocystis. Then the spread began. For a year and a half
I had been working with a statewide AIDS awareness and support group.

By this time my education about the disease had been thorough, and my encounters with it growing. Terrified when the test came out, I had taken it. I was negative. I counseled patients at risk.

"Did you bring any rubbers?" I looked at Wayne lying back on the couch, one hand half circling his hard dick, the other pulling his foreskin back and forth over the shiny head. I remembered I had none.

"Rubbers? Hey, man, you're the ho-mo-sex-u-al." He drew the word out sarcastically. "I'm the one who should fuckin' worry." He tilted his pelvis on the cushion and put his leg across me, the hairy calf resting on my shoulder. "Fuck that stuff." He pulled my head forward. "You think I'm gonna stay here all night?"

By then I could not stop. I slowly bent over him, feeling again the elastic springiness of his dick, that quality the best dicks have. There it was: all the familiar landmarks, the scent I knew so well, tasting him, touching it. My teeth pulled at his foreskin before my mouth settled around the head. I couldn't do that through a condom. I kept travelling. Dental dams? I had never even seen one. For the space of a breath I felt as if I had just thrown myself off a cliff, my eyes wide open all the way down. This was a free-range sexual predator I was in the ring with. As soon as the frenzy of orgasm evaporated I found myself in the swamp of anxiety at what I had done. At least, for a little while.

When we finished, the firelight played over us where we lay naked on the couch, legs propped on each other, clothes in two heaps on the rug. With both arms behind his head, drowsy, he told me what was going on with him. His marriage was busting up. He was still in his house, but alone. The kid came one weekend a month. He hated his job now. He swung his legs over and reached for his jeans, digging in the pocket to bring out a small glassine bag of white powder. He shook some carefully on a clean paper, lined it up with the blade of his pocket knife, then sniffed it quickly up one nostril then the other. He dusted his nose and his fingers. Holding his head back he inhaled loudly. He chased this with a beer from the two six-packs he brought with him. Lifting his butt to let a loud fart rip, he settled back and started fondling himself again. Everything he did aroused me.

And so the next eighteen months started. The telephone calls at odd times. The waits between them. The kid stayed with him on some weekends, and if he called then, usually late at night, we would have phone sex as he held the receiver so that I could hear the sound as he masturbated. If he said he couldn't come in, I would drive fifty miles one way to his house at 1:00 A.M., entertaining myself by futilely trying to analyze lust.

On one frigid winter night he called me from the Pilot Inn, a crummy little highway motel, where he rented one of the cabins for five hours, for extra kicks. Besides his pickup truck, he had a 1979 Lincoln. It was an erotic focus for him, he said, because he liked to screw his women in the wide backseat. He showed me the "pussy juice" stains. Parked in his garage, it became a place for us to have sex, too, and he carefully covered the seat with a bedspread before we got in, naked and shivering, to go at it.

While he still had his job in the field with the utility company he might appear at my house unexpectedly. Many times he came in his work clothes, heavy tan Carhartt coveralls. Coming in with his beer packs, he would flop down on the couch, boots stretched out, while I undid his overalls then peeled him out of his sweaty longjohns, his big erection sticking through the button fly, his cap jammed on his head. Later, while he showered I'd sit on the toilet seat naked, watching water stream down his belly and genitals, coursing down his hairy legs, as he soaped. I would join him and we would play with each other, pulling our soapy dicks, humping against our warm ass cracks, sliding around as we washed each other. Laughing, sometimes we pissed on each other in the hot sheets of water.

One big turn-on for him was to have sex in his kid's bunk bed at his house, our naked contortions as we tried to fit in them pushing us into all kinds of positions and mashing us together. I began to bring along my Polaroid camera. At first he wouldn't let me get his face or head in the pictures. But at heart he was an exhibitionist, and as soon as he got a little drunk or high it didn't matter. Videotapes of us together came later.

Wayne got deeper into cocaine. He became a beer alcoholic. Because he got sexually involved at work with a sixteen-year-old messenger girl, he lost his job and Rita got sole custody of his kid. He told me that the teenage girl had first put the make on him, and I believed it. It was like that more often than not. He said she had been seduced at the age of ten by a stepfather and that to have an orgasm she had to be mounted from behind and her neck bitten almost bloody as he held her as roughly as possible along the body. She liked it best up the ass, and this became his fetish and fantasy about young girls. He took the girl to a place called Tub N' Sun for a weekend (she told her parents she was at a girlfriend's) and banged her in the tubs and on the mats until, he said, she could barely walk out.

As he did more cocaine, he began to have rhythmic body spasms as he lay on the couch or the rug or the bed. His voice slurred and sometimes he couldn't get an erection. When he was like that his sex drive was as strong as ever, and he often lay jerking as he masturbated a limp dick on and off for hours, snorting coke and drinking beer. This never kept him from driving even though he rolled his pickup twice one winter, coming through with only a couple of scratches. One night I came home late to find him asleep in the driveway, half out of his truck. He had squatted in the snow right by the carport and crapped in the path to the door.

Then for weeks sometimes he pulled himself together and functioned more or less normally. He went back to short-order cooking and occasional sheetrocking; a lot of the other guys doing that kind of work were on coke and alcohol, too. He lost his house, but he found a woman to live with just as he always had before he married Rita. Rita arranged for him to go to a twenty-eight-day private drug and alcohol rehab center in Oregon. He called while he was there to say that he was going to stick it out, but as soon as he returned he went back to drugs.

One night after sex Wayne wanted to talk about himself, about his drugs and why he messed up with all the women in his life.

"My mom died when I was just a kid," he said drowsily. Then turning to me he went on. "You know, that's why I can't stay with any fuckin' woman for very long. I subconsciously put them in the role of my mom, and I'm pissed off as hell at her for leaving me." His face was serious.

"Bullshit!" I said. "You're quoting some shrink at the rehab place, aren't you. They put that in your head and you're using it to excuse yourself." I ran my finger along the row of three supernumerary nipples he had on each side, then squeezed his cock.

"What you are is just one mean motherfucker, and you know it."

He laughed. "You're right. Yeah, the shrink did gimme all that shit about me and my mother and women. Fuck, I never believed her." He spit brown juice into his empty beer bottle. "They're all cunts."

Living in the valley with his current woman, who had a job at a bank, he began to space our times together further apart. Dependent as I was on sex with him, I called the house when he stood me up time after time or when the tension grew. My preoccupation with him was an obsession, just as it had been in the past. It was an obsession that I could not, I did not want to, share with any of my friends. He frustrated me, and I felt ashamed of my weakness, his power. Feeling alone breeds desperation. He cunningly blocked any way I might find out where he lived with this ole lady. I went through every piece of paper and every card in his shiny, bulging wallet and in his pockets as he slept and found nothing helpful. And he humiliated me when I telephoned. Every time I dialed his number my anxiety became severe.

Only after he abused me thoroughly and hung up could I think of what I wanted to say.

It was about this time, fantasizing various kinds of revenge, that I thought up a way to punish him. It was blackmail with the Polaroids, and in this my ineptness equalled my desperation. I had his post office box number if not his house address. So on my office machine I copied three of the stack of Polaroids I had made. One was of Wayne walking into the bedroom naked. It wasn't one of the sexual ones, but it caught his body, the way he held himself, the way his masculinity jumped out at you; his sexual aura. In the second one he stood over the camera looking down, square hands on hips, dick nested in foreskin, balls and hairy crotch, sturdy legs disappearing. He had a beard at the time. It was from our wild night at the motel. The third was Wayne on all fours with a yellow candle stuck in his ass, taken during one of our all-night sessions. With them I concocted a typed note saying that the picture turned up in a suburban dump site and that the finder recognized him. The candle photo was comical and the note unconvincing, but I was dead serious, and the call from Wayne was gratifyingly quick. Where the hell, he wanted to know, were all those fucking Polaroids?

What did he mean? I stammered. Well, I cleaned out everything like that along with a lot of other stuff and threw it in the dump in big garbage bags. My lie was weak. What I wanted was to scare him, but mainly to get any kind of reconnection I could; I knew his body would follow. He didn't say anything about the copies or the note. His body followed, all right.

The next afternoon Wayne's battered pickup was in the drive, his legs lounging out of the driver's seat when I came home. Walking in behind me, he swung out of his canvas work coat and flipped a .357 magnum pistol out of the pocket, laying it carefully on a table by the door. He owned two pistols and three rifles of various calibers. Drunk, high, or sober, he was careful with guns. A gun was one thing he respected.

"I've been nervous as shit lately," he said, putting his palm flat on the pistol. "For some reason," he added after a pause. "My old lady says I'm more hell than usual to live with." He looked at me hard. "She acts like she knows something I don't."

I had pushed Wayne at times, but I had never pushed him like this. It had only been calling at home or at work and pissing him off, stirring up a small tantrum. I felt myself sweating. I didn't say anything.

"I know guys who owe me. Sometimes they break things. Like arms. Or a leg." He put his hands behind his head and shifted his hips. This always got my attention, which he already had. "And I hate like goddamn hell to be nervous. I can't concentrate. I can't sleep. Understand what I'm saying?" I nodded. "I thought you would," he said after a silence.

He reached down and slid each boot off. Grinning at me, he began unbuckling his belt, taking his time. He peeled his pants off and stood there in his dirty cotton socks. Then he reached for the gun and slipped it back into his jacket. As he came to the couch I knew that we wouldn't mention the subject again. There were no more Polaroids.

But it got his attention, and he was more careful about keeping our dates, and our telephone conversations were less one-sided after this. His coke intake by this time was heavy. He would start snorting as soon as we got in the TV room, and shortly after he began, the rhythmic jerking started, too. If he drank enough beer this would calm down a little, but only sleep stopped it. My God, I thought, what if he dies right here? What the hell would I do? It seemed to me that I was always reading somewhere—newspapers, medical journals, whatever—about coke heads dying of heart attacks. And young ones, too. If it happened, could I get him out and dump him someplace like Kincaid Park? But it was winter, and they'd find tire tracks in the snow. And how would I get him back into his clothes? It would have to be nude. Shit. If anything like that happened, that's the end. Would anyone, any cops, believe me if I had to call them here? It would be in the papers. And so I worried.

As time passed and nothing like this seemed likely to happen, the thought was still at the back of my mind. There were times of temporary organ failure, as I called it, when he doggedly churned on anyway, from shame, his limp dick making a loud flop-flap against his belly. But generally he could get it up and going even when he was coked to his bald spot, and drunk to boot. His powers were astonishing. Now his watery semen tasted bitter like cocaine. Poppers, which he bought at the porn shop, caused a powerful surge when he wanted to get hard, and he used them more and more. All this mixture gave me more jitters, but he could still get up and go to work after nights like these with no damage that I could see.

I bought a camcorder that winter and learned how to make videos by using it on everything. One night when Wayne was over I brought it out for him to examine, and I showed some of the tapes I had put together. After the business with the Polaroids I expected a flat negative at the idea of taping him. I underestimated his vanity, and I had forgotten how much he liked to show off his body and what he could do with it.

He was suspicious at first. I expected that. But as soon as he mellowed out on his dope and alcohol he agreed to some taping, ordering me to leave his head and face out. I followed orders for the first couple of short takes which we played back on the TV. I knew that when he saw himself performing he'd say the hell with that, and he did. From then on I taped him any way I wanted to, setting up the tripod so that both of us were in action. During these tapings I coaxed him one way or another to talk about his sex exploits.

My prize, my biggest turn-on, were the ones in which he told about his high school days with both sexes. In another one, with my relentless questions, he talked about a couple of male teachers and then about how he started with his dad. I'm as much what I call an oyeur—an excitable listener to such tales—as I am a voyeur, and Wayne was glad to oblige. He was as much a verbal exhibitionist as he was a physical one. We're made for each other and for the camcorder, I said. My little black imitation leather date book for those couple or three months has stars and Wayne's initials by those nights. As if I were ranking places to eat (and in a way I was), the stars ranged from one to four. There were always twos and threes, and five fours.

One night using the camcorder I tracked him from the TV room to the bedroom, where he was to lie down naked on the bed, under the lamp, reading a male porno magazine, playing with himself. He followed directions as he always did, no more high or drunk than he often was, until he lay down on the bed, opened the magazine, then dropped it on the floor. He looked straight at the camera, blocking it with his hand.

"That's enough," he said flatly. "Turn the fucking thing off. I ain't gonna do this anymore." By his tone I knew not to argue. He got up, stood rubbing his hair absently, then walked back in the TV room, where he pulled on his clothes. He left, grunting a good-bye.

When I went out to where he worked, he had been fired. He had no telephone, but I was a whiz at tracking him. His most recent old lady left him. He moved into two stark rooms at the top of a flimsy low-rent apartment house with his big screen TV, a couch, and a futon on the bedroom floor. His sink overflowed with a frying pan and dishes caked with grease and food. He worked a late shift, so he spent the day half awake, skimpy curtains drawn, in front of the blaring screen, changing from channel to channel when he thought about it. He was broke, but somehow he still got his drugs and beer. I washed all his dishes and cleaned up his bathroom and bedroom a bit.

In the bedroom under a heap of dirty clothes I found a Bible in a white leatherette cover, a high school yearbook, a *Hustler* magazine, and a paperback collection of stories by Dean Koontz. In the yearbook there was a photo of Wayne as a scrawny kid in thick glasses, hair cropped, as a member of the junior varsity football team. He looked shy and lost.

It was a spring evening and still chilly. The snow had melted and the birches were dusted with tiny green leaves. We got in my car and drove around Knick Arm then down the road to the site of an abandoned shallow water port. As we passed a slough a small flock of sandhill cranes flew over us, sounding like trumpets. In the days when he worked for the utility company Wayne inspected the area for lines, and he knew it well. He guided us down a dirt road to a gate closed with a heavy chain which he unhooked and pulled aside. A little further on we came to the shell of an abandoned wooden house sitting in the trees right at the shore. Just below it a large boulder sat at the water's edge. We walked through the empty house, then jumped down to the big rock and stood, looking across the half mile of water to the greening far woods.

Without saying anything Wayne started taking off his clothes. Then he turned to me and began pulling at mine. When we were naked he half lifted me against the cold, flaking stone and we made rough love as chilly dusk came on, wild Wayne laughing and growling like a satyr.

Going back we ate at an Italian restaurant. He got drunk on the wine, filling his cheeks with food and spitting on the table, chewing the spaghetti with his mouth open, white teeth grinding. He had to stop at the supermarket on the way to his apartment. I saw him stash choice cuts of meat along with packs of crackers in his deep anorak pockets while he only paid for a tin of Copenhagen snoose.

That was the last time I saw him. Within the next couple of weeks he called to tell me he was living with a woman he met at work. They were moving to Seattle that weekend. That was a surprise I was unprepared for, but that was Wayne and what could I do? I shrugged. I thought about having my own time, my own life again. It would be a relief. Then I thought about not having Wayne anymore. Hey, Wayne, I said, how about leaving your dick with me when you go? I'll take real good care of it, you know that. You can send it over in a cab, collect. He hung up laughing.

I don't know where he is. He's not in Seattle. I haven't heard from him. I didn't expect to. My determined bird-dogging couldn't flush a thing. Heart pounding, I even called Rita because I knew he'd stay in touch with his kid. She didn't want to talk about him.

To some people home movies and videos have a dead quality because they can only repeat the familiar endlessly; the action ends. If one starts it again, the sequence never varies. Real life moves on. When I slip Wayne's cassette, labelled only by the year, in the VCR I am totally Pavlovian: the familiar scenes never fail. Operant conditioning works better for lust than it does for almost any other kind of memory. The landmarks known by heart lack only touch and smell, but those surge back, too. In one sex scene the background sound is a PBS Mozart program, a piano concerto rippling through our writhings. In another, a Kip Noll video provides our gasps and groans. In the rest, the dialogue is our own. Watching it, I am going through all of it again, but this time with quiet nights, the acuteness only a memory. The lesions have scabbed over. As time passes, he becomes his video.

Wayne is a specimen now. I take him out as a pathologist might take out a slide to fasten it under a microscope, teaching the students. Focus. There. There is the agent that induces a crippling disease as widespread as the common cold. There is no cure. I have no idea what I will do when the telephone rings and I pick it up to hear, "Hey, man, what's happenin'?"

KEVIN BOURKE

BRAVO,
ROMEO . . . OR,
WELCOME
TO SEX IN
THE NINETIES

LOVE HAS LITTLE TO DO WITH GOODNESS OR PROPRIETY, OR even sanity, if it comes to that. It doesn't matter. When he is with me I drink and carry on, sometimes tearing off my clothes and jumping on the table, sometimes beating him on the chest (as if I could hurt him *that* way), sometimes accusing him of outrageous affairs and of secretly talking about me to all our friends.

When we are apart I write him love letters and weep openly in public and abuse these same friends. I've gone into debt because of the number of gifts I've presented him—little things but hundreds of them. It is permissible to spend all the money I have and more, I believe, if it's for his sake. I buy him books and CDs and little plastic trinket things; and there was a period lasting many months when I stole whole sets of dishes for him from local diners and the nicer, crowded restaurants. I regularly shoplifted from the housewares sections of department stores for flatware, embroidered linens, and kitchen appliances, by returning again and again with the same shopping bag and sales slip. I was stunning. I was brilliant. I fell in love with myself, and all for his sake.

When we are apart, even if it is during the few minutes he spends alone on the toilet, I torture myself with the thought that our last embrace will be the final one. I tremble. I pull at the hairs on my already balding head. (My hair is cropped short, so in spite of my balding I am outrageously beautiful still; no one can match me for the bright glow of my pale blue eyes with just the barest hint of gray.) I am gorgeous —he tells me so often, and he never stops touching me, not even in the streets. He has big warm strong hands and they hold me or stroke me or grasp me firmly by the waist. I have fantasies of him lifting me easily with one hand and raising me onto his shoulders. When I was a child I imagined myself swinging from the oversized biceps of the strongest men in the neighborhood like a gymnast on a parallel bar, and when I grew older these pleasant daydreams didn't leave me but became more sophisticated, more complicated, more consciously infused with libidinous cravings.

I want his arms, which are thick and muscular—even his forearms are powerful—I want his arms wrapped around me; want to use them as sites of pleasure equal to those that are more private and thus more obvious. When in public I want public pleasure. To have an orgasm in public is not difficult. He holds me fast in his terrific grip and we lick each other's faces, tenderly. All he has to do is kiss me, either softly as only a dangerously powerful man can, or as hard as his embrace, as hard as the chest he holds me against, just one kiss, twenty to twenty-five seconds, say. When he kisses me, I come. It's that easy. So when we want it to last more than twenty seconds we lick each other's faces first and thrill to the sounds of delight or disgust from the crowd, depending on which intersection we have chosen. Welcome to sex in the nineties, boys, when you come in your pants from a kiss.

But he isn't like me; and these kisses for him are exercises in power. He likes to hear me groan, and he hears it often. I groan into his mouth. I bite into his tongue. He takes forever to find *his* pleasure, but he is tireless in the search. For him we have to be alone. He is so tireless I often lag with the effort and have to let him use me like an object, which is fine with me and I'm sure he prefers it that way—to do whatever he wants with me for his own pleasure. If your partner knows what he's doing, to be treated like an object is to become like royalty—you don't have to do a thing.

We're in his apartment, say. His pleasure is deliberate and uncompromising, and he takes his time with me against the dining room table. He hasn't the interest to remove all its objects carefully and so he sweeps everything off: the papers, the crocheted placemats, the bowl of ceramic fruit, the candles in the cut-glass holders, and the potpourri basket all go crashing to the floor. He presses me onto my back, tightly against the table, and he climbs on top of me. I see his face and the look of absolute pleasure. He's the kind of man who looks good in an orgasm, the way another man might be said to look good in gray flannel. With a face not red and vein-popping and angry but showing pleasure as if from a slow release of pressure, where his face grows more serene, and he exhales a sigh, soft and relaxed, and not a sharp gasp, which some men find appealing. His embrace gets stronger, his movement gets slower. He slows with each increase in pleasure as he gets closer and closer to coming; he likes to draw it out as long as he can until, in the last moments before orgasm, he's hardly moving at all. He is moving so slightly, almost indistinctly, but it is the fact of the motion in its almost stationary state that makes it as erotic as anything a human being can experience, because his hold on you, that embrace, becomes a bear's embrace. You're locked, you can't budge an inch, and you don't want to anyway because you've never been held so tightly before and he looks at you, looks straight into your eyes; you're compelled to look back. He has bedroom eyes, although he never does out in public, where they are quite ordinary; but there's something about the approaching orgasm that shifts them, softens them, darkens them. He doesn't close them when he comes, either, doesn't shift them sideways or roll them, doesn't take himself away from you for even the slightest moment. You watch his eyes and you watch his orgasm happen in his eyes, and if you've never seen this you don't know what it feels like to be loved to the marrow of your bones, down to the smallest molecule, the absolute gentle generous quality of that, where you have no doubt the entire purpose of your life is to be under this man at this moment, and where you feel completely content. You see the absolute serenity pleasure peace in those eyes and in that open face, and anxiety leaves you, jealousy leaves you, loneliness has left long ago, there is no pain, no doubt, no doubt about yourself and your position in the world; you are exactly where you're supposed to be and you have never been more thoroughly wanted in your life.

LEIGH W. RUTLEDGE

PINK

SANTA

CLAUS

A WAVE OF BRIGHT RED LIGHT BROKE OVER ME, LIKE THE EXPLO-
sion of a bomb, and a drunk fell against me, shouting "Merry Christmas!" in my ear. He stumbled on through the crowd, shouting "Merry
Christmas!" in the ears of other men—while sometimes reaching for
their crotches—and then finally collapsed on the floor next to the video
games. The music changed to a punk rock version of "Jingle Bells," a
sleazy celebration of tradition. The dance floor filled quickly. Halfway
through the song someone dropped a champagne glass, and all of the
dancers, still dancing, moved as a group to one side: No one missed a
beat.

A good-looking young blond hesitated near me. His face was con-
genial, his eyes rather vacant. "Hello there, gorgeous," he said slowly,
swaying back and forth with a beer in one hand. "Pretty crowded
tonight."

"It always is on Christmas Eve," I replied.

Two middle-aged men in full leather burst through the front door
of the bar amidst laughter and waving and shouting to friends.

The blond turned to watch them for a moment, and then turned back to me. He looked expectant, like a little boy eyeing presents under the Christmas tree. "Can I buy you a drink?" he asked, his voice cheerful, promiscuous.

I smiled and shook my head, then finished my drink and set the empty glass on the bar. There was something much more interesting waiting for me at home. In fact, it was time to leave. "Have a nice holiday," I told him abruptly. I only briefly registered the look of disappointment on his face.

Outside, the city was wrapped in a heavy new blanket of snow. The snow seemed to cast its own light as it fell through the air and paved the streets. Earlier the flakes had been almost as big as sycamore leaves, but they'd gotten smaller and smaller with each passing hour as the air turned increasingly frigid. My car wasn't far away, but I walked slowly, savoring the winter weather and enjoying the tense, childlike feelings of anticipation inside me. Pulling my leather jacket tighter around myself, I began to think about the different men I'd spent Christmas Eve with—the quick tricks and the slow fucks, the close friends and the lovers. Thinking of them gave me the warm satisfaction of remembered pleasure. . . .

There'd been the Swedish violinist on his way to meet his wife and children in Las Vegas; he enjoyed licking beer off my ass and balls, and later he wrote me a letter saying that he and his wife had decided to try a long-term three-way relationship with another man. There had been the skinny but beautiful vegetarian who enjoyed being tied up and spanked with a ping-pong paddle. There had been the Navy fighter pilot from Florida: We had sex in his Volkswagen down by the railroad tracks, and when it was over he gave me his flight jacket as an impulsive Christmas present because it looked "so fucking hot" on me. There had been John, my first lover—we spent four glorious Christmases together, until he decided to move to San Francisco in pursuit of a teenage bodybuilder who fascinated him. And of course once, once upon a time, there was Vince. . . .

I reached my car and brushed the snow off the windshield, and listened for a moment to the sound of distant Christmas carols being played somewhere in the night. The sky was pink-orange, and the buildings around me seemed closer, more intimately connected (as if the snow somehow telescoped all distance) than they did in the daylight. I got in the car and headed for home.

I had met Vince at the bar on another snowy Christmas Eve several years earlier. When I'd first seen him, he was leaning against the cigarette machine. He had a dark, masculine face—not typically handsome, but still sexy, with a strong smile that flashed infrequently and illuminated his looks when it did. His blue shirt showed off his nipples and chest muscles through the fabric, and it was open several buttons at the throat. Around his neck, hanging down against the hair on his chest, was a thin silver chain with a small glittering Santa Claus at the end; from far away, it almost looked like dog tags.

There was something strange about him, a look in his eyes that instinctively discouraged me, as it seemed to have somehow dissuaded almost everyone in the bar. Except for a few casual greetings, no one had approached him the entire time he was there. I thought he would probably leave soon, out of boredom or thinking that the people at this bar were particularly stuck-up. Finally, though, I just went up and started talking to him. He was reasonably friendly, though a little distrustful. Initially, he maintained some distance. His answers to my questions were polite and amiable, but noncommittal and distracted. In fact, I wondered if he were cruising someone else. However, by eleven o'clock all that had changed: We were sitting together at a table, buying each other drinks and laughing heartily as he told me about his crazy childhood on Bleecker Street in New York. His full name was Vincent Christopher Martelli; he was thirty-four years old, and he told me he worked as a guidance counselor at one of the local community colleges.

By midnight, all the right things had been said and all the right moves had been made—we were in my car on our way back to my apartment. Vince's warm hand stroked my thigh, and he told me I reminded him of a kid he used to have sex with in high school. "I was afraid I was going to spend Christmas Eve alone," he added quietly.

At my apartment, everything started out fine, with no hint of the trouble to come. We drank a couple of beers and then sprawled out on the carpet, in front of the Christmas tree. Vince pulled off his shirt, revealing a firm, beautifully developed torso with slightly hairy pecs. I leaned over and started sucking on one of his nipples, then let my tongue travel up to one of his armpits. He alternately massaged and gently slapped my ass, commenting on how small and boyish it was. I was vaguely disappointed, though, that his cock wasn't hard yet.

After several minutes of this, he suddenly grabbed me by the shoulders, with a restless explosion of energy, and pulled me on top of him, giving me a fierce, hungry, open-mouthed kiss, while jamming his hand down the back of my jeans. His fingers started to push apart the smooth cheeks of my ass.

Then, just as abruptly, he stopped.

For several moments, nothing happened.

"Vince?"

He didn't answer. He was staring up at the ceiling with a dark expression on his face.

"Vince?"

"Yeah?"

"What's wrong?"

"Nothing."

"Huh?"

"Never mind. Don't worry about it."

He got up off the floor and fumbled with a lamp on a side table. Click!—the sudden harsh light shattered the mood.

By habit, my eyes swept over his body. He had a brawny, handsome body, with that rugged maturity of flesh—an insinuation of depth and experience and authority—that can often make a man in his thirties or forties more heart-poundingly sexy than one in his late teens or twenties.

"I can't do it," he suddenly said.

"I don't understand."

"I can't do it," he said again. He grabbed his shirt from the floor and started to put it on.

"Sit down," I told him.

He shook his head. "I gotta go."

"Come on, sit down. Let's talk."

"No, not that," he said. "I don't want to be understood," he added sarcastically.

He started to button his shirt, but then stopped all at once and stood utterly motionless and undecided for a moment. Finally, he said, in a low, apologetic voice, "It isn't you, if that's what you're worried about. It just . . . takes a lot to turn me on. My tastes are sort of . . . kinky."

"How kinky?"

"It doesn't matter," he said.

"Listen, I would really like to spend Christmas Eve with you, whatever it takes. . . ."

"It doesn't *matter*," he repeated emphatically.

"No, come on, tell me. I can get into almost anything."

He looked at me doubtfully.

"Everyone says that," he finally replied, softly. "But most of them run when they hear what I'm into." He hesitated and half-shrugged his shoulders. "I have weird . . . fantasies. Nothing that hurts anyone. Just . . . weird."

"How weird?"

He shook his head. There was a precipitous silence. "I . . . I sort of like . . . kids."

I didn't say anything.

"Not *real* kids," he added, as if concerned—and even slightly offended—by my lack of immediate reassurance. "I'm not into chicken. I neither would nor *could* do anything with a real kid. What I like is men who . . . act like kids, who act like boys. I like playing roles."

"That's okay," I said. "I once went home with a guy who wanted to pin diapers on me and spank me while I pissed in them. . . ."

"Did you do it?"

I could feel myself blushing. I shrugged with forced nonchalance. "Sure. Why not?"

There was a long pause.

"Relax, Vince," I finally said. "Just tell me what you want."

He thought for a minute, with the look of someone battling a deep inner constraint. At any moment the words would come tumbling out of him impetuously: He was like someone standing on a high diving board, hoping their body would make the jump while their brain wasn't looking. "Well . . ."—he hesitated—"there's one fantasy I've always had. I've never done it with anyone. You might not like it." He looked at me intensely, as if scanning my face for some sign of interest, of open-mindedness. "But you seem so right for it somehow." His face was slightly flushed. "At least, it's appropriate. . . ."

"Tell me."

"Sometimes, I've fantasized about . . ."

"Yes?"

"I've thought about pretending that I'm . . ."

"*Yes?*"

"Santa Claus," he announced in a harsh whisper.

At first, I only smiled and didn't reply. Then the smile broadened on my lips, spreading warmth into my cheeks. I tried to keep from laughing—but I just finally gave into it.

"You think it's stupid," he said.

"No," I replied. "Not stupid. I mean . . . I don't know what I mean. It isn't frightening or disgusting or anything like that, if that's what you're worried about. In fact, it's almost sort of, well, perfect."

His expression brightened a little.

"Tell me what to do," I said.

I tried to sound interested—more interested than I actually was. The fantasy didn't repel me in any way; but I confess it didn't turn me on much. Still, I was willing to try.

"Well . . ." He thought for a moment. "You're the little boy who comes into the department store to sit on Santa's lap. . . ."

I felt a renewal of laughter. I also felt a vague and unexpected stirring in my cock.

". . . and we take it from there," he said.

"What do we need?" I asked. "I mean, do you want any props or anything?"

"Well . . . it might help if I had some of Santa's clothes," he said.

For the next twenty minutes, we went through every closet and dresser drawer in my apartment trying to find the clothes for Vince's Santa Claus. I found an old pair of black pants and some snow boots; the pants were too tight and the boots were too big, but it didn't matter. I grabbed some towels for Santa's belly. The beard and moustache were a challenge we never did solve; this would be a dark, Italian Santa with the trace of a five o'clock shadow. The worst problem was the red jacket. I didn't have anything like it. Finally, after searching through the dusty corners of a back closet, I came across an old pink jacket I'd worn in high school as part of the school marching band. The huge gold buttons and gaudy epaulets made it fairly suitable to the fantasy; at least it had a flashy look to it.

Vince's Santa slowly came together, quilted from bits and pieces of old and neglected clothing. When he was dressed, I took a good look at him in the light. He made an interesting, even sexy Santa: In fact, he somehow looked like every little boy's daddy dressed up as Santa on Christmas Eve. His eyes in particular were perfect for the role: They sparkled paternally, full of amusement and masculine warmth and wisdom.

"Now what?" I asked.

"Turn on the radio," he said. "Some Christmas music will help. All you need to wear is your briefs."

The first thing I found on the radio was some opera singer wailing through Bach's "Vom Himmel Hoch."

"God, no," Vince exclaimed. "Cheap music. Department store music." I finally located a station playing traditional, Mitch Miller–type renditions of middle-class carols. "Perfect," Vince said.

Then I stripped down to my underwear. Santa's eyes glowed as he watched me peel off my jeans. He seemed fascinated by my legs and he suddenly commented, in a deep voice that was a little out of breath, "You don't have much body hair. . . ."

"The whole family's a hairless bunch," I remarked with a shrug and a short laugh. "I guess it's genetic. . . ."

"Ahh . . ." he said, with a tremolo sigh. His eyes seemed to burn.

I turned off the lamp. The only light in the room now was from the Christmas tree, with its twinkling colors and the glints of reflection from the tinsel and ornaments.

Vince sat in a chair in the middle of the room.

And then, in the space between seconds, the room began to transform itself inside my mind. There were suddenly crowds of people—harried last-minute holiday shoppers with worn and frenzied but good-natured expressions. People grabbing whatever they could find on the shelves, no longer particular, no longer concerned about matching the right gift with the right person. There were the sounds of cash registers churning with sales, and bells ringing, and people talking and laughing. There was the snow outside, and the reassuring warmth inside. There was the sparkle and glitter of cheap, oversized, department store decorations—decorations that, although garish and plastic and unabashedly commercial, still had some unaccountable power to please and excite.

And in the middle of it all was Santa, shouting a gusty, "Ho! Ho! Ho!" and patting his dark lap as he beckoned me to come closer. I walked towards him and mentally tottered on the brink between skepticism and blind faith. (Reduced to their basic elements, what sexual fantasies aren't slightly absurd and even potentially laughable?) But then I studied him, and thought: He really does look a little like Santa—pink perhaps, and lacking the usual thick, white facial hair—but Santa nonetheless. The fantasy started to enfold me.

I sat on his lap, and his warm arm slipped comfortably, lovingly, around my naked waist. In that moment, my dick started to harden.

"Have you been a good little boy this year?" Santa asked.

I smiled and nodded.

Santa smiled, too—a bit lecherously, I thought to myself.

"And have you been good to your mother and father?" he asked.

His fingers started to work themselves beneath the waistband of my briefs. At first he just gently rubbed my belly, reassuringly, right above the pubic hair; but then his hands moved slowly, furtively, down to my cock and balls. He fingered my dick and toyed with the head. Then he started stroking it as if it were a responsive lap cat.

"Yes," I said, a little short of breath. I felt an almost overwhelming rush of excitement, an unexpected mass of tingles and whirling anticipation in the pit of my stomach. This was the fantasy of being young again, of being a boy. Feelings of warm security seemed to percolate inside my brain—feelings of something wonderful and fresh, of something once lost and now regained—a feeling accentuated by being in my briefs (with an unexpected hard-on) and sitting on a man's lap with his own big erection pressing up beneath me.

I put my head against Santa's chest.

He cupped one hand around my erection and gently masturbated me, while starting to finger my ass with his other hand. His touch was sexual, but tender and caring.

Suddenly his lips came down on mine, and his tongue explored my mouth. He abruptly inserted the tip of a finger up into my asshole. I squirmed on his lap and whimpered. He smiled, and sighed with deep contentment.

"You can be as little and as small as you want with me," he whispered breathlessly in my ear.

And in the Christmas nog of lights and color and music, I let myself be sleighed away until morning, with Santa eventually ejaculating all over my thighs, and me experiencing the kind of luminous, helplessly spontaneous orgasm I hadn't had since I was thirteen years old. . . .

I drove the car into the apartment building parking lot, skidding briefly on a patch of ice. The glassy flakes were coming down more heavily than before; everywhere one looked, the details, the edges of the city were obscured and softened. The car heater felt so satisfyingly warm, I was tempted not to get out; but I finally shut off the engine.

There had been no new Christmas lovers since Vince. There had been no need for any.

I got out of the car and hiked up the steel stairs to the apartment, listening to my feet boom every step of the way, and saw that the main lights in our apartment were out. There was only the soft, unmistakable glow—slightly red—from the Christmas tree inside.

Quietly, I stood just outside the apartment door and (watching for nosy neighbors) removed my shoes, my socks, my shirt, and my pants. I folded them all neatly against the wall so that the snow wouldn't get to them.

Then I went in. . . .

The room was frantic with last-minute shoppers rushing in all directions and grabbing everything left on the department store shelves, while haggard and barely civil clerks tried to cope with the onslaught. Decorations flashed and flickered, almost blinding my eyes. There was the loud, comforting sound of Christmas carols. Even the air smelled of Christmas: of newly bought things, of spicy things, of things that were warm and musky and full of the promise of pleasure and excitement.

"Ho! Ho! Ho!" shouted Santa from a corner of the room.

The magic was as potent and mysterious as it had been the first time—even if, in the back of my mind, I understood the perfect absurdity of our annual fantasy. Sure, it's something I wouldn't want most of my friends to know about. As some obscure philosopher once observed, "Every person only understands his own love, and every other is foreign and incomprehensible to him. . . ."

My brain started to swim, and the big round head of my hard-on poked up ridiculously against the front of my underwear. For a moment I felt like an awkward little boy again—a boy who doesn't know what to do with himself or with the baffling erection coming out of his briefs. It was Christmas after all, and what child can contain himself?

I made my way towards Santa, and smiled at his admittedly atrocious pink coat. In the three years Vince and I had been together, there had been plenty of opportunities to buy him a proper red jacket—not to mention the appropriate white whiskers—but we never had.

OWEN KEEHNEN

SHAVING

KEVIN

WHEN HE ASKED IF HE COULD COME OVER I SAID OKAY, BUT things couldn't stay the way they had been. Once I got him over here I'd show him how different they would be. I was fed up with him only calling when he was drunk and horny. Time Kevin was tumbled a notch or two. Time he was taught a lesson.

Five minutes later the doorbell honked hoarsely, longer than necessary, a heavy finger. I buzzed access, went to the landing and looked over the slatted railing down the diagonal zig-zag of floors. It was an angled view, a bombardment of illusion. Kevin was moving through its belly, drunk and zig-zagging his way up. I went back inside and waited. Tonight was the night. At his knock I told him to enter. He was short of breath after scaling the stairs after cigarettes, after the night itself.

The moment he crossed the threshold I told him to take off his clothes. The wooden floor creaked to his striptease. All of it, socks, too. He smiled, thinking he knew what was coming. I smiled because he had no idea.

As he stumbled from his work pants, the scent of sweat and stale beer rose. Stenches mixed and hung in the summer heat as he raised his T. Stepping up I licked a pungent pit as his upraised arms moved the shirt beyond his elbows and wrists. His chest and paunch were hidden beneath a pelt of dark hair. When he bent to remove his socks and underwear I had a wonderful view of his ass. A whorl of black hair swirled over each luscious globe. He turned. His cock hung long and limp, just the trace of a vein visible beneath the milky surface, river in a world soon to flood.

Beauty deserves something special, something humbling. I blind-folded him with two red bandanas. He protested, then acquiesced, smirking arrogantly as if humoring me, thinking he was a real tolerant guy. I led him to the bathroom and sat him on the toilet lid. I cranked the smudged HOT knob and the water gushed; splashings and steam filled the room. I told him to get up, and studied him as he stepped into the tub.

His foot retracted. "Too hot!" I told him it's what he needed and he returned one foot, then the other, wincing as he lowered himself, reddening with shock. This will cool you in this hot weather I said.

Pockets of tension sat at the base of his neck. I massaged them as he bent to his toes. I dug my thumbs into the lumps, grown from bent dishwasher and barstool hours. I didn't have to look to know his elbows were red from being propped on the wooden bar of some tavern. I corkscrewed my knuckles down his vertebrae. He tightened, then sighed. I said to sit up and ran a washcloth over his chest; clouds of black hair assumed dancing designs with my movements. My cloth was a wave over a seaweeded beach or a shifting breeze over wheat. I made certain the terry cloth tickled and scratched his nipples. His cock floated heavy on the surface, a surfaced U-boat readying for battle. It ruled when Kevin wanted release. Tonight I would rule it. I said to let his body melt as I lathered and rinsed his arms, legs, ass, crotch, stomach, face, neck, and back. By the time I finished he was a sac of flesh. Love child of The Pillsbury Dough Boy and Cousin It.

I left him to soak a moment longer; there were things to prepare. I put Sibelius on the stereo and lit scattered candles of varying colors. I unfolded a massage table in the center of the room, placing the tools necessary for my ceremony beside it.

When I returned to the bathroom he looked like he was dozing. Tired little boy. Dangerous in a tub. His black hair was tousled, clumps curled over forehead, down upon a lean face, speckled by stubble and residual acne.

Helping him from the tub, I draped a towel over his shoulders. He was still dazed. Dry yourself and keep the blindfold on, I whispered in his ear, slipping my tongue inside at the final word. He shuddered. When he bent to dry his feet I ran a finger down his furred crack, then back up a bit deeper between. He shuddered again. I caught his arms at the wrists when he reached for the blindfold. Tonight it's my rules, I said applying pressure to my grip till he flinched a bit in a weighted drunken way. I had other things in mind. His hands lowered to his sides.

I led him to the massage table like a dog upon a leash. The floor groaned below his concentrated weight as I steadied his rise to the table, one knee at a time. Shushing him with a kiss, I gagged him with a third red paisley bandana, knotting it in a weave with locks of his hair. I loved seeing his lips stretch, pinken, whiten, crack while the bandana darkened and grew fertile with saliva.

I roped his wrists together and brought his arms elbows-to-ears over his head, securing them to the underside of the table. I spread his legs and ran a hand over his stubbly thighs, higher, till my fingers brushed his balls. Nice legs, pool hours had paid off. Kevin worked there almost every day. He was scheduled to work there tomorrow. I bound each ankle to a chrome corner. His long thin toes were sensitive, meant to be isolated, stroked, sucked, tickled. I saw a twitch higher on his leg, the slight flex of checking rope strength. I'd doubled the knots, tripled them if there was slack. Relax, Kevin, you're not going anywhere, I said.

I picked a pair of shears from the table; candlelight gleamed and slashed across them as I opened and closed the blades. I did it several times, rapidly, slowly, rapidly again. Kevin's head lifted towards the sound. His mouth fought the gag, his muscles the restraints; he became a sleek mass of tensed and corded sinew. He never looked hotter, never more translucent. If you could see yourself now is what I said to him. I ran the backside of the blade across his right nipple, his left, cold metal, nothing sharp. Leaning forward I began clipping the hair which spread like Chia grass over his barreled chest. I pruned the silken strands of his armpits to stubble and blew the thin bars of hair from his skin. Blowing into the hollow of his pit caused a tiny jerk, sensitive. I tickled him a bit. No, that wasn't tonight. Must not be sidetracked.

I began cutting to Sibelius. I clipped his calves, arms, and thighs as Kevin tensed and pulled like a pinned butterfly. When his squeamishness grew too distracting I ran the backside of the blade over his nipples again. These could puncture you if you move too much. There's greater chance for an accident, or even something intentional; my patience is not limitless.

Grabbing the butt plug from the table, I coated it with a lardish lube, bacon grease for a pig's ass. It would be a perfect pacifier. I presented it to his inner thighs, rolling it over the nook between balls and anus. His butt had been well trained our previous encounters. I poised the rubber knob at the pucker, pressed, released, pressed, released, firmly rolling the tip harder to his balls and pressing as I worked it back down to the shy bud. He wanted it, and I was getting off not giving it to him. He strained. It seemed he was continually suspended above the massage table, raising himself by resistance and arousal. Sweat coated his trim torso, the clipped hairs clung.

Are you learning your place, Kevin? Do you see how dependent you are? I said, twisting the blunt bulb into the small dark folds that filled as it widened and the butt plug slowly advanced. A large welcome guest. Kevin flipped back his head, veins rose from the lengthened sides of his neck. He gritted his teeth over the gag.

I laughed, a little different than things with Stacie huh? At the sound of her name his struggle increased, defensive. He was so worried I wouldn't keep quiet. Oh, think how awful it would be if anyone discovered the dirty little secrets this dick could tell, I said, stroking his pulsing prick.

Kneading the extra flesh of his stomach—Too much beer lately, Kevin? Too much dope and twice daily munchies?—I thrust the butt plug in, deeply. He screamed through his gurgled expression. Again, again, I played in daydream fashion with several in-and-out rhythms. He continued to fight the ropes which had broken the skin on his right wrist. He struggled less with that limb after that. A fine blue network, rivered flesh, rose along the surface of his shoulders. Weakened reserves calling reinforcements through the bloodstream. Sad, his muscles were strained, exhausted, and I'd only just begun. The gags were soaked a deep violet, even the two over his eyes. His hair dripped with sweat that seemed heavier, like oil. I spread my hand wide over his chest so the nail tips of my long fingers touched each nipple. I scratched lightly, harder, simultaneously driving the butt plug home again and again.

I shook the black can and squirted the green gel in my palm. It whitened and grew, metamorphosizing dung, yeast set to bake. I ran my hands down his chest, flattening one nub with a calloused palm while coating the other with the smooth cool foam. I pressed till they hardened for opposite reasons. Finally I began pinching them between my thumb and forefinger. I switched hands so both knobs were slick. They kept sliding through my tireless fingers. The sensations drove him to suspension. His dick was rigid and I laughed at the direct line between his nipples and cock. Kevin, I'm learning more about you all the time. Did Stacie know so much? Soon there will be nothing left to know.

I weighted my palms down his stomach, rolling his paunch, moving it about like a shoe beneath a rug. I fingered his navel and smoothed the gel into his pubic hair. I gave his cock several loose strokes. It throbbed. His ass was twitching, rising to meet my fist, seeking a constant rhythm.

Fat chance I said. If I wanted you to get off, Kevin, you would be off, but I don't so you aren't. Nothing is so simple anymore. When you're not calling the shots you just have to lie back and take it. I released his erection and watched the corn syrup collect amidst foam at his navel. Squirting more snake gel on my fingertips, I reached down and coated his balls, nearly lemons. In some ways they dwarfed his sizeable dick. Bet these fill out your swimsuit real nice, Kevin. I pulled them to a taut cluster and rolled my palm over the foamy collected sac. A lot of cum was stored in those nuts. Fun to drain. Why not take all of what he's thinking with? If I took it all what would remain? Tonight I was going to make him go dry.

I ran my gelled palms up and down his hairy legs; sketched lines of hair were apparent below the foam. I opened a six pack of disposable razors. Beginning at his feet, I rose, stroking, stroking, rinsing, stroking. It reminded me of peeling potatoes. Now I was shaving to Chopin. Now it was like conducting, like playing. His legs emerged smooth white fish from beneath the foam and hair, images from a new mythology, a lichened statue lifted from a riverbed, dipped in acid, given bleach baths. Everything about Kevin came from the water. I always said that about him. I toweled down my handiwork, smoothed lotion upon his skin.

I replenished the gel in each arm cave; five sweeps and each pit was done. An especially gratifying region; my concentration insured his ticklishness. If he weren't gagged he'd be begging me to stop, precisely why I didn't. We were beyond begging.

Lifting my blade to his wonderful chest I began with the intriguing hollow of his neck, a vulnerable, masculine place. I wove the blade down his pectorals, shaving in sweeping and ribboning strokes, circling and recircling his pebbled nipples. Like a den done white it needed two coats. The second time I worked with racing stripes. When I finished his chest his cock was purple and huge, that too-tight-cockring look from excitement alone.

I opened a third razor and worked down his stomach to his pubes, dense and wiry as a stunted thicket. I wrestled his cock out of the way, seeping velvet steel. I trimmed the hedge then shaved the stumps in short strokes, my movements the spokes of a wheel, the hub his cock. Veins now rose from his abdomen amidst the whiteness of skin, a fresh riverbed in a vast conquered land, a barren region.

Smoothing lubricant on my hand I reached down, grabbed the butt plug and began to crank its half-moon handle, winding Kevin like a jack-in-the-box about to pop. I began to thrust it lightly, then in short aggressive jabs as my lubricated hand worked him with teasing open-palmed strokings. Gratification would come at my command. He thrashed weakly, but with vigorous intent. Exhaustion was just another form of frustration and defeat for him. The gag was soggy, dripping back down his throat. The blindfolds trickled like sweating hides across his brow. His skin gleamed, hairless, perspiring. His slight gut seemed out of place, as though only recently he'd swallowed a Terrier or something of a significant size.

Banging his muscle ass with the plug, I clamped his balls to a cluster. I tsked, Sensitive after shaving, aren't they? I ran my open palm over their smooth surface.

There was no visible resistance in any muscle grouping. In his helplessness I whispered, You want it now, you fucking closet case? You want it now, so give it. Give it now. Give it to me now. I thrust, then retracted the plug from his ass and in a few firm strokes he blasted a geyser up and across his virgin pink pecs.

You're awfully proud of this, aren't you? Damn smug if you ask me. How much is there anyway? I scooped his sperm from his chest, a thick coat across my fingertips. I closed and swirled my hand around and around his cock. His body seemed relaxed, but his head was thrashing and bubbles of saliva popped at the edges of the gag. Oops, I laughed, forgot how sensitive you get after you come. But see, Kevin, I don't give a rat's ass anymore. I don't feel like stopping. Maybe I'll never stop.

Running a hand over his lotioned chest I saw them, a long hair beside each nipple. How had they eluded me? I pulled the hideaway strands into long black lines. Let's get rid of these, lie still.

He bucked immediately, then stopped. He was getting smarter. His chest was rising and not quite falling. Slowly he settled in wait.

I lifted a paraffin candle. The flame sputtered at the disturbance, a fiery tongue chastising me till it stilled and grew. I held it above his head, and tipped like a slow-motion spill over his chest. A drop died white at the edge of his left pec, another fell and froze nearer the nipple, tears of fire falling in water.

I lowered the taper slightly, causing the irregular drips to increase in temperature, a sensation multiplied being bound, shaven, and blind-folded. Poor Kevin was even unable to scream or moan at the over-stimulation. He bucked as I pumped his red erection and dripped a trail of stepping stone circles to his left nipple. Bullseye. A blob smothered the strand. The right nipple hair was a shorter version of the same story.

I returned the candle to its holder, freshened the lubricant on my pumping hand. He liked wax on his titties. That feel good? You like a little tittie pain, Kevin? I lit a cigarette. Candles sputtered with my whistling exhalation. Kevin's chest heaved in ecstasy, a mountainside of pale stone rising but tapering down, a slight knoll, a tree. He tensed when he smelled my smoke. I liked seeing him frightened and aroused by the fear. His cock throbbed, rising to meet my fist.

Neither strand snapped with the impressions I peeled from his nipples. There are simpler ways. Leaning forward, I singed each hair with my cigarette, snuffing the tiny orange ember at the second it reached his skin. His balls drew snugly against the base of his cock. I firmed my grip, increased the tempo.

Now he was a volcano straining up, up. Shoot it. Shoot it. A thick stream flew from the eye of his cock. He thrashed in his restraints and I kept stroking. Things are going to be different from now on, Kevin, I said. His breaths were titanic, earthquakes, tidal waves. I brought a pearl of jism to his lips. From the ocean inside. Is the spring going dry? Is it, Kevin? Are you beginning to worry that tonight will never end? Are you frightened that this is forever?

PATRICK CARR

GERÏON

In memory of David Weinbaum
—with all my love, as always

I HADN'T BEEN OUT IN SO LONG—PERHAPS IT HAD BEEN cabin fever that drove me to it. Though frankly I doubt it; cabin, cotton, or cleansing, no fever had ever sent me out of doors before, sent me roaming the streets I'd sworn off like a lousy lover or an unfaithful friend.

Or yeah, like a bad habit.

I suppose it was hunger that moved me that night, the strange panic-hunger I'd taken to feeling, particularly as the evening came on. Jittery, nervous, I'd get to feeling hollowness in my gut, like my bottom had fallen out. When it came on I'd try to take in what I could to fill up—I'd eat or smoke too much, maybe both. Sometimes playing with myself helped, which always struck me as a little weird. The heroin I put up my nose—and finally in my arm—was, I know, an attempt at achieving satisfaction but, well, it put me under enough, made my empty middle feel warm, finally. And I liked it, I'm not gonna say I didn't. But it jilted me fast, and took to just teasing me with the promise of going for broke, really fucking myself up enough that I was able to feel at least a little sated. And the last time, well—I guess I was disgusted enough to put myself through withdrawal, if that means anything.

But that night I wandered out, headed to the outside world with different plans, however vague. As tied as I was to the apartment, as much as I'd been through in the dingy little place, it seemed now a nagging chaperone, peevishly reminding me of the failures it had witnessed. An accomplished scold, it minimized the successes it could not altogether dismiss. The place had frowned—no, scowled—so darkly at my plans for the evening that I'd checked my several bulbs for an outage. But no—and so I wondered to myself if, perhaps, some unscheduled eclipse had begun, drawing us to its climax in total darkness. I imagined a black hole on its way, wondered if I would feel the walls crash down around me when its gravity hit.

It was about ten o'clock, and the evening was bracing autumn and exhilarating by virtue of its seeming forbidden. With the sun now gone, the cracked and broken edges of the neighborhood seemed to lose their cutting sharpness, grow softer, fuller for their bottomless shadows/evincing a new dignity for covering their threadbare shift with a hard-won evening cloak. How strange it all was, seeing those streets fresh again, after many months of doing what I could to avoid them and teach myself that they were paths to other places, not a destination in themselves.

Headed west, I turned onto Avenue A and stopped. I was surprised I had to consider street side as much as I did. I crossed the avenue and headed downtown on the commercial side.

I hadn't been to Leshko's since sometime the previous spring. I remember having pudding. I really don't know what the circumstances were. Now I was figuring on something like eggs. Home fries. That little plastic package of jelly for toast. Good, sound breakfast food was only possible in a shop like Leshko's: Cooking for myself kept me alive, but meals more complicated than pasta or oatmeal annoyed me, and I figured I'd better lay off the frozen prefab for a while—I was getting fat and probably toxic.

Was it Friday? Maybe, or Thursday. There were a lot of people on the street, more small parties wandering about than I'd expected. And traffic, which was unusual for a weeknight, so I guess it was one of the late week party nights, preparatory to harried Saturday. While the area seemed chattier than I'd anticipated, my mind quickly dulled most of the tone. I reached that strip of block above Seventh, where I passed the usual assembly clustered noisily around the shambling newsstand.

There are all sorts of sounds you get used to in New York: sirens, screeches, screams, planes, tirades and they all become easily enough ignored. But of all the unavoidables, panhandlers are the last to stand out, at least to my ear; even the most arrogant or crazy seem in some small way vulnerable, exposed by some final humbling concession to the exigencies of living.

—*Spare a quarter?* I heard: an almost offhand way, not really expecting anything.

To an extent the boy who'd spoken looked like any of the homeless-punk crew there, or perhaps more accurately, all of them. I think that's what attracted me to him—the lack of any extraordinarily striking feature that might have given him the glamour of conventional attractiveness, the elitism of individual physical beauty.

His eyes were dark, darker than his mousebrown hair seemed to ask for; it was matted into the long locks that had become a cliché of the neighborhood. His hair—well, he—was filthy.

He was sitting a little apart from the others or, who knows, maybe I'd never have noticed him. Even when he mouthed me for passing him by.

—*Hey.*

I turned my head to him, but kept walking.

—*I said got a quarter. Don't just walk by, man.*

No, I said and kept going. But then I stopped, or was stopped by that strange desire to have your worst expectation realized. I knew what he wanted money for: I had almost been in his position once; if it hadn't been for Claire I would be, though she'd made no bones about eventually cutting me off.

What for? I asked, expecting him to dismiss me. But he was a surprise, smirking first, and following with a look at: (1) feet (2) middle [my dick?] (3) face. I was flattered by what I took to be a deliberate once-over from what appeared to be an alarmingly blunt and therefore, of course, unspeakably attractive man.

Though "man" might've been pushing it. He looked to be about twenty-five (his skin was relatively clear if oily, his jaw was strong and seemed finally set, his unshaven face showed bristles that betrayed no youth by wispiness) but his eyes had the hard, tired cast of adolescent mockery. At that moment those eyes were locked on me, narrowing slightly to a probing gaze.

I could feel myself, every muscle working to turn me away from him. I had to fight it, to stiffen up to keep from going. Not yet. It was too early for that yet.

—For what? I asked him again, trying to sound like I knew his answer better than he did.

He was unimpressed. *I wanna call my ma,* he said; 'ma,' like a midwestern boy. I wondered the cliché, and tried to see his home farm, where even now ma was painting her runaway's picture on the milk jugs herself.

I offered to treat him to the call, come on I'll even dial for you if you want. Huh?

He curled his lip and blew a little *pffffffff* and turned his head away with contempt. I could tell he knew I wasn't going anywhere.

I tried to judge how much his little comrades had heard of all this: They seemed to pay no mind at all. Hitting up the passersby was daily business.

So they didn't hear my next offer, and thought little of the two of us walking off together.

I ordered the long-hoped-for eggs and potatoes. Mint jelly packets came with the toast, but I laid them aside as being too damn strange even for me.

The boy—Henry, he'd said—asked what kind of dessert they had.

The waitress slumped a little impatiently and started a litany that began with strawberry-rhubarb pie.

I watched him as he listened to the assortment of sweets being offered, watched his eyes fix on nothing some middle distance to his left. Alert. Distracted. Uncomfortable and detached.

I knew what was happening.

I knew so well that his quick, darting decision—*yeah, chocolate cake*—seemed as much a relief to me as he hoped it'd be for him.

That should help, I figured.

He ate the cake mechanically, efficiently; not savaging it but knocking it down by steady bits and pieces. I watched him, mesmerized and repelled: this dirty boy pulling at the sugary frosting that stretched and pulled like plastic wrap, and would grit between your teeth if you dared to chew it. Watched his arms, so like robot limbs in motion. But so human with their little violations. Those tiny blossoms Claire called "the pokes."

I shuddered at the thought of my own blood, and the imagined feeling of its sloppy heat glugging out of my veins. Or slipping silently, flying up the steel to pool in the syringe.

I added sugar to my suddenly bitter coffee.

I thought this had been a bad idea, maybe an awful one. What did I want? He was a pretty thing, but I churned at the sight of him. He made me feel a sexual wildness without actually making me hard for him. I sat there bouncing my leg beneath the table, tapping my fingers on its chipped top, thinking I was finally going insane. What did I want with him now? Something from the middle of him. I wanted to sate myself with him, and it felt heavy and lazy like lust, but I knew it wasn't. Flesh, man? No, not tonight. But shit, I knew where Nathan lived if that's the kind of fucking up I wanted. I'd have plenty of money, enough to buy what it'd take to quiet me down. Why was I hunting it here? Why couldn't I just leave it alone? As he finished with his sugar, Henry stared up at me; I saw his eyes add things up quickly, and fill with an uncomfortable curiosity.

—*Was it hard?* he asked finally.

And how I suddenly hated him for that question, for the way he read my mind and knew my pangs for what they were. I wanted to smack his pretty face, take a fistful of dirty hair and shake his head brainless. Hard? Yes, little Henry, it had been hard, but nothing like now. Vomit and shivers and cold rattling stones in my gut had been hard. It had all been hard and lousy and I'm hating it still. Hating its intrusion into any thought, hating the cheap, flimsy comfort I took in things now. Hating you, and the warm way you make my belly feel again, and what I want to do to you—

—Why? is all I asked.

—*'Cause I wanna know, that's all.*

I leaned forward so quickly I didn't recognize the movement.

—How brave do you feel tonight, Hank? Huh? Wanna see hell, Henry boy?

The waitress passed and slapped the check down. I fished through my wallet and watched Henry trying to figure me out. Well?

—*I've gotta go*—

—You don't have to be anywhere, I countered. He glared at that; the more sullen and suspicious he became, the more childish he looked. I liked that, and was glad I'd chosen to play mystery for a while, even with myself. So I did a little more of the inscrutable-sardonic, and I swear I gnashed my teeth:

—Come on, Henry, come home. Come on home and give me your blood, young man.

I didn't bother lighting the place at all; we'd have as much light as we needed from the street, and I thought things were appropriate with their faint green streetlamp tinge. Henry walked a little unsurely into the center of the room, without turning to me. I walked up behind him to wrap my arms round, to speak in his ear.

—What do you want to know, Henry? Huh?

I could feel him breathing hard, could hear the rush of breath grow quicker.

—You still want to know things, buddyboy? Hmm? I reached up to run my fingers over his mouth, ramble over the face I couldn't entirely see as I breathed at the back of his ear. His hair was harsh on my face, and smelled like grass. I wanted to cut him, to bleed him like a Renaissance quack.

—Can't talk, Henry? Tell me what you want to know, boy, quick—because real soon this is gonna be about what I want from you.

His mouth opened silently, and I saw his left eye slide to its corner, placing me. I ran a hand wrinkling across his shirt, then down to his jeans. Butter-soft with dirt and wear, their thinness allowing the high relief of his cock, as hard as I'd expected. I held it almost desperately: pretty, junkie kid. How I had missed him.

—*Tell me . . .*
—Yes.
—*Tell me . . .*
—Yes.
—*Please . . .*
—You know how it makes your stomach hot . . . ? You still get that, huh? Dontcha, kid? I don't. I don't get nothing now. So I want it back. . . .

I felt myself veins, snaking veins, I was wide mouth open gulping snakes, looking forward to a big prey-filled belly. Looking further forward to the moment when the burning acid ingestion of him ended, and the beginning sleepiness of my sated state. The nodding and the warmth.

He turned to me fast, pushed his mouth to mine; I searched it for something I could use, grabbing around back of his nape to hold him to me. He flailed and whimpered into my mouth. I screamed back, wordlessly. He broke my hold and showed me fear for the first time.

—Afraid, Hank? And we haven't even crossed the river yet.

Then he looked up at me, and I saw him, yes, very much afraid. His body stuck between cowering and an animal's coiling to pounce. He'd pulled back from me into a wide swath of lamplight, which turned him into some momentary seabeast as it rippled his skin. But a better focus revealed only gooseflesh—all over his arms, in response to a chill I knew was not the room's own.

I rethought. Again about this all being some terrible mistake, some cruel prank I'd chosen to play, about the sheer selfish nastiness of it. About the coming sucker punch I couldn't bring myself to stop. Alright. Alright, I thought.

—We're going down, I think I said out loud.

I held him. Or tried to, wrapped around his falling in my arms like water raining. He was all antic sloppiness that I tried unsuccessfully to still. He pushed, humped up against me hard, and pulled back, to fall to his knees and run his face over my pants, to feel with his open mouth how badly I wanted into him. To close his teeth on the fabric and pull at me with a puppy's insistence.

When I grabbed his locks he looked up noisily, rushing air out with stuttering shivers. I knelt to him, rubbing his arms fast and hard, trying to work up what fire I could manage to warm him a little. Kissed him with a wide oval mouth that tried to fill him. When I let my hands travel over back behind him and down, I felt wet as he pissed himself and watched his face go slack against its minute of warmth. When that minute waned, I pulled his wet clothes from him, and bundled him to my bed as the cold night came on.

His skin was smooth, and stretched tightly over his skinny frame. It tasted sweet as I licked roughly over him like a cat. He writhed under my tongue with short moaning sounds. Shivered as my hands ran over

him, pulling here, scratching there. He had closed his eyes, and when I
brought myself to rub my cock on his, he gasped. I wondered what he
saw behind those eyelids. Wondered what kinder man he put in my
place. I curled my lip and spit hard at his face, and then again as his
tongue moved out and mouth opened wider, thirsty, hungry. He licked
me off his lips, and pushed his head toward me for more. The greed
pleased me, made me angry, so I took his jaw in one hand and pinned
it open. With my other hand I reached in, and held his tongue down
hard. I looked at the wideopen hole of him now. Spit far into its blackness. Yes. Fuck him there.

He pulled at my skin with bony fingers, took me in his mouth in some
famished attempt at feasting. He went down on me with great pounding
plunges, pulling back in between with a great suction and burning
scrapes of teeth. He growled around on my throated cock, reached up
and scratched at my nipples carelessly. I kept my hands on him there,
resting on his dirty hair, occasionally pushdown push on him, to ram
him further onto me than he seemed to even want. But I mostly lay
still, and closed my eyes under the madness he did, the cannibalization
he frantically desired, but whose proper commencement he could not
arrange.

On his belly in front of me, writhing slowly with noises into the thin
pillow. He pulled down into himself, toward his middle, pushed his ass
to the air. I reached out to run my fingers over its paleness, its thousand
faint, raised hairs. Leaned forward to put my tongue on the skin there;
bare my teeth to it. Nip.
      He gasped at that, and I saw his hole pucker, pulling together in
a warning against my imagined advance. And so I slathered its vigilance
with spit, and pushed my tongue against the ringed muscle. Prodded.
Sealed my lips around it, sucked at its thick edges, wormed my way
between. It was there, it was way up inside there and I knew it, and
that knowledge made desperation bring a finger, then two, up into him;
there; there where it was hot. I whimpered at touching it, feeling the
heat come down out of him. My hunger gained on his, outstripped his,
finally, pushed on by cold. This was it. His shivers faded in my mind
as I probed him deep and hard. He was wet and soft and sloppy, and I
ran my fingers around his inside like I'd never possibly feel the slick
inside of his asshole enough. Plunged my dick into him at last, into the

bowels of him that were still warm dopey satiety. Fucked myself up on
fucking him then, pushing his face down hard. I felt myself bubbling
up, bubbling over, raging inside.

—that's it go ahead take it take it

I could feel our bones banging together, reached around to yank
at his cock

—my little faggot boy

pull at the way it was so hard there

—what are you gonna give me dirty little faggot boy

I slid in and out of him it was almost too easy, but for his puck-
ering hole that squeezed

—it's time kid it's time to give

I could hear him, moaning staggered by the fucking motion, but
he was holding back goddamn him

—come on now

I pushed harder, pushing prodding at something I wanted to force
out of him

—c'mon c'mon give it you fuck

I could feel it far down in him feel my dick nudge against it far
in him wanted it to just open up

—you fucking filthy

I crashed into him like some half-beast with him muffled under
me and over again pushing goading

—givityoufilthyfuckC'MONC'MON

he raised to me he raised up to me to open but it wasn't and I
grabbed him to pull him onto me reached fingers alongside my dick
clawed at him grab it to pull it out

—GIVITORISWEARI'LLFUCKING

punched him hard pounded on him to words like drums as pulled
at it ran fingers cock around stretch make it give up

—I'LLRIPYOURFUCKINGTHROATOUT

reached forward and banged his head, pushed it down hard and
then it hit like a swallowed sun.

Slow arson burned away my insides and brought me tumbling down on
him, lying hard on his clammy skin, rolling my head about knocking
on his shoulders. The surprise slowed me, stopped me. I pushed into
him again in woozy shock; how fast I went to liquid. I moved in him
again, soft thick liquid giving and withdrawing. And the giving was

taken relentlessly; my withdrawals met with small, spoiled starving cries.

—*no* and sucked me back in, and then pull back

—a small nonword as I went back in, and felt him coil about me to pull yes even one drop closer; pull back against it

—*please* I hesitated against the word, then rushed in again to meet him; the coil, tighter now; the pull, deeper again

and he shook around me, and cooled; my cock, yes and behind it, yes yes finally my bowel hot and insistent. His belly pulled at me now from inside, from deeper inside than I could possibly go. But I'd settled in now, laid back heat-drunk, and could only feel the icy serpent of him twist around me, pull me, hang on to me, slip down to some colder plain

—*please please*

I came almost without noticing but he pushed himself far onto me to catch it *please please* but no I can't I can't I can't give it back he pulled away holding his stomach curling up baby time but I didn't see him long before I closed my eyes and feel better? then yes better moans from him Henry? was far far below me there I see you Henry thank you thank you stay awhile now stay or I'll take your place again in the snow I laid on ice so long before you Henry boy y'know? y'know? where are you Henrykid huh? it's too dark where you are now y'know I can't see you there you know thaaat you know thaaaaat are you mad Hank huh? are you mad I took it huh? are you mad you're allalone there by the cold wind by yourself sorry sorrysorry but I'd do it again I can't take the cold nnoomore andyknow hell is cold Henry did ma tell you hell is colnheaven is lazy bellyfire hang on hang on don't fall my little boy the bottom's ice and hard and I left there myself so I knowI knowI know

I thought he would be gone and he was; I could trace his path to the door by the minor wreckage his last grasps had left. I pushed the gaping door shut, locked it against a mad return. And so the morning was coffee very dark and saccharine sweet. And so so hot.

And if I looked for him again? What then? Could I bring adequate apology with me, tuck something worthy in my pocket to give him in return? And so I do not look, not even at the voices that call my name from the curb.

PART SEVEN

REAL SEX

BEHIND

THE SCENES

Everybody who enjoys pornography is a voyeur. When we read an erotic story, a major part of the turn-on is being able to "watch" the characters' sexual exploits. On another level, we are turned on by the sense that we are glimpsing into the author's inner fantasy life.

Almost all gay sexual writing takes the form of the first-person, true-life confessional, but readers know this is usually a conceit, a fantasy. So when we come across the rare account that we know is in fact true, a real insider's account, the voyeuristic thrill is electrifying. These "behind the scenes" reports titillate because they speak the unspeakable, expose that which is meant to remain concealed. (I've had fans tell me that they consider my recent how-to manual, *Hustling: A Gentleman's Guide to the Fine Art of Male Prostitution*, my hottest erotica. Sure, *Mr. Benson* was a good story, but the hustler book was *real*, it made them feel that the sex was tangible, imminent.)

A few decades ago, before it was possible to have an open gay porn industry, many smut magazines passed as informational manuals with titles like "A Medical Guide to the Male Orgasm." Scott O'Hara, a prominent porn video star and sex club performer during the 1980s, recently started a magazine which updates the form, called *Steam: A Quarterly Journal for Men*. Juxtaposing the physical appearance and editorial accoutrements of an academic journal (it even prints a year-end index to each volume!) with explicit sex writing, *Steam* creates a whole new kind of porn-reading experience. The journal's bathhouse reviews and "CityScape" travel articles about public sex around the world exist on one level as highly useful informational guides. But they also make for steaming-hot fantasy material.

O'Hara's "Theatres I Have Known," which first appeared in *Steam*, is a memoir of his years performing in jackoff clubs. The fantasy that keeps customers coming back to jackoff clubs is that the performer is truly enjoying the act as much as they are. O'Hara surprises us by confessing that for him, this was true. He even went to jackoff clubs between his own nightly shows for additional entertainment.

Sandi DuBowski is one of the young writers for whom *Steam* emerged as a natural outlet. Recognizing the erotic power of peeking behind façades, DuBowski reports with tongue in cheek on the active public sex scene at his alma mater, Harvard University. Taking the cue of the journal's academic style, and spoofing the Ivy League pretensions of the institution he is describing, DuBowski even includes footnotes in his article. "The Harvard Sexposé" is a brilliant send-up of repressed intellectual sexuality, with the added bonus that it's an accurate participant-observer account.

Peeking behind the scenes of a far less venerable institution, journalist Dave Kinnick dishes up insider gossip of the gay porn video world. "Sex Secrets of the Sex Stars" captures an important historical moment in the porn industry. Originally written as a feature for *The Advocate* in 1991, the piece became the model for Kinnick's regular "Secrets of the Porn Stars" column in the *Advocate Classifieds*. Detailing such taboo subjects as pretaping enemas, Kinnick demystifies the "arduous and often boring work" of making video pornography.

Like the medical manuals, other precursors of contemporary gay porn glossies were muscle magazines glorifying the male body, such as *Physique Pictorial*. The world of male bodybuilding has alway been tinged with homoeroticism, but with the recent exception of openly gay superstars Bob and Rod Jackson-Paris, the sport has been decidedly, and defensively, "straight." A well-known reporter of the male muscle world,

"Deke Phelps" breaks the unspoken rules and exposes the gay sexual undercurrent of the bodybuilding circuit. Confessing that he is a "slut for muscle cock," Phelps documents his affair with a successful protégé whom he boosted to national success. Dripping with lust and baby oil, "The Man I Made" attests to the power of the insider's confessional.

Andrew Holleran's regular column in *Christopher Street* has for years been a place where gay men can read insider accounts of what most people won't talk about. "The Sex Vacation" is classic Holleran, giving a detailed version of his trip to the Parliament House in Orlando, an infamous motel-cum-cruising-palace. At once an explicit sexual diary and a sociological reflection on the art of cruising, the piece is an honest portrayal of a much-mythologized way that gay men have sex.

SCOTT O'HARA

THEATRES I

HAVE KNOWN

IN MAY OF '83, WHEN I MOVED TO SAN FRANCISCO, I HAD never been in a theatre that featured live jackoff shows. I don't think I'd ever considered the possibility, except perhaps in my deepest, darkest fantasies. Less than a month later, I was working in one, stripping & spurting twice nightly for an audience that sometimes numbered over a hundred. From the moment I saw the ad in the *Bay Area Reporter*, I knew it was my sort of place—but it wasn't a help-wanted ad for performers. Nosirree—I showed up at Savages the first time as a paying customer who couldn't quite believe his eyes, but knew instinctively that jerking off on stage was a great idea. I sat right up there in the front row—almost always empty, because most guys are shy enough to want a row of seat-backs to shield their crotch from the performers, Godnose why—and hauled out my meat and jerked off, and one of the strip artists, afterwards, said to me "Why don't you get up there and do a show? You'd be great!"—and so I did, and I was hooked, and they hired me. How much more right can you get than that: jerking off

onstage, being admired, turning on a hundred guys simultaneously—
and getting paid for it? I had found, you might say, my calling; and
I'd also found a family, of sorts.

Savages was not what I'd call an elegant club. The seats were ratty
& torn, many of them completely broken; the stage was seldom cleaned,
so our feet (or socks) would be black after fifteen minutes onstage. The
management (which changed at least three times during my tenure) tried
to make it a "rougher" place than the one competing theatre in town,
the Nob Hill: no velvet curtains, no plush carpeting, but both downstairs and upstairs areas were always chockfull of men having sex in the
dark. The "dressing room" was a little closetlike affair to the side of the
stage: a plywood shack, about three by three feet—with a light switch
next to it, so the performer could run his own light show. Not exactly
a class act; but it didn't have to be. It was Savages, and for a sexually-
inquisitive, eager-to-be-exploited performer like myself, it was Home;
and it was the place where, three months later, I was "discovered" for
the world of video, when I won the "Biggest Dick in S.F." contest. And
at least the patrons usually looked alive, and interested—unlike some
of the other dives I've performed in, in NYC and elsewhere, where often
as not you'd see someone sleeping in the second row.

I worked at Savages fairly steadily for the next three years; sometime in the middle of that time, it changed its name to the Campus,
underwent a change of ownership & cosmetic facelift, and installed a
video projection system and a follow-spot, so the performers could concentrate on their performance. (The follow-spot operator, coincidentally,
ended up being my closest friend for the next several years, until we
both found lovers—and I even learned the art of follow-spotting from
him, so that sometimes on his days off, I'd get up in the booth and play
the role of God to the performer's Adam.) No fundamental changes,
though. During the Great Bathhouse Scare in S.F. ('84—when the city
health department decided that baths and other sex businesses were cess-
pools of Disease & Vice), the downstairs maze (a really ingenious hon-
eycomb of hexagonal plywood booths: Some walls were plexiglass, some
were chain-link fence, some had gloryholes or peepholes; all cubicles
offered a smorgasbord of choices) was dismantled. With that concession
from the owner, the health department turned its voracious appetite to
closing the baths, instead—which was, naturally, good for business at
the theatre. I occasionally quarrelled with the owners or managers, and
stayed away for months at a time; during two of those breaks, I performed at the Nob Hill briefly, to pass the time and amuse myself.

The Nob Hill, as mentioned before, is set up for a more piss-elegant crowd. Aside from the trappings, however, it's much the same setup. Guys go onstage, do a striptease, get naked, get hard, get off. Sometimes the performers at the Nob Hill had pretensions to Performance Art, especially Scott Taylor: He had an act that could send shivers down your spine, though I don't think it got many mens' rocks off. He gave new meaning to the phrase "talk dirty to me": He'd come onstage with his dick in a vacuum pump, pumped to heroic, braunschweigerlike proportions; harangue the audience with all the invective & abuse he could come up with, play with a knife teasing his perineum, then threaten to come into the audience and use the knife on someone; and climax his act (after removing the pump) by inserting a foot-long "sparkler" into his urethra. You know, one of those clear plastic tubes with glitter inside—in this case, red glitter. The tube itself was thicker than his thumb—the man had a high tolerance for pain, I think—and once he had it halfway in, working himself into a frenzy, stroking his dick, practically foaming at the mouth, he'd let his dick flop downwards— and what appeared to be blood would come cascading out of his piss-slit, glowing in the stage lighting. I think he came at the same time. Weaker souls in the audience (if any were left) lost it at that moment. I was always entranced. Not turned-on, mind you, but certainly not about to look away, either. That's a quality I admire in any performer: mesmerization. I was told, frequently, that I had it—but I was always inclined to believe that the men who said so were just automatically hypnotized by big pee-pees. Nevertheless, getting up onstage and making grown men go ga-ga was the best fun I'd ever had, and it made the evenings pass more quickly. I seldom had much energy left to go out and find trouble afterwards; I'd barely manage to stagger back to my own bed, around 2 a.m., before quietly passing out.

And an occupation to pass the evenings, when you're a pornstar, is essential. At the height of my movie career, I only made five movies in one year; each one took a week, at most, to shoot. That left a lot of vacation time. I suspect that the famous pornstars-gone-bad who make the tabloid headlines are men who don't have an adequate avocation, and find fast-lane living to be an acceptable pastime. Shooting off onstage is more work, dollar-for-dollar, than shooting on film, but it's more rewarding in other ways. It's a job that gives some stability to an otherwise highly-unstable career; it gave me a schedule, something I could look forward to and plan around; and seeing all those men out there who wanted me, *needed* me, to shoot my load was one of the biggest ego-boosts available. After I'd finished the first song, taking off whatever fantasy-uniform I'd been wearing, and got down to the serious business of Getting Off, I'd usually parade down the runway (which extended twenty feet into the audience), looking at the guys sitting out there watching me. No pretensions, like you get in a bar: *"Oh, yeah, you'd do, but I'm really not into it tonight . . ."* No, these guys were staring at me, feasting their eyes on my skin; I could feel their gaze raising my hard-on more surely than my own fist does it.

I'd usually pick out one or two who I found especially "into" it, —and it really didn't matter how attractive or unattractive the guy was, if it was clear he was there to get his rocks off, then he was My Type —and spend the rest of the performance mentally "playing" to him, or them. Oh, I wouldn't physically single out one guy and have sex with him—some guys did that, but I couldn't quite bring myself to exclude the rest of the audience—but what went on in my head was another matter. And they never even knew the things I had them doing to me. Of course, I never knew what they were doing in their heads with me, either—though our fantasies probably weren't too divergent from each other. And sometimes, yes, the guys would get a little more personal— whisper things to me when I got close to them, requests for me to act out their favorite fetishes: Tie my boots around my balls, or stick my tongue into my armpit and chow down, or sit back on the platform's edge and spread my butthole for everyone, basically saying "Come and get it!"

You don't get that thrill when you're shooting a movie: The camera doesn't talk dirty or applaud, and the director's seen it all before; all he says is "Cut!" and "Could we shoot that one again, please, from a different angle?" And you don't get that peculiar stage-struck thrill of working in a follow-spot, knowing that as the lighting changes, you're Golden Boy, or Pink Narcissus, or a distant, moonlit, idealized Blue. And then, that perfect moment, when I knew I was at my hardest, with my dick curving up in front of my belly like a scimitar, I'd be up on stage, ignoring everyone, and I'd turn profile and give a glance up to the follow-spot booth; the light would go pure white, and suddenly my shadow was up on the movie screen in vivid silhouette, twice lifesize, with the most awesome hard-on you've ever seen. That image in itself was enough to make me shoot, sometimes.

I guess most of my coworkers in the sex biz take a different, slightly less romanticized, view of their place of employment. I don't know many of them who frequent sex-palaces on their days off. I used to, when I was working there. When I worked the Show Palace in NYC (a one-week engagement, four shows a night, $1000 per week), I dashed over to the Follies, and Eros, and the Gaiety, and the other tiny jackoff theatres scattered around Times Square, in between my own shows. I'd usually hide in the back, then, because I was there to watch, to see how other guys did it, and I didn't want to wreck the energy that the performers were creating with their audience. The medium excited me: Even if I didn't have the stamina or spunk left to jack off, I wanted to learn something about the business.

What I learned, by and large, was that most guys were not as enthusiastic about their work as I was. My coworkers at the Show Palace, the regular performers who weren't getting star billing and who were spending most of their time turning tricks on the side, were all incredibly attractive to me (I'd never laid eyes on a Puerto Rican before—and Jesus, Paris, Hector and Guillermo all made me want to melt down on the floor into a puddle of gelatinous hero-worship) and yes, I did watch their shows and "practice" jerking off to them; but I got the feeling that some of them thought it rude, as if I were trying to steal their customers away from them. Honest, I wasn't—it didn't even occur to me. I was there because I idolized them as much as any of the audience members could've. Fortunately, on the one occasion when Hector (having found no trick for the evening) allowed me to suck him off, he didn't charge me. He was even friendly about it.

That's part of the scene I was never entirely comfortable with. I've nothing against hustling *per se*; but I certainly object to the illegality. I have a horror of being arrested, especially for a "crime" that I know to be no crime; the idea of a vice cop laying his slimy hands on me gives me the screaming meemies. In an effort to overcome this fear, I did once run an ad in *Advocate Classifieds;* it was a fairly discreet ad, and produced a total of three serious responses over the three months that it ran. Also lots of late-night j/o callers. (Funny, you might think that I'd feel as positive about "getting men off" over the phone as I do in person—but I don't.) Of the three, all proved to be nice men, but I couldn't shake my paranoia (no: real, justified fear) that I was making it with a vice cop. It ruined the sex. I didn't try that route again.

I did take up one other man on his offer, a year or so later, when I was playing the Follies in Washington, D.C. (a one-week contract similar to the Show Palace). He approached me after the show, offered me money, and said breathlessly that he'd flown down from New York

City just to see my show and meet me, and could I please spare him an hour's time . . . yes, I *can* be flattered. We did it in the hallway next to the theatre, where many of the performers turned quick tricks; and he was extravagantly, obsessively lust-driven. Maniacal, even. I love it when a man is obviously devoted to his hobby. I have no idea how much he paid me; I was too busy reveling in the sensations & emotions. What a thrill—to be bought & paid for, to have a man so arrested by my mere appearance that he'll go to those lengths just to suck my dick! What made it even better was that afterwards, when he wrote down his name & address for me, he wrote it on an ATM receipt, from a NYC bank, time-stamped that afternoon. The *truth*! Truth is such a rare commodity in this business—at least, verbally. I'm confident that men's bodies are telling me the truth when they're sperming on my stomach.

The climax of my live-performance career, in a sense, came after I'd stopped making movies: the '87 and '88 Black Parties at the Saint in NYC. The Black Parties were a legend in New York, begun in the seventies and growing progressively more outrageous. The poster, one year, was a fairly severe Mapplethorpe photograph; another year, it had a condom attached to it. The Saint closed in '87, due to declining attendance; the Black Party was supposedly its last hurrah, since the building was scheduled to be demolished. The following year, they were still holding special events there—presumably due to some snafu with demolition permits. (To the best of my knowledge, it's still standing— but empty.) The Black Party, as it turned out, was too much of an institution to end: It's still going on, in various locations. Two years, though, was enough for me.

Each year, I only had to do two shows (and thank goodness—the body ages, you know), and I was one of a couple dozen major pornstars onstage over the course of the night; I wasn't carrying the show by myself, so some of the pressure was off. I could relax, most of the night, and enjoy myself. And there really is nothing like the thrill of walking around a facility as large as the old Saint was—packed wall-to-wall with gorgeous gym-built hardbodies, busting out of tanktops & spandex— and then getting up on stage and watching the crowd zero in on *me*— letting me know that whatever it was I had, they liked. There were video monitors around the club at strategic locations, just in case some people couldn't get close enough to the stage; one of my best friends first saw me performing there, that night, and told me later "everything looks more real when it's on a video screen!" I don't like to believe him, but I'm afraid that's what society's come to.

The Black Party in '88 was my last professional performance; I'm glad to say it was one of my best. The camaraderie of the occasion, the knowledge that the building was condemned, the history behind the series of Black Parties, all conspired to give the usual Bacchanalian atmosphere that special touch of Occasion: I even went out for a curtain call, at 5 a.m., and managed to blow another load, with several of my coworkers. We each wanted to make a good impression; so we groped each other, and squirmed against the bodies next to us, and from somewhere deep in my balls came that last load that's always waiting there for the right time and the right guy. In this case, the right audience. Don't even know who it was I spermed off on: someone's thigh. He loved it, and climaxed himself just seconds later. That's another of the great pluses of stagework: The guys are friendly, and I've met very few of them I didn't like. I miss those theatre days.

Of course, I still go back, whenever I'm in a city that has a sex palace (there aren't many of them), but it isn't the same. It's a blow to the ego when I'm not recognized, but it's even worse when I am: The performers coming up to me after the show who say "Wow! You were the first person I ever jerked off to, back when I was fourteen!" make me feel just a teensy bit old. Still, I think I'm a good audience. I know what a performer needs. When you're on that stage, looking for signs of life in a sleazy, half-empty theatre, it's a great help to see someone who really looks at you, likes what he sees, has a hard dick, and doesn't fall asleep. Now that's not complicated, is it?

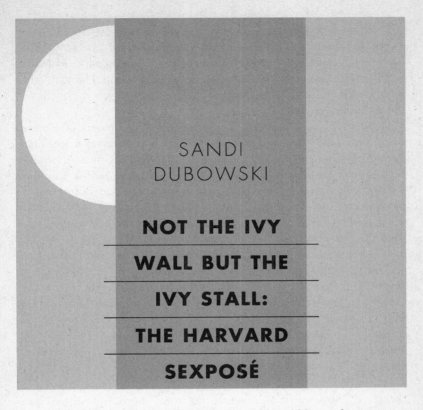

SANDI DUBOWSKI

NOT THE IVY
WALL BUT THE
IVY STALL:
THE HARVARD
SEXPOSÉ

*Harvard is a bathhouse on the Charles {where} dildos are hung up
to dry and sexually "disoriented" students begin another day in the
land of "wrong is right" morality.*

—1966 alumnus, Martin S. Wishnatsky[1]

IN A 1990 "APPEAL TO PARENTS," MAILED ONLY TO THE FA-
thers of freshmen, born-again Christian Mr. Wishnatsky warned that the
sons of Harvard were in imminent danger of becoming "pederasts" and
"sodomists." Imminent? With alumni like Boyd McDonald of *Straight
to Hell: Manhattan Review of Unnatural Acts* fame (whose twenty-fifth
Harvard Class Reunion Report lists him as "Lost,"), Charley Shively with
his series on "Cocksucking as an Act of Revolution," author Henry

---

[1] M. Sunder, "Alumnus Warns Parents About Sex at Harvard," *The Harvard Crimson*
(April 6, 1990), 1, 7.

James, and (rumor has it!) the first Dean of the Harvard Graduate School, the call to arms should have been sounded centuries ago. If, as Martin S. Wishnatsky believes, "God was excommunicated from Harvard," then it happened in 1635.[2] Just drop to your knees and ask the monks in the monastery on the Charles River.

When I was a wee boylicious thing, the bathrooms of Harvard birthed my lust. I have not been able to have horizontal sex since. Those days inspired phrases in my journal like "He had two-foot skyscraper-high nipples, and I yanked them with my teeth as one pulls a plug from a drain." Of course, on the same page I would say that Boston was "a barren wasteland of desire, a Puritan hellhole." I had my hot flashes and my bitter moments. I graduated in June '92, went cold turkey for a year, then returned this July to retaste the flavor.

There are presently four Harvard erogenous zones: the Science Center, the libraries, the Charles River Bird Sanctuary, and the Sever Quadrangle. This does not include Harvard's main pleasure spot: the mouth. One of the joys of bathroom sex at this school is to make a Harvard boy shut up. These children dissect sex, protest it, inquiry it, speechify on it, until their jawbones are so exhausted, they can't do it. Look at 1980, when the *Gay News* reported "Furor Erupts at Harvard over *Deep Throat* Showing."[3] Two hundred students demonstrated outside Quincy House, urging others to boycott the film, and two students were arrested on charges of "disseminating obscene literature." Such tight-lipped prudence of saying "no means no" but not "yes means yes" is just one side of the scholar's life. Michael Bronski recalls other oral pleasures—"My idea of heaven—spending time in a well-stocked library, discovering new novels, meeting handsome men in bathroom stalls, and then five minutes after having their cock down your throat, going out for coffee, and discussing the theoretics of the Victorian novel."[4] One friend used to spread his legs on the dinner table, tweak his nipples, moan "oh, Mami!" and as the grand finale, give a blow-job to the wooden crucifix around his neck. In typical Harvard fashion, students would walk briskly by, smile weakly (to prove their tolerance), and then fantasize about it that night for hours.

[2] Ibid.
[3] D. Sidell, "Furor at Harvard/*Deep Throat* Show," *Gay News* 7 (May 31, 1980), 44.
[4] Michael Bronski, "Cambridge, Massachusetts," in *Hometowns: Gay Men Write About Where They Belong*, ed. John Preston (New York, 1992), 174.

Fuel for such nocturnal fantasy can be easily had in Emerson Hall, Sever, and Robinson. These three buildings are technically called the *Sever Quadrangle*. To find it, sit on the grand steps of Harvard's main library, Widener. Look to your right to get the eagle-eye view of all the comings and goings from the buildings. A careful voyeur will see, for example, a figure emerge from Emerson's side doors and cut across to the basement entrance of Sever, furtively looking from side to side. Or, a lone man will climb the front steps of Sever, pretend to look at the posters hung on the boards, then cut to the right and down the steps to the bathroom.

Emerson Hall. My favorite haunt. Ripe and bursting at the cusp of the 1990s, it has quieted down a bit since. Four stalls with peepholes between. Toilet paper rolled into cigarette notes that are stuffed through the holes—from "Suk me dick" to "U R CUTE! R U HORNY? I'M NOT INTO IT HERE." Urinals across for maximum visibility, partitioned off to the unseen eye at the entrance. It is busiest at lunch hour, weekends, and after 5 p.m. Emerson's two side entrances are more discreet. Those who enter the front and zip down the stairs are action-ready. As Emerson is less trafficked than the other tearooms, especially by those who are not our comrades-in-arms, it feels like your own little hideaway. It is deserted enough that you can make your stall your Show Palace, a show-me/show-you playpen for the boy next door. Peeping through the hole is like a 3-D movie (better than Disney) with a cocktip swallowing the lens while a butt cheek or erect nipple arches out of view. These booths are great training for budding pornographers, go-go dancers, porn face-makers. And the schooling I received! You learn to pay attention to the details—scanning forearm muscles as he slides his hand to his crotch, noting how much hair is on his knuckles, how he grips his cock. Full-fisted? Fingering the piss slit? Does he lean back so you can't see his face? Emerson is very calming while you wait, like a 4' × 6' zen retreat. Just sit, listen to the air conditioning hum, the soda cans cascade down the coinslot ravine outside the door, the elevator chime, or read the soap dispenser through the crack. My little trick was to pass the boys a note or exit from the stall to the urinal, then bring them upstairs to my private lounge, the third-floor bathroom, the Philosophy Department's domain. Again, urinals partitioned off from unwarranted exposure; a quiet nook for two, especially after five. One time I met this 6'6" gruesome giant in a trenchcoat. His face was twisted into a snarl. He repulsed me. I could barely keep up with his long

sinister strides as we went to my "private office." We ran up the stairs
and into the men's room, surged to the urinals, and he unzipped. His
cock was rigid, a thick ten-incher, and he slapped the monster in his
palm. His hand shot up my shirt. He yanked me forward by the nipple
and slapped my asscheek good and hard. He stared at me, dead serious,
gauging the pace of our encounter. I moaned, he leered. My nipples and
dick were throbbing. I was soaking my pants just watching his ugliness
tower over me. Between such roughhouse utopia, slinky grad students
on dissertation breaks, Aussie beef throwing me on his barbie-Q, a jack-
booted man who sucked my ear so hard I was deaf for half an hour and
delirious for three, a Polish fuzzbear who tickled me under my balls,
and, this July, a briefcase man who encouraged me to "Fuck that ass"
—I have blissful memories of my alma mater.

Right next door to Emerson is *Sever*. It is accessible from both ends,
though I prefer the back where outside stairs lead you directly to the
spot. Two stalls. Pop into the one beside the urinals. Boys who make a
beeline to the urinal next to the stall are looking for some drama. Regulars. Sever is foot-fetish paradise, since you enter facing the stalls and
can glimpse a head-on loafer/sneaker/boot/Bass Weejun view. There used
to be a peephole between the stalls. Its edges sprouted until it was not
just a gloryhole, but a sexpig snouthole with a crust of cum. You could
almost dive to the other side. Unfortunately, Harvard maintenance work-
ers bolted and welded a metal plate to seal the gap last summer, and I
haven't yet seen enough queers with power tools who could repair the
damage. Let's send a shout-out to those Boston-area tradesmen. . . .

Next to Sever is *Robinson Hall*. In July, I saw graffiti in Sever
advertising basement BJs here on Saturdays. The urinals are blocked
from door view. This may be an emerging cumspot.

Just a one-minute walk from the Sever Quad is the *Science Center*,
where the stakes for sex are high. The Dean of Students ordered the
doors removed from the basement bathroom stalls after complaints of
"sexual harassment," "indecent exposure," and "lewd and lascivious behavior" in 1985. Such a move was supposed to cut down on play, but
it is an exhibitionist's dream. Easier access. Since the urinals run parallel
to the stalls and are in a room apart from the sinks and the door, a
urinal hogger and a toilet squatter can mutually admire and have ample
time to zip up when they hear the door creak. While the scene sputters
on, it does not seem to compare with the heydays of pre-'85. Boyd
McDonald immortalized "The Hallowed Holes of Harvard" in *Sex* when

the doors still hung: "There are no homosexuals at Harvard but if you go to the men's rooms at lunchtime you better not need to shit because the booths in the Science Center, seven in all, will all be filled and there will be men pacing the urinals looking through the cracks in the doors and waiting their turns at the cracks. One day I had a broad-dicked blondie shove it under (all the doors on the inside say KNEEL DOWN FOR ACTION, the new motto over Veritas) and I was on that dick in a second of course and the black man in the next booth over on my left . . ."[5]

In 1990, twelve men were arrested in four separate incidents by Harvard and Cambridge police, the latter wearing rubber gloves. The twelve men faced felony charges of "open and gross lewdness" and "indecent assault and battery."[6] Their names were printed in the newspapers and one high school swim coach committed suicide. Harvard's daily paper, *The Crimson*, nearly held emergency meetings on the proper spelling of "tearoom." The incident ignited campus lesbian/gay activism, protesting the administration's unnecessary entrapment and public humiliation of the men, and a committee, established to discuss police relations with the gay community, ended the arrests. One of the administration's priorities was that gay travel guides remove all mention of Harvard tearooms. And, not surprisingly, while *Damron's* lists Boston College and Boston U., a certain nameless university is overlooked. Harvard sure knows how to work the boardroom backroom.

The Science Center is a virtual institution. All types of men voyage here from all over Boston/Cambridge, yet the place seems so dangerously charged and public, some on-campus boys go elsewhere. I went only a couple of times in my four years. I remember one salt and pepper bearded Daddy . . . and I heard about an ex–football player, Lance, who used to lance his boys bent over the sink on the seventh floor. I even saw one Polo button-down flopped over in a stall, nose to knees, snoring. Walta Borawski had a poetic answer to these types—"Harvard man, Harvard man, blond for no reason."[7] These creamy white boys who don't want stains on their record (or yours) can be trouble, working out centuries of mummy and daddy. Beware, too, of the police in the Science Center

[5] *Sex*, ed. Boyd McDonald.
[6] Joshua A. Gersten, "Men Admit 'Lewdness' in Science Center Lavatory," *The Harvard Crimson* (March 17, 1990), p. 7.
[7] Walta Borawski, "Harvard Man I," in *Meat*, ed. Boyd McDonald.

more than in any other Harvard locale. There is a guard's desk at the top of the stairs leading down to the basement. Most of the time there is free flow between the floors, but access is restricted most nights to those with Harvard I.D. I met a man there once who played the game —he ripped the toilet paper, I ripped the toilet paper, I coughed, he coughed, he tapped, I tapped, rip, rip, cough, cough, rip, rip, flush, flush. He led me to a deserted classroom—then spun on me and barked, "Where's your I.D.? Are you a student?" and then reported me to the guard. I fled through the revolving doors, skirting bushes and shadows. Aside from this one episode, I have been lucky.

If you prefer social sciences and humanities to those "hard" sciences of bio and chem, try *Widener Library*. Little cruising happens here, but the cavernous reading room for size queen bibliophiles is ecstasy itself. There are small urinal-only old-fashioned marble rooms with swing-wood doors, made for one—except they lock, and can be transformed for two or more just as well. Enter from the library's back, next to Mass Ave., and just jog up the first stairs to your right. For a more distant getaway, go up two flights: marble echoes. Alumnus-pervert French Wall said that fucking in D-West, the sub-basement where, appropriately, "Minor Romance Literature" is stacked, was a "rite of passage" in the early eighties. Couples of all persuasions (but of course homos paved the way) would unscrew the light bulbs and go at it on the floor. That tradition has passed, but hey, if platform shoes and the nymphette look have returned, it's time to retro this subterranean trend. D-West, however, is only accessible with Harvard I.D. Oh well, just mug a little Harvard boy for that prize. He needs the reality check.

The X-Cage. The G-Spot of Widener and the Fine Arts Library. Each one contains nude art books of hot beefcake and porn. Bruce Weber, Mapplethorpe, etc., none of which can be checked out. They fear them being stolen. Or the librarians want them for themselves. Female nudes are on the shelves.

Lamont Library once thrived. Especially pre-seventies when Harvard was all-male and it was easier for a dog to get into the library than a woman.[8] Although Lamont was even recommended in *Steam*'s last issue, now that steel and wood cubicles with no peepholes have replaced the seventies raised stall walls and kickpanels, the pickings are slim. I've spent many an hour on the fifth floor trying to revive the glory days,

[8] Shari Rudavsky, "Radcliffe 1960; Struggling with the Dilemmas of Inequality and Feminism," *The Harvard Crimson* (June 3, 1985), p. 11.

hovering and waiting, but not once has anything happened. If, however, you get off listening to the rustle of what *you know* are porn mags while a boy jerks himself through finals, then by all means go for your aural peeps.

Before we jump to Harvard's last erogenous zone, there are a couple of spots to mention where, though the cum has dried, history was made by our fore(play)fathers.

Burr Lecture Hall has been knocked down. It is no surprise that Harvard would demolish its erotic sanctuaries (along with affordable Cambridge housing). There was so much lead time from the creaky Burr Hall door to the downstairs basement stalls, French Wall said, "you could put a tuxedo on by the time someone made their entrance." One of the men in *Sons of Harvard*, a collection of interviews with gay alumni, remembers that in the mid-sixties "all four stalls would have at least two and sometimes three people in them."[9] Unfortunately, author Marotta keeps calling this the "gay low life," and I don't think he means feet below sea level.

Adams House. Harvard has twelve houses numbering 300–400 residents. Each house has a rep, and Adams is bohemian, artsy, radical, HOMO. There's an annual Drag Night every year, where even the Mr. T doll on the Dining Hall desk goes girl (as if she isn't Missy Missy already). French Wall recalls one Loni who stood up in the Dining Hall, blew a whistle, and announced "I'm so fuckin' horny. Come have sex with me. Room B-13, 493-8317!" That was not considered abnormal. I remember Bungle in the Jungle parties where a tangled coed mass of sweaty dancing limbs allowed those hetero-plus boys to skim some skin. Before my time were naked champagne/cocaine parties, black turtleneck de rigeur. The Adams House pool was famous for its skinnydipping orgies. Adams projected an aura of decadence and decay, and many boys claimed to fear the underground tunnels. Alas, since those days Harvard has randomized its students. With Adams now a bland mix of All Types, the perversity is gone and Paradise Lost.

As dynasties fall, so do they rise. Now that a cafe has recently opened in the basement of *Lehman Hall*, the Grad Student Center, one baby dyke friend says that the bathroom is a cruisy place. I've had no chance to check it out firsthand; it's closed for the summer.

Harvard's last erogenous zone is less brick and mortar, more pas-

[9] Toby Marotta, *Sons of Harvard: Gay Men from the Class of 1967* (New York, 1982), p. 75.

toral. The Charles River is now deshrubbed and defoliated, so cruising is rare. But, if you bush-players can't get to P-Town and want a country getaway a mere ten-minute walk from campus, go to the *Bird Sanctuary*. I wish I knew about this [re]treat during my four years at the big H. Facing the river with your K-hole to the H-hole, follow it to the right (the water not your sweet ass), away from Central Square. Once you reach the second boathouse (not Harvard's but Cambridge's), turn left towards the water and go through the tunnel. Ahead will be a building and a narrow path into the forest. Veer to the right. A meadow of cattails will greet you, through which have been trampled paths of varying widths. It looks like the Everglades, and can be as muddy. When I visited, it was wet; still, there was a circle-jerk of five in a scooped-out alcove, and two pairs of boys bumping skins. It is Cambridge's version of the Fenway, slightly more vanilla, rarefied, less raunchy, but pleasant in a Sunday *New York Times* sex way. The birds provide a great audio track. I met the boy who had given me a ride home from the March on Washington, who was now attending Sex and Love Addicts Anon. I met a pec-flexing eco-wonder who was fixing a tree sapling that had fallen. Rumor has it that some homophobe is burning patches of grass, so we need to tend those gardens. AIDS Action Committee Rubbermen come to dispense their goodies, and often nudists traipse about in the afternoons. Police after dark sometimes shine their lights from the parking lot. Roving gangs of teenage boys on bicycles menaced the evening I was there (and had done so before) so be careful bush-players. At first, I was thrilled—I thought they were doing two-wheeled cruising. All in all, barrelling through the cattails fulfilled my stalker (and stalked) fantasies. The Bird Sanctuary was that perfect summer picnic—munching and grazing galore. Besides putting a little latex love in and on your basket, no preparation necessary!

Don't forget the *Yankee Clipper*, either, Amtrak's NYC/Boston route. As I criss-crossed the cars coming home, this tank-topped bull rubbed his nipple and spread out his cutoff-clad thighs, barely able to contain the juice inside. He cut into the bathroom and I followed. He grabbed me and thrust between my legs as we watched ourselves in the full-length mirror.

Bathroom sex . . . outdoor sex . . . Amtrak sex. I guess it's high time for those Harvard boys to dry off their dildos.

(Editor's note: Sandi DuBowski graduated magna cum laude.)

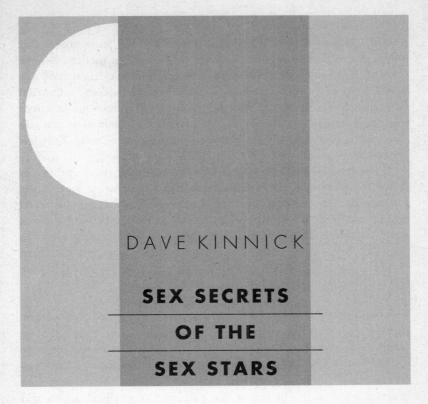

DAVE KINNICK

SEX SECRETS

OF THE

SEX STARS

AS A REVIEWER OF GAY SEX VIDEOS, THE NUMBER ONE QUES-
tion that people ask me is "What's it like on the set of one of these
movies?" Since I get this a lot at parties and upscale social functions, I
usually enjoy turning the tables and asking the asker what his impression
is. A lot of people think the scene resembles a decadent Hollywood party
as it might have been thrown by Erich von Stroheim: acres of nubile
young bodies, plenty of people of low position doling out blow-jobs to
the star players, and veritable wetacres of flowing champagne. To expand
on this fantasy, you would have to place Marlene Dietrich somewhere
in the crowd, dressed in a man's suit and tonguing every girl in sight,
then tilting her head and laughing gaily before moving on in the crowd,
leaving another heart broken. The director stands over his pets clad in
jodhpurs, cracking a whip and leering from behind his monocle. Sadly
perhaps, nothing could be further from the truth.

Making pornography is arduous and often boring work. The huge-
dicked and slow-talking performer **Tom Steele**, portraying "Tom," the

cable TV repair guy in his debut in Catalina's *Powerline*, intimated this fact in the movie when he complained to a couple of rooftop voyeurs: "Hey guys, I just got off, and I'm not feeling very sexy right now." In Tom's case, the daunting engineering feat of keeping a fleshy cylindrical solid displacing 325 cubic centimeters erect and pretty for an entire afternoon's taping requires an amazing amount of external stimuli. In short, it becomes the job of the crew and director to make Tom feel sexy.

The following is a compendium of facts, tricks, and fun that I've culled from some of the best directors in the business, as well as my own observations working on a number of sets. The question I'll try to answer is "What do video performers do to look good and perform well?" as that is the only thing that matters to industry professionals.

LE DOUCHE

Johnny Depp wouldn't let the camera lens come in for one of those face-sucking close-ups without brushing his teeth first. Similarly, a sex star won't do an anal scene without making himself wholesome inside as well as out. So, before there can be sex, there is the douche. Most prefer the classic simplicity of the Fleet brand enema. The delivery tube may be a bit daunting but it has that omni-directional action that any stripminer would envy. Some performers, like the small but hunky Philadelphia-born super-bottom **Joey Stefano**, douche "before coming to the set, once on the set, and once after the scene," explains award-winning director and performance drag diva **Chi Chi LaRue**. Now *that's* professionalism.

My friend Doug was working crew on **Jeff Lawrence**'s *Big Time* a few years back and walked in accidentally on **Chris Burns** in a bathroom off the set preparing for a scene in which he'd be playing with a variety of large latex toys (which he always carries with him in a suitcase). Burns is a muscular blond man whose work in the industry dates back to 1982. He has come to specialize in ass-challenging feats and raunch in general. On this particular occasion, Burns was perched on the toilet using the time-honored hot water bottle and rubber hose method of internal cleansing that uses gravity to deliver a healthy pint of tap water to the needed location. In the industry, men like Chris Burns are known as specialty talent. Doug, being a nice boy from the suburbs who lives with his parents, nearly fainted. The rest of the crew, waiting patiently for the arrival of the star, merely heard a slight squeal from down the hall.

Another production assistant friend worked on a different shoot for Director Lawrence last fall and was given the task of going to the market to buy both lunch and a round of douches for the cast. Taking a poll, he jotted down the ratio of burgers to chicken that the cast favored, and also uncovered a preference for Massengill's light vinegar and water internal rinse. The delivery tube on these bruisers is considerably larger —not really designed for a boy's needs, but it seems the advertised "feminine confidence" of the formula has crossover appeal that was unanticipated by the manufacturer.

Directrix Chi Chi explains that many performers, including Joey, own their own little blue squeezebulbs that they bring with them to the set (available at most finer sex stores). These medium-sized squirts have the advantage of being both portable and reuseable. "When I was doing shoots for Vivid Video," elaborates LaRue, "I used to go out and buy bulbs for all my actors and say 'Now keep this bulb and bring it with you to each set,' but no one ever remembered it. I even had to explain what a douche was for to **Matt Gunther** on the set of *Deep Inside Jon Vincent*. It was his fifth production and he had not a clue!" Though best known for his top roles, twenty-seven-year-old Matt is a sinewy, darkly tanned muscle-diva with a lovely butt which is considerably tighter in real life than his mouth, which has a tendency toward gossip. Despite the time out for tutorage, the scene was completed on schedule and, one will note, under-budget. Matt proved himself as orderly a bottom as he is adept a top.

THE PROPHYLACTIC: EVERY SEX STAR'S NEW BEST FRIEND

If the brand of douche is of major importance to some stars, their preferred brand of condom is a veritable security blanket. Ranking favorites are Maxx, Mentor, and Gold Circle. You'll almost never see a Trojan, since the white rubber they're manufactured from looks like an opera glove on camera.

One young performer a couple of years back, **Beau Childs**, brought his favorite brand with him to the set. Beautiful young Beau, who always managed to look like he was about to be sick on camera, had his mother pack a couple of Mentor brand rubbers for him before each shoot. The crew always hoped there would be an apple pie covered with a gingham towel along with it but one never materialized.

The aforementioned Tom Steele, showing up for Catalina's *Powertool II* shoot, brought with him a box of Trojan Naturalubes—which is the nice way of marketing pieces of lamb's intestine. When he went to fuck **Mark Sabre** in the shower orgy scene, he opened the foil wrapper and the cast practically passed out. Seems the little devils are packed in brine or something. Director **Josh Eliot** talked him into trying a latex brand—which, as it turns out, he had never used before. Eliot also pointed out to him that the latex brands were a lot safer in terms of viral transmission, and Tom acquiesced to the newfangled technology of rubber, and it worked just fine.

PRIMING FOR THE $$$-SHOT

To the quarterback, it's the length of the forward pass. To the television producer, it's the audience share in the overnights. To the sex star, it's cum. Lot's of it. Buckets of it, would it were possible. A weak acting or sexual performance can be overlooked, if the inevitable conclusion of the scene is a real gusher. Entire careers of lads like Seattlite **Neil Thomas** and Australian babe **Steven Gibson** have been saved by voluminous spunk levels.

In the entire history of gay sex on film and video, no other performer is more legendary for his copious wet shots than **Matt Ramsey,** now exclusively doing straight sex films under the name of **Peter North.** Legend has it that Matt/Peter, star of such classics as *The Bigger, The Better* and **William Higgins'** *Cousins*, has a "double prostrate" gland, but no one will elaborate as to what that might actually be. Since not everyone can be endowed with such a convenient, albeit enigmatic, anatomic configuration, directors commonly insist that their performers practice short-term abstinence before a shoot. **Richard Lawrence,** director of Avalon's *Devil and Danny Webster* and *Headbangers*, asks his boys for a forty-eight-hour sex-free period before they report for work—a typical request. The directors at Falcon video in San Francisco, keep their performers alone in hotel rooms before their scene, assuring that two performers who are to work together meet face-to-face for the very first time on the set just minutes before the cameras roll. This is intended to instill that hungry, "just cruised," look in their eyes.

Other directors resort to more scientific methods. Jeff Lawrence reports that blond and very Nordic looking porn legend **Leo Ford** "always used to require large amounts of milk on the set, and he drank a lot of it the day before a shoot, too. He was sure it improved his performance in terms of having more cum for the money shots." Other performers swear by a diet heavy in celery. No one seems sure where this wisdom originated, but you have to admit it can't hurt. I predict that at many gay parties after this article comes out, the crudité plate will run out of celery faster than most hosts would expect.

Lon Flexxe, chest-shaved brunette star of *He-Devils* and *Davey and the Cruisers*, heard a few months ago from an agent that supplements of zinc to a diet increased one's semen production. He tried taking 150 percent of the RDA of zinc for a week and thinks, but isn't sure, that it made a difference. At any rate, he had fun testing the theory.

Can one simply will oneself to cum more? Mocha-colored love babe **Randy Cochran,** star of *In Thrust We Trust* and *Black Force*, is a follower of Nichiren Shoshu Buddhism and chants before every shoot. He goes off in a corner by himself with a little book and does his thing until he is called to work. Randy says "it puts things into the right rhythm so that we have a nice, smooth, productive shoot."

THE AUTO-FLUFF CYCLE

Though you might think that a performer's primary source of erotic stimulation should come from his partner or partners in a scene, quite often individuals need something extra to get them going.

It's not uncommon to have a performer leave the set to get away from the lights and the crew and work himself up, either for an erection or an ejaculation. Richard Lawrence reports that young **Tony Young,** who worked for him on *Taking Care of Mike*, is one of many that jacks off in the bathroom until he's on the verge of orgasm and then tears onto the set at the crucial moment to get the shot on camera.

From the set of *Hard Rock High*, director **J. K. Jensen** remembers a kid named "**Speedster.**" He was a model for Old Reliable video, a company that specializes in products featuring street trash types in wrestling and boxing situations. Speedster performed just fine in his scene up until the time he had to come. He asked his director to slap him hard on the face several times, which got him instantly hard and near orgasm. Chi Chi LaRue reports that **Joe Simmons,** enormously tall and well-built African-American stud for both Catalina and Christopher Rage Videos, enjoys the same kind of treatment.

Chi Chi confides that "certain performers, like **Michael Brawn, Scott Bond,** and **Damien,** have to suck a dick to get turned on. If that's what it takes to get them hard, then that's the first thing we tape. Other guys need to be talked dirty to," he continues. "On *The Rise,* that little guy, **Vic Youngblood,** was like that. He needed to be talked dirty to and have Scott Bond show him his ass constantly—for eight hours. Now Scott is a very quiet, almost docile person, so for him to do that was unnatural. The scene only worked I guess because of the grace of God or something."

"Matt Gunther likes the dirty talk too," adds Josh Eliot. "And so does **Red Grecco** of *Deep Inside Jon Vincent.* He was the one in that first scene with Jon—wearing a mask." Chi Chi adds, "Red needs someone very strong and verbally abusive to make a scene work for him, so **Jon Vincent** was perfect for him. Some want it even rougher than that to get their dick hard—like **Steve Kennedy.** In his scene with Damien in *Read My Lips,* Steve wanted to be able to spit in Damien's mouth and slap him across the face with his dick and stuff. Damien obliged."

Obviously Chi Chi and Josh have some of the best dirt when it comes to how performers perform. One performer that was hyped enormously during the fall season in both 1990 and 1991, with appearances in big video releases by producer Matt Sterling, was glamour boy **Ryan Idol,** a perpetually smug and self-satisfied young creature who looks exactly like he stepped out of a 1950s drive-in picture, cast as the male lead's smart-aleck rival.

On the subject of Ryan, they report: "Rumor has it that on the set of *Idol Eyes,* he had to be alone with himself in front of a mirror in the bathroom for twenty minutes at a time to get hard. Then he could run out onto the set and do his couple of strokes and then go back and stand in front of the mirror again. That's why they finally let him do his solo scene in front of a mirror."

Of all the male porn stars to come along in the last decade, it's the king of perpetual pout, **Jeff Stryker,** that is the one name everyone knows. What most people don't realize, is that though Jeff is known as a top gay porn star, he is very reserved in his on-screen intimacy with men. LaRue insists that "Jeff doesn't like anybody taking his dick all the way in their mouth because he doesn't want people to think that such a thing is possible because it's so large. He doesn't kiss on screen either, which was a problem for Joey Stefano when they worked together in *On the Rocks* [Jeff's second self-produced gay feature] because kissing is what turns Joey on the most. Before the shoot began, Joey went up to Jeff and said, 'Why don't you kiss on film?' and Jeff said, 'Because I don't want to' and Joey said, 'Well, I'm not going to do the scene with you unless you kiss me'—and Jeff did, but only a little. They even worked that dialogue into the scene and shot it, so it's part of the story."

Another method of arousing a performer is described by LaRue using smooth, long-dicked **Matt Powers** as an example: "Matt, on the set of my *Lunch Hour,* watched a video of *Deep Throat.* It has a scene in it with two giant dicks fucking one girl. That's the scene he watches. The funny part is that all the time he was watching and getting himself up, he was also fingering [co-star] **Alex Stone**'s ass."

Playing other videos on the set is not an uncommon practice. Jeff Lawrence recalls humongous-dicked **Rick Donovan** asking specifically before a shoot on 1986's *On Top* for a lesbian video to be set up off camera while he was doing his solo scene. The technical term, by the way, for a lesbian video in the straight porn industry is a "girl-girl" tape. That goes a long way to explain why so many of the women in straight pornography have excessively large hair and practice fingernail extremism in their manicures. With the help of the video, Rick was just able to pump enough blood into his twelve-inch cock to stroke it off to orgasm. And so it goes, past the lens and onto the floor.

PET PEEVES OF THE SEX STARS

As important as helping a cast member get aroused is avoiding ticking them off and making them unwilling or unable to perform. For a look at star diplomacy, I once again turn to Chi Chi and Josh. "Some models don't want their hair touched," confides Josh. "**Brad Richardson** in *Top Man* was like that. He screamed, 'Don't touch my hair,' at **Jim Moore** when he was going down on him. In *The Big One*, he and **Kurt Bauer** hated each other. Brad was upset because he was asked to top Kurt but Kurt's body was bigger than his. They ended up switching it around."

Sometimes the slating of who is to do what to whom seems to be a big issue, which brings us to an elusive topic:

CHEMISTRY

Putting performers together who will get off on each other is also the job of the director. To do this, they show performers pictures before the shoot of who they will be working with, and get their approval. Sometimes, it is left up to fate. Lon Flexxe says of fellow performer **Chris McKenzie:** "He's just a pistol. He's real deep—not one of these think with their dick types. He's also very passionate—a real firecracker." Across town and without prompting, I asked Chris McKenzie who the one performer he would most like to work with again would be. "Lon Flexxe. He's one of those people that makes fireworks happen with me." I kid you not. Those were their words. A psychic link? Maybe.

THE GROOMING AND FEEDING OF TALENT

Josh Eliot laughs when asked about this one. "Shaving can be a major issue. We had a strict rule at Catalina for a long time. [Company founder William] Higgins really wants those butt holes shaved. Some don't like to have it done though—**Ryan Yeager** for instance."

"Others get into it. Kurt Bauer loves his butt. He's always asking, 'Is it shaved okay?' 'Does it look good?' 'Do you want me to wink it?' He would just get rock hard when he knew the crew was watching him wink his butthole."

Other performers make different demands on their employers. Chi Chi says, "Matt Powers needs to be fed every fifteen minutes—nutritional stuff—his orange juice at nine o'clock and his banana at ten. He won't shoot until he's had his meals. He's fun to work with though. Some just are. Jon Vincent is incredibly easy to work with. He used to be difficult when he was drinking but he's great now. In fact, his wife even brought lasagna to the set when we were done shooting on *Inside Jon Vincent*. They were sweet."

To some, food is just short of sexual manna. Matt Gunther says of co-star **Buck Tanner:** "He was having a few problems keeping a hard-on, and kept demanding M&M's, which he said would solve the problem. They did! M&M's are on almost every movie set because they're cheap."

ANATOMICAL CORRECTNESS

Keeping it up for a co-star is ultimately what counts in a good performer. Directors don't care how it's done, as long as an erection is ready to go when they and the cameras are. Both Lon Flexxe and Chris McKenzie, a couple we've already met, are performers who are known by industry insiders as being virtually ever-hard. **Chad Knight,** a lovely young man who is married with a wife and two kids, is the industry's current top stiffie. Despite his marital status, he comes off as gentle, sensitive, and thoroughly queer. He seems quite comfortable with his double life—and is always hard when the cameras want to roll.

For some reason beyond mere anatomy, a lot of the industry's top "studs" seem less at ease than Knight. Many of these same guys, not coincidentally, have difficulty publicly stating their sexuality. Many can exhibit behavior on screen that is decidedly homosexual, yet rigidly define themselves as "straight" and insist on playing what are known as "trade" roles. If this mindset is needed to give them the impetus to perform well, then this, too, is a sex secret.

Popular in the industry today and ranking among the straight, the confused, the vague, or the concurrently both vague and confused are: fame-bent porn legend Jeff Stryker, upstart porn pretender Ryan Idol, tiny latin boy-stud **Andrew Michaels,** long-haired go-go dude **Steve Ryder,** dirty-talking Jon Vincent, rough trade **Derek Jensen,** the perennially boy-next-door **Tim Lowe,** blond giant **Rex Chandler,** and new superstar hopeful from Catalina Video, **Lex Baldwin.** To Baldwin can be added a second layer of confusion, since when he appeared on the porn scene in 1990, he sported a gorgeous, furry chest and uncoincidentally bore a strong resemblance to Hollywood's own #1 bear-boy, Alec Baldwin. Shortly before doing his second video, though, the porn Baldwin shaved his chest smooth, making a lot of fans wonder, "What's the point?" Washed down a drain somewhere with his fleece, many feel, went a lot of his character.

STUNT PARTS ANONYMOUS

As an offshoot of the infusion of straight performers in the gay video industry, there is the phenomenon of the stunt dick and butt. In mainstream Hollywood films, you don't expect a Burt Reynolds or a Bruce Willis to do all of his own falls. That's why there is a union for stunt men and women. But you might not be as quick to question whether a Ryan Idol or a Lex Baldwin is doing all of his own fucking. Stunting has been around in the gay video industry since its inception, although it has become more popular in recent years as practiced by the bigger video companies.

An offshoot of "fluffing"—the use of a crew member or unpaid hanger-on to service the performers off camera to help conjure a hard-on, stunting takes the task a step further—unsung dicks and butts stepping in where a top star either can't or won't perform a sex act.

The most famous case arose from Matt Sterling's 1987 production of *Stryker Force*—in which supporting player **Robert Harris** stunted both dick and butt for co-lead **Steve Hammond**. Sometimes, it isn't a case of willingness so much as a case of raw talent. In 1985's *Below the Belt*, it was Chris Burns's butt that takes both **David Ashfield** and **Scott O'Hara**'s dicks in one of gay porn's few double penetration sequences, and not the considerably younger and more vulnerable looking **Michael Cummings**. Ironically, it was to be David Ashfield who dick stunted for Ryan Idol in Sterling's *Idol Eyes* five years later, poking his thick and always-hard thang into the highly bendable Joey Stefano.

In more recent examples, **Lee Jennings**'s dick stunted for **Cole Phillips** in topping young Damien in their scene shot in a ventilation duct in Catalina's 1991 *Sex in Tight Places*. The same month, Matt Gunther was called in to sub for Lex Baldwin's dick in both of his scenes for *Man of the Year*. Two months later it was Damien serving double duty as both make-up man and stunt dick for Baldwin in *Powertool II*.

Is the reason these guys need help in their performance a lack of talent or merely the canny construction of their superbutch image? Ultimately, the last thing the gay video industry is going to do is discriminate on the basis of sexuality. If for no other reason, the world of explicit homoeroticism is too preoccupied with political and economic survival to take time out for discrimination. If you mention Lex Baldwin to director Josh Eliot for instance, you get a visceral reaction that mirrors most of Lex's potential fans. "Lex is one big time juice-bomb superstar," Josh announces, enunciating each word with clear enthusiasm. "That's what he is!" It seems that good pornography maintains an open mind.

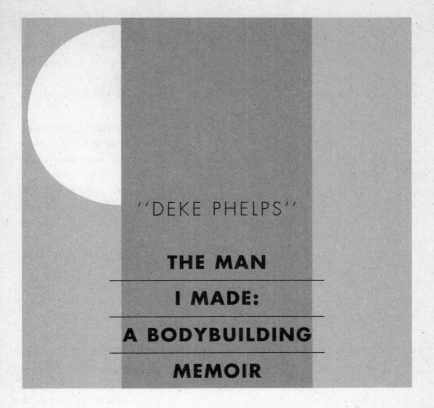

THE MAN

I MADE:

A BODYBUILDING

MEMOIR

"HEY, COACH. I WAS COUNTING ON YOU TO GET BACK AND oil me down before the show."

He damn well better! I'd been working with Darren for four years to guide him up the bodybuilding ranks, and now that he was competing in his first pro show I sure as hell wasn't going to relinquish our private little precontest ritual in which I spread a finishing coat of light oil over his heavy armor of muscle so that it would radiantly gleam under the stage's harsh lights and jerk muscle addicts in the (mostly male) audience into ecstatic cries of fealty. Darren had been at the center of such epiphanies at a couple amateur-level national contests, and it was going to happen again in his debut as a professional if I had anything to do with it—and obviously I had.

"Nobody does it like you do, man," he continued as he handed me the vial of oil. When a young, six foot, 246-pound demi-god ennobled with Herculean muscularity of ideal proportions and symmetry topped off by breathtaking handsomeness asks anything of mere mortals, there

are few men—gay *or* straight—who wouldn't rush to serve in tribute
to his masculine beauty. "Work that stuff in good. I want to look like
a chiseled work of art out there, and grab the attention of the judges,
fans, and all those magazine writers and photographers so they won't be
able to take their fuckin' eyes off me."

But Darren and I were hardly alone in our oiling-down, psyching-
up pairing. Backstage at bodybuilding contests is a beehive of anticipation that, in effect, is foreplay to the climax that will come later when
the top man emerges from the battle pitting muscle against muscle to
seize the symbol of his dominance, the victor's laurels (which tonight
will include a hefty check for his prize money). In various corners and
dressing rooms, coaches, training partners, and other buddies cluster
with their main man to charge him with ballsy energy for the fray ahead.
Elsewhere barbells and dumbbells clang and towels are pulled in tugs-
of-war as other princes of muscledom force out final muscle-swelling
pumps. But some who've gotten oiled and pumped already are trying
to cower rivals by parading around to visibly announce their own claims
to muscle mastery.

Amid all this are pairs and small groups exchanging gossip from
the constantly buzzing bodybuilding hotline, trading "secrets" on steroids or other chemical training boosters and their suppliers, and passing
along tidbits of other underground scoop brother bodybuilders might
find useful—including, more often than bodybuilding officials would
ever admit outside their narrow, self-protecting confines, the names and
phone numbers of wealthy johns who trade money for sex with muscle
studs looking for easy financing to support their obsession with what's
erroneously called a sport, in which aboveboard commercial rewards
mostly go to the elite handful of champs the 'zines publicize as turn-
ons for their slavish army of readers. Through all this, at least at major
contests, thread TV crews as well as bodybuilding scribes and lensmen
flirtatiously playing cat-and-mouse with publicity seekers, which, of
course, takes in virtually all the claimants to muscle stardom. Bodybuilding contests—and we're talking here about those for men; competitive bod exhibitions for muscular women are another matter—are
about much more than anointing the builder of the best built physique
on display. They're also muscle media happenings that supply the 'zines
with reams of fodder, and social occasions for the pumping iron tribe.
But in their largest dimension, they're celebrations of the mesmerizing
power of intense masculinity in all its outward vestiges. "Hard"—as in,

"Geez, look at the brutal mass of hard beautiful muscle packed on that dude!"—is by far the most heard word in the celebrants' lingo, and that's no coincidence. The photography historian and critic who in her book on photographers of the male nude likened the bodybuilder's hyperbolic manliness to a big throbbingly hard dick shrewdly decoded the muscular body's symbolism of virile potency.

But Darren, who was rightfully confident of his massive and tanned body's peak of contest-ready hardness, remained undistracted by the backstage sideshow as he watched my fingers massaging oil into his molded and striated pecs, across his melon-shaped delts and mountainous traps, and on down the length and huge girth of his biceps, triceps, and amazingly vascular forearms, over the deeply cut ridges—including a lower fourth-row seldom seen at contests—of abs, and on up the slabs of his widely flared lats. Kneeling, I continued by oiling his outwardly sweeping and awesomely shaped thighs whose combination of large muscles gym rats call quads before moving backward to his roped hamstrings and downward to diamond-contoured calves. Then arising, I focused my adoring labor on his broad expansive back, whose mind-blowing array of intricate muscles was set off by the "Christmas tree" pattern radiating aside the spinal erectors just above his rounded firm ass ("glutes," in bb parlance)—a hard-earned detail that separates top contenders from also-rans.

"Looking good—good enough to eat!" I exclaimed (pardon the pun) after stepping back to double-check the evenness of his mantle of oil and that the front seam of his purple posing suit was centered over the mound of his basket to emphasize its cradled fullness. (You never know what might snare the attention of judges!) While not a thong, which for some crazy reason is *verboten* in bodybuilding competition, the suit was specially tailored to ride narrowly atop his hips an inch or so under the small waist's obliques and swoop down to the base of his partially shaved pubic area while, in the rear, triangularly caressing the top and center of his glutes but revealing the striations he had ripped into the lower cheeks of that powerful—and sooo sexy—muscle group.

Delightedly, I noted too that Darren had pulled his long thick cock down over his balls to push a hint of its bulbous head against the front of his crotch at the exact spot where I had planted a good-luck kiss before giving him the suit to slip on and reassure both of us that not only did it fit superbly but the color purple indeed complemented his naturally swarthy skin tone and brown eyes. And yes, purple also underscored like an exclamation point the royal charisma glowing from his aggressive yet irresistible personality.

"Thanks, Deke," said Darren over the mounting backstage noise that indicated the contest countdown was in its final moments. "I'm going to knock their jocks off out there. This is going to be my night!" But as he pivoted to take his place in the lineup being marshaled by the contest expeditor to march forth and unleash the muscle war's pumped-up fury, he flashed me a cagey wink and added a quick, balls-churning correction: "*Our* night, man."

As I said, it had taken four years for Darren and me to get to this pivotal point in his bodybuilding career. Actually, though, his own route to get here began a few years earlier when he took up lifting to enhance his prowess on the football field as a running back and was hard bitten by the bodybuilding bug.

But when we finally connected I already knew who he was, certainly. The owner of the gym where he trained in a Louisiana town about fifty miles from where I lived had pointed Darren out to me as a determined youngster with an extraordinary potential for bodybuilding success, and I had checked him out in a local novice contest. At that point, he had been training for only a few months and didn't win. But still I was impressed enough to make a mental note to ask the gym owner to keep me current on Darren's progress.

Every few weeks I would get excited reports about his gains in weight *and* strength, and finally I decided it was time for me to step into his life if he won the larger regional contest for which he was training; no sense to rush things and raise his hopes before he had proven himself. But since he didn't win, I chose to hold my horses until the next competition season began gearing up and football was out of the way. He made All-State that year and, I read in the papers, was already being courted by college recruiters, so I didn't want to interfere with that.

But leave it to Darren to take the bull by the horns. None of this pussy-footing around stuff for him, and instead of me calling him, he called me when he got back home. A friend of mine who was a judge at the contest noted that Darren and I lived near each other and suggested he contact me for guidance if he was serious about continuing to compete. You see, as a former writer for a leading bodybuilding magazine, the promoter of my state's annual bodybuilding championships, a successful distributor of iron game products, and occasional sponsor of unusually promising young bodybuilders, I held a respectable standing in the national bodybuilding network. And having a "good guy" reputation in bodybuilding definitely opens doors; being gay has little to do with it unless gossip erupts to banish you for being "out of line" or on some other hypocritically trumped-up charge. There are lots of gay men in bodybuilding from top to bottom and probably always have been, which, of course, should hardly be unexpected given the iron game's object of glorifying the well-muscled male physique. In a tacit, if often insanely awkward, acknowledgement of this, there's a big tiptoeing around the "gay thing."

And while some nastiness crops up from time to time stemming from the homophobia that masks the sexual insecurities of bodybuilding's high (and decidedly blue collar) politicos, these days—especially since the coming out in a bodybuilding magazine of popular superstar Bob Paris (although that happened some years after the time frame I'm talking about here)—a live-and-let-live attitude generally prevails. I guess I've been lucky to have never had any trouble at all.

Fortunately, neither has the nationally accredited judge who directed Darren to me. There was a gay angle behind the referral, of course, but I'm sure my friend didn't make it explicit. Undoubtedly he was charmed by Darren's budding beauty, but instead of making a calculating play for sexual favor he sublimated desire by avuncularly encouraging a remarkably gifted young man. To be sure, that self-discipline had won him wide respect as a judge with one of bodybuilding's highest records of accuracy in picking winners, and I doubt he even allowed himself to speculate about Darren's sexual bent.

You can't always tell on sight who is and is not gay, of course, even among bodybuilders. While there *is* a disproportionately high level of homosexual orientation (acknowledged or closeted) within their ranks, there's much exuberant heterosexuality there, too. I didn't know enough about Darren to guess where he fit into the diverse sexual spectrum, nor did he drop any clues when he called me. What I heard instead was an overriding enthusiasm and motivation to go as far in competitive bodybuilding as he could. Indeed, he seemed so convinced he had what it takes to become a champ that I felt I owed it to the game to take a good look at him and offer whatever help I could to channel his dreams.

So I told him to show up at noon the next day at the gym close to my house in which I had a silent partnership. And when I arrived about ten minutes prior to that time he was already there at the front desk awaiting me, along with his girlfriend and a buddy who, I soon learned, had driven them over. Immediately, even before he changed into workout shorts and a tank top, I noticed how much larger and more impressively filled out he was than when I last saw him at his first contest. I intuited his surprisingly added size was undergirded by proportionately symmetrical muscle, a hunch confirmed soon when he and his buddy took to the gym floor to show me the stuff of their workouts.

Talk about going to the gut-busting max! And oh, that glowing smile and gleam in Darren's big brown eyes. So he's got balls, I said to myself; good, you need big ones to make it in competitive bodybuilding. Even veteran iron pumpers who think they've seen it all stopped to watch. While the sets and reps pumped-out by the well-matched partners obviously were taken from examples found in the magazines, they were adapted with an innate understanding of physiological dynamics. What that told me was that he had plenty of smarts to go with his big balls, a combination that divides the men from the boys in the body-building world. Many are called, as is written somewhere, but few are chosen.

Later, after the sweaty duo had showered and joined me in the gym's office, I asked Darren if he had any commitments back home precluding him from moving over and working under my supervision. No, he told me, graduation was out of the way and he had decided to not accept any of the football scholarships offered him but concentrate on bodybuilding. And he could give a week's notice on the summer construction job he had found, which meant he could get back next Sunday. Fine. I'd have a place for him to live, he could train here at the gym without cost, and there'd be a part-time job, something that wouldn't interfere with his training.

"Sounds good to me, coach," he exuded as he shook my hand to seal the deal, grabbed his gym bag, and strode to the front desk with his buddy in tow. Pam, the girlfriend, met them there, and together the trio danced out the front door in a playful swirl of youthful joy I watched in bemused amazement.

I spent the following week making arrangements, and promptly at the agreed-upon hour of eight Sunday night the trio knocked on my door. "Hey, coach, your future star is here," announced Darren when I greeted them and he entered like he already owned the place, followed by his buddy bringing in a few pieces of luggage and Pam bearing a couple small boxes. "Darren has a real sweet tooth," she explained, "but I told him these are the last goodies he'll get until he sees me again." At that, Darren crunched her to him and brushed her lips with a kiss as the gang—including me—chuckled at her little double entendre.

"Hey guys, none of that funny stuff here," mockingly protested his buddy. "You have to watch Darren good, Mr. Deke, and kick ass when he needs it. He can be one stubborn dude, but underneath it all my man's got what it takes. I want to be able to tell my babies I was the first workout partner of the strongest and baddest muscle stud ever to come from our hometown, hear?"

But Darren had his own goals in mind. "Oh damn, y'all get out of here. Me and Mr. Deke got lots of work in front of us. Do I have to put up a 'Men at Work' sign?" Pushing them out the door, he gave his buddy a high-five and, turning to Pam, shouldered her again in his arm and rewarded her with another kiss. "I'll see you soon, babe," I heard him tell her, "but don't call me. I'll call you."

Closing the door behind them he began anxiously chatting. "They're good guys, coach. But what about us? You're the boss, and I'm here to learn. They're yesterday, man, but you and me, we're tomorrow." For beginners, I told him, he'd be living here in my house, and I showed him the layout—kitchen, phones, TV and VCR, stereo and tape deck, and so forth—before heading down the hall to show him his room while pointing out his bath and john two doors down. But my master bedroom was across the hall from where he would be bunking, and I said he was welcome to use the adjoining bathroom in case of an emergency since it was closer than the other one.

"Great, man. So what's tomorrow's schedule like?" Well, it was going to be a long day. He'd be meeting the trainer I had found for him at the gym, a nutritionist at the local college to set up his diet, a doctor to devise and keep close tabs on his steroids program (legally), and the owner of a construction company for whom he'd be working part-time.

"Sounds great, coach," he assured me. "But, oh man, I see I'm going to need all my energy to get off on the right foot, so if it's okay with you I'm going to hit the sack and get a long night's sleep." I was tuckered out also from being keyed up all week, so I followed his lead by bidding him good night and turning into my bedroom.

And I slept like the proverbial log, not awakening until the dawn from the flushing toilet in my bathroom. Coming out of my grogginess,

I realized it was Darren. I guess he heard my waking-up rustling, too, since soon he called out, "It's only me, Mr. Deke. I woke up with a dick full of piss and didn't think I could make it down the hall."

Daylight was peeping through the blinds, but it was light enough for me to see the sheepish grin on his face when he stepped out of the bathroom. Like me, he must enjoy sleeping in the nude because the only thing he was wearing was an invitingly full hard-on.

"Sorry, didn't mean to wake you, Mr. Deke," he apologized, moving closer to my bed. "Pam's always been there to help me handle this, but I guess I'll have to get used to doing it with a hand job."

"There's no need for that," I calmly objected, trying hard to muffle my boldness. Nonetheless, I could see from the no-longer-grinning look on his face that what I said perplexed him, and after a pause he asked what I had in mind.

"We can probably come up with another solution if we think about it. Does Pam ever suck you off?"

"Oh no, Sir. I keep asking her to, but she's a good Catholic girl and thinks that's dirty. The priests and nuns in the school we went to taught us that."

"Do you?"

"Well, to be honest, Sir, I never bought that," he answered still in the deferential mode well-mannered southern boys muster in the presence of older men (not that I was *that* much older!). "Football players horse around a lot in the locker room, and I got my first blow-job from my co-captain. He played center, and we made All-State together. Then my big brother told me when he was a Marine in boot camp at Parris Island, one of his drill instructors used to call him up to the DI duty hut so he could chomp on bro's dick. You think I'm big? You ought to see him, and he's a real ladies' man, too. But he said he'd never found a woman yet who could suck dick as good as that sergeant. So I've learned those nuns and priests were real wrong. You don't have to be a damn sissy or sex pervert to be a cocksucker or like getting blown. You ever tried it?"

"You be honest with me, and I'll be honest with you," I told him. "I admit to having tasted that pleasure. But fucking or sucking, it's all about sex—just, as they say, different strokes for different folks."

"Hey, Mr. Deke, I just thought about something. You're not a fag, are you? I don't want you to get the wrong idea about me. I've heard lots of talk about fags who like to hang around bodybuilders. But, man, I like pussy too much for that."

"Was your buddy the football player or the DI your brother told you about a fag?"

"Okay, that's cool, I see what you mean. But just so you know where I'm coming from. I trust you, man, or I wouldn't be here. I asked around about you, and nobody had anything but good to say. You know what you're doing. I want to keep us on the same wavelength, that's all."

But as he talked, I could see that his cock was still standing stiffly at attention. "Come here, Darren," I summoned sternly, and propped myself up against my pillow while he moved closer and finally was looking down at me, his sexual curiosity obviously intact. I returned his gaze, and then leaned forward to flick his throbbing cock head with my tongue and sniff the intoxicating musk of his late-adolescent maleness. My hands reached to cup his sack of balls, and as I tingled from their touch I spread my lips to swallow the shaft of his big dick and strokingly feast on its lusty bounty.

"Careful, coach," I heard him cautioning me. "I come easy when I'm fired up and I'd hate to strangle you with my load." But in my ravenous hunger that was the furthest thing from my mind. Instead I spread my lips wider and swallowed him deeper, speeding up my range of friction to feel the thrusts of his shaft digging farther and farther down my throat. Reaching around to grab the taut cheeks of his ass, I pushed him deeper into me as he leaned over to buttress his already big arms—nineteen-inch biceps, I would guess—upon my shoulders. And amid his quickening gasps of breath, I felt the building tenseness of his body and tasted the delicious precum signalling his readiness to erupt into me.

"I'm coming, man, I'm coming!" he yelled at the height of my frenzy. "God damn! Fuck! You're gonna get it all, cocksucker!" And that's just what I got as payback for my worship, every drop of which I greedily supped. Emotionally drained, he fell across me as if to snuff out my lust, too, with the pressure of his heavy spent body. But the weight of this emerging muscle divinity was heaven upon me, and I held tightly to him. Resting, with his bulk still draped over me while my mouth cleaned his softened cock, he caught his breath and rolled off onto the bed, from where he reached up to pull me down aside him.

We lay that way in the quiet together, our eyes closed and each savoring the climb down from the peak to which my thrashing mouth had led us. But I felt him move, and opened my eyes to look directly into his above me. "I've got to tell you," he intimated, "you've already shown me something new, coach. I guess I went a little crazy with that yelling and cocksucker stuff, but, man, that was the greatest. Bro was right, nothing like being sucked off by a man who's an expert at it. Y'know, you got what he calls a velvet mouth. It's almost as good as getting into a juicy hot pussy."

"What's this 'almost' shit?"

"I thought that would get a rise out of you," shot back his retort, punctuated with a chuckle and wink I would soon come to adore. "Yeh, almost. Guess you'll just have to work on it."

Darren took to his sharpened-up training program and living with me as naturally as a duck takes to water, and by fall we began choosing contests for him to target the next year. But first he wanted to return to the regional show he had narrowly lost in the spring and win it before moving up to higher-level competition. Yes, I agreed, it would be good strategy for him to get a regional title under his belt before casting his net more widely. Fortunately, the junior national championships would follow a couple months later, time enough for him to make whatever fine-tuning was needed before he came up against other regional and state title winners from across the country.

As expected, he aced the regional competition and easily won his first bodybuilding title. Undistracted by that success, though, Darren remained focused on moving ahead, and by the time the juniors rolled around he was ready. And his spirits were buoyant, too. But while I would like to claim credit for that, I must in candor share it with Pam, who flew up to the juniors with us.

Except for his Christmas break, Darren had spent little time with her since the night he was delivered to me, and the contest weekend, he convincingly argued, would be both a good opportunity for them to have some "quality time" together and a chance for her to learn more about the bodybuilding lifestyle. He had already taught her a few things about caring for a bodybuilder, such as how to prepare his meals with the precise ratio of carbs, proteins, and fats, the method of shaving his body to reveal unadorned the structure of its muscularity, and the way to oil him down. And certainly she had down pat the basic essential which many of the female gender ironically lack—an appreciation of the bodybuilding physique—and was primed to build further on that bedrock of devotion to her man.

On the flight up the three of us were happy campers, chock-full of eager anticipation for what lay ahead. When we got to the hotel, they veered off to their room while I went my separate way. And I heard no more from them until the night before the contest, when Darren called to ask me to come up and show Pam how to apply his artificial tan so its golden bronze coloring would seep into his skin overnight to insure the size and depth of his muscles wouldn't be smoothed out by the contest lights—another detail he had mastered.

When I arrived, they were ready to begin. Pam was wearing thin running shorts and a tank top revealing a more rounded, fuller-breasted figure than I recalled seeing last spring. And Darren, who had been practicing his posing routine in front of the bathroom's tall mirror, had on the satiny teal posing suit we had selected for the juniors. Okay, I instructed to get things under way, the first thing to learn about applying skin bronzer to a bodybuilder's body is that he should be totally nude so not a fraction of an inch anywhere is left uncovered. Posing suits jiggle as the body moves, and you don't want to see any unsightly lines marking him when he is on stage trying to win attention to the physique he's worked damn hard to build.

They looked at each other for a few seconds with hesitant embarrassment. But Darren broke their silence and urged her to do as I said, while he forthrightly pulled down his suit and stepped out of it. "I see I've got a lot to learn," she responded with a nervous giggle, and picked up the applicator as if to ask "Where do I begin?"

Patiently, I showed her. Placing Darren back in front of the bathroom mirror, I directed her to begin at the neck and work down, concentrating on evenly covering the whole body from top to bottom. Following this guidance, she kept her eyes intently on her gorgeous field of labor and Darren looked down to follow her progress. As for my eyes, they switched back and forth to check Pam's thoroughness and see Darren's reaction.

She was a quick learner, too. " 'Atta girl, you're doing good, babe," he coaxed her, which seemed to increase her confidence, especially when she got to his hips, butt, and pubic area. It was touching to watch her dutifulness, and I could see Darren was affected, too; already his cock was rising to a hard-on.

"Easy does it," I cautioned, trying to calm both of them as she headed down to his well-defined quads and on to his calves. "Anything for you, Darren," she pledged, admiring the sculpted—and now thoroughly bronzed—vastness she was kneeling in front of. "God, you're so beautiful and I just want to make you happy."

"Show her how to suck cock, coach. We've been working at it, but

she's still got a long ways to go and I want her to learn from the best."
If that acknowledgment of her ardor stunned Pam, her eyes betrayed
neither surprise nor revulsion. Instead, she looked up at me meekly and
awaited her second lesson.

Whatever Darren wants, Darren gets, so I dropped to my knees,
figuring the best way to teach this was by example and that he would
supply such commentary as he felt was needed. Pulling Pam up to him,
he gentled her with a smooth lover's kiss and directed her attention to
how I was inching his cock into my mouth and cupping his balls in my
hands.

"See, babe, the trick is in keeping your lips relaxed, like Deke's
are. Don't stop breathing, either; I don't want to gag you. Your mouth
is smaller than his, but you can take my big dick by slowly working
up to it. See how he's starting out by first swallowing my cock head,
then inching up deeper with his lips? Just open wide and let my dick
slide in, nice and easy, resting on your pointed tongue." And as I began
building my rhythm, he told her that was an important part of the head
action. "Don't be jerky. Keep your strokes smooth and even. And no
teeth, babe; I don't want you to bite my dong. Once it's in, keep your
head angled so it just slides down your throat. We'll have a ball."

I was having a ball, certainly, and the curtailment of Darren's commentary told me he was getting pleasure, too. Now the only sounds in
the room were coming from my slurping mouth and the couple's lapping
kisses. But just when my head was slipping into overdrive, he pulled
out of me.

What the hell? I'm sure the look on my face surprised them. "Sorry,
Deke," he explained, "but Pam's been real good and I told her she's
going to get my load. She's between her baby making periods and really
hot for me." He didn't just leave me kneeling there on the floor, though,
like some disappointed beau at party's end. Rather than packing me out
the door, either, he gave me an invitation I couldn't resist: "You get
out of your clothes, and take the other bed. I want you to stay and watch
us. You're not the only teacher here, man, and now I'm going to show
you a thing or two."

I began tearing away my clothes—somewhat frantically, I recall—
and saw him lead her by the hand to their bed, where he sat down to
slip off her shorts and tank top. This was going to be much more
exciting than watching some raunchy porn video; I was getting ready
to see a real-life muscle stud sleekly fucking his lady love. .

But first, he wanted to know how well she had mastered her sucking lesson. "Show me, babe, how much you want my dick," I could barely hear him whispering to her while his hands explored her naked body. He lay down and reached out for her to come to him, and she quickly began proving how totally she craved him.

"Good girl, sweetheart," he said to her bobbing head. "My pretty lady's gonna be a cocksucking pro." But Pam's newly adept sucking, of course, was only a prelude to the big show Darren was going to treat her—and me—to. Pulling her up and sliding her body across his rippling torso, he held her atop him in his arms and tenderly showered her neck, ears, and face with kisses. Then gently laying her beside him, he dove down to tongue her nipples and small belly before descending to her triangular muff and clit, where he *really* went to work. Flat out, he had her moaning and pleading, "Fuck me, Darren, fuck me!"

"Hold on, babe," he calmed her as he spread his body back over hers and opened her legs to wrap them around his lower back. And from my bed, I watched her hands guiding Darren's dick into its mount, then shoot up to grasp his biceps. I heard a gasp from him, too, as he broke through to the promised land.

"Oh yeh, honey, grab your man's muscle and feel my power. I'm going to shoot us to the fuckin' moon, babe."

And I was going with them. Pam's delirious cries of pleasure and Darren's pulsating domination of her also aroused me, and I was jerking off in sync to his heaving plunges deeper and deeper into her. But it didn't take us long to reach our destination. Pam's ecstatic shrieks and the tightening muscles in his back along with the dimples sucking into the cheeks of his ass heralded that the moon's landscape was within sight. Finally, neither my young muscle turk, Pam, nor I could hold our intense longing to get there any longer, and I shot my wad as he stove his with a culminating thrust into his woman. As for Pam, her yells were proof that her lust was more than satisfactorily satiated.

Exhausted from the heat of the ride, I fell back on my bed while they embraced in theirs, the three of us drenched in sweat. And I lay there, lulled by their anticlimatic love murmurs. "God, that was the best ever, Darren," I remember hearing Pam tell him before I drifted into a peaceful reverie of my own.

But before I had time to get very far away, I was brought back by a tug on my worn-out cock and a peck on my forehead. Realizing it was Darren, I thought he was up for more after exhausting Pam and recovering his amazing energy. After all, his virtually unquenchable potency had kept me up more nights than I can count. But who's complaining? When my eyes opened, though, I saw from his mischievous smile that this time he was only joking.

"Hey, coach, what you dreaming about? Must be good from that happy look on your face. That was some trip you just watched, huh? Pam thinks you're pretty cool, and she's real proud you taught her how to suck. And, man, she's come a long way and couldn't have done it without you. But, hey, you got to admit I'm the best fucker."

Hey, he had just shown me that, and I wouldn't even think of competing with him. Still, I pointed out, he had a big problem. "Now your tan is all splotched, and Pam's magic fingers are going to have to get back to work and smooth you out. Otherwise, the best fucker will be laughed off the stage tomorrow as the biggest fuck-up when he shows up with his big beautiful bod all messed up."

"Oh shit!" he hollered and ran to the mirror to see the damage. "Damn, babe! The party's over. Looks like you got lots of work to do."

But there was no laughing when Darren showed up for the contest. Pam did an expert repair job, and he dominated the large lineup so forcefully that when the judges' sheets were tabulated no one was surprised he won with a perfect score—the first in the show's history. So much for this bullshit about bodybuilders not having sex the night before a contest to save their energy for the next day. Hell, a lot of guys stick with such rigid card-depleting diets and other body-defining ploys (including diuretics) in the quest to lose excess body fat and water around the muscles that even if the vaunted "thin skin" look comes as a result to sharpen the physique with super-definition, the unhealthy process saps energy so completely these dumb asses couldn't get their dicks up if they tried. None of that stupidity for Darren. The cock I had worked up to delight Pam proved how well he had listened to the nutritionist and doctor who kept close check on what he put into the temple of his body.

As expected, Darren's unprecedented triumph became the topic-of-the-week on the bodybuilding hotline (where he was benighted "Darren the Detonator") and brought him lots of magazine publicity. One went so far as to rave he had "the stuff" to shoot directly to the top of bodybuilding and already was a prime candidate for the heavyweight lineup at the fall's senior nationals. His win at the juniors qualified him to compete in that top amateur-level competition, of course, and he was eager to do so. But I didn't think that was the best thing for him at this point in his career, and urged him instead to be patient and put another year of progress behind him so when he finally got to the nationals his added size and muscle density would dazzle jaded judges who're only impressed by bodybuilders showing pronounced improvement since last seen. However sensational a competitor may have been on his previous outing doesn't count with those hawk-eyed birds, a fact innumerable bodybuilders fail to learn until it's too late.

Happily, Darren bought my line of reasoning. And after spending a few weeks with Pam, he returned to map out a revised program with his trainer, nutritionist, and doctor designed to achieve what would be needed when he entered next year's nationals. Before the juniors, I had told him that if he won he could quit his part-time job and I would support him until he won the nationals and earned his pro card. So now there was nothing to prevent him from totally concentrating on pushing his body to a higher and more mature plateau of development, and he and his new workout partner—a comely blond heavyweight from Texas named Greg whom Darren met at the juniors and had moved over to train with him—were soon burning up the gym like a pair of obsessed demons. We even had to buy some additional equipment to take care of their heavy-duty needs.

Yet despite all that, a distraction cropped up a few months later when Pam wrote to tell Darren she had found someone else to quench the sexual fire he had set burning but didn't have time to keep stoked. Ironically, the stud she turned to was his hometown buddy who tagged along for our first momentous meeting. But it wasn't just a fling; they were already married—which made me wonder if the buddy would be telling *their* babies about the time he trained with Darren.

After spending some time being sorry for himself, though, Darren bounced back and picked back up on his momentum. The only result of Pam's exit I could see was that it cemented a tighter bond between Darren and Greg, for whom I had found a sponsor from my network of friends with the means to underwrite promising young bodybuilders. Greg was set up in his own apartment, but when he and Darren weren't at the gym they were together at my much better furnished and more comfortable house. And once when I came home and found the door to Darren's room shut, I heard the unmistakable sounds of an energetic sexual coupling coming from the other side.

But that was fine with me, and I went quietly about my business. Sexual exclusivity, of course, wasn't part of my deal with Darren, and actually the vision of him and Greg getting it on together was a rather exciting fantasy. One of the things I've learned from my bodybuilding involvement is that the camaraderie of the gym meshes a closeness, especially in workout partners, that carries over beyond. There's much evidence to validate the adage that a good workout partnership hones the closeness of a tight marriage.

Still, I hoped he would continue to find his way into my bedroom. I rejoice to say he did—and often, since he still had a "problem" in waking up with a powerful morning hard-on. I never asked what he and Greg did outside the gym, but I also benefited from the deepening emotional sensitivity Darren derived from the relationship. In tandem with the muscle growth he was pumping out, he was becoming a more assured and assertive lover which meant that I was no longer the initiator—well, not always, anyway. The strutting ballsiness of adolescence groping toward manhood, in other words, gave way to an authoritative masculine maturity.

Indeed, he was bursting with manly confidence as the date for the targeted nationals drew near, having used the past year to pack on about twenty pounds of heavy muscle, bring up lagging areas of his physique we analyzed were needed after the juniors' excitement died down, and perfect a new posing routine to dramatically showcase his dazzling achievement. Timing is everything, his trainer kept repeating, and bearing that firmly in mind Darren deftly paced himself to hit his peak on the day the nationals would be judged.

When we, together with Greg and his sponsor (a sports agent named Dave who represented some of the country's highest-paid football and baseball stars) flew up to the contest city, each of us knew the Detonator was going to do serious damage to the plans of his competitors. I had made reservations at a hotel away from the one designated as the contest headquarters to keep him under wraps until he showed up at the weigh-in and shocked everyone. The other couple went to their own room, while Darren and I took separate ones since I didn't want any salacious questions asked in case some gossipy spy saw us there together. Then after we stashed our gear, I met him back in the lobby to take him to a nearby sauna to force out the last bit of excess moisture between his skin and underlying muscles.

Greg went along, too, and the two beauties set off a riot of lascivious stares when they stripped to expose their bodies to the vaporous heat. I instructed the attendants, whom I knew from previous visits, to not let *anyone* hassle my guests, and told Darren when I would meet him in his room to rub in the bronzer to his already deep tan and give a final check-through to his posing routine.

"Man," piped up Greg, "while you guys work, me and Dave are going to be out partying. He's got some big stuff lined up for us, going to show me around."

I just bet he is, I thought, but said instead, "That's okay, wiseguy. Go ahead and wear your dick out that way. But Darren's the one who's going to have something big to celebrate, and he and I'll get in our partying when he wins tomorrow. And you and Dave won't be invited, either. Don't even think about it."

I had some business to take care of before the banks in the city closed for the day, so I left them to soak up the heat. And later when I got to Darren's room, I could see the sauna-induced sweat had carved out the intended effect. Holy shit, I was stunned at the sight! His huge body's galaxy of muscle was incredibly defined with the hardness of granite.

Beholding him standing there in the doorway wearing only the purple posing suit we had finally settled on, I paused in fear that he was a fantasy, a transcendent apparition that would disappear when I reached out to touch it.

But, of course, he was real, and I was brought back to the world when he smiled and threw me one of his winks. "Think this is good enough for those demanding judges, Deke?" he asked.

Oh my, yes! He was going to have them panting, to say nothing of the havoc he was going to wreak among the blind-sided lineup. As for the magazine writers, his magnificence would dash them into a panic to toss out their tired lexicon of praise and come up with new phrases to describe him. But I didn't say any of this, not wanting him to lose his competitive edge. What I actually said, as I recall, was something noncommittal yet, I hoped, positive, like "Well, you've certainly done all you can."

But I hadn't yet done all I could, so seeing the container of bronzing fluid on the room's dresser I grabbed it and went to work to prepare him, proceeding pretty much as I had taught Pam to do. He stepped out of his posing suit for my polishing job, of course, but when I finished I told him to put it back on so we could run through his posing choreography the way the judges would see it.

The compact cassette player he had brought for this purpose was on the dresser, also, and I flipped in the cassette of his posing music. We let it run through to get him in the mood and play the routine's timing back in his head. But when he was focused, I reversed it to begin all over. From an opening lat spread with his hands on his hips and pecs tensed, he glided from one statuesque pose to another, all the while keeping his body sensually aligned as he drew attention to each muscle area and triumphally ended with an over-the-head extension of his arms.

Noncompetitors, even judges, don't realize how much energy is expended in posing, and while Darren recovered his breath I calmed myself to submerge my excitement and retain at least a shred of objectivity. Although his execution was well-nigh perfect (and hypnotically sexy!), one detail wasn't yet quite right. The angle of his flexed arms when he turned to display his back from the rear was a tad off, just enough to detract from the impact of his raised biceps.

But it's best to show rather than tell, as I said, so I led him into the bathroom where he could watch himself in the full-size mirror there while I helped him correct the flaw. Keep your elbows back and your triceps parallel to the floor, I reminded him when he's holding the wrists outward to fully flex the biceps. A little more. There, that's it. Perfect. Oh beautiful!

I could hold back my worship no longer, though, and bent down to kiss his spectacularly peaked left bicep. Then looking up, my eyes locked with his in the mirror and he turned to sweep those astonishing arms around me and reciprocated my devotion with a deep kiss of his own.

Like some swooning damsel surrendering to her lord, I submitted to his masculine desire and meekly followed him to his bed. Laying me down there, he stood over me, stripped off his posing suit, and knelt down atop my hips, which sent my hands into a frenzy to fondle the wonders of his chest, abs, and, yes, swollen cock.

But now Darren was the master, and he pulled my head forward and silently ordered me to suck him. Holding me up to him, he thrust into my anxious mouth and my hands rested on his godly quads. Truth to tell, he had a slut for muscle cock on his hands.

A good suck, though, wasn't all he wanted from his bitch in heat. Soon I felt his hands on my shoulders, pressing me back upon the bed. He repositioned his body over mine, and I shivered to feel his hands caressing my ass and a finger lubricating my queer pussy. Instinctively I opened my legs to take him, and he lifted them outward to hold them there, spread-eagle style. "Guide me in," he commanded, "and hold on." I reached down to grab his hips, feeling the delicious pain of his en- gorged shaft entering me. And when he was deeply in, he bent down to tongue me a kiss. But sensing that my tight hole was now stretched wide enough to take his heaving fuck, he pulled his body back up to captain our own trip to the moon. But God, he shot us way past that and on into the outer reaches of the universe.

Maybe precontest sex was Darren's good-luck charm, because he over- whelmed the nationals even more effectively than he did the juniors. Judges were indeed spellbound by the enormous gains he had made since that earlier contest, and soon he landed up on several magazine covers. Overnight, he became the hottest new ticket in bodybuilding and offers came pouring in from contest promoters clamoring to sign him on as the guest poser at their events since his name guaranteed sold-out houses. But the most important thing for his future was finally getting a pro card. Now he was poised to enter competitive bodybuilding's inner sanc- tum, the pantheon of its gods.

As I watched the lineup take to the stage with a thunderous wel- come, it was impossible, even from my backstage vantage point, not to be stirred by the pandemonium his introduction evoked. But what was truly amazing was how this initial enthusiasm for Darren not only stayed with him but actually rose during the contest's succeeding rounds. While this and that lesser champ was relegated to the sidelines to watch the action of more skillful muscle warriors, he stayed right in the eye of the battle. And if any doubts remained about his superiority, he annihilated them in the free-posing round.

From that stellar performance, he advanced into the select cadre of finalists. But he outmaneuvered them, too, and when the emcee reeled off the names of place winners his was the last to be announced. The man I made from the driven youngster who showed up at my house had arrived at his destiny, a champion of champions.

I spotted Greg and Dave in their expensive front-row seats yelling their gonads off when Darren stood on top of the winners' platform to accept the spoils of victory and reward his loyal following with an encore of choice poses. I knew that cocky cowboy couldn't wait to get his hands on his training partner. Already he had been dropping hints about get- ting into a threesome with Darren and me, and maybe—probably— that would happen. But later, not here. Tonight was for my man and me, and the universe was still up there beckoning us back to explore its limits.

Note: The delightful carefree years I've recalled here happened just before the pall of AIDS tempered sexual exchange between bodybuilders and the men who love them. Even so, ironically, bodybuilding's swift rise in popularity has brought muscle worship out into the open and indeed given it a stamp of approval in today's hip culture. But that's a story for another time and place.

ANDREW HOLLERAN

THE SEX

VACATION

AT FIRST I GOT COLD FEET—AFTER RENTING THE CAR FOR A week, it sat in my driveway in north Florida for three days, eating money while I faced the fact that what had always been a fantasy was, in real life, not. When the time came to set out on my sex vacation, it seemed to me suddenly depressing and sordid. Why get on the road, spend nights in strange motels, eat by yourself in restaurants, just to cruise? Why cruise at all, for a solid week? Looking at the car through the window of my bedroom, this blue Mercury that was to bear me away to Sexual Bliss, I felt homesick before I'd even left, and very lonely; a lesson, perhaps, in choosing one's fantasies more carefully, because some-day you may have to carry them out.

On the fourth day, nevertheless, I made myself get on the road—if only to use the car—drove to the baths in Jacksonville, stayed most of Saturday night (not that different from other visits), and then checked into a nearby motel at four a.m. (Depressing; all motels you stay in by yourself are.) The next day I went to the gay beach in South Ponte

Vedra—deserted, under a drizzling gray sky—and by the time I'd finished my solitary swim, I was debating whether or not to continue to
the final stop: Orlando. Only having paid for the car kept me going, I
think; that, and the prospect of driving through a town whose name
appealed to me—Bunnell. ("There isn't a man in Bunnell who isn't
handsome," said a friend.) And the fact that once I made it past Bunnell
I was almost in our version of L.A.—Orlando—and once I was in Orlando, I was at the Parliament House. The P-House is technically a
motel—that used to advertise itself as the world's largest gay complex.
Whether that's true or not, it is a place people down here go when they
want to get away from it all—meaning their lives in small towns; small
towns which do not offer what the Parliament House does.

And not only small towns—the first men I spotted in a room near
mine when I passed their plate-glass window had, on a table next to the
glass, a book by Paul Monette called, I think, *Lustleven*. A bearded, bald
man was reading in a chair by the window; another on the bed. They
must be European, I thought; the usual window display here includes a
television someone is pretending to watch, and sex. Here were two men,
at dusk, in their room, reading books. They seemed annoyed, however,
when they looked up at the sound of my knuckle tapping on the glass.
I tapped again. The man on the bed finally told the bearded fellow to
open the door; I said I'd noticed the book by Paul Monette, and wondered which one it was, in translation; the man on the bed looked for
the copyright page, finally found it, and snapped, *"Afterlife!"* I thanked
him and, my attempt at transatlantic friendship rebuffed, fled to Cal's
room—a place of refuge—and told him what had happened.

I went to Cal's room a lot during my two days at the P-House—
because he's a friend, because he'd been there a couple of days already,
visits frequently, and could explain the place in less time than I'd need
to figure it out. It takes time, he said, to adjust. When you first get to
the P-House, you're overwhelmed; I felt that way myself, and saw the
same unease in the faces of new arrivals, including a very handsome
Dutch boy when he first came out onto the balcony facing the lake with
his friend and they stared, with parted lips, at the sun setting over the
lake, the palm trees, the men. Cal, who comes here periodically, claims
we are all starved for genital contact, panic-stricken that each dick may
be our last, participants in a search whose desperation people assured of
regular, if not domestic, sex, never experience. Whatever the reason,
when you get to the Parliament House, you're stunned. All those men,

in some incredible hormonal buzz, some cloud of pheromones that make the place radioactive. The minute you drive in, you feel it. It's not like going to the baths—it's much more intense—it's like landing on a desert island populated by homosexuals who have been stranded for months. Cal estimates he recognizes sixty percent of the people—regulars, like the Eternal Nine at the Jacksonville baths: locals, who stop in on their way to work, or on their lunch hour. But you can't tell the difference between them and the tourists when you get there. You just see . . . men . . . walking across the parking lot, lying by the pool, clustered in the bars, standing on the balcony, sitting behind plate-glass windows in their rooms. It takes time to adjust, to get your cruising goggles on, to decide what you want, and when. That is: If you can have sex twenty-four hours a day, when do you have it? Cal's friend John, who drove here from his home an hour away to have lunch, fled afterwards in terror at the thought of the place; fat and celibate, not knowing how, after ten years in New York, he is still alive, he does not want to be near temptation. So he secludes himself in a small town and eats. The rest of us come to the P-House from other towns, or cities, in this country and Europe, in various states of optimism or despair, proud or ashamed of our physical selves, in midlife crisis or the bloom of youth, each one having made his ethical, psychological, physical contract with the fact of AIDS. ("I bet a lot of positives come here," says Cal. One assumes so; one of the 9,658 ironies of AIDS is that it's the HIV-antibody-positives who are out tricking, and the negatives who have withdrawn. Ironic, from an ethical standpoint, perhaps, though not a psychological one.) His first night he encounters a young man from Gainesville so terrified of AIDS, he is afraid to do anything; till Cal slips a rubber on his dick. "You're the right person for him to have run into," I tell Cal, who says: "I wanted him to know he can have a sex life, that he doesn't have to live without sex."

My first night there, I ran around the place, as if on speed. My room was on the ground floor facing the lake near a stairwell; a sort of backwater, though it was on the most heavily trafficked wing. I hardly used the room, however, until it was time to sleep. Mostly, I kept walking past other voices, other rooms. The P-House is a voyeur's paradise. (In the morning you awaken, and find palm prints and smudges on the window, like frost on a winter morning, where people have been cupping their hands and putting their noses to the glass to see you, as you lay there sleeping.) It's like that street in Amsterdam, where the whores sit in lighted windows. It's a place for *tableaux vivantes*. ("I want a *scene*!" said a bored friend of Cal's the previous evening, when Cal asked what he wanted.) The real difference between people there is not between tourists and locals, but between those who have a room (about $50 a night) and those who don't; those who do, it seems to me, have a lot of clout—are exchanging, you might say, money for sex. With a room, you feel like a john; without one, I suspect, you feel like a prostitute. Sometimes two people will ask for the use of your room, Cal says, and allow you to watch; he considers this a thinly veiled insult. To me the idea is thrilling. As I wander around I keep thinking, like some opera director, of the cast I'd like to put together; one person no longer seems enough. (Sexual deprivation followed by sexual greed.) That's one reason I walk the balcony, at least.

It's a bit difficult to do—like everything there—at first. (Staying at the P-House is a gradual process of discarding inhibitions.) You walk by quickly and barely glance in at first; a split second is all you get. Glances are held, or broken, very fast—rejection, or acceptance, so immediate you really have no time to decide whether you want the person. (So fragile is the ego-offering, you lose people this way whom you decide later on you wish you'd gone with. People here are really very shy, a local tells me, till about two a.m.; "If you want someone," he says, "reach out and *trip* them.")

The degree to which the curtain is drawn back varies from room to room—as does whether the door is open, open with the chain still on, whether the person is lying on his bed fully dressed, or naked. Through one window, with a small crowd, I watch one man screwing another; they lie at an angle across the bed, like two beached whales—two big white backsides. It's like watching nature films: mammals mating. In another room, from which earlier I saw a man emerge bare-chested in full leather—the picture of The Leather Queen, easy to dismiss—I now see the same man stark naked, in the pale, spectral light of his TV, with a gigantic sausage of a penis dangling between his legs. A minute later, a beefy dark-haired man in jeans and T-shirt takes a position beside me at the railing, looking back, and in another moment, enters the room. The curtain is drawn, and I hear slaps. (I think of this image all the way home, and can't get it out of my mind; it is probably what will draw me back to the P-House.) The truth is, however, people feel embarrassed, looking in and looking out of the rooms. The expression on the faces of people looking into my room is strained, pained, or carefully cool; I cannot look in unless I'm passing at a good clip.

In one room, completely dark, a naked man is seated next to the window so that the light from the courtyard reveals his genitals. In another, there is nothing but a table spread with Al Parker magazines, while its occupant comes and goes to see who has paused to stare at them, like a fisherman checking his trap. One man lies in bed, with the sheets and blankets pulled up to his chin; I have watched him in various stages—lying on the same bed fully dressed, reading a book; standing in front of his TV selecting a channel in jockstrap and T-shirt; and now, apparently with no success, like a child waiting to be tucked in with cookies and milk. Of course, the luxury of the P-House is that the cookies and milk are cock. This is the House of Penis. I can only stand in my room for a few minutes, fully dressed, with the curtain open a little bit, before I feel embarrassed and leave it to wander. With so many men it's impossible to choose. I lose a great opportunity when, standing outside my room toward the end of the evening, two men I am attracted to, but hesitant to approach, take up positions on either side of me. This is the moment, I tell myself; though I can't tell for sure who is attracted to whom. Open your door, I tell myself, and see what happens. I can't. Too proud. Too nervous. The next day, I ask Cal: "But what should I have said?" Cal: "Simply, 'If you two would like to get together, I have a room.' " It sounds very Emily Post. A surprisingly high percentage of people here are actually as constrained, as frightened, as I am. It's not easy, for one thing, when you are drawn to someone, to figure out what they want; what you'd do together. Rilke says we should kiss the frog, because it may turn into a prince. Connie Cruising says: Figure out what they're after before you get involved. (Cal: "You can never get some of them out of your room!") Better to do nothing, than to make a mistake. You're always safe, not having sex at all. Sex "solves" nothing; but what is life without it?

I finally draw the curtain, and go to bed, hearing the footfalls of people passing. When it comes time to check out the next day—one p.m.—I can't decide whether to spend another night; so I check out, as if this will tell me. I move my car to another part of the parking lot, under a shady oak tree, and tell myself I'll wait till Cal awakens from his nap to say good-bye to him, and watch, meanwhile, one of the staff—a shirtless hunk—mow the lawn on the adjacent lot.

Checking out of the Parliament House is like stepping off a cruise ship—one of those gay cruises I was always afraid to take, thinking they'd be claustrophobic. At the P-House, of course, all you have to do is turn in your key and drive away. This big oak in whose breezy shade

I now stand, leaning against my car, is a spot from which to get some
objectivity about the place. It's hot, the breeze feels good, the motel
looks somnolent in the brilliant sunshine. The first man I note is the
beefy guy in khaki shorts and black tank top who passed my room twice,
and looked in, as I was getting ready to check out. I did not return his
glance. Now he stands across the asphalt parking lot, leaning on the
railing in the sunshine, looking better than ever. (The P-House, which
could supply someone's thesis on the Psychology of Cruising, eventually
illustrates all its laws, including the one that says, as in life, what you
can't have, you want; what you can, you don't.) Looking at him now, I
tell myself that if I check back in and he's still available, I'll refuse
again. He's too young, good-looking, hunky; it would be work, adoring
him. (Later that day, around dusk, I pass him again at the bottom of
the stairs having the inside of his arm licked by a big puppy of a blond
his own age who doesn't find it work.) Finally, the hunk in the black
tank top walks off, and a slender Indian or Pakistani in a red-and-black
polo shirt, jeans, and glasses takes his place at the railing of the balcony—keys on the right, gray on his temples. He will be here for hours
today, exhibiting a patience I find extraordinary. He will also make me
think, eventually, that there is nothing so poignant as a bottom who's
aging; where is he to find the topman who will want to plunder him?
(The problem women have as they age that men, ostensibly, do not; the
passive partner, that is, must be alluring; the dominant retains virility
as he ages.) I watch another man, shirtless, stocky, bearded, leaving his
room to check on his laundry in the little laundromat next door. He
isn't even that attractive to me, but seeing him go in and out of his
room, watching him turn on his TV, stand there in the air-conditioned
dimness looking out, makes me suddenly feel I want him; in other
words, there is something erotic about the context—the room; the man
in a room you can enter.

Eventually, a security guard comes over and says hello; I tell him
I've just checked out, and am waiting for a friend of mine to wake up
from a nap so I can say good-bye to him. That is the official reason—
had Cal not been napping, I don't know what excuse I'd have used to
delay a departure I was finding difficult. Neurotic is as neurotic does. It
is very pleasant under that tree, in the breeze, watching the motel. I
now begin to notice a very handsome man I'll call the Riverboat Gam-
bler walking the corridor-balcony. He's obviously on a lunch break,
dressed in pale-gray slacks, a long-sleeved white shirt with the sleeves

rolled up, smoking a cigarette nervously as he walks—fast. Each time
he comes to a room with the curtain drawn back, he stops, cups his
hands beside his eyes to block out the glare, and peers inside. Then he
draws back, and moves on to the next window. It's like watching a
butterfly stop at flowers; something I've just been doing a lot, since it's
late August in Florida, and the butterflies are active. Each time he
straightens up, after peering in the window, he does something to restore
his equilibrium; he either takes a puff on his cigarette, pats his hair, or
draws a hand across his nose. The actions are linked: cupping his hands
to peer inside, and smoking, patting, or wiping. He's very handsome.
Beautiful wavy hair, moustache, the works. Eventually, after almost an
hour of circling the balconies, he gets in his car and drives off.

I decide to do the same: What is the point, after all, of spending
a second night? One will have to leave eventually. With that in mind,
I walk over to the motel, and go 'round the corridor to the back wing,
climb the stairs, and head towards Cal's to tell him I am leaving, if he
is awake. When I get there, I see, through the patch of window the
parted curtain has left bare, two legs hanging off the end of his bed,
like the limbs of people disappearing into the mouth of a giant fish in
Bosch's *Garden of Earthly Delights*, and realize he is blowing someone I
cannot see. All my objectivity, the distance I've gained by staring at the
motel for two hours from a nearby tree, dissolves instantly, and I rush
down to the front desk and rent myself another room.

The minute I do, I feel like a child on Christmas morning. I feel
much, much better; I don't have to leave, after all. My second room
overlooks the tree under which I stood for two hours watching other
people. It faces an exterior parking lot, the nondescript strip of car and
boat dealers on Orange Blossom Trail, and above some trees, two post-
modern skyscrapers of downtown Orlando. It feels open, breezy, quieter,
far less intense than the other wings. I open my door and sit there,
reading the paper. (There seems no point in staging a tableau; one might
as well be oneself.) Two young men come up the stairs and stop before
my door, one a young blond alcoholic-in-the-making with a drink in
his hand. He says to his friend: "Never send an older person to pay for
the room." His friend replies: "He's not *my* lover, he's yours!" And they
move on. Age is a factor at the P-House, as it is in life, but there are
so many people, of such different sorts, varying ages, it doesn't really
matter: You'll get someone. The wonderful democracy missing in so
much of gay life is here. The clientele's too various, ever-changing, the

place is too much an oasis in a desert to segregate people according to age, race, or looks.

Two doors down from me, I notice a sexy guy in his thirties, I'd guess; his hair is thinning, he wears glasses, he's a nerd with a skinny body, tight stomach dusted with black hair, a band of underwear showing above his shorts. Before long, a thin, handsome young blond with premature bags under his eyes and a pained, perturbed expression takes up a position outside his room. I stand beside my curtain, unnoticed, and watch the blond's mouth begin to move with, I assume from the expression on his face, dirty talk; then he pulls out his erect cock, pink in the daylight. It's very exciting. The door closes, the curtain is drawn, they're having sex. Love in the afternoon. The skinny blond leaves forty minutes later with the same perturbed expression he wore when he first appeared. (Maybe it wasn't Love.) There are a lot of emotions in this place, and one of them is the gloom of Lust, and quite possibly, a sense of Shame.

But it's also very friendly. I meet a man from Jacksonville who tells me about a new bar there full of people "our age." A very well-built bald man with gray hair and a friendly face—so humpy he looks like a professional scuba diver, a Navy SEAL—comes by and stops, but he's so massive I can't think what I'd do with him, and he moves on. He's followed by another older man, in shorts, and bare chest—a magnificent chest, beautiful eyes, silver hair; he nods, and I nod back, stunned, and he disappears. You have to make your decisions very quickly here. The old joke is "Men are like streetcars; there's always another in five minutes." At the P-House, it's more like five seconds. Next comes a stocky black man with an angry expression; he leans against the railing outside my window, and within moments has massaged himself into a fat erection showing plainly against his shorts. His expression is so sour, however, I let him go by. Later Cal tells me he's a very, very nice man from the British West Indies who couldn't be sweeter and just wants to get blown. Which makes me think: We are never ourselves when we cruise. We almost always assume an expression of indifference, or gloom, or anxiety, when in fact most of us are something else entirely. The few people I know who are friendly when they cruise I've always admired. Even the Dutch boy looks cold and frozen when we pass, till I see him rubbing his head and otherwise portraying a tableau of Traveler's Weariness when I spot him later that night at a picnic table in the courtyard, and go down and ask him if he's tired.

He comes to life immediately; he couldn't be friendlier. I talk to him in a happy trance. Every time he laughs, every time he turns his face toward mine, I marvel. He has just come from two days in Miami. He thinks Americans are very well-behaved drivers compared to Europeans. He is interested in both cities and nature. He and his friend plan to go to Disney World, then Tampa, then the Everglades, then Key West. He lives about sixty miles south of Rotterdam, which is not very beautiful, he says, since it was almost completely destroyed during the War, though it once looked like Amsterdam. He worries about the rise of the skinheads in Germany; he likes Antwerp, Ghent, Brussels. He uses condoms for both oral and anal sex, and even kissing makes him nervous, he says, because the virus is constantly mutating and there are cases where no one can explain the method of transmission. "You can never, ever, have oral or anal sex without condoms," he says calmly, his arms locked around his drawn-up legs. "Never. Ever." He says it with such calm good humor I ask him if it is not frustrating; he says, "No." As in: What's the alternative? He is waiting for his friend to wake up so they can go to see the strip show in the discotheque. Afterwards, I think I should have said: "Wouldn't you rather strip yourself, for me, in my room? I promise to applaud." But I don't. I take it instead that this precludes my asking him up to the room, and so, since I'm exhausted anyway, I shake his hand and say good-night. The minute I get up and walk toward my room, I feel I've fallen into a pit—of depression: I'm in love, walking away from someone I don't want to leave.

There are a few people outside my room when I turn off the light; the night before, I could hardly fall asleep, since each time I heard a footstep, I got up and pulled aside the curtain to look out—but tonight I fall asleep, surfeited by my hour with the Dutch dentist.

In the morning I wake up, pull the curtain back, and feel a sense of profound luxury lying on the big clean bed looking out at a soft gray rainy sky. Then the first offering appears: a stocky young man with glasses, a twentysomething in a short-sleeved white shirt on his way to work. He frowns at me and stops. I like everything but the shoes; the sort you wear with a tuxedo, I believe, perforated, like wingtips, with the sort of tasseled flap you see on golf shoes. The shoes are insurmountable. But he keeps coming back, and the idea of having sex when you wake up is so luxurious, I'm thrilled. I'm also shocked when someone I saw the previous night, cruising for hours, walks by; today he wears a different outfit, highlighting his excellent legs, but I'm too stunned to

see him there again to feel much lust. Then another man appears: tall,
with beautiful brown eyes and wavy brown hair, and a good tan; wearing
nothing but a short-sleeved green shirt, and a jockstrap. He stops and
begins massaging his cock. I let him go on, too: too hardcore. Then he
comes back, and does it again; the penis begins to assume an outline
against the cloth, and with a quick jerk of my head, I indicate that he
should come inside. He does so immediately, pulling a bottle out of his
shirt pocket; the first words I hear that day are: "Want a hit?"

       We have poppers and tit clamps and cock for breakfast. It's like
finding yourself, after high winds, driving rain, bent trees, in the eye of
the hurricane. All is still. Sex is so powerful an urge, a dream, a lure,
that when you finally get it, you're like the crying baby stilled with its
mother's nipple. You're thrown into another state altogether. Your desire
is satisfied. The hunt, that is, calls for one set of emotions; possession,
another. The second is both calming, and anticlimactic. One wonders
what all the excitement was about; even if this is all that matters in life.
At the same time, there are practical considerations: Is he enjoying this?
Can I keep doing it? Do I want to do anything more? Is this it, or will
it lead to something else? Slumped at the foot of the bed, having slid
down off the mattress, I find myself facing, when I do open my eyes,
two thighs and a hand—a large graceful hand, which is now applying
a tit clamp to my nipple. I've finally found the pornographic tableau.
Like all pornographic sex, there is no particular emotion—hence the
feeling of stillness, of quiet. Only the furious enactment of a fantasy. A
priest saying Mass in his motel room. I pause to look down at the spit
falling in gobs onto my own chest. I worry about the stocky young man
in the expensive shoes; wonder if he saw this man come in, close the
door, and—most exciting of all—pull the curtain closed. There is at
the P-House this cruel and humiliating sense that we are all just tricks,
interchangeable, since new people are constantly checking in, or driving
over, to cruise. One handsome hippie the night before, after having sex
with Cal, said to him as he left: "Well, now you can get someone
bigger." Bitter, bitter! The daily requiem of gay life, the feeling that
we are merely our cocks. In fact, this man's hand is more erotic than
his penis. When we stop, he bends forward, clutching the back of his
thigh; a hamstring cramp, he explains. He's a jogger, he gets cramps.
(The marvelous contradiction of gay men: He runs to stay in shape, then
takes amyl nitrite. Poppers are everywhere in the House of Pleasure.) I
watch him knead the cramp out—he endured it politely during sex,

rather than interrupt—then he goes to the washbasin, washes himself, puts his jockstrap, thongs, and shirt back on, and leaves. It was all very friendly. Nobody came. I go down to the restaurant to have breakfast with Cal. The same patient, smiling woman with a permanent sits at the counter of the tour-desk, reading a novel by Danielle Steel. The previous evening, dining in a nearby Vietnamese restaurant, both Cal and I spoke of Orlando in glowing terms; all because I'd decided to stay a second night, and we were both anticipating sex. Now I'm calm. If we vacation to relax, there is nothing more relaxing than sex. Yet I'm also aware that the sex I had was hardly with the person I liked most; and after explaining to Cal how I'd failed to turn the conversation with the Dutch dentist into a sexual invitation, I bemoan the fact that once again I'd failed to unite Love and Sex. "Oh, darling," Cal cackles as he reaches for the Sweet'n Low, "you'll die before you ever do that! I've given up, myself. Don't expect to do it in this lifetime!"

This is the problem, of course, as I drive north a few hours later over the hills of central Florida.

Driving back from the Parliament House, I keep talking to the dentist. He is at Disney World at that moment, with his friend from Belgium, but in my imagination, I am telling him all the things about Key West I'd forgotten to recommend the night before (rent a bike, take a trip with The Mosquito Coast, snorkel the reef). I realize now I have no way of getting in touch with him. (Hence those ads you see in the Personals: *Man in red baseball cap I talked to Wednesday in Atlantic City, please call Bob at 555-6793.*) I have no way of finding out how his trip will go; whether he'll tube the Ichetucknee (as I recommended) or do Tampa instead (as he planned); what he will think of the Everglades or Key West. But that's not all I recall.

The P-House forces you to define your desires. Driving over the ribbon of pale concrete above the orange groves, I think not only of the dentist, but of the huge dick in the light of the TV the first night, and of the fact that we compartmentalize our personalities so much in this society that we need rental cars to connect them all. We're going to end up renting everything in this country, I think; owning nothing, committing to no one, because nobody wants to settle for just one thing where there is So Much. Meanwhile, postcoital reflection fills the time allotted to it: two hours on I-75. Sex—all sex—produces contemplation. The way to the soul is through the body. Driving north I try to remember what Kierkegaard said about the Seducer; how he can never be happy. How life is really a choice between two ways—an Either/Or—but Americans want to have it all. But it's so jerry-built, in the end. It's like the old joke about Los Angeles: You have to drive 150 miles to assemble the ingredients for dinner. Whereas Socrates said: Happiness is Virtue. That's all. No driving required. (Make a list, I tell myself, of what you consider a virtuous life, for a man your age, now; then look at it, and see how many or how few, if any, of those things you practice—that is the measure of your happiness or unhappiness: the distance between your actions and Virtue.) A few miles later, I wonder: Is that all nonsense? Is life just animal instinct, not virtue?

When I eventually reach Gainesville, and reenter my own piece of Florida, my nonvacation life, I feel I'm returning from a distant planet. It takes just as much adjustment leaving the Planet Sex as it did landing on it. In fact, it's so difficult, the first thing I do after I get home is call Cal, who's staying another day. He answers, and tells me in a thick, tired voice—the main problem of the P-House is relinquishing its opportunities long enough to sleep—what's happened since I left. (The cute boy with the tight body and ponytail turned out to have an enormous dick, and wanted twenty dollars to have it played with; after he left, a man with an even bigger dick had sex with Cal for nothing.) In the middle of the call, the fatigue, the sexual heaviness in his voice turn suddenly urgent. "I have to go," he gasps. "Someone's here!" He hangs up, and I imagine him sinking back into the delicious ooze, the primeval mud, the salubrious swamp of sex. Which leaves me wondering: What am I, without the pursuit of sex? Traveling is a fool's paradise, said Emerson, for you always come back to yourself in the end. Around me, the emptiness of the house I'm in could not be more complete, or shocking.

PART EIGHT

POST-AIDS:

SEX AND

GRIEF

At a panel on pornography and AIDS at a recent gay writers conference, one speaker stated, "Let's face it: AIDS isn't sexy." The other panelists and audience members agreed without much thought. The stories in this section defy that conventional wisdom.

Our lives in the past decade and a half have become thoroughly imbued with AIDS and grief—it only follows that our sexual fantasies would also become intertwined with the complicated emotions surrounding sexual danger, the specter of death, and disease. The grim physical details of HIV illness itself are not necessarily fodder for arousal (although these stories demonstrate that they can be), but the entire milieu of the disease is brimming with sexuality.

Will Leber from San Francisco is one of the very best new writers at depicting the way urban gay men have sex in the 1990s. Often setting his stories in the new sexual venues that have been created in response to AIDS, he uses these contrived atmospheres to heighten the complicated and conflicting emotions surrounding sex in an epidemic. In

"Trouble," Leber depicts a man who after a decade of monogamy is propelled into a safe sex club for the first time. The man has just attended the funeral of a close friend who had AIDS, and the proximity of the events is not accidental. Grief, fear, and arousal swirl together until the moment of climax, when they become a single, all-consuming emotion. Leber poses the question: Where are our sexual and emotional breaking points?

"Hollywood Squared" by Brandon Judell is another piece of writing that captures the essential connections between sexual arousal and sexual worry. The jumbled and oddly juxtaposed form of the story's sections mimicks the experience of having sex in the age of AIDS: erotic details and medical facts are inseparable; encounters that should be entirely sensual or humorous are tinged with a foreboding undercurrent. The story's abrupt and inconclusive ending is at once dark and hopeful. The epidemic rages on, but so do life and sex.

People with AIDS have been objects of scorn, of pity, of fear, of love . . . but never, at least in the public imagination, of sexual attraction. When Benetton tried to use the image of a man's muscular arm, tattooed with the words "HIV Positive," to promote the company's line of clothing, public outcry from various camps quickly killed the campaign. The bodily connection between AIDS and sexual attraction is simply too dangerous.

Stephen Greco and Michael Lowenthal are two writers who have boldly confronted this taboo subject matter and created truly transgressive stories. In "The Last Blowjob," Greco's setting is one now intimately familiar to many gay men, a hospital room. What is often a frightening and impersonal space is reclaimed by the act of sex, just as the narrator's attraction to his lover's wasted body saves the dying man from being simply a medical object. The radical element here is that the narrator is not attracted to his dying lover *despite* his illness; the illness and its physical manifestations enhance and reinforce the lover's attractiveness.

Lowenthal's story "Going Away" also eroticizes the stark physical realities of AIDS, addressing the complicated relationship between sex and death from a sexually transmitted disease. Sex is both an antidote to grief and a means of grieving, a way of forgetting and a way of remembering. By mixing erotic activity into the rituals of mourning, Lowenthal affirms the central place of the sexual in all phases of the life cycle. Sex brings us into the world, and since the advent of AIDS it can clearly kill us, but it can also be what allows us to survive.

WILL LEBER

TROUBLE

I PARK MY CAR ACROSS THE ONE-WAY STREET. I SIT AND
watch who goes in—and out—of the club for fifteen minutes. The
parking lot beside the shabby, two-story structure crams to capacity.
Traffic passes in thinning waves. Saturday night bleeds into Sunday
morning. Finally, I muster the courage to cross over.

As I approach, a shirtless hunk startles me. He slides out from
behind the dark, unmarked door as I reach to knock.

"Are you looking for trouble?" he asks with a smirk. His practiced
double entendre strips my intentions bare: This men-only sex club is
called Trouble and, yes, I nod, trouble is exactly what I'm looking for.

"Well, you've found it!" he arches an eyebrow and sweeps me inside
with his gigantic arm. "Check in at the desk."

As he propels me through the door, I marvel at the super hero
proportions of his chest, the tight grip of the studded leather strap across
his left biceps. His confident wide-legged stance exudes a compelling
sexuality. I watch him greet a twosome rushing in behind me. "Welcome!" he booms out. "Are you looking for trouble?"

I wait in a short line at the reception desk. In the room beyond, the dance floor's light show hypnotizes me, the deep pump of bass rhythm massages my heart. I could still turn back. I cross-examine myself about what has led me here. I rationalize that I just want to *see* what it is like; that I don't intend to *do* anything; that I'm not getting any younger and had better *experience* life; that it is time I *overcome* my fears. But I know I have been running toward trouble since early afternoon. I saw it clearly ahead as I stood in that hot, midday California sun and listened to a talentless, born-again preacher eulogize my friend Tommy's too-short life.

"Have you been here before?" asks the young guy behind the desk. Three necklaces hang down his chest: regulation dog-tags, gay freedom rings and a long knotted strand of simulated pearls. He wears tattered shorts, a T-shirt with the sleeves rolled. I'm certain he would call himself a "queer" rather than a "gay." Unlike me, he could never pass as straight.

"It's my first time," I answer.

"Well, we're a membership club, read this, sign at the bottom and it's ten dollars." He hands me a form and a ballpoint pen as I reach into my pocket.

There is no light to read by, but I make out some phrases about releasing liability, about private membership and about promising to have only safe sex. I work as a paralegal, so the business side of me wants to read it thoroughly, but my emotional side is screaming, "Go!" Though I intend to assume an alias, I do it automatically—quickly sign my real name, Brian Collier. The guy pulls away the sheet and the ten dollar bill. "Have fun!" He slides me a membership card and a packaged condom.

I stumble across a central dance floor, so dark each beam of light burns a path through the smoky haze. There is little decoration. The large warehouse space is shrouded in black. Crude figures depicting phallic worship are etched on the walls like cave paintings. The beams flash by regularly like headlights on the highway. A mirrored ball casts a net of shadow and light over a row of men against the wall. I imagine them lurking in the brush under a full moon. I follow a perilous path between them and the dance floor back to the bar. Their hungry eyes peer out from the thicket. This is serious, I think, thirsty for the comfort of a cocktail.

I gesture to the skinny bartender. "Scotch and soda." His T-shirt is pulled through a beltloop and hangs like a dish rag on his thigh.

"Sorry, no mixed drinks." He leans toward me. "How about a vodka punch, or a soda?" He's smiling at me! "Or will it be, coffee, tea or me?"

"Punch," I blurt out. I'm so inept that I can't return the kindness of his flirt. He ladles it out. I hold up a five and ask, "How much?"

"Oh, there's no charge. It's all included," he explains and I flush like a first-time fool. I stuff the bill in a big mason jar marked TIPS, and he winks at me. I flash him a grin. I study my plastic-cupped drink. Little particles float atop the fluorescent yellow depth. I sip it and confirm it's vodka-spiked lemonade. This reminds me, perversely, of a high school dance.

I leave the brighter space of the bar and head back down that dangerous alley between the lined-up men and the writhing dancers. I sense, more than see, a break along the wall and fall into the slot. To my right two leather guys make out. The naked ass of the one nearest me pokes out of black leather chaps. A thin strap runs down the cleavage of the buns. He's so close that his curly haired butt occasionally brushes my hand. As they neck, his friend's thick arms circle his back. In a moment of red illumination I make out an eagle tattoo on the muscled forearm. I gulp down my drink as I watch the dance floor.

I cruise every man that passes. A guy in a floppy, court-jester hat slides by me and leans into my ear, "Want some X?" I refuse the offer to purchase that designer drug. More men shuffle by without connection. Do I look that bad? I don't have gym-pumped tits, I reason, but I'm trim. People tell me I have a nice smile. But I know I lack the essential salesman aggression to really score. I expect Mister Right to just walk up and introduce himself, say, "Hi, I'm Stud. I like your eyes, let's get out of here and go home to my place where I'll be nice to you and we'll play safe but naughty games and I'll promise not to ask you if you have a lover and I won't say I'm too tired and roll over after the first time and I'll wish this would go on forever though I'll make no fuss when we kiss a passionate departure because we know in our hearts something so special could never happen again."

Surprisingly, fewer men dance shirtless here than at the disco I just left. I had called the sex club's hotline before leaving the house. The recorded message finished with a statement I found reassuring, "Optional clothes check, *come* as you like!" I've never been to a bath, never exposed myself in that—this—sort of place.

Across the room I watch wide-eyed men pass in and out of dark doorways. I feel glued to the wall, unsure of my next move. Why am I here?

I remember how I felt trapped at Tommy's funeral and how I plotted my escape. In a horrible black suit, I suffered the stifling stillness of our hometown. In the neat yet dusty cemetery, when all the others shut their eyes and bowed their heads in prayer, I stared wide-eyed and head-up at the cheap porcelain pot that contained the ashen remains of Thomas Evan Johnson. One more friend murdered in his prime by AIDS.

We should never have let Tommy out of our sight . . . we should never have allowed him to leave us, his real family, at Christmas! He shot himself two days ago. It was that place that made him do it, those repentant fools who provided the weapon, their hatred that he loaded into the chamber.

He must have struggled with the hunting rifle, a high-caliber Bambi-blaster. The family saw fit to show me the weapon. They had discouraged my visits while he lived, but insisted I come and share the ugly details of his death. When I reached out in a gesture of comfort to hold his mother's trembling hand, she pulled back from me. I saw her eyes brimming with blame. I recalled her rage years ago when Tommy followed my lead and moved to the city. She accused me of turning him gay. Now, she undoubtedly held me responsible for his getting AIDS.

When I told my lover Robert the horrible news over the phone, he was on the opposite coast in New York with pressing business. "My God," he said. He wanted to fly back for the service, but the family had already cremated the body and scheduled the interment for the next morning. "No," I advised him, "by the time you got back it would be all over. It's better if we plan a memorial when all his friends can make it."

During the service I became a kid again, desperate to leave behind that claustrophobic, god-fearing, fag-hating world of my adolescence. I imagined jumping into my car and driving as fast as I could back to San Francisco and going *out*. I saw myself falling into a stranger's big manly arms and sucking his tongue down my throat.

The music invades my revery, chases it away with an insistent beat, *ba-boom, ba-boom*, an answer in itself, *ba-boom, ba-boom*, the irresistible compulsion to live in the here and now.

The same queasy anticipation I experienced the first time I stepped foot in a gay bar boils in my bowels. My world is about to rupture.

Will I explode or implode? Blast-off or self-destruct? The bass in this club pounds pure and hard, booms in my bladder until I realize that metaphysics aside, I've got to pee.

I push off to search for the john. My head spins in the middle of the dance floor and I imagine I'm caught in that classic but trite tale in which you must choose the correct door. Through which does the man-eating tiger await? The twist to my tale: I want to unlock the tiger. I want him to leap out and maul my flesh.

While the tiger may crouch inside the dark dens across from me, intuition tells me the bathroom isn't there. On the opposite ends of the room parallel stairways ascend to a second floor. Men march up and down both sides. I choose the stairs to my left and follow up to the top the tight, blue-jeaned, beefcake butt of what we used to call a clone. I resist the temptation to bite.

At the upper landing he slips to my right and settles into a shapeless sofa against the wall. My eyes have begun to adjust to the dim light and I can see that the guy beside him has a large rod sticking out of his pants that he occasionally strokes as if his hand were a windshield wiper set on intermittent. I glance around to find all the seating—an assortment of recliners, loveseats and sofas—occupied. All eyes fixate on the soundless, fuzzy-pictured porno that flickers on a twenty-five-inch console color TV.

Along the opposite wall I notice a vacancy along a row of threadbare, fold-down seats. Matted stuffing oozes out of the wounded cushions. A squat man slides stealthily into the seat beside an anxious, knee-bouncing boy. He spreads his legs, widens his territory, bumps knees, and finally chances a hand slinking over the armrest.

The club's dance music sifts in, but seems distant. A strange electric video haze, a hum in which a long-dicked pizza delivery boy solemnly fucks a lonely accountant who's been burning the midnight oil veils the room. He rams him on top of a desk covered with ledgers and IRS forms. He pulls out in time for the prolonged multi-camera-angled climax—gushing spurts onto tax tables, schedules A thru Z, across the blurred ink of taxes due and tedium payable. I stay long enough to see the size of the delivery boy's tip. As I turn, the tanned clone crosses the room. His arm zaps me with a static charge as he glides by bare-chested and descends. I follow, but lose him into the swell of sweating, swinging men.

I ascend the opposite stairs and find a familiar line at the top. It seems I'm not the only one with the urge. Inside the room it's a little too bright. I'm accustomed to the dark now. A white claw-footed bathtub crouches to the left wall, two stalls angle to the right. A couple of dudes in combat boots, jeans and lumberjack plaid shirts, shorn of their sleeves, hunker up to the tub and let loose from firehose thick pricks.

I enter a stall. The weight of my penis surprises me, flops out of the slit in my underwear. I will it to wilt and plead with it to pee. A hand gestures from the adjoining stall through a hole in the partition. At the sink, I run cold water over my hands, rub it on my face. As I wipe with a paper towel I watch a very dark man beside me take a bottle from a shelf, pour a yellow liquid into a tiny paper cup. He leans his head back and gargles. He has a beautiful throat with a sharp adams apple cleaving the center, a strong jawline, a bountiful and curly black mustache. When he spits, I turn and leave. I wonder, does Listerine kill HIV?

Across the hall another room fills with the shuffle of men. I file in and a familiar smell hits me at once: the sharp scent of poppers, like the biting whiff of gunpowder after firing a shot. No, we don't do poppers anymore. . . . I'm pushed in deeper by the entering crowd. A single red light bulb hangs from the ceiling. Against the black walls, a flank of flesh. Passing hands nudge nipples, explore extremities. A couple deep kiss, the blond's pants fall down, pool at his ankles. His partner drops to his knees, curly locks sway around his bobbing head. A group forms around them, a mound of men, orifices opening, whose? which? impossible to tell, too tight. An octopus propels itself with undulation and stroking tentacles through a blood-red sea. The room is steamy, sexy and smelly. Sweat, cum and poppers. It closes in on me. Offer me a snort, I'll take it. Show me your shaft, I'll ride it. I'm turned on, but I run like an open faucet, hot and cold, never a comfortable warm flow, unable to find the right mix. Now I'm looking, looking for it. I flee from what I am drawn to. Red-faced, I head for the stairs and descend quickly. My cock is rock hard.

Sexy, sweltering, shirtless men grind and thrust on the dance floor. Little T-shirts whip like tails from their back pockets. Tight bodies twist from side to side. I join the dance, frantic and frustrated.

I dance without a partner. I've watched the "raving" homosexuals, a younger ecstatic breed, dancing alone, face into the loudspeakers. But I'm an old-fashioned homo who likes to watch the sexual beating of bodies.

I surrender to music that's so evolved it can only be described in hyphenations like techno-house-funk-hi-n-r-g-rave-toon-primal-retro-future-beat-or-maybe-even-disco-sound? If you can tap your foot to it, fags can funky-groove-twist-swing-disco-dance-or-fuck to it.

It's four a.m. and I'm wired for sound. The club continues to serve alcohol because legally it is a private party. I order another lemonade banger. I stand between doorway number one and doorway number two ready to find my man-eating tiger. I slide into number one, drink in hand. A big guy, six-feet-four with cantaloupe melon halves for tits, stands before me. I could eat him for breakfast, orange, sweet flesh. I watch around me. I'm a quick learner, the system is easy. Basic cruising principle applies, it works like this: Start with heavy eye contact. If a glance is returned, escalate. Turn your body fully around and make eye contact appropriate to the message you want to convey. Blink: *Let me get a better look at you.* Wink: *You're hot!* Stare: *Right now and any way I want you.*

I wander along a short dark maze. I notice most of the men have doffed their shirts. But I'm not ready for that yet. I pass through a narrow short corridor, hands glide across my chest, they pinch my tits, they palm my straining crotch, cup my ass. Ahead a short guy in cowboy boots leans back in a corner. A slim boy in cutoff jeans and tan construction boots kneels, face into his belly. The boy's long hair conceals his face, the man's crotch.

I hug the wall. A well-tanned man moves close beside me. He's a few inches shorter than I. He is mostly torso, like a satyr. He's all chest with quartersized nipples and a stomach with twenty ripples. I glance at him and he begins to unbutton my shirt. His fingers wander inside and tickle a nipple. I literally jump and it startles him at first, then amuses him, my little jerking motions every time he flicks the tit-tip. I close my eyes and trace my right fingers over his chest. I encounter a prickly field of stubble and my excitement deflates, *he shaves his chest.* Then as quickly reinflates, *does he shave his pubes?* But before I can even fully explore down the hills and valleys of his abs, let alone check so far below, he moves silently along. Did I disappoint him? Or did he sense me withdraw?

In any case, he's paid me a tremendous favor. He has set off an intense tingling in my libido. I finish the job he started, unbutton my shirt and pull out the tails. I'm thirty, but retain a nearly hairless chest. My lover tells me I have a boy's body—slim, supple, willing. I'm also a bit shy, so why am I suddenly so brazen?

I move opposite doorway number two. Further along I can see

doorway number three and I realize that it is really a very simple maze and that the tiger is free to roam, not confined, and liable to leap out at any turn. Men pass by, quick glances, but no flare or spark of interest. Near me a cute-enough guy leans back, legs crossed. I won't approach him, and he won't move toward me. Right now, we are both quarry, not hunters. A broad-shouldered profile comes through doorway number two, crosses toward me. His skin is a deep mahogany. He smiles. I grin. He reaches inside my shirt flap. His caress vibrates through my ribs. He looks back once as he moves on.

Why am I doing this? I stand shirt open, legs spread, welcoming any and all comers. My God, I've been like Ivory soap for almost ten years, 99.44% pure. I've been more or less monogamous, only a few stealthy slips. Out of fear? Yes! Or cowardice?

"Hi!" A thirtysomething man in tight jeans and running shoes moves in beside me. He inches closer, ventures a wordless caress of my pecs. I stand my ground. He faces me, all smiles, flicks my nipples lightly and I am instantly erect in my pants.

"We all have to get started sometime, don't we? Might as well get started, huh? You're cute," he says. He's very quick and one hand is already at my privates. "And hard." He leans against me, exploring inside the waistband of my jeans, into the underwear. "Is that all yours!"

What a trite thing to say, I think, though it works. I am complimented. He already has my belt undone. He slips out of his tight T-shirt. He drops to his knees, peeling down my Jockeys. He takes my swollen self into his warm, moist mouth and I suddenly panic, "Hey, not that, ah, come on." Shouldn't. It feels good. . . . It's his choice, if he wants to take the risk.

No. Not safe . . . but it's never been safe. Men fucking in public restrooms, risking a dose of VD? Men beating it in park bushes, courting the sexual rush of guilt and fear? Men stalking alleyways, seeking expiation of sin in the blank, blackout moment when desire triumphs like the popping of a champagne cork from a too warm bottle?

"Stand up, not so fast." I urge him to rise, using his armpits as my handholds.

He looks into my eyes, "I'm Tom, so what's your first name?" His name paralyzes me. Tommy. . . . If we had just held you tighter, closer, longer!

"What's your name?" He squeezes my crotch.

"What?" I return, not sure of my answer. I ponder, what is my name?

"Jim," I lie.

"Jeff," he says, "Jeff, that's a cute name. I want to cum, Jeff— you're cute, Jeff." He begins to jerk himself.

I lightly tweak his tits, run loose palms over the severe hardness of his pecs, trace down to his dick which he mercilessly beats the life out of. I tickle back against the base of the shaft, happen upon a studded leather cockring. I tease his shrunken ballsac bound up by the leather strap. His balls are marblesized.

Jaded queen, I think, too gym-toned, entranced by some hackneyed fantasy. But I distractedly manipulate his balls with my left hand, while my right pinches his nipples, while my cock sadly sags.

"Yeah, I'm getting close, man. You're a hot man . . . I'm gonna shoot, man!" He whacks it hard and I give into his need, apply my mouth to the too perfect globe of the nearest pec.

Into the wall he shoots a rapid-fire spray of jizz, bucks and cries, "Ah, ahh, I'm cumming!" Rat-a-tat. A-tat. A-tat. A-tat. A neat row of splats dribble toward the floor.

And wasn't it the least I could do, given the circumstances? To help him get rid of that unwanted stuff—disinterested, aloof, my own dick dead? I slip off through smoky fog back onto the dance floor, gone before he's even buttoned up.

Now I am Jeff. I've taken that name—jerky Jeff, jiffy Jeff, jittery Jeff. Jeff is a hunter.

I spot a guy I admired when dancing. He's coming my way. I catch a glance, return a glare. He's heading up the stairs. I follow. He wears a backwards baseball cap, an oversized T-shirt that drapes from his broad shoulders, hugs his square pectorals and loosely folds at his slim waist. He is stud-meat and I want him obsessively. He enters the red-light room and I am hot on his tail. He saunters up toward a macho-macho man, maybe forty-five, crew-cut hair, big biceps with a little tattoo, a dark stain on his right shoulder. It's an immediate liplock, "Come to daddy!" They're sucking tongues and I am repulsed. No, I am not repulsed, I'm rejected and I'm horny and I want to be in the middle of them. I want all those hands, elbows, boot toes, tongues, fists, knees, legs and cocks inside my each and every hole, now! It's too much, I'm overwhelmed. It's all too steamy, sexy, smelly. Sweat, cum and poppers. Jumbled Jeff had better go.

I bounce on the balls of my feet beside the dance floor. The crowd presses me into the treacherous terrain separating the dancers and cruisers. As bodies squeeze by I lean into them and they fleetingly rub my naked flesh.

A hot number snakes closer. At arm's length he faces me and I give him the eye—the hard cruise. He is dark: brown eyed, thick black eyebrows almost touching together above the square bridge of his nose, a dense stubble across his cheeks, short black spikes of sweat-gelled hair. His hairy arm slithers against my abdomen, his fingers scratch across my crotch as he passes. He turns back to gauge my reaction. He jerks his head toward doorway number three. I pursue, swoop in behind him.

I'm now delirious and desperate to join in the rituals of the tribe. He's turned from me as I near. I struggle against a human stream entering from the side door. In the momentary delay doubt sprouts into questions. Will he be safe enough? Will he go far enough? Am I afraid of dying without ever having lived?

More bodies push between us. I lose him. A group has formed near the far corner. I look over shoulders of a crowd already two deep. On a narrow bunk bed a Latino looking guy, rusty brown with jet black hair, pounds it between a pair of white legs scissored above his head. The toes point up from legs thin and tense. I think they truly look sharp and dangerous. I imagine that at any moment they might slice closed and snip off his head.

I stand on tiptoes, look down to the lower bunk and spy two bodies, jeans bunched at knees, in a sixty-nine. The guys in the front row are beating their meat. One performer's dick pops sideways from the eager mouth. A tightrope of spit stretches from the heartshaped head to the still-open, pleading lips. It is unsheathed. I'm seized by danger signals, train-crossing bells, flashing red lights.

I turn to leave and I am face to face with a Haight Street-queer type. He's exactly my height. He stares straight into my heart and I hear those words ringing in my ears, *right now and any way I want you.* His passionate, sky-blue eyes levitate me toward him. Though he turns toward the door, the eye contact never breaks. He's a little rough around the edges, both ears pierced, hair a little wild, a bit lean and very hungry. My sexual rebel.

He wears a denim shirt with cutaway sleeves. The frayed armholes expose his milky white shoulders, the natural roundness of biceps sculpted by labor. His shirtfront is unbuttoned and the collar lies a couple of inches back from his vulnerable neck. A very light spray of black hair blossoms between his pecs.

He leads me back toward the swirling lights and dance floor then quickly through doorway number two, my arms already circling around his waist. As we enter all eyes watch us. Our desperation is obvious. I am against him along a dim and sticky wall, my teeth at his neck. He takes hold of both my nipples, turns them like knobs on a stereo, all the way up, full-volume.

I bump up the sides of his ribcage with probing palms, delve into his armpits, grab fistfuls of his tits. I lick a flat, hot tongue around the shaft of his larynx, suck on the bump of his Adam's apple, rub my nose in his sharp beard. My tiger's tongue laps at his parting lips. He twists his head like a ferret, noses up my jaw, tongue wet on my cheek. He nibbles at my left ear, swallows it fully into his mouth, opens and whispers, "Let's fuck."

His right hand unbuckles my belt while left detours behind, down and deftly into—there. When he touches—there—I quiver. He slips just in, then out and around the waistband. I undo his big, black belt. The leather strap slides softly through my hand. He pops one, two, three metal buttons open on my jeans and grips me like he means it. His eyes into my eyes. I unzip his shorts and they fall to the floor with a clatter. No underwear. His dick springs free, slapping my hand. He slides the elastic band of my white shorts beneath my hairy balls.

I have queer-boy up against the wall, pinned by the waist. I spar with him cock to slippery cock. I'm aware of shadows around us. I know that as a sex act starts, a group might form, create a scene, but we have shut out their participation—this is one-on-one—they keep an observant distance, lurk and leer at our show.

Sex standing up is bad-boy sex, it's fast sex, sinful sex that you need to get over before you get caught. His dick sticks straight up, back against his belly, mine juts out, waves in the air. My right fist jerks the loose skin up over the head of his cock. It starts to slick up with precum oozing with each stroke. I lick at his nipple, rub it under my chin, grip it with my teeth and chew while I milk him. I pump, squeeze and jerk him to the rhythm of the music. I stop momentarily then frantically start again. I kneel to it. I nose into the cleft between his legs, lave his velvet sack, work my way up it, press full-face to the perfect statue of his erection. *Anyway I want you.* I angle it downward and slip my lips just over the flared head. My palms press into the contours of his flanks, fingertips spread the crack of his ass. I swallow him whole, suck him into me. He becomes my world, the entire globe twirling on my tongue—all that matters. It is mine . . . all mine.

I try to hold on, but he resists me and pulls back. He takes hold of my forearms and brings me to my feet. He saves me from myself.

He takes me by the scruff of my neck and forces my mouth to his. He offers his thick tongue, a pacifier. It throbs in and out. He grips the root of my cock, angles the head down, points the arrowhead into the cleavage between his legs, beneath his balls. His body's strongest appendages part in a V for my entry, slide closed. I fuck this tender spot, below his beautiful butt, beneath his boyish cock. This place almost as wondrous as I imagine his forbidden passageway, behind, beyond. My forefinger probes that magical opening which leads into the deep, dark forest.

I have him in my fist—ferocious in my fist. I lap up the beaded sweat, beneath, between his breasts. My tongue searches for succor. I suck his tit. His breaths shorten and his cock throbs with blood. His hips heave forward and I bite and lick him and slap his butt as he shoots again and again a stinging, hot tribute to his pleasure.

I hump him as he cums. I reach back and tweak my own tit, he pinches at my other. We somehow invite the crowd to join in. I am compelled to contact as many of them as possible. They come as if from nowhere, they come from everywhere, from behind bushes, from under beds, out of dingy alleys and closets, off the streets, from foreign lands, from hometowns and out of the jungle they come. I imagine their thin hands, hairy arms, jean-clad thighs, the love-handles around their stomachs, the bumps of their spinal cords, calloused thumbs, the bends of their necks, the cleavage of butts—and I passionately want to have and to hold them. I want to involve, incorporate and dissolve them without judgment or commitment into my experience and my release.

I pull my cock into the open air and wrap my slimy fist around queer-boy's hand. We jerk my cock, hand-in-hand, together. Strange fingers pinch my nipples, scratchy palms caress my thighs. A dozen hands possess me. Into the darkness I shout, into the cacophony I erupt from within shaking like an earthquake, spewing smoke and rock into the atmosphere. Flows of molten lava cascade over our intertwined fists, relentlessly incinerate the tropical jungle, flow into the cool tide and sizzle in the sea.

I stand with my pants around my ankles, my eyes wide open, my hands all slippery and wet. We are alone.

I quickly pull up my pants. He tucks in his shirt. I wrap my less wretched hand around his back and say, "Hey, thanks." It's all I can think to say. And as I look down to buckle my belt, he disappears.

I sweep out of the place, still buttoning my shirt, tails flying. I half-run to my car. I squeal away, round the corner and gun out onto the deserted avenue. It's almost dawn as I head toward the safety of home, the comfort of a hot shower, the crazy notion of a cleansing— gargling with mouthwash, bathing in rubbing alcohol. How will I explain this to Robert, flying back to my waiting arms, already halfway home in the sky over Kansas? How could he understand what I cannot?

I speed past the offices and warehouses that bustle in the day and now stand vacant in the deep cool night. The regular traffic signals have been turned off and red lights flash at the intersections. Guilt and worry haunt me. I drive carefully, wary of police cars, in a panic that I have committed a crime, will be chased, apprehended and tried. Passing streetlamps transform into interrogator's spotlights shining in my eyes.

I hold the shiftknob with a gooey hand. My solitary vehicle slices through the city streets. I click by hundreds of parking meters, all bearing silent witness, their red flags up. I recoil from their unanimous declaration that time is up. They read: EXPIRED.

BRANDON JUDELL

HOLLYWOOD

SQUARED

I THINK I HAVE AIDS TODAY, EVEN THOUGH I HAVE BEEN
tested about thirty-two times and have always come up negative. For
the last two or three months my stool has always been soft and long—
like long snakes decomposing. Today I stared at one of these boalike
creations for a rather long time, searching for parasites. I also think I
might have worms. I found maggots in Pumpkin's food last week. I
thought maybe she ate a maggot and transferred it to me.

But anyway, I picked up a man on the cross-town bus at 86th
Street the other day, and maybe we'll fall in love. He called me the
very next day. He has gray hair and eyes that don't open all the
way. He appears to be a failed novelist and playwright, the type of
person who once you know him well will be totally neurotic. I can't
wait.

I'm reading the letters section of *Harper's* right now. Someone tearing apart Raymond Carver throws in some distasteful words for David
Leavitt, too. David's probably getting very depressed in Spain right now.

He can't handle interviewers who criticize his clothes, so he must be
foaming that his psyche is getting a trouncing, too.

I think my breath is terrible all the time. How can I kiss a man with
a tongue tasting like moldy chopped liver? I keep mints under the
mattress in case I get a guy home. Then I stuff my face while I'm going
down on him.

That's how Louis gave his girlfriend her wedding ring. He was
performing cunnilingus between her thighs (which is the best place to
perform it), when he started choking. He said in a garbled voice,
"There's something in there that I swallowed."

Denise replied in a panicked tone, "What?"

Louis went, "Mmmwhawhawhammmwhawha!"

"What's wrong?" Denise shouted.

"I'm choking. There's something inside of you!" gurgled Louis.
Then he pulled the $6000 designer ring out of his mouth. "Look!" After
Denise realized it wasn't a dislodged IUD, she started laughing. That's
so romantic, but I'm not supposed to know about it.

Another idle Sunday. If I had a salaried job with coffee breaks, I wouldn't
feel guilty about doing nothing. Just made rice pasta and topped it with
French salad dressing. I'm out of butter. Out of sauce. Too lazy to do
anything but play this Columns game on the computer. You get three
blocks of the same color abutting each other and they disappear.

Called Kenny Lasser, my possible love interest. He's the guy from
the bus. We might get together tonight. Cleaned the living room floor.
It's the only room where you can now walk and your feet actually touch
the linoleum.

Haven't masturbated for days, either. I'm going through my non-
sexual phase again. Clint Eastwood is on the living room TV.

My stool still hasn't hardened. I guess nothing puts a damper more
on erotic thoughts than shit problems. Haven't really been exercising.
Maybe forty minutes this week.

I think my life is getting a bit too passionless. I did let a strange
Hispanic suck my cock in the George Washington Bus Terminal bathroom this week. I pulled out before I came, yet he spit into a tissue
anyway. I felt great.

Someone had actually wanted to mouth my organ, play my har-
monica, wet my whistle. . . . I'm a sex object again. Thank you, Lord.
Thank you, anonymous Hispanic.

I'm getting exhausted. . . .

Kenny just called. We're meeting at Pumpkin Eater's at seven. He's a vegetarian. This story might actually get off the ground. A true gray-haired love interest. He's young, just prematurely gray. I wonder if I have enough time to henna. But then I'll have that henna smell. I guess I should do the mudpack to tighten my pores and exercise a bit so my tits swell.

This kind of fiction is a real headache to write because it's basically fact with names changed—and a few inches added to the cocks. If nothing happens in my real life, we're *both* out of luck.

The positive side of writing about factual orgasms is that if a critic writes, "This is unbelievable crap," I can say, "Fuck you, asshole. Everything here is the whole truth. I *was* gang-banged by twenty albino pygmies and have Polaroids of their footprints on my ass to prove it."

The problem is that Kenny looks like the kind of guy who doesn't leave behind any marks.

Two years later, maybe.

I've just discovered this piece and I hardly remember this Kenny. Anyway, I recall I walked him home. I think he lived in the Ansonia or someplace near. I started grabbing his crotch, and he warned me that he might not be able to get it up because he takes Prozac. I accepted the challenge. So after he lit the incense and rearranged the Indian print bedspreads around the room, plus put on the mood music, I got to business. He might have come. I don't remember. I don't care. I probably jerked off.

Maybe I should reread *The 120 Days of Sodom*.

I just remembered about a guy I blew in San Francisco in the seventies. He was coked out and couldn't get hard. Blond with looks good enough to make him appear average in dark light. He said, "Don't worry. It feels good even if I'm not hard." So there I was on my elbows for hours giving this guy I didn't want to be with a great blow-job. Well, at least an immensely long one. I recall my jaws locking, my cheek hollows aching, and my back stiffening. I think I finally said I had to go and pick up my schnauzer or something. Otherwise, I'd probably still be there like one of those Walt Disney automatons at the 1964 World's Fair going through some very precise but limited movements.

New York Times just did an article on penises and impotency. It said in so many words that if you don't have sex regularly, not enough air gets into your cock, and some type of skin cell grows and the veins get clogged, and you have trouble getting an erection. Now I'm going to have to masturbate twice a day.

Nowadays, I just masturbate before I sleep. I jerk off to an old issue of *Drummer* or *Stroke*, then I answer a few clues in *New York* magazine or the *New York Times* crossword puzzle. Immediately, I conk out. That's why I'm afraid to jerk off during the day, since I've trained my body to snooze about six minutes after ejaculation.

Anyway, before I get to my hot experience in Turkey, Carl, one of my tattooed nephews (I have four) pointed out a beautiful black girl to me that he had sex with in the past.

"My friend and I met her in a bar. Then we danced with her. Then she blew us. I wound up going home and to bed with her. Almost, at least. Because when I put my hand in her pants, I found out she had a dick. I was freaked out. A dick, man. I yelled at her, 'You should have told me!' She said, 'Then you wouldn't be here right now.' I said, 'Right you are!' "

He was freaked it seemed because when he was eleven or so, his evil stepmother used to go around to his friends' parents and say that he was gay. So even though he's as straight as a Buckingham Palace guard's spine, that accusation had always made him slightly uptight about homosexuality.

I'll be right back. I have two of those new sandwich-sized Thomas' English muffins in the toaster. Also I should masturbate to get some air in my cock.

So, anyway, I was lying on one of those filthy cots in the old Everard bathhouse when who should come swishing in but Paul Lynde. He said in as butch a voice as he could muster, "Baby, you're beautiful, and I'm going to make you feel good." He was wearing a towel and a gold chain with some oversized medallion hanging from it, and there was a pack of cigarettes stuffed between the towel and his waist.

I thought to myself, Well, he is a celebrity and maybe I could use this sometime in the future. Then I thought, Well, I'll probably be too embarrassed to tell anyone I *schtupped* with Mr. Lynde. But it was too late. He had closed the door and had thrown his towel to the ground. His locker key was around his right ankle.

Mr. Lynde's stomach was more than a little fleshy and his legs were calveless, but he surprisingly had some tits. Also his cock looked to be close to eight inches and was thickish. He also had big balls that hung low.

(I usually don't remember these details, unless they're about a celebrity or the sex is exquisite.)

Anyway, I'm lying there and he starts licking me from my balls to my chin. Then he sticks his thick tongue down my throat. I remember wishing he hadn't worn so much cologne. Anyway, I close my eyes and I imagine myself lying on the desk of the center square of *Hollywood Squares* as Paul Lynde rims me in front of an appreciatively applauding audience. The other squares are filled with the likes of Joan Rivers, Oscar Wilde, Marcel Proust, Fabian, the Gabor sisters, Eddie Cantor, Ann Sothern and I can't remember who else. They're screaming, "Do it, Paul! Do it, Paul!" Suddenly, I open my eyes to Paul and reality, and I see the *Bye Bye Birdie* star lifting my legs over his shoulders, spitting on my asshole and on his cock. "Oh no! Now I can't tell anyone this story. It would be all right to fuck Mr. Lynde, but to be fucked by the queen of queens? Shit!"

So I close my eyes again, but he slaps my face and says, "When you get fucked by Lynde, baby, you keep your eyes open." And, truthfully, it was a great fuck. Lasting for over twenty minutes or so. I was moaning and screaming. It felt like he was hitting my prostate with every stroke. Sadly, the medallion kept hitting my nose, but I didn't care.

"Chew my nipples," he ordered. I did.

Then he screamed, "I'm coming, baby. I'm coming." But instead of coming inside of me, he shot all over my face . . . drop after drop after drop. Then he licked the cum splatter all up. "I love how I taste, baby. Now turn over."

I did. Suddenly I felt him writing on my ass. He must have had a pen or tiny marker or something in that cigarette case. He then turned me over and kissed me good-bye.

Ten minutes later, I ran to the bathroom and checked out what he wrote.

It said on my firm left ass cheek: FUCKED BY PAUL LYNDE.

Anyway, what I really want to write about is Turkey, which was where my first sexual bout of this year with another human being took place. Except I just want to quickly mention last night. I had called up (212) 550-1000 and listened to sex messages left by others with the hornies. Well, someone was having an orgy on the Upper West Side and they needed a fifth. I passed phone inspection and headed over there.

I was the second best looking person there with possibly the first or second best body, which tells you this was not some chic group with membership at the World Gym.

Everyone there sucked, and a few fucked with condomed penises and dildos, and we had to blow the host, who was overweight with a small penis, but friendly.

Anyway, the next morning I'm looking into the mirror. I have my glasses on, and my vision is blurry . . . *schmutzy*. For some reason I can't figure out what is wrong. Are my glasses smeared, is the bathroom mirror dirty, or is something floating on my pupils? Instead of solving the problem, I just keep staring at the messy visage, unable to function. But I'm often like this after lots of sexual activity. My brain cells which are no doubt connected to my penis get burnt out.

It's been about four months since I last looked at this piece. I wonder if I'll ever finish it. I just got an invite in the mail to a water sports party in two weeks. Maybe I'll go. That'll make a good ending.

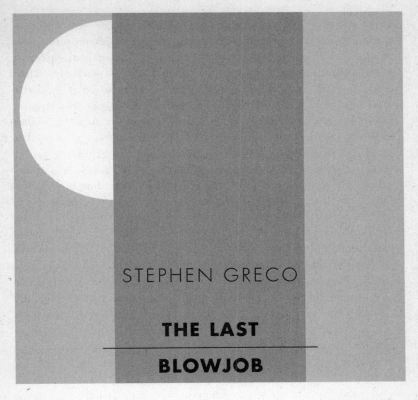

STEPHEN GRECO

THE LAST

BLOWJOB

BY MAY, A MONTH AND A HALF AFTER MY LOVER HENRY WAS admitted to Sacred Heart, it was clear that he wasn't going to come home as quickly as we had been hoping. They eliminated the pneumonia within the first few weeks and knocked out the peskiest of the other, "little" infections that had bloomed under its influence. But Dr. Ehrlich said that before we could think of transferring Henry to a "home set-ting," his mysterious low-grade fever and recurring cough would have to be brought under control. But this didn't happen right away and, by late spring, it didn't seem likely to happen at all. Managing Henry's condition had begun to look as difficult as shoring up a big plate of softening Jell-O.

Still, Henry remained optimistic. Attached to an IV pole, he con-tinued to produce his TV talk show by staying in constant touch with his office by phone. He had a small fax machine installed on the table next to his bed, received and dispatched several messengers a day, and even had prospective guests for the show come by the hospital for the standard interview—something he always took mischievous pleasure in suggesting to them. His universe, like that of all hospital patients, may have shrunk to the size of a room, but Henry's room—private of course, we had the best medical insurance possible—encompassed the world.

There was a steady stream of friends and colleagues who stopped by—visitors whose appointments it was my responsibility, as Chief Care Partner, to coordinate. Henry was, after all, not as strong as he used to be and needed to conserve his energy for crucial things, like breathing and thinking and praying. His attitude about being sick was philosophical. He accepted the death that was clearly impending but tried to embrace life as vigorously as ever, since it was still in progress. Not only did I never hear Henry curse the sex-in-the-fast-lane lifestyle that some mistook as the cause of this whole mess; more than once, both to me and among friends who loved to hear him talk this way, he affirmed his faith in eros. Eros is not what got us into all this, he would say; eros is what can get us beyond it. Not that he expected his disease to be cured by this force, nor did he think his body would be "healed" by it (to use a term he found annoyingly unscientific). There was simply nothing Henry had discovered in his predicament to put him off the conviction that what Freud described as "binding together" with others, whether for work or pleasure, was the highest expression of the life instinct.

I guess that's why I was so disappointed when, after the pneumonia was over and he began to gain back a few of the fifty pounds he had lost, Henry rebuffed a gentle request I made to bind with me. We were slouched together in his bed one night, watching TV, and I fell into the kind of lovey-dovey nuzzlings that had been typical of late-night rerun-watching behavior in our home over the last ten years. But Henry wasn't interested. He stopped me with a limp squeeze of his hand. I let it go at that, not wanting to tax him with a conference, but the next day, as I was shaving him, I brought up the question of sex.

"Honey, do you ever jerk off after I go home?"

"Uh-uh."

"Have you done it at all since you've been here?"

"No."

"Why not? Not enough privacy?"

"There's enough privacy. I just haven't felt like it."

It struck me as odd that the man who had gone to so much trouble to reconstitute his work life around his newly diminished capacities should not have done the same thing with his sex life, which was just as important to him.

"I tried once," Henry continued, "but I got interrupted by Rachel." Rachel was the head nurse. "I know she's seen everything, but still I felt weird. Another time, I couldn't stay awake long enough to do it. And then once I thought I was getting turned on by a muscle magazine that somebody brought, and that was the moment when a patient down the hall decided to go Code Blue. The commotion killed the mood for me."

I put down the electric razor and took his face in my palms.

"I could help you feel like it," I whispered.

He smiled wanly. Shaving now not only made my Henry look neat but, since the structure of his handsome skull was so much more visible than before, it also brought a focus and clarity to his looks that I had never imagined.

"Can I tell you," I purred, "that I'm as totally turned on by you as ever?"

"Baby, you can tell me anything you want," he said, his smile disappearing suddenly into a fit of coughing.

We'd always been creative with sex. When Henry had his wisdom teeth taken out, when I broke my leg, when we were both paralyzed with sunburn, we were still able to figure out some way to do it when both of us felt like doing it. And we were proud of our secret history of making love in romantic places on storybook occasions, like the garden of the Taj Mahal at midnight during a full moon in July, or a cramped compartment aboard the Orient Express in the middle of the Alps on New Year's Eve. I was sure there must be some way for me now to be with my lover sexually—pacifically, of course; only so far as his energy and strength would allow; in a modulated manner, the same way I got him to eat in the hospital by dining with him slowly or, when the meals put before him looked too enormous or too monolithic, by cutting things up and putting them individually into his mouth.

I knew the problem: Henry needed time to adjust to the fact that if he wanted sex, as with work, he was going to have to do it here, in this sanitary environment, because he might never see our Joe Durso bed or the antique oak kitchen table again. It might take time; it might also never happen. I would have to try and remain understanding.

"Well, I want us to keep talking about this, okay?"

"Us having sex? Maybe someday, honey," he said. "I just . . . don't know how. I promise I'll work on it."

He reached over to give my pec an appreciative tug, then turned away abruptly as the coughing started again.

Henry was the one who got me going to the gym. He was one of the original converts to the pectoral lifestyle, at the dawn of the Nautilus Age, and was one of the first people I knew to fill out the sleeve of a polo shirt with a properly pumped tricep. Now, installed for weeks in his bed at Sacred Heart—perhaps never to stand up unaided again, as a physical therapist rather insensitively blurted to both of us—Henry continued to take great care in his appearance. He made sure I shaved him three times a week and insisted I speak with a nurse if there was the slightest delay in his sponge bath. He groomed his fingernails daily—much more than they needed it—and somehow managed to contort his semiwasted self into a position to tend to his toenails, too.

And his body, I thought, still looked great. Was I only seeing him through the eyes of a devoted lover, or was Henry beautiful in a new way? Of course there were detriments galore for us in this damned hospitalization, but there were benefits, too: new strengths, new ways of looking at things. We'd made a pact when he was first admitted to be aware of whatever unexpected good could be found in this new phase of our life together. I thought Henry looked like a statue of the emaciated Buddha we'd seen in Japan, a sexy/saintly figure whose every muscle, vein, and bone was legible beneath a shrink-wrap of skin that seemed a gracious concession to corporeality. Most of the weight that Henry had lost was unsuspected fat, I swear; there was a new tautness that gave his impeccably gymmed physique a refined, essential look— as if he'd been madly training for some bodybuilding contest in which bulk meant nothing and definition everything. His complexion was radiant—probably the side-effect of drugs he was taking, Ehrlich told me—and when Henry sat there in bed, now that it was spring, draped casually with a sheet over his waist, no shirt on, his chest looking like something out of a George Platt Lynes photograph, his feet out of a Michelangelo drawing, I could hardly deflect the thought that these were nipples I still wanted to lick, toes I still wanted to suck. And I was not ashamed of this thought, because desire was the only way I could think of to keep sanctified this piece of flesh that had been turned by diagnosis into an object to be poked and prodded and palpated by an endless parade of technicians.

Henry often said how glad he was to have suffered only pneumonia so far and no skin mutilations. He detested any kind of physical disfigurement and was horrified when I told him about the guy down the hall who had been so transformed by black-and-purple lesions that he was unrecognizable as the cute boy-next-door in a snapshot his mother had put in a frame near the bed. Henry was intact and proud of the fact.

I, on the other hand, felt like I was disintegrating, physically. Cramming a full day's work into four hours at my own office, then rushing to the hospital to serve as traffic cop, baby-sitter, physical therapist, and master of ceremonies; squeezing in quick workouts now and then; getting home late and sleeping fitfully, because I couldn't adjust to going to bed alone for the first time in a decade; I was often so tuckered out that even looking twice at boners bulging invitingly under sweatpants in the street seemed too hard to do, let alone striking up a conversation and going home with someone—which I almost felt I *should* do, since I hadn't had sex with Henry in months and sex is usually one way for me to refresh myself. Anyway, it was Henry I wanted— *those* arms, *that* face. Despite brief escapades that we agreed must remain "only physical," could never take time away from the relationship, and were not to be spoken of, Henry and I had always been true to each other, and now that our relationship was probably in its final months I felt less like hooking up with a stranger than ever.

I hope I don't have to explain why sex in a hospital is such a thinkable proposition. Hell, it's got to be the most therapeutic thing in the world. Other longtime companions I was meeting in the corridors of Sacred Heart told me about salutary bouts of lovemaking they'd enjoyed with their sick boyfriends on hospital beds. In fact, to hear some of them tell it, hospitals are hopping with sex. One had a friend who, over the years, had been a faithful client of one of the city's top pornstar-hustlers. Now that the hustler was ill and occasionally installed in hospital rooms, the client made it a point to go on seeing him. It wasn't so much about money being exchanged for services but a special kind of friendship remaining intact, I was told. The client would arrive for a visit with a bouquet; the two of them would chat aimlessly for a while, then swing into a highly verbal bodyworship scene that centered on the hustler's cock; those famous ten fat inches would inflate and be deflated in a manner that was usual for them; and the cash would be found later in a get-well card tucked into the flowers. Gay men are nothing if not adaptable.

Another guy told me that the ritual group of men he belongs to had recently visited one of their members who was hospitalized in coma. After words being spoken and hands being laid on, the group masturbated onto the man's motionless body, exactly as he had asked them to do when he was able. And *everyone* tells me that there are nights now on the phone sex lines when it simply isn't possible to avoid at least one connection with someone whose conversation testifies to bed confinement. One guy I was talking to recently told me he had to hang up because an orderly had arrived to wheel him away for an X ray.

I was trimming Henry's hair one day, finishing up with a little peck on the cheek, when he pulled me close to him and inserted his hand under the waistband of my jeans.

"Oh, really?" I said. "Frisky today?"

"I don't know," he said with coyness that outside the room would have seemed inconsequential but here seemed practically monumental. "You're so good to me."

"You're good to *me*," I said, "letting me take care of you. . . ."

"Hmmm," he said, snuggling into my armpit.

After a moment he reached over to get his wallet from a drawer in the night table and took out a twenty dollar bill.

"Listen, it's not five-thirty yet, is it? Go out to where they keep the linens and give this to that cute nurse with the crewcut and goatee. His name is Eric. Ask him to watch our door for twenty minutes. He's cool."

When I returned, Henry had kicked down the bedding and was stroking himself through his Brooks Brothers boxer shorts. I perched next to him and slipped a hand over his chest and down around his back. He smelled very old but reassuringly Henry-like.

"He's cute, right?

"Very," I said, kissing Henry's ear. But I was nervous. "Has Rachel stopped by with the afternoon meds yet?"

"She came at four. Ehrlich's due around six. Now, I can't guarantee that someone's not going to come barging past Eric, wanting a cup of my blood or a picture of my brain . . ."

"Let me check once more."

I hopped down and went to the door. The corridor was quiet. Eric smiled confidently when I peeked out. He reassured me that this was a good time and shooed me back into the room. Inside, it was suddenly the baths. There was this sexy guy spread out on a bed, giving me a look and a half. I bee-lined over to him and applied my skull deftly to his cock.

It was like conversing in your native language again after a year among foreigners. Henry's cock was big, but it was articulate. It spoke to me. And I was very good at listening to it. The language was that subtle, nonverbal kind that occurs between body parts that are lavishly endowed with a zillion times more receptor nerve cells than other parts. With the delicate skin of head of cock nestled into the lining of mouth and throat, both of us were acutely attuned, like human polygraphs, to minute fluctuations in each other's temperature, electrolytic balance, and galvanic response, forget grosser signs like pelvic thrust and breathing rate. The taste of him drove me crazy; the very elements he was made of, in their exact proportion to each other, I have craved since the day I met him. And he simply *looked* hot: Mr. Big TV Producer lying there on his back, his weak little limbs as immobile as if they had been fettered by leather straps. Now, Henry and I had never done much bondage, but I think what really worked for us this time was this expression of his passivity, with an undertone of resignation.

He took no longer to come than he ever did. Maybe fifteen minutes. If Ehrlich had burst in with his chart, or Rachel with a needle, or that perky, surrealistically well-groomed patients' advocate woman with one more questionnaire, what they would have seen was me kneeling over this muscular skinny guy, his head thrown back in ecstasy, the plastic urinal bottle empty on the floor, where it had fallen when knocked from its hook on the bed rail. What they would not have seen, but surmised, was the presence of the thick, warm, veiny shaft plugged up inside my head, emptying itself. Henry gave my hair a little tousel when we'd finished. He was beaming like Howdy Doody. I kissed his navel and covered him with the sheet.

"Cold?" I asked.

"Hot," he said, letting me tuck him in. "I've so much missed being that close to you. Listen, honey, can I say something serious? I want you to make sure you have another lover when I'm gone. . . ."

"What?! Henry, I can't believe you're giving me that speech. It's entirely premature."

"Just remember that I said it. Be sad when I'm gone, but get another lover. Think of my saying that as a little gift to you, like the one you just gave me."

STEPHEN GRECO

We talked for a minute about my not wanting to talk about the matter, then it was time for Henry's nap. I put the room back in order and took off. Eric said good-bye as I left.

That was the last time Henry and I had sex. The *last* last time, that is. The time before that—which I remember fearing, when it happened, could itself be the last—took place a month before Henry went into the hospital. We were in London for the opening of a new play. He had already begun to lose weight "mysteriously" and sleep through any performance we got tickets to. We'd returned to our hotel room in the afternoon for a nap, and upon waking fell into each other's arms with a hunger I recall from our college days, which is when we met. Another lover! That was the last thing I wanted to think about.

Henry never came home from Sacred Heart. Less than a month after our little escapade, Rachel found him one morning wailing about being "at the wrong gate" and waving a towel like a flag to someone on the horizon. Dementia had set in and from there everything got worse. We lost him in August. I am glad to think that, during the last days, though he seldom knew who I was, he still favored me with a kind of infantile sexual intimacy, as if through gathering shadows there shined the memory of love. In the midst of throwing food at the walls and ripping off his diapers, he'd grasp me affectionately and grin as if to say, "I know who you are and I think you're wonderful." And I would feel completely wonderful.

I was surprised when Eric showed up at the memorial service I arranged for Henry that fall. It was a giant affair. Friends and relatives flew in from all over the country. Dr. Ehrlich was there. Rachel came. And then there was Eric, who strode in looking incredibly cute in a smart linen blazer over a tight T-shirt that definitely showed "something going on" underneath, as Henry liked to say. After the ceremony he came up to me and told me something amazing.

"He was a great guy," Eric said, gathering me into a warm embrace. No, I hadn't realized how muscular he was. "I'm sorry I didn't get to know him until so late. But I thought you should know . . . that is, he wanted me to tell you, after he was gone like this . . . that we fooled around in the hospital. A little bit."

At first, I didn't know what he was talking about.

"Fooled around."

"Sex. He said you'd approve."

Oh, I thought.

"He loved you so much," Eric went on. "He always said that. He and I used to see each other at the gym all the time, before he got sick. I always thought he was totally hot, and he used to look at me in the shower like, 'Someday, mister.' I'd drop the soap, spend four minutes picking it up, that kind of thing. Well, when he checked into the room on my floor at Sacred Heart, it was natural that we should talk to each other, spend time with each other. You know."

"So how did you fool around?" I asked.

"We felt each other up a few times, jerked off," Eric said brightly, "and once I blew him. Mainly in the room, when I knew there would be no one around. Once he asked me to put him in a wheelchair and take him to the solarium. We did it right there, next to a visitor guy who was asleep on the sofa. Your lover was a very sexy man. Now, he said that this would be good for you to hear. . . ."

"Yeah, yeah, it's good," I said after a moment. "So the day you watched out for us. . . ."

"He told me later that until then he hadn't been able to feel aroused in the hospital. It was only after that that he and I did anything. He said that you had, quote, restored his body to him and that after he was gone I should buy you a drink and tell you all the details."

So it was not with me that Henry had his last sexual experience. Well. It would take some getting used to, but I realized even then, in my stressed out state, that Eric's story hardly detracted from my memory of Henry. It embellished it, really: Heroes of Eros, welcome Henry into your midst.

I wanted to hear more, but I was being summoned by the rabbi. I asked Eric to call me. We would have a drink, talk more. And I was thinking: I'm as happy to go out with Eric as Henry thought I would be. Any excuse to keep talking about my lover was okay with me.

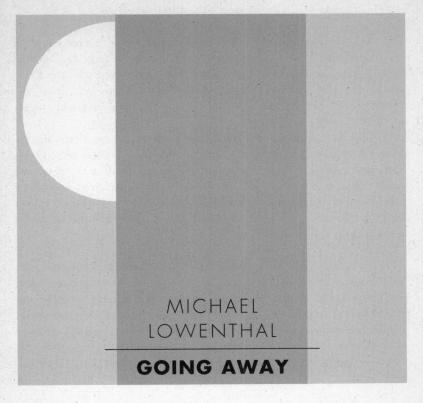

MICHAEL LOWENTHAL

GOING AWAY

"ENOUGH OF THIS SLOW STUFF. TAKE OFF YOUR SHIRT."

Michael stands at the foot of the bed. He hesitates, looks down at his fully clothed body.

"Go ahead. I put up with this cold room for long enough. You can stand having your chest bare for a while."

He slips his hand to the bottom edge of his old chamois shirt, fingers the soft and fraying fabric.

"Grab your nipples. Dig your fingernails into the skin. Twist them hard while you walk over to my closet."

Michael's feet stay planted on the wide pine floorboards. His shirt is still on, buttoned to the neck.

He steps forward and slams down his hand, smothering the stop button with too many fingers. The portable recorder crushes an image of itself into the down pillow it was propped against. Michael presses eject and removes the tape, holding it with just his fingertips as if it were one of the hummingbirds he finds sometimes, dead outside the kitchen's bay window.

As he walks across the bedroom he is shaking, his throat weak the way it gets just before vomiting. He sits down at the huge maple desk, Scott's desk, the one Scott built when they first moved into the farmhouse. The gray tool box, stained with streaks of motor oil, sits in the center of the polished slab of wood. The top is tipped back like the lid of a casket open for display.

Without looking at the rest of the contents, Michael carefully replaces the cassette and shuts the box. He flips the metal latches on both sides and pushes it away, making room for his head, which he leans forward and rests on the desk. He feels the tears start to gather in the sacs below his tired eyes. A bubble of grief rises in his throat, chokes him for an instant. How could Scott ask this of him? Why did he always have to push things so far?

This morning, after Scott's parents and closest friends had been notified, after a few hours of hugs and tears, after the hearse had come and taken the body to the funeral home, Michael asked everybody to leave and forwarded his calls to Carrie, who as they had arranged long ago would handle the logistics of the funeral. He locked the door, turned off most of the lights, and walked into the empty bedroom.

The smell was the first thing, so familiar by now, but at the same time painfully unexpected. That odd mix of antiseptic freshness with fermenting body odors: sweat-soaked sheets, the diapers filled with black ooze still resting in the bottom of the trashcan. Michael bit his cheek to keep from gagging.

The room was strangely dark, even with the new windows Scott had knocked into the wall just before he got sick the first time. The October Vermont light came in grainy, at too low an angle, making everything look like a faded black-and-white photo. Nothing had been taken yet. The oxygen tanks were still clustered in the corner, like a minyan huddling to pray. The IV drip stood watch over the bed, the plastic tube dangling down like a rope from the gallows. A half-empty can of Sustecal waited on the night table, ready to be poured. Michael imagined it as one of his own meticulous still lifes: "Recent AIDS Death, 1993."

Michael stared at the bed for just a moment, certain he could make out the indentations in the mattress from Scott's shoulder blades. Then he reached underneath, where he'd seen Scott stash the box dozens of times. It was heavier than he had imagined, as if it were still filled with

socket wrenches, pliers, vise grips. He hoisted the box and carried it
over to the big desk, clearing a space to set it down.

First he ran his fingers over the cool metal, the rounded edges and
hinged black handle. He noticed the slight change in temperature when
his fingers reached the strip of masking tape. He traced the smooth
length of the tape, the ragged ends where it had been torn from the
roll. Then he read the words written carefully in red magic marker:
WHEN I GO.

When I go. *When.* Michael had always wanted it to be *if*, wanted
to hold out for the possibility of some miracle. But Scott had been
realistic, practical-minded. When he knew he wouldn't be driving any
more and sold the S-10, Scott had emptied the box of the auto repair
kit that had been a high school graduation present from his grandfather.
He'd given the tools to a kid down the road who had his own jacked-
up pickup, but kept the box and marked its new function with his crude
masking tape label.

For all these months, Michael had not been allowed to look into
the box. He hadn't wanted to know what was in there anyway. But he
had given his word that when Scott died, he would open the box that
very same day. Scott always made him repeat that part of the promise.
It was a strange request, to start looking through his lover's mementos
before the funeral had even taken place, but Michael wanted to do everything he could to make Scott feel more secure about his death.

He unclipped the latches and opened the box warily, as if it were
a magician's trick box and a snake might leap out at his face. On the
very top of the pile was a handwritten note on Scott's personal stationery.

Michael:

    Just when you thought it was safe . . .

    *Sorry. I know how much it bugs you when I'm not being serious
enough. So how are you doing so far? Make sure to take time for
yourself. Let Carrie deal with my parents, and you do that sit-and-
shiver thing—whatever it's called—that your people do. (Just don't
cover the mirrors; what would all the queens at the reception do
without a place to check their hair?)*

    *Listen. Darling. I don't know how to say this without sounding
like an Ann Landers column, or worse yet the Cliff Notes to Kübler-
Ross. But you have to move on. Promise me you will. That doesn't
mean you should forget me. (You better not, kiddo, 'cause I'm watch-*

ing your ass.) But you know my thing about restriction. If I thought
after everything I was the one holding you back, I would just die.
(Get it?)

    Well, this is getting as long as the basketball season. Here's
the deal. Most of what's in the box can wait. Some sentimental stuff.
Letters to Milton, Sandra, and a couple other friends. An extra copy
of the will. But the tape on top is for now. Right now. Use the
portable box we usually take to the beach, prop it up on the pillow
on my bed, and press play. Remember, you promised. Do it for me.

    All my love, always,
    Scott

Michael opens the box again now and unfolds the letter. It's quintessential Scott: full of jokes, as if nothing's a big deal. But if the smallest demand was violated, look out! And that line about "restriction."

Michael studies Scott's slanted lefty scrawl. It's even messier than usual in this note, as if he wanted to make sure Michael would be the only one capable of deciphering it. He thinks back six years ago to when they were at B.U., Scott a junior and he a senior, and they went shopping together for the first time. At one point Scott had stopped the cart and stood there, examining the grocery list he had written. "Let's see," he'd muttered to himself. "What's next. I can barely read my own writing." Michael had ripped the paper out of Scott's hands and read aloud: "Raisins. Chocolate chips. Vanilla ice cream." Scott had stared at him, amazed, then kissed him full on the lips, right there in the frozen foods aisle of the Stop & Shop. "Wow," he'd said. "I think I just might have to marry you."

Michael places the letter back in the box and stares at the cassette. It's old and a little scratched; Scott must have recycled it from the used tapes pile. Yankee frugality, he'd probably claim. Just plain cheap was the truth. But cheap and lovable. Michael picks up the cassette. The plastic is cold in his hands, weighs almost nothing. The exposed ribbon of brown magnetic tape is thin, fragile as a strand of hair. Could this be all he has left?

He takes the tape and stands up, walks back to the bed. He has to. He gave Scott his word.

Michael snaps the tape into the player and hits rewind before fear might allow him to hesitate. The recorder whirs for a few seconds, clicks twice as the auto-reverse activates, and then the room fills with Scott's voice.

"He's baaack! Hi, Michael. It's me. The recently deceased. And you thought you'd gotten rid of me.

"I know you'll think I'm doing my Marlene impression, but this is just the way my voice is these days. You'll have to bear with me."

Judging from the throatiness, the frequency of pauses for breath, Michael figures Scott must have recorded this two or three weeks ago, just as the last bout of pneumonia was setting in. He pictures Scott with the tubes in his nose, the mucous caking on his lip, green like mold. He blinks hard, tries to shake the image.

"Listen, I know you have trouble following instructions. You always have to do things your own way. The rebel artiste. Well, this time, you have to go my way, kiddo. You wouldn't want to disobey the dead."

Michael can't help cracking a smile. He thinks of the way Scott said he imagined heaven, as one eternal taping of "The Gong Show." All the dead sit at a long table, watching over the earth. Whenever one of the living does something disrespectful, the dead person who's been blasphemed gets to stand up and smash the giant gong, which Scott said manifested in the offending earthling as a splitting sinus headache.

"Now, I want you to stand at the foot of the bed. Stand there like you would some Saturday mornings when you'd come back to the bedroom after painting for a couple of hours. I wake up and you're just standing there, reeking of turpentine, watching me with that distant look in your eyes. You don't make a move, you just stand there, teasing me. Even when I pull down the sheets and show you my chest, you just watch. I can't tell you how horny that always made me.

"Rub your hands through your hair. Lightly, just barely touch it. Imagine it's my tongue, tickling your scalp. It's my tongue nibbling at the wave of your widow's peak, biting your neck, around to your Adam's apple, leaving a trail of miniature hickies."

Michael moves his hand absentmindedly to the back of his head, grabs a handful of short bristles. He hasn't showered in three days. The hair is slick and soft with oil. He is thinking about when Scott discovered the first spot of KS as he was buttoning his collar one morning. They'd had fierce, acrobatic sex the night before, and Scott thought the lesion was just a hickie. He teased Michael about it, saying that was the problem with painters: They always had to make their feelings visible before they believed they were real. Michael remembers wanting to tackle Scott then and bite him hard on the hickie, to draw blood and say, *"That's* how I feel." What instinct had held him back?

"Move your hand down, slowly. Let it linger on your chest. Then go down, circle past your crotch, trail your fingers lightly down your left thigh. Go ahead and grab if you want, squeeze the muscle. Think about when I first discovered your leg thing."

The first time through, Michael hadn't been able to touch himself. He'd stood there, frozen, resisting the memory. He didn't want to let Scott manipulate him the way he so often did, as if his emotions were wires Scott could connect and disconnect as easily as the ones in the pickup truck engines he customized.

Now, as he listens to the same words again, Michael's fingers rub softly on the loose fabric of his khaki pants. He glances at the small wooden table next to the bed—"the shrine," as Scott always called it. Photographs of both their parents, Scott's namesake nephew, and, front and center, the happy couple in their favorite spot, the bleachers at Fenway. It was the first picture ever taken of the two of them together. They stand just barely balanced on their seats, blue caps turned at crazy angles on their heads, their giant K signs held in the air in tribute to Roger Clemens's copious strikeouts. They're beaming because the Red Sox have won and because they're about to have the best sex either of them has ever had.

Michael moves his hand lower, forcing himself to comply with Scott's disembodied voice.

"I think it was the third or fourth date. At your place after the Sox beat the Tigers in extra innings. Remember? I made you lie down on the bed and promise to let go of all your muscles, like a puppet. Then I gave you a tongue bath even though you still had all your clothes on, starting at your sneakers and working my way up. I sucked on your ankles, letting my spit soak through the cotton socks, then your calves, turning the blue jeans black with wetness. When I got to your knee you flinched the way you do when a doctor tests you with that little hammer. I darted my tongue back to the same spot and you flinched again and tried to twist away. I had to punish you for breaking the rules. I had to hold you down and nibble at the underside of your knee. I'd never seen anybody writhe like that before. Even through your jeans, it made you shout so loud the upstairs neighbor banged on the floor. That's when I first fantasized about tying you to the bed, face down, and keeping you that way all night long. Go ahead now. Touch the back of your knee."

Michael's hand has already been there for a few seconds, ahead of the tape, his index finger flicking back and forth at his most sensitive spot. His eyes are rolled to the ceiling and he's not seeing anything, just feeling the tingle in his nerves.

"Touch the other knee. Back and forth, the way I always tortured you. All right. Enough of this slow stuff. Take off your shirt."

This time he does. He unhooks the buttons quickly, two at a time, rushing to keep up with the tape.

"Go ahead. I put up with this cold room for long enough. You can stand having your chest bare for a while."

Michael tosses the chamois shirt to the floor. It does seem cold in the room. He starts to feel guilty until he remembers it was Scott who refused to use the space heater, saying the electric bill would be too high. His nipples stiffen, turn crimson with the infusion of blood. His chest pricks with goosebumps, each separate follicle buzzing, alive. It's been so long since his chest has been touched this way. He always forgets to when he masturbates, concentrating instead on the quick route to pleasure between his legs. Now he reaches a hand up to the right nipple, presses the stiff bump between his thumb and forefinger.

"Grab your nipples. Dig your fingernails into the skin. Twist them hard while you walk over to my closet."

They kept separate closets. Scott's hasn't been opened in weeks because he couldn't get out of bed, let alone get dressed. Michael pulls the sliding wooden door and he is overwhelmed with the smell of Scott: the old Scott, Scott before the sickness. It's the smell of wet leaves, deep inside a raked-up pile. The smell of a wool jacket that's been draped over a chair near the smoking woodstove. More pungent, personal odors as well: old boot liners, urine-stained boxer shorts. Michael breathes in as deeply as he can, the way he used to suck the air around Scott's underarms.

"The leather jacket is on the far left. Get it. Put it on."

The stiff leather creaks as he pulls it from the hanger. The jacket is heavy, feels almost solid. Michael slips his arms into the sleeves, then hunches fully into the jacket and his chest juts forward, a reflex against the cold animal skin.

"I bet that leather feels good on your bare chest. Think of it as a little piece of me on top of you. Think of what I would do if I was there."

He imagines Scott coming in after a morning of splitting firewood, surprising him from behind with his cold, raw hands. Scott would hold them there, palms pressed against Michael's sensitive spine, until finally they warmed to normal body temperature. Then, just when Michael had adjusted and let down his guard, Scott would flip them, nuzzle the still-freezing backs of his hands into Michael's skin, up into his armpits.

A chill shakes him, collects in his groin. He never thought he would let himself go this far.

"Walk back to the bed. Climb onto it and kneel at the foot, facing down where I would be. Yeah, I can see you. Just kneel there, arch your back some, feel the leather rubbing against your skin. Reach in and touch your nipples again."

Michael is on the bed. He is kneeling, his feet tucked under him, leaning back against the cold brass rail. With both hands he kneads his own chest, squeezing chunks of flesh and skin. He slaps one flat palm over his heart, leaving a stinging red handprint on the pale skin. He flicks the left nipple with the back of his fingernail, then again, and again until it is purple.

"Now unzip your pants and pull them down. Not too far! Pull back the underwear, just a little. Pretend you're putting on a show. You love that. You always act shy, like you don't want me to see. But I know you do. You want to sit on me. Right?"

Michael unveils his stiff penis and shakes it seductively in the direction where Scott's face would be. He always did like to show it off, liked to get it from on top so he could watch Scott's eyes, riveted to every move.

"Go ahead." Scott's breathing is deeper now, more labored. "Go ahead and pump it. Take yourself all the way."

Michael's right hand tugs quickly, pushing blood to the tip. He jerks himself with the head pointed down, almost touching his thigh, the way Scott liked to see it.

There is a knocking sound as the headboard hits up against the wall. Over and over, the hollow plaster answering each thrust of Michael's hips. It's a comforting sound, familiar as his own heartbeat. The photos on the night table shake and threaten to topple, but he knows from experience that they won't. He thinks of all the times they had sex on this bed. The first time, with all their clothes on. A few days later, when he finally stayed the night. Then he remembers the time in the truck. He hasn't thought of this in months.

It was when they were moving from Boston up to Vermont. They had hired a Mayflower crew with a huge semi, and they were supposed to follow behind in the old Subaru. But just past Springfield the Subaru blew a rod. They had to abandon it on the side of the highway and ride the rest of the way in the back of the moving truck.

It was pitch dark and cold, the air thick with dust from the blankets draped over their belongings. The bed was against one wall, piled with boxes of clothes. There was just enough room for Michael to lie down with Scott on top of him.

As the truck whined through the gears and came up to speed on I-91, Scott readied Michael with a spit-covered finger, skipping the usual foreplay. Then he jerked himself quickly, fumbled to get the condom on, and pushed against the tight opening. When he was all the way inside he just lay there on top of Michael, not moving at all, and not saying a word, letting the bump of the tires over each section of pavement be their rhythm. For fifteen minutes they lay there, completely at the mercy of the road. Finally, they entered a construction area where the highway was grooved, waiting to be repaved. With the metal sides of the truck rattling as if they would pop their rivets, the rush of cars in the passing lane, the hum of the engine pounding in their ears, they came within seconds of each other.

Michael picks up the speed of his jerking. He pulls his cock hard, yanks on the skin until it folds in on itself and appears suddenly uncircumcised, like Scott's. He rams his hand down to the base, then jerks up again, then again, faster. He's getting really close. He makes his cock look uncut again and imagines Scott's dick inside him the way it was that night in the truck. He leans back, listens for the voice. He wants to come to the sound of Scott's voice.

Suddenly he realizes there's nothing coming from the tape. He tries to remember the last thing Scott said, but he can't. He was so lost in his own pleasure that he didn't notice when it stopped. Now he pauses, listens again for the voice. He peers through the plastic window of the cassette player to see if the tape is still rolling. He can see the sprockets turning, but the only sound it emits is static.

Now he hears something, a faint noise. It could be the creaking of a bed, or a door slowly opening. He realizes it's a human voice. A single, high-pitched sob and then a painful gasp for air.

With one hand Michael reaches out instinctively toward the cassette player, as if he could comfort Scott, run his fingers reassuringly through the soft blond hair. He realizes his other hand is still gripping his penis and he drops it like something poisonous, lets it fall limp against his thigh.

Michael starts to cry, the tears pooling in his eyelids until they

sting and his eyelashes mat together. The recorder appears to him now
as just a fuzzy black rectangle. He wants to punch it, wants to smash
the plastic into a thousand pieces. How could he be doing this now,
today? But it's not his fault. Why did Scott always have to make a show
of everything, always have to orchestrate things so he was the center of
attention? Like when he banished Michael's paintings from the bedroom,
saying they were too gloomy. "I'm the sick one," he'd said. "Why should
I have to stare all day at *your* grief."

He never should have promised Scott he would listen to the tape.
He moves to slam it off but just as he does, the voice resumes.

"I'm sorry, Michael. Shit. I'm really sorry. Pull yourself together,
Scottie.

"What was I thinking about? This was supposed to be for you, not
for me."

Michael hovers midway across the bed, his hand still reaching toward the tape player. He wants to stop it, but he's terrified by the
prospect of silence.

"I just couldn't let go of this fantasy, you know? That we'd come
together, at the same moment, one last time. I was sure I could get it
together for one last triumphant burst.

"Leave it to a Red Sox fan, I guess. It's like I actually believed Yaz
would hit a home run in the playoff game in '78, instead of popping
up. What was I, crazy? I haven't even been able to get a hard-on in two
months! So I'm sitting here, fixating on trying to rouse this useless piece
of flesh, and I forget all about you.

"Who knows? Maybe I'm getting all worked up over nothing.
Maybe you've already come, shot your load all over the bed. Or maybe
you got disgusted and turned off the tape ten minutes ago. How am I
supposed to know? It's like having phone sex with somebody's answering
machine."

Michael smiles just a crack, involuntarily, and the tears run in at
the corners of his mouth. He licks the salt away.

"I guess this whole thing was a dumb idea anyway. It could never
work. But I just wanted to leave you with . . . I don't know. Something
more than an empty room, a closet full of clothes, and that depressing
photo shrine. I couldn't bear it if you became one of those dreadful
AIDS widows.

"All right. I'll get off that trip. I know you've heard it all before.
All I'm saying is, don't turn off any part of yourself on my account.

And don't turn off any memories of me either, don't just think of me
as the gorgeous young stud I was. Think of me like this, too. You know,
the diapers, everything. It's all me. But don't forget to remember me
how I was when I was making love to you. Yeah. I guess that's my last
request. Think of me as sexy."

Michael flinches at the last word, a silent sob shuddering through
him. He makes himself hold it in, makes himself listen for anything
else Scott might need to say. There is the sound of strained breathing,
then the creak of the old bed, something metal shifting on the floor.

"Well, I'm exhausted. Need a shot of this oxygen. This has been
a bit much for a man on his last legs, so to speak.

"I don't know what else to say, honey. I think this has really gone
on long enough. I love you, Michael. I love you now and always. Take
care of yourself."

His eyes are closed. He is still kneeling with his feet tucked under
him but he can't feel his legs, can't feel the bed under him. He is in
zero gravity, spinning through space. He hears background noise but
it's as if both ears are covered with giant seashells. He hears an ocean
that's not an ocean, a nonexistent wind.

Random snapshots of memory rush through Michael's mind: Scott
bent over into the hood of the truck, the view of just his butt and legs,
the single greasy handprint on his thigh; Scott and his nephew—the
two Scotts, Scott squared—lying head to head on the living room rug
over a game of Monopoly; Scott on his back in the bathtub, so far gone
that you can see the outline of his spine just by looking at his stomach.
Then Michael tries to remember what Scott was wearing the first time
he ever saw him. He should know this, he has to, but he can't bring it
to mind. Everything goes blank. He can't remember anything, not
Scott's hair, not his eyes or his face. Just as quickly it all comes back,
more vivid than ever. Michael is dizzy, confused by the tricks his brain
is playing.

Now he is rocking. Back and forth with his whole body, like a
Hasid davening in prayer. He is rocking, holding his stomach with both
hands as if his intestines could spill out. The motion soothes him, makes
his head feel light and good. It's a rhythm, something to hold onto.

The sound brings him back into the room. The high-pitched
squeak of the bedsprings giving way, the steady knock-knock of the
headboard against the plaster wall. He can't help it. He can't. The sound
makes him remember.

He's hasn't allowed himself to admit it until just now, but even at the very end, Scott never stopped turning him on. He had thought he knew every inch of Scott's body, but when that body started falling apart, started changing and doing unexpected things, it was like learning a new lover from scratch. He would turn Scott over to give him a warm sponge bath and he would explore every fold of rashy skin, every corner of bone. What could be more intimate than wiping the crud from somebody's ass, or picking the lint from between their toes? How could he ever be that close to another body?

He wishes things could be clean, could stay in their proper compartments. But he can't keep anything straight anymore. One second he sees Scott's emaciated chest, each rib poking through the skin like some picked-over carcass in a nature film, and the next instant he's remembering the smooth pearly foreskin that he loved to play with so much.

He thinks of the time Scott called him in from the studio over the intercom they'd set up. "Come quick. Come right away." Michael had panicked, dropped his palette paint-side down, assuming the IV had pulled loose again. When he got there Scott was propped up on his elbows, the sheets pulled midway down his thighs. "It's hard," he said, with a child's amazement. "It's hard." And together, with Michael's right hand on the bottom, Scott's left hand on top, they gently massaged the shaft, laughing, careful not to disturb the tubes that criss-crossed the bed, until Scott came in three small bursts.

Michael is startled by a sharp noise and the sound of a voice. It must be Carrie, or Scott's parents. But it seems early for them to have come with dinner. He listens closely and he realizes that it's his own voice. It's coming from the tape.

He opens his eyes, wipes the residue of tears so he can focus. He stares at the small black box from which he speaks to himself in his grandiose Prince Charles impression: "A quarter century. The silver plateau. It is, friends, a remarkable achievement." It's Scott's twenty-fifth birthday party, two years ago. He doesn't even remember that they taped the festivities. But they must have, and Scott must have recorded over the old tape by accident.

Scott's chimes in, doing Princess Di. The voice is different from the tape Michael's just been listening to: clearer in tone, no rasp in the throat. "We thank our lovely husband the Prince, but remind him that our quarter century pales in comparison to his own abundant achievement of years." A group of people in the background howls with laughter. They were in top form, Michael thinks, their timing perfect as an old vaudeville act.

Then they're singing "Happy Birthday" in warbling falsettos, the whole group of them, everybody laughing, trying to spit out the words. Michael remembers feeling drunk even though he'd only had one glass of champagne, remembers falling against Scott's chest and pressing his ear to the solid rib cage, being tickled by the vibrations as Scott sang. And then the surreptitious hand that slipped into his jeans, Scott's fingers circling the base and tugging just a bit while the others sang on around them, oblivious.

Michael's entire body stirs with the memory. His knees grind into the firm mattress, making a tangle of the sheets. He should have stripped the bed this morning, but now he's glad he didn't. These are the sheets Scott slept in, the last thing that covered his living body. Michael grabs a handful of fabric and holds it to his nose. The smell gags him for an instant, sweat mixed with traces of shit and puke. But he holds the sheet to his face, inhales deeply again.

It all smells good to Michael right now. It all smells of Scott, of his body. Michael keeps the sheets in place with one hand and with the other, reaches down. His cock is already hard and wet with clear fluid gathering at the slit. The skin still tingles from being so close before. He knows it won't take long.

He wraps his fingers around the base just as Scott had at the birthday party and moves quickly in strong, even strokes. His eyes are open, looking to the head of the bed, and he can see Scott clearly. He sees the expression that would bloom on Scott's face when he was just on the verge of orgasm: the lips slightly curled back, the eyes closed to fluttering slits, a combination of strain and relief. It's the same expression, it occurs to him now, that he found on Scott this morning.

Michael jerks one last time and releases, two spurts of fluid shooting out over the dirty sheets, the rest dripping onto his hand, running between his fingers. He squeezes out a few more drops and then lets himself fall forward onto the bed. His head lands on the pillow, bumping up against the cold plastic of the cassette player.

On the tape they've moved on to the second part of the song. *How old are you now? How old are you now?* Michael hears his own voice soaring above the others. And then Scott's voice. Competing divas. The other partygoers drop out and are silent as Michael and Scott slow to a grand finale. The two voices jar for a moment as they waver in and out of harmony, straining against each other. *Happy birthday to . . .* The voices soar up together on the last word, each man assuming the other would stay on the melody note, both instead singing the harmonic third, and Michael can't tell whose voice is whose.

PART NINE

CLOSING

MANIFESTO

Michael Bronski has long been one of the most astute observers of gay culture. In his book *Culture Clash: The Making of Gay Sensibility*, and in his frequent essays and reviews, he has consistently provided clear analysis of the lives we are still in the process of creating. I end the collection with his landmark essay, "Why Gay Men Can't Really Talk About Sex," as both a mark of how far gay sexual writing has come and a gauge of how much further it could go.

Bronski argues that while gay men perhaps talk about sex more, and more publicly, than any other group in society, we still have great difficulty discussing our private, personal, sexual desires. One might think that the proliferation of gay pornography would help counteract this deficiency, but Bronski takes the porn industry to task for commercializing sex. Rather than enhancing our abilities to fantasize creatively, he contends, mass market pornography has homogenized our sexual language to the point when "honest discussion about sex is as scarce as good acting in a porno movie."

Bronksi's closing challenge is particularly crucial. He calls for gay men to talk and write stories about our most personal, our most transgressive, our most frightening fantasies, and in language that is the honest speech of confessional, not the borrowed clichés of genre dialogue.

I suggest that all of us gay erotic writers cut out the essay's last paragraph, have it enlarged at the local copy shop, and tape it above our desks. If we all rise to the challenge, there will be enough cutting-edge dirty stories to fill an entire series of anthologies like the one you have in your hands.

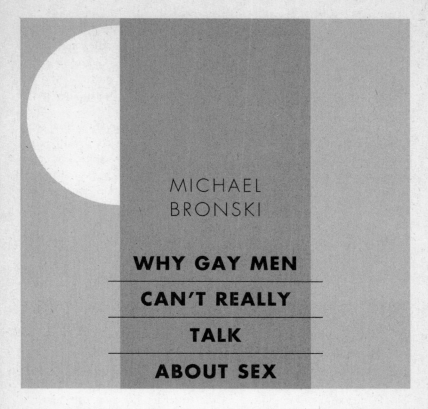

MICHAEL
BRONSKI

WHY GAY MEN
CAN'T REALLY
TALK
ABOUT SEX

GAY MEN ARE ACCUSED OF A LOT OF FAILINGS IN OUR CUL-
ture, but the inability to talk about sex is never one of them. I mean,
after all, gay men *talk* about sex. It's something we do. We do it well.
We do it a lot. At least that's what I've thought over the past twenty-
five years. But recently I'm coming to the conclusion that most of our
sexual talk is simply an attempt to avoid really talking about sex. The
discussions of what, or who, we do in bed, of how big someone's dick
is, of who we want to fuck, or what went on in the bushes last night
are fine as far as they go, but they are more posturing than professional,
more obfuscating than observing, more pruriently licentious than pro-
foundly liberating.

It is rare, in my experience, for gay men to discuss honestly their
sexual feelings, their sexual needs or their sexual fantasies. This isn't
about gay men being unable to open themselves up emotionally—problems in expressing intimacy are endemic to being human, although their
manifestations are certainly influenced by a wide array of gender, race,

ethnicity and class factors—but about how sex, sexuality and sexual activity have shaped and been shaped in gay male life. The irony is that while talk about sex has always been a salient, vital part of gay male culture, honest discussion about sex is as scarce as good acting in a porno movie.

I first started to think seriously about gay men's inability to discuss sex after I started presenting a piece I had written entitled "Death, AIDS and the Transfiguration of Grief: Thoughts on the Sexualization of Mourning" at conferences. The piece (which originally appeared in *Gay Community News* in 1988) talked about the physical connections between sex and grief, about my sexual fantasies about my ex-lover Jim who had recently died of AIDS, and how I discovered, for me, the reality that sexual fantasy and activity had become inextricably intertwined with dealing with the miasma of death and grief with which I found myself surrounded. The piece began with a description of my jerking off on Jim's brass bed a few hours after he had died—an image which, though shocking, conveyed both the visceral and emotional sense of my ideas.

When I wrote the piece I was aware that some of the images and ideas might be challenging. I had no idea that they would disturb listeners so much. The first time I read "Death, AIDS and the Transfiguration of Grief" in public was at a panel on AIDS writing at the 1990 Gay Games in Vancouver. Each of the panelists did their presentations and received appropriate applause. When I finished my piece there was a sort of stunned, embarrassed silence. I thought maybe it was because they felt I was not taking AIDS seriously, or perhaps because my solution to the grief that immediately followed a hospital visit was to go and cruise Boston's outdoor, reedy Fenway area. But it became clear to me later on that much of the distress was caused simply by my elaborating on sexual fantasies concerning Jim's doctors and other sick PWAs on this hospital floor.

This I thought was most curious since most gay men I knew will be more than willing to tell you how big last night's trick's dick was, how many people they blew in the bushes and exactly what they would like to do if they ever got porn star Jeff Stryker in bed, or over a kitchen table. Why should my sexual fantasies—and rather mild sexual fantasies at that—be so threatening? Of course it was possible that I had broken some gay cultural taboo by talking about AIDS and positive sexuality in the same breath, but it seemed that the problem was deeper, that by simply recounting actual, masturbatory fantasies I had crossed some un-spoken line of sexual and social demarcation: sure, everyone agrees, sex fantasies are great—we just don't want to get too personal about it.

Keeping this in mind the next time I presented "Death, AIDS and the Transfiguration of Grief," I built my presentation around the idea that men needed to talk more openly and honestly about their sexuality. The venue was perfect—a panel called "Gay Men and Sex" at the 1991 Creating Change conference. I began with a short rap about how hard it is to talk about sex and read portions of the article (once again to great discomfort in the room). Then I spoke about how gay men, myself included, found it hard to talk about the more intimate aspects of our sexual lives: not how many times we got porked the other night, but what it meant to us, how we felt about it. I talked about how we never really talk about jerking off—perhaps the most common private sexual act we all perform with astonishing regularity—and asked how many men jerked off last night? (some hands were raised), how many men jerked off this morning? (a few more hands went up) and then I asked how many men were willing to tell us, as a group, what they had thought about while they were jerking off. Most of the hands disap-peared. This was, obviously, moving into the more dangerous territory. A few hands lingered, and when their owners spoke the results were amazing: almost all of their private, intimate, personal masturbatory fantasies sounded like tired scenarios from a porn film or a dog-eared copy of *Honcho*. The audience seemed pleased; sex was being spoken about in the most explicit terms and everyone (but me) seemed to think that gay men had no problem being open and honest about their sexual fantasies, desires and needs.

What puzzled me most about that episode was that I could never figure out if the men who presented their fantasies were avoiding the truth or were, in fact, simply recounting it. Did they mask their real thoughts with shop-worn, store-bought erotic fantasies or—a more frightening thought—were these mundane, commercialized, processed images and actions really their fantasy life? If either one is correct, what does this tell us about gay men, about our ability to fantasize and explore our erotic needs and desires? What does it tell us about gay male culture and what does it tell us about our lives?

The ease with which gay men can talk sex—probably better than any other cultural group—emanates from a desire for self-expression, a need for public space and an urge to be socially rebellious. In a culture that tells us that our sexual lives and feelings are bad, or nonexistent, gay male talk about sex is a form of survival. The articulation of sexual desires—"I want to suck your cock," one man says to another in a bar —is the first step to action and satisfaction. The articulation and gesticulation of gay male sex in public—queers talking loudly on the street, softcore gay porn on newsstands, blatant cruising, sex in restrooms or in the bushes, openly sexual modes of dress like the leather queen, the clone, the drag queen—are all a reclamation of a public space that we would be denied. All of these actions are—in the broader scheme of things—a form of social and sexual protest, an attempt to break down those social boundaries of "private" and "public" that have enforced silence and shame for so many for so long.

Gay men have learned how to use their sexuality as a social marker, as a disrupter of the social and sexual status quo and as a way to make their presence felt in the world. The problem is that we have begun to see these actions and effects as ends in themselves. The blatant public sexual persona has obscured the need, the desire and the ability to talk about a more private sexuality. Gay men have learned to talk sex by emulating the bravado of straight male locker-room talk and mixing that with the rhetoric, conventions, language and images of commercialized pornography. By adopting this ready-made set of attitudes, words, phrases, postures and desires—a one-size-fits-all notion of gay sexuality—gay men can talk sex all they want without ever revealing anything about themselves.

Over the past forty years porn has played an important part in gay male culture. It has given us a visibility, it has given clear imagining to gay male desire and it has made it perfectly clear to both gay men, as well as to heterosexuals, the answer to "what *is* it that they do in bed?" For many gay men softcore and hardcore porn was one of the ways that they validated their sexual desires. Be it paintings by George Quantice in the *Physique Pictorial* of the 1950s, the famed *Song of the Loon* by Richard Amory in the 1960s, or the newest Falcon video of last week, porn not only gets us hard but shows us new possibilities; it is incitive as well as instructional.

But porn has also had a deeply destructive effect on gay male sexuality. The increasing commercialization of porn over the decades— *Physique Pictorial* gave way to *Mandate* and *Honcho*, 8mm porn loops have given way to the assembly line productions of Falcon and Bijou Studios—has left us with a porn world of homogenized, mass-produced images that have little emotional or sexual resonance. Sure, porn stars are well-built with big dicks and fashionable haircuts but they have little connection with real life. They are commodities like new cars, expensive shoes or Gap fashions. It is no surprise that the men who appear in Bruce Weber's early photographs for Calvin Klein advertisements have become one of the basic molds for porn stars: Calvin Klein is selling clothes, pornography is selling sex. The same is true of other male porn-star types: the boy next door, the Marky Mark clone, the gym body. And it is no surprise that they all have made-up, generic names: Corey, Scott, Lane, Rod, Casey, Erik, Rob, Mitch, Ty, Alex.

The commercialization, and codification, of gay male sexual fantasy is a powerful social force. As with all merchandising, "the market" has rules and parameters; it stipulates what is "hot" and what is not, it sets standards and it promotes what sells. The problem is that our general culture is so homophobic that none of us are encouraged to cultivate, stimulate or act upon our own incredible wealth of sexual fantasies. In such a context the fantasy factory of porn rushes in to fill a need created by fear, ignorance and lack of encouragement. I don't mean to imply that pornography has completely stolen our inner erotic resources— everyone's libidinous mind is always working constantly, spurred on by some man on line in the supermarket, a photograph of a Missouri flood worker in *Time* magazine, or the fleeting remembrance of a trick from twelve years ago—but it has made it far easier to rely on prepackaged, physically approved and commercially available images.

This is not only true of sexual images but of sexual language as well. Everyone has a story of going home with someone who—once sex began—fell into porno-talk: "Yeah, take that big dick," "Bite those tits," "Yeah, that's right, suck it, yeah." The frightening thing is that this happens far more often than people will admit. An intimate, personal language of passion and desire and physical heat has been supplanted by the dialogue of porno films and novels. When our culture tells us that it is not all right to talk about sex, it makes sense that we would not be very good at it. The language of passion must be as practiced, experimented with and honed as any other type of communication. I have a friend who recently was being picked up in a bar. When he asked what the other man, who was slightly younger, was interested in he replied, "You know, like having a hot time." And what would that entail? my friend asked. "You know, like two hot dudes doing it. Like, you know, getting together and like making it . . ."

What struck my friend the most was that the other man's language was nothing more than a series of porno-phrases combined with advertising slogans. It was communication for the nineties—all pitch and no substance, evocative without ever being provocative.

None of this is a recent problem. John Preston remembers that in the late 1970s when he was working on magazines like *Mandate* and *Honcho* it was not uncommon to hear of men in urban centers simulating specific looks that the magazines published each month: the cowboy, the mechanic, the biker. John speaks of this to illustrate how few models men have in their lives to teach them how to be sexual. The lesson for me is a little more frightening. Did these images—really, just a series of half-put-together costume accessories—really resonate with these men's inner lives or were they simply responding to what they had been told by the media they read was "in" or "hot"? This is not a uniquely gay male problem—did all those straight men *really* want to look like John Travolta in 1978, did all those women *really* want to look like Marilyn Monroe in the 1960s? The lure, and the trap, of the media image has always been with us. A consumer culture tells us we are not good enough (in any number of ways) and that we have to buy something—anything—to make us different.

Some might argue that "fantasies"—and porn is, like all imaginative creations, a fantasy—*don't* have any relationship with real life, but this misses the essential point: Our fantasy life is as integral to our emotional, psychological and material life as eating and sleeping and fucking. The problem with almost all gay male porn (and most other porn for that matter) is that it has little connection with our real fantasy lives. The gay artist Blade talks about how, in the 1940s and early 1950s, his erotic drawings were so rare and so legally dangerous, they would be left in bus-station lockers or in sealed, plain envelopes behind bars to be passed from one man to the next. Such early porn had far more personal energy and honesty to it than anything mass produced later in the century. Look at the early drawings of Tom of Finland and then at his later work—it is the difference between an artist and an industry.

The power of pornography is that it can arouse us (and thus, generally make us forget how boring it is) and that it offers us social visibility. But like other mass produced genres of commercial writing—the mystery, the romance—it also allows us to forget that we have an inner life that is more varied, more exciting and dirtier than most of what we might read and see. We are told by porn (and TV, movies, advertising), as well as by heterosexual culture, that this inner erotic life—different for every man, completely idiosyncratic for his desires and needs, fantasies and longings—is inferior to the approved (and sanitized) sexual images that are made for popular consumption.

I think one of the reasons why my piece "Death, AIDS and the Transfiguration of Grief" was so disconcerting to gay male listeners was that, for a few minutes, it broke through the silence of gay men's fantasy lives—it actually said what was on someone's mind in images and terms that were not represented in porn films or *Drummer* magazine. It connected sex with the real world—in this case the world of friendship and AIDS—and it did so explicitly but without the usual language and rhetoric that makes other writings about sexual fantasy acceptable and emotionally safe.

The prevalence of causal, nonimportant sexual talk in gay men's lives has been, in many ways, a completely positive presence. It has helped us form visible communities, it has helped us formulate safe sex education skills and techniques, it has—in the long run—challenged the all-encompassing antisex attitudes that have so long been the bulwark of western culture. But it has also prevented us from exploring the many ways in which our sexual desires and ideas, longings and needs do manifest themselves in our lives. How many of us are willing to talk freely about the whole *range* of sexual fantasies we choose to have—not to mention those that occur to us in sleeping or waking dreams, or while we are in the midst of masturbating, or having sex or coming.

What about those dreams of sex with a best friend whom we have never before thought of as sexual, or about sex with a family member, or with women, or a daydream about an s/m activity we would never (well, probably never) really do, or fantasies about underage boys, or with animals, or with lovers who have died of AIDS, or men who are very ill, or sex that is not, or might not be, consensual, or sex that occurs in connection with extreme violence . . . the list goes on and on and on. There are whole areas of sexual fantasy and imagination which are never discussed because we are embarrassed by them, either because they are "taboo," or too personal, or too frightening. If we are to grow as people and as a community we have to find ways to discuss our actual sexual lives and thoughts, our real sexual fears and longings. And not in the language or the posturing of porno novels or the images of porn videos, but in honest, open discussions with ourselves and with others until we have broken through the inhibitions and the embarrassments, the anxieties and the terrors of really knowing—without fear and without shame—the complexity and the glory of who we are and who we might become as fully sexual beings.

CONTRIBUTORS

KEVIN BOURKE's other published works include "Helen's First Tri-mester." He is best known, if he is known at all, for the public per-formance of his story "Dave and Barbara, All the Way from Guam," and for the underground versions of "Caroline Clay Falls Apart" and "What Do You Do for an Encore?" He has participated in the late Pamela Pratt's In Our Own Write sessions, and has studied writing with an improbable assortment of instructors that includes Jay Cantor, Frank Conroy, and Paul Carter Harrison.

MICHAEL BRONSKI is the author of *Culture Clash: The Making of Gay Sensibility.* His articles on sexuality, culture, AIDS, and politics have appeared in *Gay Community News, Z Magazine, Fag Rag, The Boston Globe, The Advocate, The Village Voice,* and *Radical America.* His essays have appeared in more than a dozen anthologies, including *Gay Spirit: Myth and Meaning, Taking Liberties: AIDS and Cultural Politics, Hometowns: Gay Men Write About Where They Belong, Personal Dispatches: Writers Confront*

AIDS, and *Flesh and the Word 2*. He has been involved in gay liberation for more than twenty-five years.

TOM CAFFREY is the author of the short story collections *Hitting Home and Other Stories* (Badboy) and *Tales from the Men's Room*. His writing appears regularly in the pages of magazines, including *Advocate MEN*, *Fresh MEN*, *Advocate Classifieds*, *Torso*, and *Pucker Up*, and is included in the anthologies *Ritual Sex* and *The Best American Erotica 1995*. He became a member of the Episcopal church after an encounter with a very handsome and persuasive priest.

PATRICK CARR was previously published in *Flesh and the Word 2* and is currently slacking off a novel. He received a degree in theater from Rutgers University and now lives in Brooklyn. He does what he does for David, even now.

JEFF DeCHARNEY is the pseudonym of a woman who lives and writes in the Northeast. The original Geoffroi DeCharney was the commander (Preceptor) of the Knights Templar in Normandy and was burned at the stake for (among other things) heresy and sodomy, together with the Templar Grand Master, on March 18, 1314. The novel about the fugitive Templar referred to in her story is an actual work in progress.

JOHN DIBELKA is an essayist, magazine editor, and author of children's books who has published four collections of adult short fiction, including *Animal Handlers* and the upcoming *Shooters*, under the pen name Jay Shaffer.

SANDI DuBOWSKI is currently distributing *Tomboychik*, his dragesque video made with his eighty-eight-year-old grandmother. He is also in production on a Hasidic go-go drag featurette shot in Israel and Brooklyn. He works with MIX: The New York Lesbian and Gay Experimental Film/Video Festival, has published in *Ten Percent* and *Steam*, and has been profiled in *Esquire* and interviewed in *The New York Times*, *The Boston Globe*, and on PBS. His Harvard class, Women's Studies 105, "Pornography and the Politics of Culture," met in Sever Hall, preparing him for *Flesh and the Word 3*.

LARS EIGHNER is the author of *Travels with Lizbeth*, a memoir of life on the streets, as well as several collections of essays and erotic fiction. He lives in Austin, Texas, and is a member of the Texas Institute of letters.

STEPHEN GRECO is a former senior editor of *Interview*. His story "Good with Words" appears in *The Penguin Book of Gay Short Stories* and was previously published in *Flesh and the Word*.

ANDREW HOLLERAN is the author of the novels *Dancer from the Dance* and *Nights in Aruba*, and *Ground Zero*, a book of essays.

JOHN M. ISON, using various pseudonyms, has written erotic fiction for such magazines as *Torso*, *Fresh MEN*, *Honcho*, and *Advocate MEN*. His poetry has appeared in *Evergreen Chronicles*, and he has published articles in *California*, the *New York Native*, and *The Advocate*. A graduate of UCLA and California State University, Los Angeles, he plans to earn an advanced degree in American literature.

BRANDON JUDELL barely exists in the borough of Manhattan. He has been anthologized in *Lavender Culture*, *A Member of the Family*, and *Contemporary Literary Criticism*. He currently hosts the weekly "Arts Magazine" on WBAI-FM radio, and has written for *The Village Voice*, the New York *Daily News*, *Bay Area Reporter*, *Detour*, *Au Courant*, and *Art and Antiques*. Formerly he was vice-president of the Gay and Lesbian Press Association, chairman of the Gay Caucus of the National Writers Union, and host for six years of the Gay Cable Network's "The Right Stuff." He will next be seen in director Rosa von Praunheim's film *Neurosia* and Philip B. Roth's autobiographical short about an erotic masseur. His story is dedicated to Jim Moody, his lover of one week, the longest relationship he's experienced this decade.

OWEN KEEHNEN is a nationally syndicated interviewer, as well as a columnist for *Penthouse Forum*. His fiction has appeared in such periodicals as *Christopher Street*, *Iris*, *Thing*, *Holy Titclamps*, and *The Evergreen Chronicles*. Recently he completed a short story collection entitled *Doing Time in Bayetteville*. He currently resides in Chicago.

DAVE KINNICK began a career in erotic journalism in 1982 while managing UCLA's gay newspaper, *TenPercent*. He has been the monthly video review columnist for *Advocate MEN* magazine since 1988, and chronicles the small world of pornography and its denizens for magazines such as *The Advocate*, *Advocate Classifieds*, and *Fresh MEN*, and is an editor for the *Adam Gay Video* publications and *Steam*. His first book, *Sorry I Asked: Intimate Interviews with Gay Porn's Rank and File*, was released by Badboy Books in 1993. Dave also makes occasional forays into video production, hoping someday to be considered the world's most beloved pornographer.

WILL LEBER is a native Californian and a graduate of Stanford University. He worked for many years in the garment industry in New York and now lives with his lover in San Francisco. His story "Sucked In" appeared in *Flesh and the Word 2*. He is at work on a collection of erotic short stories set in San Francisco and a novel about fashion models.

KEY LINCOLN grew up in the Midwest, served in the U.S. Navy, and now lives in California. He has written stories under various pen names for *Advocate MEN*, *Fresh MEN*, *Hot/Shots*, *Options*, *Torso*, *Playguy*, *Guys*, *FirstHand*, *Stallion*, *Beau*, *Mandate*, *Cavalier*, and *Honcho Overload*. A collection of his stories, *Submission Holds*, has recently been published by Masquerade Books.

MICHAEL LOWENTHAL is a writer and editor living in Boston. His story "Better Safe" appeared in *Flesh and the Word 2* and was selected for Susie Bright's *Best American Erotica 1994*. His writing has also appeared in the anthologies *Men on Men 5*, *Sister and Brother*, *Friends and Lovers*, and *Wrestling with the Angel*, as well as in more than twenty periodicals, including *The Advocate*, *Lambda Book Report*, *The James White Review*, *Yellow Silk*, *Art & Understanding*, *The Evergreen Chronicles*, and the *Boston Phoenix*. He edited a volume of gay men's pornography entitled *The Best of the Bad Boys* (Richard Kasak Books, 1994) and is currently working on a short story collection and a novel.

V. K. McCARTY, who writes as Victor King and Mam'selle Victoire, is John Preston's godchild.

DAVID MAY was born in Honolulu, Hawaii, in 1956. The son of a naval officer, he grew up in Hawaii; Monterey, California; Washington, D.C.; and Southern California; before moving to San Francisco in 1974. He received a B.A. in dramatic literature from UC Santa Cruz (specializing in medieval religious theater) in 1978. He started publishing in *Drummer* in 1984 and his writing has since appeared in *Mach*, *Honcho*, and *Advocate MEN*, as well as in the anthologies *Rogues of San Francisco* and *Meltdown!* Not limited to erotica, his work has also appeared in such wholesome magazines as *Cat Fancy*. In 1992 David May lost his lover of eight years, bisexual activist David Lourea, to AIDS.

JAMES MEDLEY began writing in 1990 after working in "their" world for thirty-odd years. His work regularly appears in virtually all the skin magazines, as well as *Christopher Street*, *RFD*, and *Signs of the Times*. Two of his stories appear in the anthology *Insatiable*, edited by John Patrick. Medley has a novel, *Huck and Billy*, published by Badboy Books and another from Starbrooks Press, *City Boys and Country Boys*. A third novel, entitled *Gypsy Boy*, is scheduled for publication in 1995 by Starbooks. Contrarily, he has published children's fiction in *Highlights for Children*. He lives with Harry, his lover of thirty-four years, in a small town in Central Florida.

SCOTT O'HARA, retired pornstar, is now editor of *Steam* magazine. Other pieces of him have appeared in *Flesh and the Word 1* and *2*, *Diseased Pariah News*, *The James White Review*, and many skin magazines. He can be reached at Route 2, Box 1215, Cazenovia WI 53924. He is not single.

RON OLIVER is a writer/director who has produced several notorious horror movies and a few dozen television episodes. He began writing fiction at the urging of his boyhood pal Michael Rowe, who insisted they do something better with their time than ogle strippers and eat Häagen-Dazs—or vice versa. "Monster Cock" is his first published fiction and will soon be a novel, furtively shoved under a pillow near you. A native of Canada, Ron now lives in West Hollywood and prowls the streets late at night in search of inspiration . . . and body parts.

MARTIN PALMER lives in Anchorage, Alaska, where he writes, teaches, and practices medicine. He has had pieces in *Men on Men 3*, *Hometowns*, *A Member of the Family*, and *Sister and Brother*.

ROBERT PATRICK has more than fifty plays in print, including *Untold Decades: Seven Gay Comedies* (St. Martin's) and *Michelangelo's Models* (Dialogus). "After Hours at the Buono" was cut from his first novel, *Temple Slave*, published by Richard Kasak Books. Mr. Patrick welcomes correspondence at 1837 N. Alexandria Avenue #211, Los Angeles, CA 90027. He is not the same Robert Patrick who appeared in *Terminator 2*.

"DEKE PHELPS" is the pseudonym of a life-long muscle worshipper who's served his gods variously as a sponsor, widely published body-building writer, contest promoter, and accredited physique judge.

JOHN PRESTON was born in 1945 in Medfield, Massachusetts, and lived for many years in Portland, Maine. He was a pioneer in the early gay rights movement, cofounding Gay House, Inc., in Minneapolis—the nation's first gay community center—and editing *The Advocate*. He was the author or editor of more than twenty-five acclaimed gay books, including such erotic landmarks as *Mr. Benson* and *I Once Had a Master*, and the anthologies *Personal Dispatches, Hometowns, A Member of the Family, Sister and Brother*, and the *Flesh and the Word* series. He died of AIDS complications in 1994.

ANNE RICE was born in New Orleans, where she now lives with her husband, the poet Stan Rice, and their son, Christopher.

MICHAEL ROWE was born in Ottawa, Ontario, in 1962. A journalist and essayist, his work has appeared in *The James White Review, The Body Politic, Xtra!* and numerous mainstream publications. He is a contributor to the anthologies *Sister and Brother: Lesbians and Gay Men Write About Their Lives Together* and *Friends and Lovers*. He is the author of a volume of poetry, *When the Town Sleeps*, and a nonfiction book, *Writing Below the Belt: Conversations with Erotic Authors*. He recently moved to Toronto from Milton, Ontario, with his life-partner, Brian, and their two golden retrievers, Valentine and Ben.

LEIGH W. RUTLEDGE was raised in northern California and currently makes his home in Colorado. He is the author of *The Gay Book of Lists, Unnatural Quotations, The Gay Fireside Companion*, and *The Gay Decades*. He is also the author of seven other books, including *Cat Love Letters, A*

Cat's Little Instruction Book, and *It Seemed Like a Good Idea at the Time*. He lives with his lover of seventeen years; they share their home with thirty housecats and four dogs.

D. V. SADERO is a private investigator who writes erotic stories in his spare time. A collection of them has been printed by Badboy Books under the title *In the Alley*. The same publisher will soon release his erotic science fiction novel, *Revolt of the Naked*.

STEVEN SAYLOR is the creator of the ancient Roman sleuth Gordianus the Finder, hero of a series of novels which began in 1991 with *Roman Blood*. Under the pen name Aaron Travis, his erotic fiction includes the novel *Slaves of the Empire* and several short story collections. He divides his time between homes in Berkeley, California, and Amethyst, Texas.

CARO SOLES writes gay erotica under the pseudonym Kyle Stone and is the author of the novels *The Initiation of P.B. 500*, *Rituals*, *The Citadel*, and *Fantasy Board*, as well as short stories in magazines like *Torso, Honcho Overload, Fresh MEN, In Touch for Men*, and several anthologies. Caro is the co-editor of the erotic dark fantasy anthology *Bizarre Dreams* and the editor of the erotic science fiction/dark fantasy collection *Meltdown!* Caro/Kyle lives in Toronto, Canada.